ANNA DAUGHERTY

Outside of Grace

Black Rose Writing | Texas

Second printing

ISBN: 978-1-68513-070-1
PUBLISHED BY BLACK ROSE WRITING
www.blackrosewriting.com

Printed in the United States of America
Suggested Retail Price (SRP) $22.95

Outside of Grace is printed in Garamond Pro

*As a planet-friendly publisher, Black Rose Writing does its best to eliminate unnecessary waste to reduce paper usage and energy costs, while never compromising the reading experience. As a result, the final word count vs. page count may not meet common expectations.

Cover Artwork by Michelle Esguerra Wilson

"The God of all grace, who called you to his eternal glory in Christ, will himself restore, establish, strengthen, and support you after you have suffered a little while."

–1 Peter 5:10

Outside of Grace

Chapter 1

Standing on the stage, eyes forced closed in prayer, Ava could sense the weight of 200 people in front of her—surely a few were peeking. Her dad had prayed for her on this stage before, for mission trips and graduate blessings. This was the first time she stood alone, though. College students studying abroad were not typically the congregation's concern, but what happened to the Sanford family happened to the entire church.

A row of hot, yellow lights hit her as she tried not to fidget. The middle school auditorium where they met was stuffy, the heaters blowing against the January chill outside. Ava tried to focus on his words. "—That she would be a light to all."

The moment he finished the prayer, her eyes flicked open. Probably too soon. She should have waited so nobody would think she had her eyes open during the prayer. Risking a quick look at the college group, she caught Jack's blue eyes wrinkling in a smirk—no doubt at her embarrassment.

Well-wishers congregated before she could move away. They all knew her, at least as the pastor's kid, if nothing else. The Newtons were first, then an assortment of family friends, offering kind words and handshakes like she was a missionary heading to a war-torn country rather than a student going to Scotland for a semester.

When the area finally cleared out, Ava headed to the back of the auditorium. The other students stood outside the doors, debating where to go for lunch. Talia caught sight of her and started a slow clap as Ava approached. A few others joined in with a whistle or cheer. Ava complied with a bow.

"Our international hero," Jack said with a sweeping motion in her direction.

"Stop." Ava kicked at his shoe. "It was all I could do to keep him from having everybody lay hands on me."

Talia stepped into the middle of the circle to hug Ava, perfectly straight black hair swinging above her shoulders. "It was adorable, mija. We're excited for you."

Others joined in, noting their jealousy or sharing their own study abroad stories. For once, she could almost imagine being a normal college student, and not the still-living-at-home pastor's kid. When she caught Jack's eyes rolling, she waved off the comments and redirected the conversation back to lunch.

"Your pick," Talia said. "It's your last good American lunch."

"Cracker Barrel?" Ava suggested. Everybody except Talia groaned. Ava raised her hands in surrender. "Okay, okay. Anywhere with mac and cheese is fine with me."

"Nope, you heard the woman," Talia said. Her best friend since childhood always came to her defense. "It's her last lunch with us. Stop complaining."

"That sounds pretty fatalistic. You know I plan on coming back, right?"

Talia patted her head like a mother. "It won't be the same. You'll finally be a grownup."

Ava laughed and pulled away from her. "You'll lose your ride with comments like that."

"No, I won't." Talia looped her arm through Ava's. She could never lose her ride.

When they arrived at the restaurant, they pressed two round tables together in an awkward figure eight. It was a small group today—most of the students were still gone on winter break. The students left behind were a hodgepodge; either working students, international students, or locals who never left, like Ava.

"Everybody else here is getting the senior discount, Aves," Jack said as they sat.

Ava shushed him and elbowed his side. "We represent Grace. Be nice."

Her parents had drilled it into her head from birth. She represented the church, and she had to do it well. When she entered college with the name Sanford, she was the assumed leader of the group. Her last name was a birthright and a responsibility.

Conversation flowed rapidly around the table, breaking off into rivulets and rejoining again. Ava let it wash over her. It was the last time she would see this particular group. When she returned to Ridley Bay in five months, some would have graduated, others left for the summer. There would be new students too, new faces. They would have all moved through an entire semester without her. Sentimentality threatened to ruin her last lunch; Ava forced herself back into the conversation as Talia retold the story of her uncle's Great Dane ruining Christmas.

Eventually, the checks were passed around and takeaway boxes were packed. The guys at the table sat back, rubbing their stomachs like Thanksgiving afternoon, while the girls picked at the cornbread. Talia left first, catching a ride to a babysitting job that afternoon. The rest slowly disbanded. Ava sat rooted in place, not willing to see it end. Eventually, Jack and Ava were the only ones remaining.

"You gonna stay here the rest of the day?" Jack asked.

"I don't want it to end."

"Nobody's making you go."

Ava laughed. "That's not helpful. You're supposed to tell me to go. Tease me for still living with my parents. Didn't you say I should leave home?"

"I didn't mean across the Atlantic." Jack's shoulders fell.

"Why is everybody talking like I'm never coming back?" Ava asked with a laugh.

He flicked a butter packet at her. "We're just happy we can finally act like heathens without our walking conscience here."

"No way. I'm passing the baton to you."

His laugh was genuine and contagious, and it always made Ava smile. "Then we're a lost cause."

"*You* might be."

She followed him to the front, and they meandered through the restaurant's old-fashioned store on their way out. When Jack made a joke about a ridiculous hat in the front window, she let it slide, ignoring the instinct to hush him. She should have practiced this sooner—loosening her grip, sinking into the background. But she needed them as much as they needed her.

The coastal wind beat against the door, resisting their exit. Ava crossed her arms tightly as they stepped outside. The wind whipped her hair from barely contained waves into a long, tangled, brown mess. Jack was apparently unaffected by the wind that flapped through his blue plaid button up.

They reached her car, and he leaned against it. "Coffee before group on Wednesday?"

"I'm not sure I'll make it," Ava said, stalling. It had been their weekly routine for over a year. If today was hard, coffee with Jack would crush her. "I fly out on Thursday. I might need to pack."

"Don't skip your last small group because you're afraid of crying. Go out swinging, Aves."

"It's not even a real Bible study, it's just the meet and greet. Won't people think it's weird or rude if I show up for that and I'm not actually joining?"

"You've always been part of the group. Besides, who cares what people think?" Jack shoved his hands in his pockets.

Me. I care. "Maybe... If I'm packed and everything."

"You will be. Or else I'm coming over and packing for you."

Ava grinned. "I actually believe you. Fine, coffee at five."

"Good. I'll see you later." With a wave over his shoulder, he strode off to his truck. Some goodbye.

Ava sank into the driver's seat of her beat up sedan. It was really ending. Everything she had ever known. Despite the sense of loss, it was time. Everything here was not enough. There had to be more. Whatever more there was, Ava knew it was in Scotland.

• • •

She parked on the street in front of the white house that had been home for twelve years. The farmhouse-style structure with black shutters, plopped in the middle of a suburb, begged to be surrounded by acres of freedom. The window at the top right was hers.

After a quick hello to her parents, Ava headed upstairs to pack. Four days gave her plenty of time to pack, but she needed the activity now, to keep her mind busy, to balance the goodbyes with excitement.

A matching set of green suitcases, a Christmas gift from her parents, waited to be filled. One was a carry-on, the other a behemoth, promising to hold her entire life for a semester. She had packed for mission trips and vacations before, but nothing longer than a week or two at most. This was more like moving.

She looked around her room, layered with evidence of many stages of life, her value system shifting. The books meticulously arranged into a rainbow were meaningless now, while the small porcelain angel sitting on top of the bookcase suddenly seemed priceless, chipped wing and all. It had been a baptism gift from her dad. Ava picked up the angel as she continued pacing the room, reevaluating everything in it. *"He will command his angels concerning you."*[1]

"Can I come in?" her dad called from the hallway as he walked towards Ava's room. The door was already open.

"Sure." Ava set the angel down, but not before her dad saw it.

Turning it over, he examined the jagged wing. "I remember when Ezra broke this."

"Me too."

"You were so mad. We had to convince you that your brother was worth keeping."

Ava smiled. "Yeah, I wanted to trade a brother for a new angel, but you refused the deal."

"We learned a few things about grace that day." He looked around the room as he lowered the angel. "It'll be strange not having you here."

Ava nodded and sat on the foot of the bed. The oldest of three Sanford kids, she was the first to fly the nest. A sophomore in Grace Church's college ministry, she was the last. She would turn 20 this semester and even students younger than her were living on their own. Life was moving on without her. Time to catch up.

"It'll be good though." Her dad sat next to her. "You'll get to experience new things. And focus on school for a bit, without worrying about church and your crazy brothers for once."

Ava laughed. "I'm sure I'll still worry about it all."

"I'm proud of you, Avie." He draped an arm over her shoulders. "The semester's going to fly by."

"Are you trying to convince yourself or me?"

"Both." He smiled and stood, crossing to the door again. "Your mom's making spaghetti for dinner, if you want to join."

"Thanks, dad. I will." The smell of roasted garlic and tomatoes was already making its way upstairs. Routines like dinner were mandatory for her siblings, but when she started college, they became optional for Ava. Her parents let her have as much space and freedom as possible while living in their house. It was never quite enough.

Alone again, Ava ran a hand over the angel one last time. Childish mementos had no place in a college dorm room. She took a few pictures down from the wall instead and carefully tucked them between the pages of her Bible. With the suitcase half full, she snapped a picture and sent it to Jack as proof of effort. She was ready.

Chapter 2

The coffee shop was unusually crowded on Wednesday night. Texas Gulf students packed into the spot at the end of the dated strip mall. They were all coming back to town and waiting for the spring semester to start. Every table inside was claimed, so Jack and Ava took their coffees to a wrought iron table outside in the chilled, wet wind.

Jack pushed his chair back onto two legs. "Good practice for Scotland, right?"

Ava hugged her core. "I'm gonna freeze before I make it to my first class."

He laughed. "You better make it to every single class, ma'am. They aren't cheap over there."

"I know that," Ava sighed. "I never miss class. I'll be there even if I'm hypothermic."

"It wouldn't be that bad if you'd wear a real jacket." He tossed his chin up at her.

"What? It's cute." Ava crossed her arms over her cropped denim jacket.

Jack scoffed and watched a group of girls walk into the coffee shop instead of responding. "Who else is going to Scotland?"

"A few architecture undergrads and a couple of graduate students. The only person I know is Benjamin Rath."

Jack made a disgusted face. Of course. "I didn't know Benj was going. Bet you're happy."

"Why yes, I am glad another Christian will be there." Ava added a glare for emphasis. *One time.* That was all it took. She had called Benj cute once and Jack never let it go. He had dated at least three other girls throughout their friendship, but she couldn't call one guy cute.

Jack gave a dry laugh. "Being part of C3 doesn't mean he's a Christian."

The biggest student ministry at Texas Gulf University, nearly all of Grace Church's college students were involved in the Campus Christian Coalition. Ava had made several friends there too. Including Benj. "Ever heard that 'judge not' verse?"

"Where's the verse about trusting your friends? And don't forget, he has a girlfriend."

"Shut up," Ava groaned. Obviously she wouldn't forget Benj's girlfriend. Changing the topic usually helped. "Have you started work yet?"

He narrowed his eyes at her before deciding to let it slide. "We start back this weekend. I'm leading an orientation for the newbies."

"You're in charge?"

"I am now. The other guy graduated in December." Jack shrugged. Accidentally moving up was his style.

"Good for you. And for the athletic department. Maybe you can finally get them in line."

His was the best smile—when it wasn't sarcastic. "I'm not sure anybody can."

Ava rubbed her arms and craned to look through the window next to them. "I'm freezing. Has anything opened yet?"

"Nobody's left." Jack slid his keys across the table. "Go get a real jacket. I've got one in the back seat."

Ava grabbed the keys and bounded across the parking lot towards his pickup truck. A parking lot light had burned out, and the sky was darkening, but his white truck stood out like a beacon. She sifted through athletic gear, books, and loose papers until she found the black fleece. Tossing her jean jacket into the passenger seat, she tugged on the pullover with the small *Texas Gulf University Athl. Dept.* logo embroidered on the top left.

"You need to clean out your truck," Ava said as she tossed the keys back to Jack.

"If I had, you would still be freezing."

"At least I wouldn't smell like Taco Bell."

"That's it, you lost your jacket privileges—" Jack lunged across the table as Ava shrieked and curled her legs to her chest to block herself in.

"No," she whined with her best pout. "It's a compliment. Taco Bell is my favorite smell. I spray it on every morning."

Jack lifted his wrist dramatically to check his watch. "Can you catch an earlier flight?"

"I'll be out of your way soon enough, promise."

Jack gave her a small smile and turned his attention to the parking lot next to them as he took a long drink of coffee. He'd never admit that he would miss her. Maybe he wouldn't.

"You could visit," Ava said. "Come to Edinburgh for spring break."

Jack raked a hand through his light brown waves; by the time she returned, his hair would be sun-streaked blond like a surfer's. "Right. If I suddenly have a couple grand to throw away, I'll be there."

"There are worse ways to spend money," Ava said in defense. She shouldn't push the issue, but calling it a throw away was insulting.

"Yeah, and better ways to not drown in student debt," he said, twisting his coffee cup in his hands.

Before she dug the pit any deeper, they were interrupted by a quick hello from someone Jack knew. Afterwards, they easily slipped back into their usual mode: comparing notes on class schedules, complaining about textbooks, and people watching. It was a mode less affected by their stalled goodbye.

Half an hour later, they threw away their cups and headed to the truck. They were five minutes early when they pulled up to Katie and Isaac Torres' house for small group. The front door was already propped open. Their five-year-old twin daughters greeted Ava, their favorite babysitter, with squeals and hugs around her legs. Katie waved them in with one hand while holding baby Gabe in the other.

Jack headed outside to the grill with Isaac while Ava joined Katie in the kitchen, scooping up Gabe while Katie set out drinks and cups.

"He is the chunkiest thing," Ava cooed as she tickled his cheeks.

"You're telling me, " Katie said. "My back is sore from holding him all day."

Before Ava could reply, a loud group of students entered. Quinton, Val, and Isabella from Grace Church, plus a couple others Ava recognized from C3. Every week was a new mix as college students floated in and out of groups, finding their place in the city. She introduced herself to the newcomers.

"You play sports?" one of them asked, pointing to the jacket's Athletic Department logo.

"She definitely does not," Jack answered first, walking inside with a plate of hamburgers.

Ava shrugged in concession. Jack set the plate down and joined the group. He already knew the new faces. He knew everybody at TGU.

They started on dinner as more people from church trickled in. A mixed group showed up—young adults, college students, and one other young family. Soon, the house was packed with people scattered around the dining table, the living room couch, and a folding table in between.

Ava finished eating first and grabbed a fussing Gabe from his high chair. She quickly calmed him, letting Katie finish her dinner. Walking around and checking on kids, helping with refills and getting napkins came naturally. Serving was another Sanford requirement. Who would she help tomorrow? That no one would need her was thrilling and terrifying.

After dinner, they all piled into the living room to chat. The evening was short and social, a simple welcome meeting before Bible studies started next week.

"Will you look for a church in Scotland?" Katie asked Ava.

"Of course. I mean, it's mostly Saint Somebody and Somewhere's Parish, but I'll try."

"Perishing somewhere sounds promising," Jack said dryly.

One of the new students joined in their conversation. "What's in Scotland? Scotch and bagpipes?"

"Well, Ava's gonna miss out on the Scotch," Jack said.

"Isn't the drinking age 18 over there?"

"Doesn't matter, she's a Sanford." Jack's eyes were on her, eyebrow raised in challenge. "She won't even sit at a bar in a restaurant."

"Okay, that was one time, and I didn't know you could just walk right up to it."

Everybody else laughed. It was always the same story. Everything she did was measured by her last name. In 24 hours, that would change. She would fly to a land where nobody knew the name Sanford.

As the group disbanded, Ava and Jack prolonged the goodbye, helping clean. The Torres kids had all gone to bed when Katie and Isaac said a quick prayer for Ava's flight tomorrow.

They were quiet on the drive back to her house. He parked on the curb. Neither of them moved for a moment.

"Here—" Ava started to pull the fleece over her head.

"Keep it. It's gonna be a lot colder over there.

"I've got jackets."

"You don't have an athletic department one that makes you look like a total poser."

Ava tugged the fleece back down and squashed the rising hope that lending her a jacket meant something. She buried her nose in the top collar of it and breathed Jack. "You're right. That's exactly what I need. To repeatedly explain that I'm not actually athletic."

"That's not true. You can hold your own on a basketball court."

Compliments from Jack were too rare—she never knew how to handle them. Rather than respond, Ava slouched in her seat and propped her feet up on his dashboard. Jack swatted at her feet, but she didn't move and he didn't make her.

"Nobody will know me," she said.

"They'll get to know you."

"I can't even remember the last time I was the new person somewhere."

"It's only a semester, Aves. You don't have to be everybody's friend."

"Will everybody here forget about me?" A stupid question, granted, but she wanted to hear him promise he wouldn't.

"Of course we will. There's an Eva at C3. We'll recruit her to replace you."

"You're the worst," Ava groaned as she sat straighter. Of course that backfired. Jack laughed and climbed out of the truck. Ava followed him up the sidewalk to the house. He stepped onto the front porch and turned to lean over the railing.

"Are you coming in?" she asked.

"No, I gotta go," he said, facing the dark yard. "But… call me if you ever need anything."

"And you'll come rushing to Scotland?"

Jack chuckled under his breath and shifted to look at her. "Just be careful over there. It'll be different from Grace."

"I know that."

Jack stepped closer to her and wrapped his arms around her. Ava tucked her head into his shoulder. Real hugs were another rarity for him. It was a second too long and too short before he let her go. "Tell your parents I said hi. And good luck explaining how you got that jacket when you can't even throw a football."

"Can too. And next time I'll chunk it at your truck."

He raised an eyebrow and pointed at her. "Nobody touches my truck."

Ava spread her hands out and put on her best innocent look. "Footballs don't leave fingerprints."

With one last boyish grin, he shook his head. For a second, Ava thought he would hug her again, but he turned away. "I'll see you in May, Aves."

That was it.

Throwing back a wave, Jack crossed the yard. She hesitated; hoping, giving him one last chance to say anything else. He didn't.

May. It sounded impossibly far away.

Chapter 3

After two layovers, one long night in a cramped airplane seat, and a confusing trip through campus to retrieve dorm keys, Ava had arrived. The dorm room welcomed her on one side with an explosion of twinkle lights, pink, and paisley. The other side, presumably hers, was entirely bare. A green mattress topped the loft bed. Underneath it was a bookcase and small desk, with a wooden chair. An afternoon nap tempted her, but with no bedding or pillows, Ava forced herself to stay awake.

Hauling her suitcases into the space under the bed, she stood back to examine it again, as if the addition of two bags might have changed things. It was hers. She hadn't had a blank slate in years. Now this one extended to every part of her. Here, she could create a home for herself. A temporary one, but home nonetheless.

Unzipping her suitcase, Ava laid clothes out on the bed. She pulled open a closet door and found it already near-bursting. The clothes that filled it were sparkling, shimmering, and silky. Most of which looked impractical for the weather here.

The moment she laid a hand on a sheer white top, the room door burst open and Ava jumped back. Someone entered the room in a fit of giggles.

"Och, I hae ta go," the blonde said into her phone and tossed it on her bed. She bounced up to Ava and stuck her hand out. "Ye must be the Texan. I'm Rosie."

"Yes, Ava." She took the handshake with a smile. This was the pink and paisley roommate.

"Thank god yer here. I had ta sleep in here last night and it's pure hackit like that—" Rosie waved her hand towards Ava's side of the room. "Ye hae to make it pretty."

Ava laughed. "I'll do my best. I don't have much yet. I need to go shopping today and get some bed sheets, at least."

"Shopping, now that's something I can help with," Rosie called over her shoulder as she walked into the bathroom that joined their room to the next. Without bothering to close the door, Rosie sat on the toilet. Ava spun away and tried to focus on something besides the sound of a roommate who didn't use doors.

"I tried to save ye some space," Rosie said, pointing to the closet as she walked back into the room, zipping her ripped jeans. "We look close to the same size, so what's mine is yours, hen."

"Hen? Like, chicken?"

"What?" Rosie laughed. "Like, girl."

"Oh. Well, thanks, same to you." Sharing clothes was familiar, like she and Talia had at times. But in every way different. This new instant-friend had the look and energy of Tinker Bell. Or a cheerleader. A combination of the two, really.

With a high-pitched, lilting chirp, Rosie filled Ava in on the details of her life: born and raised in the highlands, the youngest of five sisters, and a second-year student at the University of Edinburgh, majoring in architecture and planning to go to graduate school next. Rosie's former roommate, also her best friend, was studying abroad in France this semester, so Ava was filling in for both roles. There was no interview for the part, only absolute confidence from Rosie.

She could talk a mile a minute. Ava didn't mind listening to her and learning the accent—the way she only slightly rolled her "R" or added a syllable to words like girl. Soon Rosie stood and grabbed her hand. "'Mon, let's get you to Argos before they close."

The sky was already dark, the days were shorter this far north. A slight drizzle fell and Ava zipped her jacket all the way, flipping the hood over her hair. Rosie bounded down the dorm building's front steps with her jacket flailing open as if 35 degrees meant nothing to her. She led the way to the store, while Ava stared up at the surrounding buildings, assessing the materials and styles, running dates in her mind, and tripping over curbs and stones.

"Watch yerself, hen," Rosie said with a laugh as she pulled Ava into the store.

A quarter of the size of any superstore in America, Argos managed to pack plenty on its shelves. Rosie went straight to the bedding section of the small store. Ava ran her fingers over the selection of bedding sets, landing on a pin-tucked teal duvet.

"Naw, where's your sparkle, lass? How about this?" Rosie pointed to a pink set with yellow flowers.

"It would clash with your paisley. This teal will set off the colors in yours."

Rosie tapped her chin for a moment, debating it. "A'right, that'll do."

Their arms were filled with toiletries and linens by the time they left. They squeezed in a quick stop at the market for Ava to grab enough food to make it through the next day or two.

The dorm room seemed even smaller when they arrived with the bags of things. Once everything was unloaded and organized, it would feel better—more like a home. A tiny one, but enough.

Ava began unpacking bags while Rosie went to reapply mascara. "What're ye doin' with architecture?" Rosie called from the bathroom.

"My degree is actually in interior design, but it's under the School of Architecture," Ava said.

Rosie's head popped out of the bathroom, lipstick in hand. "Interior design? Are there any boys in that?"

Ava laughed. "Only two."

"And they're gay," Rosie said dryly. She wasn't wrong. "This is college, not a convent, hen. Don't forget yer in school for more than a degree."

"There are other places to meet boys." Ava said with a shrug and little conviction. Roommate and love advisor, apparently. She could use one.

"Mmm, speaking of which, ye need to get ready."

Rosie stepped out, lips fully covered, along with the rest of her face. Her hair was in tousled waves, a deceptively casual look, carefully perfected.

"Ready?" Ava asked as she opened her carry-on bag to finish unpacking.

"Ta go out," Rosie whined, as if it were painfully obvious. "We're goin' to AltBrew. It's the first night out this term. If you miss it, you'll never catch up."

So that was Rosie's type. Ava hesitated. No one had ever invited her out drinking before. Maybe because she was 19, but probably more so because she was the pastor's daughter. "No thanks, bars aren't really my scene."

Rosie barked out a laugh. "They are here. 'Mon, let's get ye dressed." The strength of her accent seemed to cut in and out, like a Southern Belle who knew how to play it up as needed.

"I don't drink, sorry." Ava ignored Rosie's dramatic jaw drop. "Besides, I have a school meeting tomorrow."

"On a Saturday? Americans," Rosie huffed and gave up. She paused at the door. "Yer sure? That ye don't want any friends?"

Ava laughed off the comment. "I'm sure I'll be able to make some elsewhere." *Better ones.* She waved Rosie out.

Alone again, Ava sat back on her heels and blew out a breath. She was too tired to unpack, but if she went to bed now, she would have jet lag for days. She reached for her phone instead. A quick phone call home would help.

• • •

Saturday afternoon was a special orientation on campus for international students. Ava had already explored some of the campus on her own that morning, but she arrived 10 minutes early to make sure she had a spot at the front of the group anyway. The skies were gray and the cold cut through Jack's black fleece and her jeans. She kept an eye out for TGU students in the group. One girl approached the group, looking at her phone. Ava recognized her from a class they'd both had back home, but she hadn't met her yet.

"Hey, you're from Texas Gulf right?" Ava walked up and held out her hand.

The girl looked bored. She returned the handshake and introduced herself as Sloane. Two more girls walked over together and Sloane's bored stare turned into an instant smile as she greeted the other girls and they started talking. Ava stood awkwardly outside of the circle, attempting to immerse herself in it. Before she could introduce herself, the leader of the tour stood on a nearby stone bench and began calling for attention.

He pointed out the buildings around where they were standing, before waving for everyone to follow him towards the library and administration offices. The TGU girls fell back in the group and continued their conversations. Ava joined them. From what she gathered, they had all traveled here together. Sloane and one of the girls were roomed together. The other groaned about how jealous she was, roomed with someone who spoke little English.

"Mine's a little wild, but she helped me find a store yesterday," Ava cut in, skipping introductions. The girls looked at her like they had no idea she had been there at all. "Oh sorry, I'm Ava, I'm from TGU too."

"I can tell," one of the girls said, pointing to the TGU Athl. Dept. pullover. Ava couldn't tell if she was sneering or if that was just her face. "What year are you?"

"Sophomore. Sort of, I've taken extra courses so I'm kind of in between sophomore and junior. You?"

"Junior. The real kind," the girl said and turned her attention back to her friends with a laugh.

Ava pressed her lips tightly and let herself fall out of step with the group. That wasn't going well. Introductions would have to wait until the TGU meeting after the tour. She glanced around the group as they stopped at the library, a late-modernist beauty, held together with concrete and polished black granite. Ava focused on the guide as he spoke about the millions of books inside the acre-sized building.

When the tour ended, she attempted to join the group of girls again for the walk to the architecture building. If by pity alone, they seemed to allow her into their circle this time. It was a long walk, crossing back through the campus. Ava surveyed the buildings more than she participated in the conversation. She might be an interior design major, but spending all her time with architecture students had rubbed off.

The sun was already dipping behind the buildings when they arrived. Two guys from the tour group joined them as they climbed three flights of stairs to a small classroom. Ava found a familiar face at last—Benj. He was talking with three other students and Professor Garcia.

"Come on in, everybody," Professor Garcia said, waving them into the room. Rumored to be one of the best professors in TGU's architecture school, he only taught upper-level courses, so this was the first time Ava had a class with him. She scanned the tiny room, there was no front row to claim, only two white tables with a smattering of folding chairs; each of which were already claimed. Ava stood at the back with a guy she hadn't met yet.

Professor Garcia had everyone go around the room and introduce themselves. Ava did her best to memorize names; a required skill for a Sanford. Sloane, Georgia, Emma, Grayson, Carter, Bailey, Paul—she repeated their names in her head. Three were graduate students. The boy next to her was Leo, a junior in architecture. Ava introduced herself as a junior, with no further explanation, despite a snicker from one of the girls. She couldn't risk being the youngest in the group.

They went over some basic school policies and conduct expectations. He passed out a folder with the University of Edinburgh's resources, phone numbers, and maps. They reviewed the materials they would need to turn in for TGU and he dismissed them.

Ava turned to shake hands with Leo but he was already heading out the door. She pulled her hand back in and grabbed a now vacant chair opposite the table from Benj and another undergrad.

"Skipped the campus tour, huh?" she asked with a smile. Benjamin looked at her blankly. She swallowed. "Ava Sanford, we've met at The Campus Christian Coalition..."

"Right," he said with a nod and no recognition. Of course. "Do you go to Ridley Bible Church?"

"Grace Church," she corrected, trying not to let a blush sneak into her cheeks. They had met three times at various C3 functions and he didn't remember her at all? Handsome boys with blue eyes and black hair had a free pass to forget anyone they wanted.

His eyes finally lit. "Oh yeah, you're the pastor's kid."

"Yeah," Ava smiled and turned her attention to the other guy at the table. "It's Grayson, right?"

Grayson half-stood from his seat to reach a hand across the table. "Pastors let their kids study abroad?"

"Why not?" Ava shrugged.

"It's probably part mission trip for her," Benj said with a crooked smile as he leaned back in his chair.

"Just school," Ava said. "When did y'all get here?"

"Yesterday," they answered simultaneously.

Grayson pushed his chair back and slapped a hand on Benj's shoulder. "Fish and chips?"

"Let's do it," Benj said.

Ava stood as well, they were the last ones in the room. She followed them out, silently hoping for an invitation, but none came. They talked between themselves about some TGU football drama and Ava let her step fall short, giving them some distance until she was alone.

The campus was dark. Cold. Wet. Ava shivered and wrapped her arms across her chest. A microwave dinner waited for her in her room. And probably a roommate who wanted to give her more love advice. Neither were wanted right now.

Ava diverted toward a street packed with restaurants and pubs. She wasn't used to eating alone, but in the anonymity of this place, it was no different from anything else she was doing. *"Two are better than one."*[2] The verse popped into her head, but it wasn't helpful. One was fine.

After ordering at the counter of a quiet pizza spot, she sat on a barstool facing the street. The city was beautiful, even in the dark drizzle. The mist around the street lamps made it look even more magical. She ate her pizza in silence, pulling out her phone for company.

Finished with dinner, Ava wandered slowly towards the dorm, stopping at Argos again. The silky duvet hadn't kept her warm last night, so she found a small row of fuzzy blankets—most with a busy pattern or dark color. She found a single cream one at the bottom. The perfect peace to a room filled with Rosie's chaos.

The dorm building was quiet, only a few students sat scattered around the downstairs lounge area, each with headphones and laptops. Everything was quieter than she had imagined it. Student living was supposed to be busy, loud… Maybe the building would come alive once classes started. The ping-pong table sat off to the side, as dejected as Ava.

Room 407 greeted her with its dull brown face. A room down the hall had a pom garland around their door. She could do something similar. A wreath would breathe life into the drab hallway. Ava unlocked the door and stepped inside to a cloud of perfume.

"Good grief," she coughed and waved it away from her face. Rosie laughed from the bathroom and called out an apology.

Another voice was in there with her. A new face popped out and introduced herself as Molly from the room that shared their bathroom. Ava declined another invitation to a bar. Those weren't her people.

Grabbing her laptop, notepad and pencils, she climbed into her loft bed. She had a short list of Christian churches within walking distance of the campus. The closest one would work for tomorrow. Sundays were for church, regardless of where she was. Monday, she would go to the Christian Student Union and find out where other students went. She would find her people.

Chapter 4

Ava sat in the front row of her Modern History of Architecture class, five minutes early. She had already met the professor, along with a handful of other early arrivals. It was a large class, the professor estimated 150 students. At least, that's what Ava thought he said. He was Irish, and at times his accent was so thick, Ava wasn't sure if he was still speaking English.

Benjamin and Grayson walked into the room, and Ava lifted a small wave to them. Grayson returned it. Benj didn't seem to see her as he made his way up the steps to the back of the lecture hall. Sloane came rushing through the door at the last minute. Maybe they could all swap notes to make up for the accent struggles. If any of the others were the note-taking type.

The professor was entertaining to watch. He made more hand gestures than any syllabus ever deserved. By the end of class, he had assigned 50 pages of reading.

As students filed down the steps and out of the room, Ava packed her bag slowly, hoping to catch the Texans. The three of them were already talking as they headed for the door. Ava fell into step with them.

"I didn't buy all the books," Sloane said. "There's no way he can assign that much reading."

"You can borrow any of mine," Grayson said.

"Same," Ava said. "But hopefully you're right and he doesn't get to it all."

"Says Miss Front Row," Sloane laughed.

Ava shrugged. "It helps the grade."

"I wouldn't know, I never needed it," Sloane replied without looking at her. "What other classes are you guys taking?"

Ava listened in. She was the only one with interior design courses, so her schedule varied the most, but she noticed she shared one other class with Benjamin. She didn't admit it out loud. Sloane seemed capable of taking anything she said and making her look dumb.

When they exited the building, Sloane and Grayson headed off to a shared class together. Ava was going to the Christian Student Union for their kickoff luncheon and invited Benj to join her. With a quick head shake, his sapphire eyes looked like they just now noticed she was there.

"No thanks. Later." With that, he turned down a sidewalk, all lean six feet of him. Ava groaned inwardly and hiked her canvas backpack strap higher onto her shoulder.

The campus spread out, cutting in and out of the city, interspersed with touristy streets and parks. It was nothing like Texas Gulf, where the university claimed its 40 acres with a perfectly contained layout. Ava had studied the bus maps and schedules but still didn't understand it. She decided to walk the half-mile to the union rather than waste time waiting at the wrong bus stop.

The union occupied the second floor of a modern building that stood in stark, glassy contrast to the central campus' historic stone. Glaring against its Reformation-era surroundings, it was out of place.

Seeing nowhere to check in, Ava stepped into the short line at the buffet tables and added a sandwich and fruit cup to her plate. At the end of the self-serve line, she turned and faced the room of round tables.

It was seventh grade all over again. She had started at a new private school, walking into a sea of new faces. And she had been okay. Of course, she had already been friends with Talia, and one friend was all you needed to break in at a small private school. Here, she was on her own.

Nobody else sat alone. No groups had an obvious open spot. Everyone seemed well established. The cliques were already set on the first day of the semester? Maybe this was more of a reconnecting lunch than a welcome lunch. If she stood here any longer, it would only get more awkward.

Ava took a step towards a table with a few girls and a couple of empty chairs when a middle-aged woman cut her off.

"Hello there," she sang out as she walked up to Ava. "I don't believe I've seen you here before. I'm Linda."

"Ava Sanford, nice to meet you. I'm new to UE this semester."

"Welcome, welcome. We're always glad to see new students. Where did you transfer from?" Linda guided them towards an empty table to the right.

"Texas. I didn't transfer though, I'm studying abroad."

Linda's mouth opened but nothing came out. She tried again. "How long are you staying?"

"This semester."

"Oh dear." She nodded slowly and twisted her lips. "Well, you are welcome to stay for lunch. But I'm afraid to register with CSU, you have to be a permanent student."

"Really?" Ava asked with a frown. "I'll be here for the entire semester…"

"Yes, dear. We work to provide a stable community here, so we don't want too many faces changing out," Linda said with a plastered smile. "The university has some wonderful resources for study abroad students though, have you visited their international student center?"

Ava buried her frustration and forced her jaw into a similarly fake smile. "I have… But they didn't have many religious resources." Their first meeting of the semester was at a pub.

Linda shrugged and looked like she was about to move on to the next new face. Ava stopped her with one more question. "Could you recommend a Christian church around here? Where do most of the students go?"

"Oh, I think most of them are too busy on weekends. You could try the Redeemed Christian Church, they're down the street."

The same place she had been yesterday morning. The same one that was definitely not a student spot. Everyone else there had either been under 10 or over 40.

"Thank you, Linda," Ava said politely, she was obviously losing the woman's attention and waved a quick goodbye.

The woman left her alone at the table. Ava stared at her lunch. She could move tables. Would that be weirder? Was there a point in staying here anymore? She scarfed the lunch as quickly as possible. A swing and a miss, as Jack would say. It didn't mean she was out yet. *"I am continually with you,"*[3] repeated in her mind as she silently started praying for something to change.

• • •

With another glance at her phone, Ava slowed her walk to the Environmental Design class Tuesday morning. If she had heard Benj right, he was in this class. And if heaven smiled on her today, she might snag a seat next to him, even if it meant skipping the front row. Though some other TGU undergrad would probably claim that spot. She had to time her entry perfectly.

It was still early when she arrived at the building. Habit. Ava stalled, fidgeting with her backpack, a shoelace, her water bottle. Two minutes to class time. The sweet spot between too early and late. She straightened and walked down the hall towards the classroom. It was a small classroom with five rows of desks. She spotted Benjamin in the back. He waved to her and nodded slightly toward the empty desk to his right. *Thank heavens.* With a quiet hello, Ava dropped her backpack and slid into the desk.

The professor introduced herself and told everyone to read the syllabus on their own time. "I don't take attendance and it's not part of your grade, but if you want to pass the tests, you'll be in your seats." With that, she dove into the lesson, jotting terms onto the chalkboard.

Ava had barely pulled her notebook and pen out of her bag when the first hints were dropped to "remember this for the test next week." Ava's hand flew across her page. She noticed Benj seemed to keep pace as well. He wasn't the sit-back, too-cool type after all.

When the whirlwind hour finished, her brain felt like it had been in a train wreck. The professor dismissed them and left the room before anyone else. Ava hadn't even introduced herself.

"Better get here earlier Thursday for that front row spot," Benj said with a dimpled half smile as they packed their notes into their bags.

"Yeah, looks like I'm going to have to work a little harder for this grade."

"And Sloane thought assigned reading was bad." Benj shook his head.

"She would hate this," Ava laughed and shouldered her backpack as they headed out of the classroom.

"How's Jack and the gym staff?" Benj asked.

Her mind and step stuttered. "What?"

"You're friends with Jack Shields, right?"

"Yeah…" *I thought you didn't remember me?* "Um, I don't know. Fine, I guess."

"I heard some football guys showed up to the gym drunk and trashed the locker room."

"Wow. I didn't hear about that. I hope the staff didn't get in trouble." Why hadn't Jack told her?

"Yeah, the entire football team got suspended from the gym for two weeks."

"Gosh, I might actually use that gym if they kept them out."

Benj laughed as they stepped outside. "My next class isn't for another hour. Wanna grab coffee?"

"Oh… Um, yeah, sure. Coffee?" She couldn't remember how to use words. "Where's the closest spot?"

"I found one yesterday," Benj said, putting a hand on her shoulder and pointing her towards the south end of the square. His touch was electric, vibrating and numbing. "It's not too far. Come on."

Ava followed him, focusing on the sidewalk. *"Don't forget, he has a girlfriend."* "Have you talked to Cassandra?"

Benj gave her his signature half smile. "Yeah, she requires it pretty much daily. If she could have made me sign a contract, she would have." Ava laughed.

They walked half a block when Benj stopped short at a tiny storefront tucked between a bank and a souvenir shop. He opened the door for Ava and they walked inside to a shop the size of a hallway. Two-top tables were crammed along one wall, while the other housed the coffee equipment. They each ordered and squeezed past the first few tables to an empty one at the back of the shop.

"So I went by the Christian Student Union yesterday," Ava said, needing to fill the space with conversation. She had never been around Benjamin one-on-one before. "Save yourself the walk. They don't let study abroad students into their programs."

Benjamin laughed and, like his smile, it managed to land somewhere between a genuinely happy sound and a snicker, as if everything only slightly amused him. "I wasn't planning to try at all, but thanks for the heads up."

"Not at all? No church or anything?"

"This is a break from all that." Benjamin shrugged. "If the church is sponsoring your mission trip, shouldn't you be around non-Christians anyway?"

"It's not sponsoring me, and it's not a mission trip," Ava said, though the defense was useless. "I just want to find some decent friends here."

"Don't try so hard," Benj countered, his gaze wandering around the coffee shop. Ava leaned back in her chair, trying to borrow his nonchalance. "Be the foreigner. It has its own charm. Throw out a cute southern *y'all* and you'll have boys lining up."

Ava dropped her head in a nervous laugh. "I'm not trying to get boys lined up."

"Oh, the girls then?"

"No—" She answered too quickly and caught the flash of a dimple around Benjamin's mouth. He was teasing her. Ava tried to send him a quick glare, but wasn't sure if the nervousness had worn off enough for it to work. She blew out a breath. "Forget it."

"Relax." He gave her hand a quick squeeze, long enough to squeeze out her ability to think straight. "Nobody here knows Ava Sanford and they aren't expecting anything from you either. Just have fun."

Ava brushed a hand over her hair, hoping the waves would hold, instead of giving into a humidity-induced frizz. She needed something to say, something that covered how nervous he made her. "I am having fun. The campus is gorgeous. My roommate is Tinker Bell. And it's cold and wet all the time."

"Living the dream." Benj winked.

She managed to hold a normal conversation for another 20 minutes, talking about mutual acquaintances and their plans for their time in Edinburgh until they had to leave for classes. Outside, rare rays of sunshine were peeking through the clouds. Each patch of light like a kiss of warmth. Once they got to the campus, they split ways and Ava made it to her class in the perfect five-minute window.

After the interior design class ended, she had the day to herself. Winding outside of the campus for her walk back to her dorm, Ava followed the shop-lined streets. She stopped at a floral shop and a woman called a hello from behind a towering bouquet of dried grasses. Two neat rows of bouquets lined the front, while the back of the shop held an untamed jungle.

"Can I help you?" The woman came around the counter wearing a white apron over her green sweater.

After explaining her plans for a homemade wreath, the woman led her to the jungle at the back wall. Ava pulled eucalyptus and cedar leaves, and was reaching for a few stems of baby's breath when the woman returned with a wreath form.

"Why not make it a bit more Scottish?" she asked, snagging a few branches of a purple bloom.

"Lavender?" Ava asked, sniffing the flower.

"Heather. It covers the moors in the summer."

It was a beautiful touch to the wreath. Ava checked out, noting that the cost of growing plants through the winter must be much higher in Scotland, and carried her bouquet back to her building.

Rosie was lounging on her bed when Ava walked in. "Bought me flowers, did ye?"

"A wreath for our door." Ava held up the arrangement. "What do you think?"

"Perfect, more memorable than a room number for the boys."

Ava wrinkled her nose. Not her goal. She dropped her backpack on her bed and scattered the arrangement on the floor. Weaving greenery in first, she covered the wire circle before filling it in with blooms of heather and baby's breath. *"The grass withers, and the flower falls, but the word of the Lord remains forever."*[4]

"Here." Rosie hopped down from her bed and fished through the bins that filled her bookcase. She grabbed a random string and pulled a pushpin from her cork board.

"Perfect." Ava hung the wreath on the door and both girls stood back to admire it, like a great work of art. It might as well have been, compared to the dull hallway. It added a touch of home. Ava's own touch.

Chapter 5

Jack had finished sanitizing the last of the intramural softball gear and stacking it in the athletic department's storage room when the gym music cut off, leaving an empty, welcome silence. The two-hour playlist was long enough for anyone working out, but short enough that the songs were permanently etched into an employee's brain.

When Jack walked back into the main area, the lights were dimmed and the gym was cleared out. Natalie wiped down equipment and stacked weights. Jack went through the locker rooms for one last check. The stupid football player incident wasn't his fault and his boss knew it, but he still had to triple check everything now.

"All clean, Cap'n Jack," Natalie called as she walked to the front and dropped her spray bottle and rag into the bin by the desk.

"Thanks, Nat. Everybody scanned out?"

"Yep. Isn't the gym great now? Can we get the team permanently banned?"

Jack laughed. She was right. The gym was more peaceful now, but he couldn't admit that out loud. "It would be pretty boring around here without the gym rats. Gotta start recruiting other students."

"Need some pretty ladies in here? I'll see what I can do," Natalie said, laughing as she clocked out.

Jack rubbed the back of his neck and reached for the computer. Being a supervisor was weird, he had to watch everything he said now. He didn't bother to reply to Natalie. She had worked with him last semester and didn't care at all about his title change.

They walked out of the gym together and Jack double checked the lock. Natalie looped an arm through his. "A few of us are going to Draft Haus tonight. You coming?"

"On a Tuesday?" Jack shot her his most disapproving, supervisorial look.

"There's no homework yet." Natalie shrugged.

"I've got class at eight, I'll pass."

She booed him. "Why would you take one that early? You're a junior, you should have a better schedule."

"Blame my advisor." Jack pulled out the key to the truck and unlocked it. The blame was actually his, for running the five-year track to graduation—and slowly, at that. Every semester, he took the minimum number of hours required by financial aid. He had to save time in his schedule for work or else he would completely drown in loans. He had been slowly falling behind since the day he started school.

While giving Natalie a ride back to her apartment, she chided him the entire way about his business degree. Half of the students working in the athletic department were kinesiology majors and were always teasing Jack for throwing his life away. But he knew firsthand how all-consuming sports could be. And how easily those dreams could be torn apart. He refused to fall for it again.

His roommate wasn't home when Jack got there. He tossed his keys on the beat up IKEA table and headed for the shower. The running clock in his mind gave him a maximum six hours of sleep if he powered through tonight's homework.

Halfway through the first research assignment, his phone buzzed with a useless notification. Before he knew it, he was watching a live video from Natalie. Anything to distract him from the boredom of more accounting. A quick flick through his feed took him to Ava's latest post. An elaborate green and purple wreath hung on an otherwise dingy door, with a caption about making it more like home. Jack liked the photo and kept scrolling.

Another friend studying abroad in Norway posted a picture of a columned building covered in snow, with a caption rattling on about a winter wonderland. Half the people he knew were studying abroad right now. Apparently, this was the semester to go. It was the "can't-miss experience" for everyone who assumed a college degree was a given. And an impossibility for a student paying his way through every single day.

By the time Jack glanced at the clock, it was well after midnight. He groaned and tossed the phone across the bed. The days were too carefully measured, scheduled, and balanced for distractions. Two more years and he would be done. He would have a degree and a job. Any job.

• • •

Wednesday went by in a blur, the morning was filled with a core-level history class, mind-numbing accounting, and business law. The afternoon wasn't much better. Jack spent it trapped in the athletic department offices, setting up practice schedules for the intramural fields, confirming equipment requests, and answering questions from new students. Halfway through scheduling staff, his phone buzzed with a text.

Ava
Wednesdays are still for coffee, right?
Jack
Like watch each other drink coffee on a video call? Weirdo...
Ava
I never said video anything, creep.
Jack
I work till 5.
Ava
Ugh that's 11 here.
Fine. Call me when you get off.

The hours somehow simultaneously dragged, yet weren't enough to get everything done. The moment the clock hit five, he packed out of the office. He waved bye to Natalie and Victor at the front desk of the gym, stopping himself from telling them to double check the locker rooms and doors tonight. He wasn't a "double check" kind of supervisor. Besides, someone in Scotland waited for a phone call. He climbed into his truck and put in earbuds before tapping Ava's name.

"Jack!" Her voice rang out, surprisingly chipper for someone who whined about staying up until 11.

"Wow, I expected whispers and crying about it being bedtime."

"Well, my roommate's gone, so no whispers needed," Ava said.

"What'd you do with her body?"

"Ha, ha. She's never here. She's kind of wild. I think she's at ladies' night at some pub right now."

"And you skipped it?" Jack asked without an ounce of sincerity.

"Yeah, she reminds me regularly that I'm failing all of my roommate duties. I think she has roommate confused for wingman."

"They're basically the same."

"You would not believe how much everybody drinks here. You only have to be 18 and they act like it's their sole source of life."

Jack couldn't help but smile at Ava's first taste of the real world. "Yeah, Aves, that's not Scotland. That's college outside of Grace Church."

Ava groaned. "Don't tell me that. I was going to join the international student group here, but they were going out drinking tonight too. How am I supposed to find any decent people here?"

"Who's the judgmental one now?" Jack laughed. Plenty of decent people drank a little, and plenty not-so-decent ones drank a lot. "Go get a soda or something. Doesn't mean you have to get drunk."

Ava made a noncommittal sound. Really, he was fine with that, and ready to pull back his own advice at the mental image of Ava in a bar. "What about the other TGU students?" Jack asked, waiting to hear a certain name.

"I think they all came together as their own clique. I don't know... Hey, Benj told me about the football players messing up the gym."

There was the name. Jack's grip tightened on the steering wheel. "Those guys are tools." The football players and Benj.

"Did anybody on staff get in trouble?"

"Not really, but we have to track who's there now and triple check everything when we close."

Jack pulled up to his apartment and headed inside. He tossed his chin in greeting to Quinton, his roommate, watching TV from the couch. Jack headed into his room, answering Ava's list of questions about church on Sunday, mutual friends, and C3 events. He had expected the phone call to be filled with stories about Scotland and how he was missing out on everything good.

"Okay Aves, home is the same," he said. "When are you going to start talking about how amazing Edinburgh is?"

"Oh… It's okay."

"Not incredible, spectacular, best semester ever? Come on."

"It's kinda weird. Not what I expected. I thought it'd be easier to make friends."

Was this the same girl who could become best friends with anyone she met? Jack scrambled for the confidence she seemed to have suddenly dropped and tried to give it back. "It's only been a week, you'll be fine. Just don't trap yourself in your room."

"I'm not, or not on purpose."

"Hey, quit moping."

"I'm not moping," she whined.

"Yes, you are. You only get flowers when you're moping. I saw the wreath."

The laugh sounded more like her. "Whatever. I need them to remind me of the sun. I haven't seen it much lately."

"Still shining here. Want a picture?" Jack tucked the phone into his shoulder and pulled out a fresh shirt for tonight's Bible study group.

"I'm good. By the way, did Katie send out the email with prayer requests and study notes this week?"

"Yeah. Did you not get it?"

"No. I mean, I'm not in the group anymore. It makes sense. I guess I just miss being part of it."

"You're still part of the group," he said. "I'll ask her about it."

The line was quiet for a moment. "Thanks… Give baby Gabe a squeeze for me."

"No way. I'm a guy, that's weird. I don't do babies."

"It is not weird and you can do it for me," Ava said. Jack only grunted. "Photo proof or it never happened."

"We'll see."

"Okay, I know you need to go. Thanks for talking..."

"Anytime," Jack said. "Aves, the first week is always a wash."

"Yeah. You're right." She sighed. "Next week? Same time, same place?"

"You got it."

He set the phone down and reached for a snack in the refrigerator when he got a text from Micah Sanford. Micah invited Jack to stop by their house before small group that evening to pick up a textbook. Ava was loaning him one for his history class. Despite the fact that she had graduated high school a year after him, she had practically caught up to him in college and finished the class first.

Jack groaned and rushed through the apartment, throwing on the new shirt and grabbing his Bible before heading out the door, half-starved.

Chapter 6

Church Number Two was another flop. They were so full, they turned her away for not having reserved a seat. She had never even heard of a church requiring reservations. So back at her dorm room, Ava watched her dad's sermon from last week and cried.

The second week of classes was more of the same: dead ends and blank stares. Everywhere she went, she was in the wrong place. She went out with the international students at their second meeting, trying to take Jack's advice. They had already split into two groups: the ones who spoke Mandarin and the ones who spoke French. Ava knew they all spoke English, that's what the classes were taught in, but no one engaged with her. It made sense. Anyone would choose a taste of home when offered.

Katie sent her the email of prayer requests for the week. Ava added hers in Christian code: good community. It sounded less pitiful than asking for a friend. If her last name was her identity in Ridley Bay, her anonymity was her identity in Edinburgh. She even caved and accepted her parents' offer to send a package of things from home. The requests were mostly comfort food items she couldn't find. Peanut butter and Trix cereal. So much for growing up.

She finished her homework in the empty lounge downstairs, without a soul in sight. She repacked her backpack and climbed the steps to her room. Weekends were dead. She had just kicked off her shoes when Rosie came in behind her like a whirlwind, blonde waves flying around her face.

"Yer comin' oot tonight," Rosie said, ripping her jacket and scarf off and tossing them on the bed. "I dinnae care about yer protests. Ah need a buffer."

"I don't drink," Ava said.

"Ye do tonight, hen."

A loud knock sounded from inside of their bathroom before the door opened and their shared-bathroom-mates, Molly and Liliana, spilled into the room.

Breathless, Liliana spoke first. "The rugby club is going to St. Bart's tonight."

"Ah ken, get her ready," Rosie replied with a jerk of her head towards Ava.

"You cannot wear that, Miss Texas," Molly said to Ava.

"I'm not going—"

Rosie grabbed Ava by the shoulders, turning her face to face. "Do ye want friends or not?"

Ava hesitated.

"Aye. The Puritan act is cute, but get yer bahooky out of this room. Drink water for all I care, but no more moping."

"Okay, okay—"

Molly grabbed Ava and pulled her through the bathroom into her room. "You don't own a proper shirt. Pick one of mine." She opened a crammed closet and started pulling out hangers, tossing them on the bed. Her own light skin was already clad in a skin-tight green dress that matched her eyes.

Ava studied the four tops in various shades and cuts. None of them looked like anything she would wear. "I'll be fine in what I have…"

"Haud yer wheesht!" Rosie shouted from the bathroom.

"What?" Ava squeaked, eyes wide.

"It means shut up," Molly laughed.

Running her fingers over them once more, Ava opted for a plum wrap sweater with a wide boat neck. It was the most reasonable option, considering the weather.

Molly nodded. "Jewel tones for brown eyes, perfect."

Ava took the shirt back into her room and changed. "You can see my bra straps," she said to the mirror as she fidgeted with the wide neckline, trying to pull it higher on her shoulders.

"Yer in uni," Rosie said. "Everybody knows yer wearin' a bra."

The bathroom was the center of makeup and hair madness and it sucked Ava in. Her idea of going out involved restaurants and coffee shops, and bars were unknown territory. Within an hour, she was styled, curled, and powdered. They all slipped on coats and hustled down the stairs into the frigid night air before she gave it a second thought.

"Have you seen him yet this term?" Liliana asked Rosie. Liliana's gold top took the term "v-neck" to new extremes, plunging nearly to her belly button. The shirt reflected her amber hair in a way that made the entire ensemble exotic.

Rosie shook her head of curls.

"Who?" Ava asked.

"Callan, my ex. Or he was," Rosie said with a wicked smile and a wink.

Ava wore boots instead of heels like the others, yet she could hardly match their pace. The tempo kept her warm in the frigid air. "How do y'all afford going out this much?" She asked, half laughing, half grumbling.

Rosie's high-pitched laugh filled the air. "Doll, it's the boys who have to worry about that."

After two quick blocks, they entered a red brick pub packed with people. Ava stuck close to the girls as they pushed their way between the crowded barstools and ordered four beers. The wall behind the bar was a dizzying array of mirrors and colorful glass bottles without a focal point.

"Here," Molly handed Ava a beer. "Take a sip so you don't slosh it."

Doesn't mean you have to get drunk. It tasted terrible. Molly must have caught the face Ava made. Molly laughed at her and promised it was just a starter until the boys bought them something better. Ava had never felt so out of place in her life. Carefully holding the glass away from her borrowed shirt, she followed the girls, weaving through the crowd to the couches and armchairs at the back, filled with people.

Rosie abandoned their group to make contact with her obvious target, leaning over the couch and whispering something in his ear, surprising him. Liliana and Molly struck up a conversation with a small circle of guys standing to the side. They knew most of the guys in the group; introductions were made for the rest. All athletes. All holding drinks.

Molly looped an arm around Ava's waist and introduced her as "little Miss Texas." Several eyebrows shot up and a couple of the guys shot each other looks. Maybe Benj had been right about being the foreigner.

"Do you own a horse?" one boy asked, probably the youngest in the group. His wavy, tawny hair reminded her of Jack.

Ava smiled. It was the most common question whenever she left the states. "No, but I do know how to ride."

Somebody whooped, and another whistled before Ava heard her own comment through a different filter and her cheeks warmed. "—A horse," she tried to add, but the damage was done. Liliana failed to bite back a laugh. Molly smirked but saved her with a comment directed at the boy about needing some lessons.

Suddenly the music volume rose until the windows nearly shook. Ava glanced at her phone—11 on the dot. Apparently that was when St. Bart's went from pub to club. Conversation was limited to those closest, and even then, it was difficult. The guy to Ava's left bent down towards her ear and said something to her.

"What?"

"What's wrong with your drink?" he asked again, pointing to the still-full beer in her hand.

"Oh—I don't really drink."

"You haven't found the right one then," he said, with a smile that touched his dark brown eyes more than his lips. It wrinkled the one freckle under his left eye. "What do you like to drink?"

"Um… Tea, coffee, soda…" Ava said with a shrug. The answer was lame. She was completely out of her comfort zone. Especially talking to someone tall and handsome, and who filled out his button up until it stretched across his chest.

"Got it," he said. He took the beer from her hand and brushed against her shoulder as he turned and walked toward the bar.

When he returned, he held out a small glass with what looked like soda. Ava accepted it and took a sip. It was good. Coke with a smokey flavor.

"That's better. What is it?" Ava asked. His eyes tightened and flicked over hers like he wasn't sure if she was serious. Was it a dumb question?

"Whisky and Coke." This time his smile reached his lips, curving up the crisp outline of a stubble beard. He reached a hand out to her. "Oliver."

She returned the hand shake. "Ava."

"That's a pretty Scottish name for a Texan."

Liliana chose that moment to pull Oliver into a very Scottish exchange of witticisms and sarcasms that Ava didn't understand. She moved towards Molly, right as Rosie came bounding over to them, throwing her arms around their shoulders and breaking the circle.

"I think he properly regrets himself now," she said with a satisfied grin. "There's some Americans at the bar, doll. Cute too. Know 'em?"

With a discrete glance at the bar, she saw Grayson from TGU sitting with a few other people, one she recognized as a grad student, but the others had their backs turned. "I do, actually."

"Introduce me," Rosie begged and pulled her towards the bar.

Ava looked back over her shoulder in time to make eye contact with Oliver over Liliana's head. She immediately spun away and kept her eyes straight ahead on Grayson. It wasn't until she was stepping right in between the barstools that she realized who was sitting next to Grayson.

"Benjamin," she said, surprised by the proximity to him as he turned towards her. He drank?

"Ava... Sanford," he said her last name slowly as his eyes fell from hers to her drink. His half smile played at the corner of his mouth. "What are you drinking?"

Ava stammered for a second as warmth spread up her neck and she suddenly remembered the black bra straps that were probably showing. *Do not touch your bra straps right now.*

"Coke and whisky—"

Rosie cut in, introducing herself. Benjamin returned the introduction without much attention. The bubbly pixie roommate worked the area and held the TGU students captive. Except Benjamin.

"Who got you the drink?" he asked, stepping off the barstool, getting closer to Ava to speak over the noise.

"What?" She had heard him but didn't want to answer the question. "Why?"

Benj's smile was measured. Always. "Watch your drinks, girl. Don't let them out of your sight."

Of course… Bars might be new to her, but she wasn't born yesterday. She shouldn't have taken a drink from a stranger. Ava studied the cup in her hand and frowned, setting it on the bar behind Benjamin. He watched smugly.

"You're here with her?" he asked, motioning towards Rosie. Ava nodded. Benj put a hand on Rosie's arm and she instantly sprang to his side. He said something in her ear that made her nose wrinkle and she laughed.

"You got it, Cowboy," Rosie said, leaning onto his arm. "What are the terms? Does she have to go home alone?"

"Not necessarily," Benj said, looking back at Ava with a brow raised in question. Ava groaned and crossed her arms. The pixie had already turned her attention back to Grayson and Ava nudged Benj's arm.

"Don't be gross," she said.

"How is that gross? You can go home with whoever you want. I'm just making sure it's not because of something in your drink."

Ava shook her head and pointed at Rosie. "Look at her, Benj. I'll be the one getting her home."

"I'm looking, and I'm pretty sure she can handle herself." Benj flagged the bartender and ordering a new whisky and Coke for Ava. This time, she watched it until it was in her hand.

"What are you doing here, anyway?" she asked.

"Same thing as you," Benj replied with a quick scan over her that made her conscious of the bra straps again. "End of the week. Why not?"

A few reasons ran through her mind: about testimonies, transparency, and the appearance of evil. But his grin was convincing. And he was actually talking to her in front of other TGU students. It was progress—up until now, he had only been friendly in private. So her reasons slipped away.

Rosie grabbed her arm before she gave an intelligent response. "A'ight lads, Miss Texas has a few more Scots to meet." She waved goodbye to the group and Ava followed.

"Always leave them wanting more," Rosie said in Ava's ear as she hauled her back towards their former group.

Being attached to Rosie thrust Ava into the center of attention. Suddenly, she was part of the pixie and they were a shining duo. Either the energy emanating from Rosie or the second glass of whisky did the job, and Ava was finally relaxing.

The former Ava could run a room at a church event. Why not at a bar too? Nobody else thought she shouldn't be there. Nobody but Ava. All the places she *should* be had turned her down. She could be here. *Why not?*

Molly and Liliana had moved on to another group when Oliver reappeared. His arrival nearly evaporated her fledgling confidence. Rosie dragged Ava towards him.

"Ye met Ava yet, Oliver?" Rosie asked, finally dropping Ava's arm.

"I have." He winked.

"O' course ye have," Rosie laughed. "You're always the fastest at finding a new bonnie lass."

"I had to save her from your beer choices."

"What she drinks isn't my job, now is it? Keep an eye on her, I'm gaunnae take one more stab at Callan." And she was gone.

Oliver leaned down to cover their height difference and said something in her ear. His voice was too low and soft and Ava missed it again.

"I'm sorry, it's so loud—"

"Come on," he took her hand and zig zagged through the crowd towards the front door before Ava even thought about removing her hand.

They stepped outside and the cold air rushed into her lungs, a welcome change. She hadn't realized how crowded she had felt inside until she was free. The music poured onto the street, but the bass no longer set the tempo of her heartbeat.

"Better?" Oliver asked. His black hair was cropped close on the sides and longer on top. It reminded Ava of the soccer players her brothers watched.

"It is… But I probably shouldn't ditch Rosie—"

"Ah, now that I can actually hear it, you have a lovely voice."

"Oh—Thanks…" Benjamin's warnings about getting home floated into her mind, but Oliver had already dropped her hand. And they were only standing outside. "So you go to UE?"

He smiled again, like she was missing some joke. "Yeah. I play rugby. Callan's my roommate."

The cold was reaching her bones and Ava awkwardly attempted to slip her coat back on while hanging onto her glass. Oliver reached out and held it for her while she buttoned up.

"What year are you?" he asked.

"Junior." Graduation dates weren't relevant.

"Same." He lifted his glass in cheers and Ava met it. "It's the best one. You know what you want, but there's no pressure or big commitment yet."

The door swung open behind them, releasing a burst of warm air and pounding music. Ava turned and found herself face to face with Benjamin. And the female grad student from TGU with a hand on his arm.

"Ava," he said coolly, looking past her.

"Benj… This is Oliver," Ava motioned towards him and Benj gave him a quick handshake before introducing Bailey as well.

"Where's your roommate?" Benjamin asked with obvious disdain.

"Rosie? Inside…" Ava stood frozen in place. He was mercurial, and adding alcohol to the mix only made him more confusing.

"We're heading to Devil's Glen down the street if y'all want to come," Benj said casually. He leaned in close to Ava and whispered. "Careful who you go home with."

"I'm just getting some air—"

"See you later." He waved her off and turned his back. The only options her eyes could find were watching Benjamin and Bailey walk away or staring at Oliver. Neither worked.

"You going to join them?" Oliver asked, entirely unfazed, standing in the same wide stance he'd had since they stepped outside, one hand in his jeans pocket, the other holding his drink. His question gave her permission to look at him again. To study him from half a foot below.

"It's up to Rosie and the other girls. I'm only along for the ride." Ava shrugged, and the motion turned into a shiver.

"Rosie should be done having her fun with Callan. Wanna go back in?" he asked. Ava nodded and Oliver proved the gentleman, holding the door open for her and following her back inside.

They found Rosie straddling Callan's lap on the couch and making out with him. Ava's eyes went wide, and she spun away from the scene.

"Not done then," Oliver laughed. He touched her back, and she straightened an inch taller, letting him direct her towards another set of tables at the back. Oliver motioned towards her empty glass. "You're out. Can I get you another?"

She was only one and a half drinks in, but she wasn't sure how much a first-timer should drink. Or how much longer she would be here. Or if it was the reason her face was so warm. "No, thanks."

Two other guys from the rugby club approached and started talking about the states. None had been to Texas, but they had all been somewhere in the U.S. and compared travel notes over the music. Ava became the expert, called on to decide important matters like whether true American pizza came from Chicago or New York. She caught sight of Liliana sending glances her way every so often. Just when she was about to cave to getting another drink, Molly and Liliana walked up to her.

"Sorry to steal your newest thing, lads," Molly said, hooking an arm through Ava's. "I've got to get this wee bonnie back home."

"Are y'all leaving?" Ava asked. Someone snickered at the word y'all. "Where's Rosie?"

"She already left, but she's not going home," Liliana said.

"Oh? Oh… Okay." Realization dawned awkwardly. Ava turned back to the guys and thanked them for the chat.

"Till next time," Oliver said too softly, so that Ava questioned if she had heard him correctly. She only smiled in response.

The girls bundled into their jackets and ducked their heads against the light drizzle coming down, misting over the lights and darkening the street.

"Had to go straight for Oliver, did you?" Liliana asked with a laugh.

"No, not at all, I didn't mean to…" Ava jabbed her hands deeper into her coat pockets. "I'm not here for a boyfriend. He's all yours."

Liliana shrugged and patted Ava's shoulder. "I'm teasing you, doll. Besides, he only likes new girls."

Ava was quiet as they walked. It was well after midnight when they made it back. She washed up and went to bed, alone in the room. For the first time in two weeks, there was no lying awake for an hour, staring at the ceiling. No, she fell asleep within minutes, and stayed asleep.

Chapter 7

By the third week of classes, Ava completely understood why everyone loved Professor Garcia. He was more like a sweet, encouraging grandparent than a professor. Their Friday lab was essentially a study hall—a weekly pause to check in with everyone and review papers or projects.

She was always the first one there, usually followed by the grad students, while the undergrads came last. Those few minutes alone with Garcia gave her a chance to connect with him and talk about her school plans and career goals. The free, five-minute mentoring was the highlight of her week. This week, it offered a break from a four-day headache Ava blamed on the Scottish weather.

When everyone had arrived, Garcia asked the group for some of their favorite buildings in the area. After the grad students listed off some, Ava volunteered hers: St. Mary's Cathedral, west of campus.

"Oh, for the love," Sloane sighed. "Of course you would pick a church for your mission trip."

The mission trip joke had spread, like the blush on Ava's neck now. "I'm not, it's a beautiful—"

"If she's on a mission trip, she did a great job reaching out to some Scottish guys at St. Bart's last week," Bailey said with a laugh.

Ava went dumb and mute, blinking at her shoes. Being teased by petty undergrads was one thing, but an attack from a graduate student? Sloane and the other undergrads were laughing.

"Is St. Bart's a church?" Garcia asked innocently, arms crossed as he watched the conversation unfold.

"It's a bar," Grayson volunteered. "With the entire UE rugby team at it last week."

Sloane swore, dragging the word out slowly. "Ava goes all in. Wonder how many converts she can bag in a single night."

Ava wanted to defend herself but knew any and everything she said would be used against her. Her eyes stayed on her pen and notebook, unable to look up. Benj wasn't saying anything, and Ava couldn't tell if she heard his laugh in the mix or not. Ava almost wanted to pray for wisdom, but God was probably laughing too. She had made her own decisions, she was on her own now.

"Okay, what y'all do in your off time is not the discussion right now," Garcia said. "Grayson, we haven't heard your favorite yet."

The room quieted for a moment as the others finished sharing theirs. They had 20 minutes left and Ava had already submitted all of her TGU work. She pretended to be absorbed in editing a paper until Garcia dismissed them early. She closed her laptop and tossed it in her bag, making it out the door before anyone else.

But they weren't going to let her off the hook that easily.

"Ava," Sloane shouted down the hallway.

If only Ava could pretend she hadn't heard. But she had already faltered. Ignoring someone wasn't in her repertoire, regardless of who they were.

"Why didn't we get an invite to St. Bart's?" Sloane asked.

"My roommate forced me to go out at the last minute," Ava said, deciding on a need-to-know policy for this conversation.

"You didn't look too forced," Benj said with a signature smirk. Ava narrowed her eyes at him. *Why are you like this?*

"I wish I had a local roommate," Sloane groaned. "No offense, Georgia."

"None taken," Georgia said. "We need an insider."

"Ask Benj or Grayson then," Ava said. "They were there. Bailey too."

"Not willing to share your rugby team?" Sloane asked.

"You can have the whole team for all I care."

Sloane laughed and placed a hand on Ava's shoulder as she walked past. "Okay, you clearly need to get laid."

Grayson and Sloane took the lead, and the others walked on with them. Ava didn't even get a chance to defend herself. To tell them she wasn't the "get laid" type. Rather than chase them down, she focused on the crack in the concrete floor and willed it to open and swallow her. Or swallow Sloane at the very least. But the voices of the grad students echoed down the hallway and she didn't want a repeat conversation with Bailey. Ava followed the first group out of the building, maintaining a careful distance.

She had to drop off an interior design project today, and diverted from the TGU students to head to her professor's office. After dropping it off and visiting for a while, she wandered slowly through campus. Aimlessly. Avoiding her dorm. Her room would either be empty and lonely, or filled with Rosie's mindless chatter. At least Rosie was friendly.

"Ava," a voice rang out ahead of her and her head jerked up. Benj walked towards her—alone.

"Hey…" She met him halfway in the small courtyard.

"You okay?"

Ava watched him without answering. She knew his pattern by now but couldn't resist him. It was like watching a snake rising out of a basket—charming and deceptive. She never knew when he would change moods again.

"Grayson, Leo and I are going out tonight. You wanna come?"

An invitation from the cutest guy at C3 should have made her happy, but she only felt gullible. "Are the other TGU girls going?"

Benj shifted his backpack on his shoulder. "Sloane just wants to sleep with Grayson and he's not interested."

"Well, apparently I'm out there to sleep with everybody too, so I should probably pass."

"We all know you aren't. That's why it was funny."

"It wasn't. That's not something I joke about."

Benjamin laughed and looked at the sky for a moment. "We get it, sweetie, you're a virgin. The last one in the club. It's really not much of a club."

Ava's mouth formed soundless words as she alternated between staring at him and the ground. Jack had been right. Being in C3 didn't mean being a Christian. Or maybe being a Christian didn't mean being a virgin.

Benj was the one guy she knew here. And she knew nothing. "Can we not talk about this anymore?" Her headache returned with reinforcements.

"It's just sex, Ava." His familiar smirk returned. "Don't get so defensive about it."

She shook her head to shake off the conversation. "Okay. Fine. Whatever."

"Is that a no for tonight?"

The weekend loomed with unfilled hours and nonexistent plans. Her room loomed. The buildings around her loomed. If there was any more freaking looming, she would faint. Claustrophobia set in. Maybe another drink wouldn't be such a bad thing.

"Where are you going?"

"Devil's Glen."

"Rather ominous."

"I understand if it doesn't fit in with the mission trip," Benjamin's smile crept higher, bringing out the dimples again. "I'll buy you a drink so you won't have to file the receipt with the church."

"Oh, shut up."

Benjamin's smile broke into an actual laugh this time. "Nine o'clock, ma'am. Feel free to bring the blonde chaperone."

"Keep talking boy, and I won't go."

Benj motioned to zip his lips and waved to her, walking on through the courtyard while Ava headed back to her dorm, somehow giddy, gullible and guilty all at once. However briefly, she had held a normal conversation. She had felt confident, like the world had righted itself and she had fallen back into place.

When she made it back to her room, Rosie was there, tucked under her covers, watching a movie on her laptop and sipping tea like the very picture of hygge.

"The tables have turned, Rosie," Ava called out as she entered. "I've got an invite tonight."

Rosie popped up with an instant sparkle in her blue eyes. "Oh, thank god, I was running low this weekend. Well, Callan invited me out, but we can't do that too often. Gotta keep 'em on the line."

Ava laughed and shook her head. "The guys from Texas Gulf are going out."

"Okay, and you've got Benjamin claimed. Are the other two available?"

"I do not have Benjamin claimed. He has a girlfriend back home."

Rosie shrugged. "And he's away from her for, what, four months? If you don't claim him, I will," She winked conspiratorially.

"Aren't you dating Callan again?"

"No, and don't ye go sayin' things like that."

Ava shook her head. "Relationships are weird."

Rosie laughed. "You're one to say so. Who's that boy you talk to all the time?"

"What? Nobody—"

"Mmm, nobodies don't call every week and text every day. Nobodies don't give you their jackets."

Ava's throat seemed to close in around her words. "Jack? No, we're friends. Good friends."

"Boys aren't good friends, hen. Did you ever date him?"

"No. I haven't dated anyone…"

Rosie gasped as her eyes grew wide, saucers in her porcelain face. "That's what's wrong with you."

"What? Good grief, can you be a little more subtle with the insults?"

"Why in heaven's name have ye not dated anyone?"

Ava shrugged. "I don't know… Small, private high school. Poor selection. Nobody asked." *Bra size too small, not funny enough, pastor's kid, high school braces…*

Rosie jumped down and studied Ava, tapping her lip. If Rosie could give her the once over and figure out her problem, Ava would welcome it.

"Nobody ever asked?" Rosie circled Ava for her investigation. She snapped. "I've got it."

Ava crossed her arms. "What is it, doctor? Am I ugly? Unloveable?"

"Yer gorgeous, hen, but yer frigid. Have you at least kissed anyone? Slept with anyone?"

"Oh for heaven's sake, why is this the topic of the day?" Ava groaned and started fishing papers out of her backpack for distraction.

"I'll take that as a no. So there's your problem. You need to be more available."

"Are you kidding me? Sleeping with someone is the last step, not the first."

Rosie's diagnostic tone turned into something closer to horror. "No, don't tell me you're a 'wait till marriage' type."

"Yes, and I think there's a handful of guys left on this planet who agree."

"I sincerely doubt that. But at least it explains why you're permanently single."

Rosie was prodding the wounds and self-doubts that needed no help. Every time a friend of hers started dating someone, every time a guy from church or C3 asked another girl out, Ava wondered why it wasn't her. Her mom said not to rush it. To keep the standards high. That it was a good thing. But heading into her twenties without a single date didn't seem like a good thing.

"Okay, thanks for the pep talk. I think I'll get my relationship advice elsewhere."

"Your loss," Rosie said. "Where are we going tonight?"

Ava sighed. "I don't know if we should. The guys were jerks today."

"That's a good sign, hen, it means they notice you. And yes, we have to go. You'll look fabulous and rub it in their faces."

It did sound promising. "Devil's Glen."

Rosie crinkled her nose. "Fine. We'll start there and move them on as quickly as possible." She walked to the closet and started sifting through tops. She pulled out a sheer black shirt.

"You're wearing this."

"Not without a tank top underneath."

"Och, naw. What about this?" Rosie tossed her a white crop top.

Ava wasn't allowed to show a midriff. "It's freezing outside."

"Yer in luck, the bars in Scotland have heaters. Do you want to be dateable or not?"

Ava bit her lip. The crop top wouldn't reveal as much as the sheer shirt. She could pull it off with high waisted jeans.

"Fine." Maybe she could test out a little of the love advice. It seemed to work for Rosie.

Chapter 8

There was one last church on her list, Dumfries Parish. The fourth and last Christian church within walking distance of her building. The preacher had an out-of-place Australian accent and delivered a heavy-handed fire and brimstone message.

"*You must not associate with anyone who claims to be a brother or sister but is sexually immoral or greedy, an idolater or slanderer, a drunkard or swindler. Do not even eat with such people.*"[5]

"Expel, it says!" he shouted. "'Expel the wicked person from among you!' Wickedness fills the world with its darkness, the devil prowls to devour, the gates of hell may be unleashed; but in this church, we have the Kingdom of Heaven. In this church, there is no place for the wicked."

If Ava's dad had an opposite, it was this man. She sat alone in a row at the back and was tempted to sneak out, but the traditional church had ushers standing at the back, watching everyone. Her mind wandered to her promise to her family—that she would try to find a church. She had given no promise that she would be successful.

After the sermon ended, everyone stood for an old hymn and then carefully filed out of the church. The preacher stood at the back, greeting people as they left.

"And what's your name?" he asked, reaching a hand towards her. There was something to be said for that; none of the other churches had acknowledged her.

Ava lifted her chin and shook his hand. "Ava."

"Ah, a form of Eve. The original sinner. Strange choice for a name, isn't it?"

Maybe being ignored was better. "No stranger than Adam."

His smile soured. "I suppose we all need a reminder of evil's presence." He nodded curtly and turned to greet someone behind her.

Did he just call me evil? Ava held back a shiver as she left. Strike four. One too many. Four weeks of this was enough. Like Benjamin said, this trip was a break from all of that.

When she made it to the bottom of the steps in front of the church, she stopped next to the rose bushes and studied the building. It had been built, rebuilt, and expanded over centuries. Replaced stones and mismatched styles left it medieval on one corner and Baroque on the other. Ava huffed out a heavy sigh. Like the building, she was structurally lost, borrowed, pieced together, and now without category or type.

The Bible verses she heard today, the ones she had grown up with, promised that sin led to a life of darkness and despair. The Christian was supposed to have life abundantly. Yet here, all the sins she had been carefully coached against were housed in happy, confident faces. In pixie-like roommates and their worldly friends who were kinder than the Christians. Here, the gates of hell were more welcoming than the churches.

And this was no mission trip. No, here, Ava was the project. She was the miserable one, and they held all the answers.

That afternoon, she watched Grace's live stream online. That would suffice as church. No more visiting. It was home, even if she only watched from the outside. Even if it was followed by a silent, empty room instead of hugs and lunch with friends.

She needed to talk to someone. Anyone from home. Ava tapped Talia's name on her phone. It rang several times before going to voicemail. She tried Jack's next.

"Hey." His voice had never been more welcome. She heard the sounds of several other voices behind him.

"Hey, what are you doing?"

"Having lunch," Jack said. "What's up?"

"Oh, sorry, I forgot what time it was there."

"Do you need something?"

Ava was taken back by the curt tone. "Oh, no. Nothing. Just wanted to talk. Call me later?"

"Sure."

"Okay… Enjoy your lunch."

"Bye." Ava hung up and frowned at her phone. He was never that short with her.

Before she could overthink it, Rosie spilled into the room, a perfectly welcome distraction. She hauled a duffel bag on her shoulder and dumped it on the floor the moment she got into the room.

"Hey girl," Ava said, climbing off her bed to stretch and clear floor space for Rosie's stuff. "Where were you yesterday?"

"Went camping in Cairngorms with Callan."

Jealousy pricked at her. Everybody had plans except her. She had spent her entire weekend in this stupid room. "So are you and Callan back together or what?"

"Last night we were," Rosie said with a wink as she pulled outfits from her bag that did not look suited for camping in the Scottish winter.

Ava could only laugh. They were yin and yang, Ava was restraint and repression, Rosie was pep and perk. They could find a middle ground. "I want to get out of Edinburgh. We should do a day trip or weekend trip or something."

Rosie raised her eyebrows. "Weekend trip, as in you would skip church?"

"Yes. I'm allowed to skip church. I'm not that weird."

Rosie wrinkled her nose and laughed. "Okay, let's do it. See if Liliana and Molly want to go too. We'll figure something out."

Ava clapped her hands and welcomed the pep that snuck back into her. A trip could redeem this whole stupid trip.

The phone never rang again. Neither Talia nor Jack called. They were too busy. They still had friends. She was the one who left, they didn't owe her any of their time. Ava waited until Rosie had gone out for dinner and then called her parents.

Mom answered. Ava vented about her many attempts at church and her final decision to stick with Grace online. Her mom was quietly supportive, clearly trying to let Ava have the freedom to find her own way.

"Of course, a big part of church is the community," her mom said. It was a gentle chide.

"Yeah... Well, I'm finding my own. And I mean, I'll only be here for a few months."

"That's true. Although, being around people with similar values can be encouraging."

"Right." Similar to whose values, though? Ava's, or her mom's? Ava's were shifting. "So where's dad?"

"You know Val from the college group?"

"Yeah, of course." Val's family had recently joined their church; Val attended irregularly and always wore dresses that were too short.

"Her dad had a heart attack. He's in intensive care in the hospital and your father's visiting him."

"What? When? I should call her or something."

"You don't need to worry about these things, hon. There's enough on your plate over there. Focus on where you are. The college group is really stepping up."

"Okay. Okay. Thanks for the update." They finished the phone call and Ava started going through social media posts. Val hadn't posted anything about it online, but Talia did post about taking care of friends.

All of that had been her role. The presumed head of college outreach, reminding others about birthdays, hard days, and everything between. Selfishly, she had believed it would all fall apart without her. Ava had to laugh at herself. Of course they would be fine. They had been fine for years before her. She was replaceable and unmissable. No one needed her at home, and no one wanted her in Scotland.

The walls around her seemed to be closing in and the room felt too small, too big, too empty, and too crammed. Her entire trip was being wasted in this room. She hauled herself out of bed and pulled on a coat and boots. She needed to eat dinner and couldn't handle another microwave meal in this room. She knew how to cook, and a perfectly good, full kitchen waited downstairs, with the potential to meet people.

After a trip to the market down the street, Ava returned to the dorm kitchen with the makings of beef stew—the perfect comfort food. The kitchen was entirely hers tonight. Students passed in and out of the main area, but none stopped.

Everything was simmering on the stove when she heard two familiar giggles. Ava glanced up to see Liliana and Molly coming down the stairs.

"What's for dinner, mum?" Liliana asked.

"Stew. There's plenty if y'all want some."

"It smells delicious," Molly said, walking into the kitchen, while Liliana stayed between the stairs and the front door. "We were about to go out for dinner though."

"Come on, Molls," Liliana said in a high-pitched whine.

"I haven't had a home-cooked meal in forever." Molly mirrored her pout.

"It's dorm-cooked, not the same," Liliana said.

"I think it'll taste as good as home cooked," Ava said. "Seriously, you can stay."

"No thanks, I didn't put on makeup to eat in a dorm. I'm leaving, Molly."

"Okay, gosh, I'm coming," Molly said. "Next time, Miss Texas."

After waving them out, Ava sat with a steaming bowl of beef and broth. She stared at it, realizing she didn't actually have much of an appetite. Comfort was in the cooking, not the food, and now she had lost the will to eat it.

The sound of the front door slamming jolted her and Ava picked up a spoon to at least pretend to be eating like a normal person, while a group of students walked past her. It was only eight, and they were obviously half drunk already. Once they were gone, she set the spoon back down and stared at the bowl. Life abundantly was life alone.

Chapter 9

The next weekend, Ava watched Edinburgh flying by from the rear windows of Molly's red hatchback. It had taken a month of boring weekends but she was finally doing it—getting out of the city, seeing Scotland. Sitting on the right side of the car, disorientingly behind Molly as she drove. Rosie sat in the back with Ava. In the left-sided passenger seat was Molly's "boy friend, not boyfriend," Harris, from a campus arts club they both attended.

They drove across the Queensferry bridge, with its enormous towers and cables supporting them. Out the window, running parallel to Queensferry, was a red cantilever bridge that rose and fell like waves on a shore. Ridley Bay's basic concrete excuses for bridges couldn't hold a candle to these two.

After a lot of back and forth, the girls had decided on Inverness. Ava pushed hard for the trip north through the countryside, playing the tourist card with her sweetest Texan twang. The plan was to enjoy the trip there, stop at any little town or trail that caught their eyes, and then visit Loch Ness tomorrow. Rosie had griped that Loch Ness was an absolute tourist trap. When she finally admitted she hadn't even seen it herself, Ava won out.

Ava quickly warmed to Harris. He turned out to be her biggest advocate and Molly was a willing participant. They pulled over in every cute town to walk down rows of cobblestones and peek inside overpriced boutiques. Harris spotted every good lookout point and insisted on a long sidetrack to the Falls of Moness.

"Haven't you ever heard of the Birks of Aberfeldy?" he asked, looking over his shoulder at Ava.

"Not at all," Ava laughed.

"We're going then." The designated DJ in the car, he switched the music to an old-fashioned song with bagpipe undertones and a soft, Scottish male voice singing about a bonnie lassie going to the Birks. Rosie and Molly groaned, but Ava thought the music was a perfect soundtrack to the rolling hills.

When they reached the trailhead, they were the only ones there. It wasn't tourist season in Scotland yet—the weather was still too cold. A northern storm had blown in a few days before, coating the place in a light layer of snow. The scenery wasn't the lush, green Scotland she had pictured; it was better. Snow clothed the bare birch branches in white and drew her like Lucy into Narnia. The trail was untouched, pure white without a track. It almost seemed wrong to mark it.

As they went further into the woods, the snow's silencing effect was broken by the trickle of a river that at times turned into a rush. The trail was slick in places and they slowly crossed the narrow portions, following the growing sound of the falls.

"'Mon Miss Texas," Molly called back to her as the group took a curve out of sight.

Ava snapped one more quick photo and hurried to catch up. She lagged behind the entire way, stopping to lick an icicle or catch a snowflake. "Sorry, we don't get snow on the Texas coast. I have to appreciate it any chance I get."

Molly threw an arm around her with a grin. "I'll admit it's a fine bit better than the slush we get in Edinburgh."

When they reached the overlook, Ava blew out a long breath that fogged around her. Water rushed angrily down the center of the falls, fighting against the frost, swirling around chunks of ice at the bottom. "It's so beautiful. Why aren't we out here every weekend?"

Rosie made a backhanded comment about her social life, but Ava ignored her as she took a dozen pictures. None could capture the boom of crashing water, the intricate icicles adorning the rocks, or the wisps of snow that occasionally fluttered from the trees. Even Rosie was losing some of her indifference in the setting. She started taking selfies with the waterfall in the background.

They took photos with each other until they each had something worth sharing. Ava's photo-worthiness declined rapidly in the cold; her nose and cheeks turning red as she shoved her hands into her coat pockets and bounced to keep warm.

"Our wee Texan is freezing," Molly called out to Harris and Rosie. "Let's keep going."

Molly hooked an arm through one of Ava's as they trekked back towards the car. The cold was so wet, it soaked into her bones, where the car's heater couldn't reach.

They drove through Cairngorms National Park as a heavy fog descended, shielding the views. Molly slowed, carefully navigating the curves and bridges endlessly. They pulled up to a little lighthouse outside of Inverness by the late afternoon. Harris had picked it as their last sightseeing spot before it got too dark. The fog had lifted but the remaining clouds nearly blocked out the last of the sunlight.

The wind was ferocious on the coastline, battering the car and rocking it when they parked. Rosie and Molly opted to stay in the car, but Harris and Ava hopped out.

The wind threatened to rip the car door from Ava's hand. It stung her face like ice—actually, it was ice. The wind slashed the drizzle sideways at her and she followed Harris as he sprinted towards the lighthouse. They huddled next to the building, edging around the side for a slight reprieve.

"Too bad the weather's turned," Harris said over the roar of wind. "On a clear day, you can watch the dolphins swimming in the firth."

"Is there ever a clear day in Scotland?" Ava asked, holding her coat hood over her head.

Harris just laughed. They ran to the pier and squinted at the water, but it disappeared into the fog. Ava was chilled through, it would be impossible to warm up again without a hot shower.

"I'm going back to the car," Ava said through the din.

"Be there in a minute," Harris said.

Ava shrugged off her coat at the car for one bitter moment before ripping the door open and hopping in. Rosie squealed as a blast of cold, wet air came in with Ava.

"Great day for sightseeing, huh?" Rosie asked as she passed Ava the blanket she had been cuddled up in.

"It's the full Scottish experience, right?" Ava laughed, burying herself in the blanket.

"Where's Harris?" Molly asked from the front.

"He said he'd be here in a minute. I don't think he even feels the cold."

Molly shrugged. "Probably not."

"He's sweet, Molls," Rosie said, shooting a wink to Ava, who echoed her conspiratorially.

"I know..." Molly said.

"You gonna do anything about it?" Rosie asked.

"Shut up, he's here."

The girls went awkwardly silent as Harris climbed into the car. He glanced around at them all and Rosie finally busted out laughing but no one said anything else. Harris shrugged it off and Molly drove them back into the city center to their hotel.

Being broke students, they split the cost of the room four ways, dividing the two queen-size beds amongst them. Ava had never slept in a room with a guy, aside from her brothers on the occasional family vacation. Nobody here needed to know that. In unspoken agreement, Ava and Rosie tossed their bags beside one of the beds while Molly and Harris set theirs by the other.

Taking a seat on the floor directly in front of the radiator, its warmth gradually began to thaw her, starting at her nose. "I could use a hot cup of tea right about now," she said to no one in particular, raising her hands towards the radiator.

"I'd prefer a hot toddy," Rosie said, taking a seat next to Ava and holding her hands out as well.

Warmth from the moment spread through her, emotions matching her body. This was the trip she wanted. Making new friends, exploring

Scotland with them, making memories. This was the trip she could talk about when she returned home.

Once they were warm and dry again, they were ready for dinner. The sleet had stopped, so they walked the few blocks to downtown. Rosie voted for an upscale diner while Harris championed a cheeky Scottish pub. Molly and Ava were willing to go anywhere, and let the other two decide. Harris won, citing Ava's need for a proper haggis. It was probably the live band that actually won over Rosie.

They grabbed a table in the back and listened to a four-man band play everything from Scottish folk to indie rock. Everyone convinced Ava to order the haggis, neeps and tatties, without telling her what a single one of those items was.

"Can I at least Google it?" Ava asked.

"No!" They all said it in unison.

"Tatties are potatoes," Molly cut in but the other two hushed her.

Harris sent an entirely unmissable smile towards Molly before answering Ava. "It's a surprise. But trust me, it's quintessential Scotland."

The server brought out their plates. The others had ordered hamburgers, while Ava's plate had mashed potatoes, something that looked similar but with an orange tint, and a serving of some sort of meat. It looked like a cross between ground beef and meatloaf. She stuck a fork in it and scooped up the meat. Everyone watched her.

The meat was bearable, peppery and dry, but with an off-putting liver flavor. Ava coughed and covered her mouth with a napkin as she forced it down and chugged water. Molly and Rosie broke out laughing while Harris tried to cover his smile.

"Okay, you guys are the worst," Ava said. "What is it?"

"Sheep heart, lungs and liver," Rosie said.

"Boiled in sheep stomach, if they made it properly," Harris added.

Ava made a face but took another bite out of curiosity. "It tastes worse now that I know. You shouldn't have told me."

"It's a rite of passage," Rosie said, sliding her plate towards Ava. "Here, have some burger."

Ava cut off a slice and moved it to her plate, as far from the haggis as possible. "Okay, what are neeps and why are they yellow?"

"Turnips," Harris said.

She took a bite suspiciously, but they were delicious. Ava forced everyone at the table to take a bite of haggis so they didn't waste too much. She kept the neeps and tatties to herself.

After their meal, Rosie steered them all to the covered rooftop, partially enclosed, with heat lamps lining the edges. There was a full bar there, and everyone stepped up to order drinks. Ava hesitated and asked the bartender for recommendations.

"What do ye like?" he asked, eyeing her.

"I don't really know."

He tapped his lips for a moment and suggested something he promised was light and fruity. Ava's first reaction to it was less than stellar, though not as bad as the sour beer at St. Bart's. The bartender offered to replace it, but Ava warmed up to it with a second sip.

The rooftop had music coming through large speakers and a younger crowd. Already on her second drink, Rosie began chatting with a guy at the bar, while Molly and Harris wandered to the edge of the rooftop, looking at the city. Ava sat back in her barstool, content from a whirlwind day.

Her phone buzzed, surprising her with Jack's name.

"Hey," she plugged one ear and pressed her phone into the other as if it could block out the noise if she pressed harder. She couldn't hear anything this close to the speakers. Ava moved away from the bar, wandering to a far corner of the rooftop and outside of the partition, into the frigid air. The wind wasn't much quieter than the music.

"Hey, sorry, I couldn't hear you," Ava said. "What's up?"

"Where are you?" Jack asked.

"Inverness… On a road trip with my roommate and a couple friends."

"Time out—the party crazy roommate? She's got you out with her?"

Ava frowned at his description. "Rosie. Her name's Rosie."

"And you couldn't find anyone else to go on a road trip with?" Jack asked.

"No, I couldn't," Ava spat back. "I asked the Texas Gulf students, and they acted like I was an idiot. Rosie's great."

"So now you're out at a bar with her?"

"Yes. You're the one who said I should go out."

"I said go out to meet some people from the international group. You already knew your roommate. And I'm pretty sure I specifically said not to get drunk."

"I'm not drunk. What is your problem? Did you call me just to lecture me?"

"Nothing," he said. "Never mind. I'll talk to you later."

"Jack—" The line went dead. Ava twisted her mouth, staring at the phone for a minute, debating calling him back. He had missed their Wednesday call. Their schedules never lined up anymore. He hadn't texted her back for two days either.

A chill ran through her and she stuck the phone in her pocket, heading back towards the heat lamps—but they did nothing for the internal chill. Rosie waved her over to the bar. Ava headed that way, feebly trying to put Jack out of her mind. It was impossible. Anger and confusion churned on a full stomach.

In an instant, Rosie introduced Ava to her new friend and his brother. She made it clear which one she had claimed. Ava had been called over to play wingman, but she didn't know how. Not that Rosie needed any help. Within a few minutes, she and the new guy were exchanging saliva.

Kissing a stranger wasn't Ava's goal for the night, but she had to wonder at Rosie's ability. Rosie could get herself into somebody's arms in five minutes flat. It was both impressive and frightening. Ava, on the other hand, had never been kissed. Or properly asked out. She shook her head and tried to care about the weak conversation with the brother. He was equally uninterested. Because she was Ava.

An hour later, Molly and Harris were ready to call it a night. It was hours earlier than Rosie's usual, but she agreed and joined them on the walk back to the hotel. Molly and Harris walked at the front while Ava and Rosie fell behind.

"Didn't find anyone that caught your interest?" Rosie asked, poking Ava's arm.

"No. I don't know how you do it."

"Just try to have a little fun sometime, hen."

"I have fun… Besides, what about Callan?"

Rosie rolled her eyes dramatically. "That wasn't anything serious. Only a wee flirting game. Haven't ye ever flirted a bit, for no good reason? To feel good? Hell, it's good for any relationship if ye go out an' flirt a bit."

When Ava hesitated too long, Rosie put an arm around her waist. "You can't keep being scared of yer own body. Yer scaring the boys off, too. You're gorgeous, hen, enjoy it a little more."

They made it back to their hotel room and flicked on a movie. The moment Harris stepped into the restroom, Molly and Rosie pulled off their clothes and switched into tank tops and tiny shorts to sleep in. Ava played the role of prude, waiting for her turn in the bathroom to don her pajama pants and a large shirt, hyper-aware of the male presence in the room.

When the movie ended, Rosie poked Ava and nodded towards the other bed. Molly and Harris were asleep, cuddled in a decidedly "boyfriend, not boy friend" way. Ava and Rosie shared a silent laugh.

"I told you boys don't make good friends," Rosie whispered. The reminder of Jack erased Ava's smile and Rosie caught it. "Is that who you were talking to? The illustrious Jack?"

"Yeah. He was being rude."

"Because he likes you," Rosie said.

"We've been friends for five years. If he liked me, he would have asked me out by now."

"Yer frigid, remember? Any man would be scared to ask you out."

"Shut up," Ava pushed Rosie's arm. "I am not."

"And what would you say if he did ask?" Rosie asked. Ava shrugged, sick of this stupid hypothetical conversation. Jack had dated other girls throughout the years. He didn't see her like that. And Ava didn't want to think about it anymore.

"Why don't you like him?" Rosie asked. "Is he ugly?"

"Oh my gawd," Ava drawled, biting back a grin. Rosie insisted on seeing a picture, so Ava opened a social app on her phone. "Jack Shields. Find him yourself, I'm not helping you."

And she wouldn't share the picture Katie had sent her of Jack reluctantly holding baby Gabe. It was too precious.

Rosie tapped in the name and started gawking. "Ye diddy, why haven't you asked him out yerself? I'm studying abroad in Texas next year."

Ava peeked over Rosie's shoulder and saw the picture from last year's church retreat. His summer surfer hair was windblown and his arms were crossed, showing off muscles that he barely had to lift a finger to earn. He was only half smiling, but his eyes gave away a brighter happiness. One that hadn't always been there. Suddenly, it clicked. Jack's phone call. Ava's heart fell, and she cursed, lunging for the phone.

"Watch yer mouth, Puritan," Rosie said, lifting the phone away from Ava.

"What day is it?" Ava asked in a panic. "What's the date?"

"What? Picking a wedding date?" Rosie asked, still teasing.

"Rosie, give me the phone. That's why he was calling. I've never skipped talking to him today."

"Yer off yer trolly," Rosie handed back the phone. "What are ye haverin' about?"

"I have to call him," Ava said, but she was already out the door. The moment she was in the hallway, she dialed his number. It rang eight times before going to voicemail. She tried again immediately. It rang twice before going to voicemail. He declined her call?

Ava

I'm so sorry, I just realized what day it is. Call me.

She sank against the wall and waited. And waited. She called again, but he ignored it.

Jack

Having dinner.

Ava

Call me later?

Nothing.

Ava called Talia in desperation.

"Hey mija, what's up?" Talia answered.

"Talia, it's the anniversary of Jack's mom's death," Ava rushed the words out, needing to backtrack, to make up for time. She always kept up with these things.

"I know," Talia sounded confused.

"Are you with him?"

"We're having dinner now. Val got a group together."

"Val did?"

"Yeah, she..." Talia made a sound like she was about to say something and stopped.

"What? Val what?"

"Nothing. Having fun over there?"

Ava ran a hand over her face. "Yeah. Sure."

"Okay... Well, I better go. Talk later?"

"Sure." Ava hung up the phone and stared at the stained, outdated, swirl-patterned carpet, trying to remember what year it was. Jack had been 12. So nine years now. His mom died before they had met, but once she knew the date, she spent the day with him every year. Until this year, when she told him off.

Ava cursed herself again and waited in the hallway until she was sure Jack wouldn't call. And sure that Rosie had fallen asleep. Slinking into the far corner of the bed, away from Molly and Harris, away from Rosie, she stared at the clock on the bedside table until sleep finally stole her away from herself.

Chapter 10

There was too much to do today. Too many rituals. Jack always took the day off work so he could go through all the motions. The day started with a run. He could handle today once he burned off the stress. Next were chocolate chip pancakes, a specialty from his childhood, though his would never taste as good as his mom's.

After that he drove to the beach. There was no gravesite, her ashes had been scattered in the sea, at her request. His dad took him to the beach the first few years. As soon as Jack could drive himself, his dad stopped going. He tended to drink the day away instead. This year his dad had a new girlfriend; there was no telling if he would even remember the day.

Jack stretched his legs out on the sand, leaning back on his arms. He was alone this year. Like most years. Ava had been here with him twice. One year he had brought a high school girlfriend. But being alone was fine. It gave him the space to think. To remember. The memories brought back both parents. He had lost both to cancer. One had died, the other had simply given up.

He had lost church too. His mom had taken him as a kid, but he stopped going when she died. His dad wouldn't take him. Besides, Jack had been too angry to go. Nearly five years later, he ran out of anger at God and found himself at Grace Church, thanks to a friend. By now, he had run out of emotions. The day was routine. He liked it better that way.

After leaving the beach, Jack called his dad and invited him to lunch at the burger spot his mom loved. His dad gave an excuse—working on a car. But at least it sounded like he hadn't forgotten. He invited Jack to dinner instead. Jack agreed to an early dinner before a second one with the Grace group. His bases were covered. His day was filled.

• • •

Four hours later, Jack drove to his dad's house outside of town, white-knuckling the steering wheel. The horrible phone call with Ava was ringing in his ears and he couldn't figure out who to blame. Who had been the rude one? He never should have called her in the first place, but he had been so sure she would call at some point. Everything about the call was so unlike her.

Two dinners could keep him distracted. He needed to get to his dad's house already. Listen to him talk about cars. Maybe even answer some of the new girlfriend's lame attempts to talk to him. Anything but Ava.

He slowed down on the caliche road that led to his dad's house. Lion, the lab-mix they had adopted shortly before his mom died, greeted him when he parked. The dog wasn't quite as bouncy when he jumped on Jack these days. After a quick ear rub, Jack headed to the garage. It looked messy, but his dad always knew exactly where to find things. Jack peeked at the engine of the vintage truck sitting in the garage and headed inside the house.

Jack sighed the moment he heard a female voice call out a hello. The new girlfriend stood by the stove in the kitchen, a few years too young for his dad and dressed for a yoga class. With her around, it would be too awkward to talk about mom. Her presence today seemed sacrilegious.

His dad walked into the room, looking like he had just showered.

"What's wrong with the truck?" Jack asked. It didn't matter if the girlfriend was here or not, they probably wouldn't have talked about mom, anyway.

"Had to replace the serpentine belt," his dad said. Working on engines was both a hobby and a job for him. When he wasn't at the body shop, he flipped cars. His dad started walking towards the garage and waved for Jack to follow.

"Dinner will be ready in five minutes," the girlfriend called out after them.

Nobody saw Jack's shudder. She would be jealous of any moment that Jack's father spent with anyone else besides her, even if it was his own son.

They poked around the vintage engine for a moment before turning their attention to Jack's truck.

"How's it running?" his dad asked, walking around the truck, inspecting the body.

"Fine," Jack said. "The steering wheel is cracking and the seats are faded. But the engine is solid."

"Yeah, it's been that way since I passed it on to you," his dad said, rubbing the back of his head. The truck was his high school graduation gift to Jack. A final send off to the real world and the end of his parental duties. "Sorry, I don't do interiors."

"That's okay. Doesn't affect how it drives."

"Gets you from Point A to Point B, right?"

"Exactly."

His dad opened the driver's door and popped the hood of the truck. He gave everything a quick look over, checking fluids and oil levels. It was the only love language he spoke. He didn't offer much else. Once satisfied that the truck passed inspection, he closed the hood and stared at it for a moment with his arms crossed.

"I miss her too," he said. The moment the words were out, he turned and headed back into the house. "Our five minutes is up, come on in. Yvonne's a good cook."

Jack nodded and followed him into the house. It was the most his dad would say on the topic for another year.

The spread of roasted chicken and kale salad wasn't Jack's taste, but his dad was right, she was a decent cook. Maybe the healthy foods would balance out his dad's habit of drinking too many beers and keep him alive a little longer.

They made halting conversation, attempting to find common ground and failing. Jack's world included school, athletic department, and church.

His dad's world was exactly what it had been for Jack's entire life: cars and beer. The girlfriend's world had something to do with drama at yoga class.

When they finished eating, Jack helped clear the table before heading to his old room. It was more of a storage room now, but memories were buried under the boxes. There were posters on the wall that had never been taken down, a calendar from four years ago, and a large plastic bin of Legos under the bed. Jack shoved boxes around until he could reach the other side of the bed and hunted for a specific bin. It wasn't there.

He turned to the closet and found a few boxes marked "Jack" in his dad's girlfriend's handwriting. He pulled the boxes out and opened one. Old clothes and a stack of car magazines. Jack glanced at his watch. He didn't have time to go through it all now.

"Hey dad," he shouted out the door. "Can you help me with these?"

His dad showed up and frowned. "Sorry about the mess. Are you sure you want to take those? I mean, I know you don't have much space at your apartment."

"It's fine. I want to go through them later."

They made two trips to haul the boxes out to the truck. Jack waved a goodbye to the girlfriend and walked with his dad out to the truck. The light was failing as he rubbed Lion's yellow ears while the lab slobbered on his shoes.

"You can stay if you want," his dad said, rubbing at the back of his head again.

"I've got plans," Jack said. *And not much interest in drinking with you.* "Thanks though."

His dad gave him a slow, awkward pat on the back. They didn't hug. "Thanks for coming out, Jack. We… I'm glad… Anytime."

Jack gave a quick nod. "Yeah. We'll do it again. I've been working a lot these days."

"Good," his dad said and crossed his arms again. "That's good, son. Work keeps you honest."

"Learned it from the best," Jack said as he opened the truck door. He climbed in and gave a quick wave to his dad before turning the truck in the gravelly drive.

Love and pride were emotions that were probably too strong for his dad. But *"that's good, son,"* was dad code for something close enough.

Jack recognized a couple other cars in the Mexican restaurant's parking lot. The whole dinner was under the pretense of planning a spring break trip, but he knew by now it was really for him. Ava had started the charade, putting together a "high school picnic" the year they had met. She meant it as more than a distraction—it was about making sure he wasn't alone. And he played along, pretending it was about whatever theme they picked that year.

Val waved him over to the table when he walked inside. It was a small group, just the core students that were at church every Sunday. Not all the others that came in and out, thankfully.

Val had sent him the details. She was barely more than a week out from the scare of her dad's heart attack and somehow she had remembered this. A few hours ago, Jack would have suspected that Ava had played a hand in it behind the scenes, but now he knew that wasn't true.

Their waitress was walking away with their order when his phone rang. When he saw the name, Jack stuck it back in his pocket. She called a second time, and he sent it to voicemail. When her text appeared, annoyance bubbled up.

Jack
Having dinner.
Ava
Call me later?

"What do you think, Jack?" Val was asking. "Is Big Bend too far of a drive?"

Blonde curls and hazel eyes leaned close into his space, and he dropped the phone back into his lap. "How far is it?"

"Okay guys start the entire conversation over—" Talia said with a laugh before getting distracted by her own phone. She shooed the others out of the booth so she could answer it. "Hey mija, what's up?"

Jack shot her a look. He knew who that tone was for and wondered if Ava would snap at Talia too.

"—Eight hours would use an entire day of spring break," Fisher said.

Jack tried to refocus on the conversation. "I'm not putting that many miles on my truck," he said.

"We could pool our money and rent a van." Val was still enthusiastic.

They debated it for a little longer, tossing around more destinations and the usual beach camping trip that they would probably default to because it was cheap. Talia was back in a minute and ruthlessly eliminated the worst ideas, championing her personal favorites as being the best for the entire group. Jack sat back, letting them work it out. Val kept trying to get Jack to have an opinion but the whole concept of a spring break trip seemed pointless. He would be working anyway. He didn't tell her that yet though. She was doing this for him.

Nearly two hours later, Jack was back in his apartment, with the boxes hauled into his already-cramped room. He only wanted one, for reasons he couldn't explain. It was the fourth box he opened. Unwrapping the football jersey from around a coffee mug that wasn't his, Jack sat back against the bed.

He always wondered if his mom would have been at every high school game. Would she have been a cheerer? Or the quiet type? Maybe the snack mom. Without a doubt, he knew she would have been there. Unlike his dad. If she had lived though, would he have been as good as he was? Football had been therapy for him in high school—an obsession and distraction.

Everything had been about football. Every hope and dream, every high school party, every morning on the field. Football had become a god. Then, early in his junior year, a torn ACL cut off his season. When it was taken away, he'd had nothing. Until weeks into physical therapy when, driven by boredom and desperation, he'd agreed to visit Grace Church with a friend. Finding a real God had given him hope again.

The small scar on his right knee was a reminder of how easily dreams could be torn apart. Of the lost college scholarships, the bad decisions and the misplaced priorities. Of how God had finally taken away the demigod of football. Just like he had taken Jack's mom. Wadding up the jersey, Jack shot it back into the box. He would never take the field again. If God and football couldn't coexist, he knew which one he would choose.

• • •

Four days later, arriving home from work, his phone rang. Jack's thumb hesitated over the answer button. He wasn't sure if they were still doing this. It seemed like she needed space. "Hey."

"Hey, is this a good time?" Ava asked.

"Yeah, sure, I've got an hour before group. Should probably shower before then though." He pulled into the parking lot and hopped out of the truck.

"Definitely, I can smell you from here," Ava said, with a forced laugh that fell flat. "I won't take too much of your time."

"You're fine. It's Wednesday. This is what we do."

"I'm sorry about Saturday. I was… We were road tripping. I totally lost track of everything."

"It's okay." He didn't want to talk about Saturday. He walked inside and flicked through a neglected stack of mail on the countertop. "You don't owe me anything."

"Right," Ava sighed. "So I heard y'all made spring break plans?"

"Yeah, Val pulled your move." Val had managed it, even after spending a week with her dad in the hospital.

"Good… Wait, no, I don't know what you're talking about. I don't have moves."

She said it so sincerely it made Jack laugh. "That's the truth."

"How is Val? Why didn't you tell me about her dad's heart attack?"

Because you don't care about anyone back home anymore. Jack blew out a breath. That wasn't fair. "Figured you didn't need to worry about it. You're taking a break from it all, right?"

"You sound like Benj," Ava muttered.

"What?" Alarm bells rang. How much time was she spending with him?

"Never mind."

"I'm going to pretend I didn't hear that. Anyway. Val was pretty shaken up. Her dad was in ICU for a week, but he's out now. She's fine."

"Okay, well, still check on her. Sometimes people around you move on before you're ready. She might still be stressed about it."

"I know that. I am the one with experience, after all." He didn't mean for that sound as curt as it did. "We got lunch again today."

"Again? Oh. Okay."

He didn't want to keep talking about Val either. "How's the beer in Scotland?"

"Kinda bitt—" Ava switched to a tone of mock innocence. "What beer?"

Jack laughed. "Right."

"Oh come on, you've gone out for a drink before. You're jealous that I'm getting to do it before I'm 21."

"Just be careful."

"Yeah, I know, watch my drink and such." Ava sounded bored.

"That's not what I meant..." But now it was all he could think about, and it was disturbing. Who was she around these days? "How's the hunt for a parish going?"

"Perishing. I'm done with it."

"Really? No church or anything?"

"It's only for a few months," she said. "It's not like my soul will perish that fast."

Jack mimicked a drum cymbal for the lame joke. "Are you still following the small group Bible study?"

She hesitated. "Not really."

"Going for a full-on prodigal vibe?"

Ava laughed. "I haven't demanded my inheritance yet."

"I guess you're just a lost sheep then. Should've gone for that inheritance."

"Ha. Ha. I'll read some tonight. What chapter?"

"Second Timothy, chapter 3. It starts out with a long list of people not to hang out with. You might want to read it." Benj qualified for at least eight of the descriptions.

Ava sighed. "I'm so tired of lists of people not to hang out with. What happened to 'judge not'?"

"Pretty sure judgment and discernment are different things." Silence. He sensed the seething through the phone. He had pushed her. "You're gonna have to take that up with God."

"I would, if he ever answered."

Jack felt her words in his gut, uncomfortable and out of place. Like biting into an apple and finding it rotten inside. She wasn't supposed to say those sorts of things. She had always been the strong one, the reassuring one. Jack had to backtrack and get out of the conversation. "He might. Anyway, I've got to get ready for group..."

"Yeah, sorry. Thanks for talking. I'm sorry again, about Saturday."

"It's okay. It... Hey, are you okay, Aves?"

Her silence answered the question without any words. "I'm fine. Maybe I'm homesick."

With several months to go. "Maybe you can come back for a few days."

"Or you could come here," Ava said quietly.

"Buy me a ticket."

"I'll talk to you later, Jack."

"Aves—" he stopped her from hanging up. "Call me if you need anything."

Ava let out a weak laugh. "You're too busy."

"Not for you."

"Even for me."

Dead end. Everything was a dead end. Their friendship was hanging on by threads and it had only been a little over a month. Three more would kill their friendship and he couldn't let that happen. "I'll do better," he promised.

Chapter 11

At Jack's prompting, Ava had tried to read through the Bible study, but stopped at the long list of sins that sounded more like Rosie's idea of a good night. She laughed at it, if only to hold off the inevitable guilt trip.

By now, February was almost over, and Rosie declared that a cause for celebration. Every night held potential in that girl's eyes. Ava had to agree that the noisy, crowded bars were better than another quiet weekend alone in her room—even if they were filled with more sins and guilt.

Besides, Ava had a new top she had bought with Rosie that week. It was finally a "proper" top as the girls said, though Ava couldn't help thinking that wasn't the right word. Nearly invisible straps held up the clingy red silk blouse. Ava paired it with black high-waisted pants and gave a few slow spins in front of the mirror. She had never owned anything like this. "Showing off her assets," as Rosie put it, was not something the pastor's daughter did.

Molly walked into the room and whistled. "Now that's a shirt. It's your color," she said with a grin.

It did seem to set off her dark eyes and hair. Molly tossed her some lipstick and promised it would be the perfect match.

Liliana declared everyone needed to preload and passed around a case of cheap beer. They raised their bottles to social lubricant, and Ava choked down a few sips. She still didn't have the taste for it.

An hour later, they were on their way to AltBrew. Ava had invited Benj via text, not risking any interactions with TGU students in classes lately. Only after she had sent it did Rosie mention the possible appearance of certain rugby players as well. One in particular came to mind. It made buying the new top seem worth it.

They arrived at the bar and shrugged off their coats. Ava eyed the open floor plan warily; it looked like the type of place that might have dancing. Something that sounded very Rosie and very not-Ava. The girls ordered beers while Ava tested out white wine—better than the beer. The night started slowly. None of them knew anybody else there, so they chatted together at a table. Ava enjoyed the smaller gathering, but Rosie and Liliana were obviously checking the door every minute for male faces.

Rosie must have spotted the ones she was looking for. Her pixie grin spread slowly across her face. She lifted a bottle in Ava's direction. "You're going to practice yer flirt tonight, hen."

Ava wrinkled her brow and turned to see who had prompted this pep talk. More than six feet of muscle, dark hair and brooding eyes were walking through the door, wearing a dark green cowl neck sweater. Oliver peeled off his sports coat slowly, scanning the room and undoubtedly the dozen people watching him. Ava spun back around to the table before he saw her and gripped her wine glass for confidence.

Rosie clicked her tongue at Ava. "No more hiding."

"Maybe we can start with someone a little more… in my league?" Ava asked weakly.

"To Ava's confidence," Liliana raised her glass ruefully. They all laughed and downed another sip.

"You guys hit it off pretty well a few weeks ago," Molly said. "See what happens."

"I mean, I can't date somebody here, I'm leaving in…" Ava's mind scrambled for excuses, while she snuck another peek behind her shoulder.

"I saw that," Rosie laughed. "Nobody said date him. Just have fun, for once. I'm determined to send you home a little less frigid."

Ava swirled the last wine in her glass around and emptied it. She would need plenty of social lubricant to pull this off. Before she could think about it anymore, Rosie waved the guys over to their table and everyone scooted barstools around to make room. Oliver and two more guys from the team came over.

"Hey guys, you remember Molly, Liliana, and Ava, right?" Rosie ran the table, abandoning her post to give a cheek kiss and hug to each guy. To Ava's disappointment, Oliver circled the table and took a spot on the opposite side instead of beside her. He struck up a conversation with Liliana. So much for her chance to practice flirting.

"I'm getting another," Ava said, lifting her empty glass and excusing herself from the table.

She approached the bar shyly, waiting for a spot to open, in no rush to get back to the table and prove her ineptitude. Finally, a bartender came over to take her order. Ava hesitated. She almost asked for a glass of wine, but changed course at the last second. "Whisky, please. With Coke."

"You got it."

A moment later, the small glass was in her hand. But she wasn't ready to socialize yet. Ava stalled, downing half the drink at the bar. The moment she was ready to go, a hand landed on her back.

"Sticking to whisky and Coke?" the low voice murmured, always too quietly.

Ava blinked back her surprise and turned towards the body next to her. Heat emanated from him. "Still a favorite."

"The next step is to drink it neat, so you can taste the subtler flavors," Oliver said with a slight smile. "You can't leave Scotland without getting the full experience."

"That would be a shame," Ava said into her glass as she lifted it to her lips. A low buzz ran through her head and she was pretty sure it wasn't the alcohol.

The way Oliver smiled always made her feel like she was missing the joke. He raised two fingers in the direction of a bartender and ordered two glasses of a local whisky by name. The bartender set the golden liquor in front of them. Oliver lifted it slowly with an eyebrow raised at Ava. She followed suit, catching a smoky whiff of the drink first before guiding it back to her lips. It burned her nose and throat but she refused to cough. She wouldn't look like a newbie.

"You're properly Scottish now," Oliver laughed. "We can top the rest with Coke if you need."

"It's strong, but you're right, you can get more of the flavor."

"It gets better every time."

Ava tried another sip with a slight grimace. "It's like drinking fire."

"You'll come around," he said, looping a finger through his pants belt loop. Oliver straightened and threw a nod and smile to someone walking into the bar. He excused himself and brushed a hand on Ava's bare shoulder as he walked away.

Ava watched him from the corner of her eye as he greeted a group of girls at the door. With a groan, she turned back to her table. Ava squeezed into a spot next to Rosie, leaning her head on Rosie's shoulder.

"I'm terrible at this," Ava said.

Frowning, Rosie scanned the room, analyzing it. "You need more practice. Cowboy's here, let's go practice on him."

"Who?" Ava followed Rosie's line of sight and spotted Benj and Grayson… And Sloane. She dropped her head forward. "No way, Sloane's here. She hates me and makes me look like an idiot, no matter what I say."

Rosie's lips twisted and she grabbed Ava's hand. "'Mon, I can handle her."

Ava protested, but let Rosie pull her along. She was a step behind as Rosie walked to Benj's table and leaned across it. "Hey Cowboy," Rosie said, grabbing Benj's beer and taking a sip for herself.

Sloane looked horrified. "Do you know her?"

Benj's half smile teased a hint of dimple and Rosie walked around the table and grabbed onto his arm before he answered. "'Course he does. Nobody forgets a night out with the dream team." Rosie winked at Ava.

"Hey Rosie," Benj said, smirk in full effect. It seemed Rosie was the one getting some practice, and she certainly didn't need any.

"Y'all went out together?" Sloane asked.

"A couple times," Ava said, finally inserting herself fully into the circle instead of watching dumbly from the background. Rosie tugged her closer and Ava prayed she didn't say anything stupid.

"Miss Texas and I give ye braws a pure barry night at Double Cross and ye forgot to tell yer friend all about it?" Rosie leaned heavily into her accent and laughed. She gave a pitying look to Sloane. "Poor lass. Now I see why Miss Texas prefers to spend her time with us Scots."

With that, Rosie gave Ava an unexpected kiss on the cheek. She dropped Benj's arm and swapped Ava into her former place next to him as she went around the table to stand between Sloane and Grayson.

"I think it's part of her mission trip," Sloane said to Rosie. "You must be her latest project."

"Actually, I think I'm her project," Ava said. Benj looked at her like he just realized she was there.

"Fine art project," Rosie said with a grin. She reached across the table to steal another sip of Benj's drink. He didn't seem to care. "You boys are my next one. Ava's got ye beat on taste. You'll have to teach them how to appreciate our fine whiskys, hen."

Benj ran his eyes down Ava to the glass in her hand. "Cut the Coke, huh?"

"When in Scotland, do as the Scots, right?" Ava smiled. Rosie's confidence was contagious. Or maybe it was the whisky. "You get the full range of flavor."

"And what flavors are in this one?" Benj asked, reaching for the glass and lifting it to his nose.

"Hmm, caramel, oak, a touch of spice," Ava scrambled and hoped Benj wasn't a whisky connoisseur to disagree.

He took a small sip and passed it back to her. "Okay, I obviously have something to learn."

"Come on," Ava said, stepping back and holding a hand out to Benj. "I'll make a proper Scot out of you, too."

Benj's smile spread enough to hit both dimples as he took her hand and stood. They walked to the bar and Ava's confidence grew with every step. She could steal Oliver's and Rosie's, they had enough to spare.

Stepping up to the bar, she asked the bartender for a recommendation that could top the Glenfiddich she had finished. The bartender poured them two glasses of Ledaig and promised it tasted like the western isles. Ava tapped her glass lightly against Benj's and they each took a sip. The flavor was lighter, earthy with a touch of honey.

"Thanks for showing me your ways, Miss Texas," Benj said, drawing out the nickname with a tease in his eyes.

"My pleasure," Ava said, stealing energy now from the drink in her hand, letting it warm everything from her face to her toes. "I've learned a thing or two on this mission trip."

Benj laughed. "I see that. You're finally having fun."

"Maybe if you spent a little time away from killjoy herself, you'd have some too," Ava said. Benj raised an eyebrow at her. She might be leaning into this too hard. "Sorry, whisky talking."

A smile transformed Benj's face and he tapped his glass on hers again. "No worries, I like you more like this. What else have you learned?"

He leaned in perilously close, and Ava used another sip of whisky to keep her cool. "Always leave them wanting more." She let her own smirk cross her lips as she backed up. This time, she would be the one to walk away.

No wonder people always did that to her. It felt amazing.

And she couldn't have left a moment sooner. Rugby's finest was a few feet away, walking towards her. He glanced at her glass, resting a hand on her elbow. "I see your friend got you a new one. What is it?"

"I can buy my own drinks, thank you very much," Ava said, keeping the smirk in place. "Ledaig. Want a taste?"

She tried to lift her glass, but Oliver's body blocked her arm. He closed the gap between them and his lips were against hers before a coherent thought could form. None were possible now. Ava froze in place as Oliver ran his tongue along her lips. She had never been kissed and had no idea what to do. This wasn't how she ever pictured her first kiss, but at least this one was happening.

"Oak and pepper," he said against her mouth, slight scruff rubbing against her lips. He leaned back slowly. "I like it."

Any confidence she had stolen from him, he took back with interest. Ava couldn't trust her mouth to work out words. But Oliver took over the silence, meeting her lips with another kiss. He kept one hand on her elbow and the other rested on her exposed shoulder at the base of her neck. Ava stood there dumbly, tasting the forbidden fruit, and processing what could very well be her first and last kiss at her rate.

"Finest whisky I've ever tasted." Oliver ran a hand through her hair—she had left it down, letting it cover what her shirt lacked.

Ava grinned and dropped her eyes to the ground. Her mind raced for something Rosie would say. Probably walk away, but the warmth of whisky and Oliver had mixed in her stomach and she was dizzy. The music suddenly got louder, saving her from needing to talk.

"I'm guessing you don't dance?" Oliver asked.

"I don't really know how."

"So many things to teach you, Ava."

She could do this. "I'm a quick learner."

Oliver was already leading her by the hand, and he tossed a quick smile over his shoulder at her. "And I'm an excellent teacher," he said, though it was lost in the noise.

• • •

Classes were strange the next week. Sloane was vicious, throwing every insult she had missed at AltBrew, and Ava struggled to tune it out. She left classes as soon as they were over. Pouring her energy into other outlets helped—she refreshed the wreath on their door with yellow daffodils to make up for the lack of sunshine. March hadn't brought a single hint of spring to Edinburgh.

The weekends were a bright spot in the week. A night out with Rosie meant another boost of liquid courage, even if it left her in the morning. And next weekend, they would be taking a road trip to the isles.

After a night out, Ava slept late Sunday morning, embracing the lazy day before the week of birthday festivities that Rosie had promised. The buzzing of her phone woke her at noon. She cracked heavy eyelids and lifted the phone to her ear. "Mom?"

"Hi, hon. How are you?" Her mom's tone was weird. Or maybe it was Ava's still-dreaming brain.

"Um, I'm good," she tried not to sound like she had just woken. It had to be the crack of dawn in Texas. "Are you okay?"

"I am. Yeah. I was just looking at the pictures you've shared. Those stone buildings are so beautiful."

Ava sat and stretched her neck. "Aren't they? It's the perfect city for studying architecture."

"Good, good. I saw you were tagged in some pictures, too. It looks like you're having… fun."

Rosie's pictures. Ava had finally stopped fighting her on it and let her start posting pictures with her in them. She made sure to remove the tag from anything too incriminating. "I am…"

"Who's the guy in the group picture?" That was a tone Ava knew—though it was usually used on her brothers. She was rarely the one in trouble.

"Which picture?" Ava lowered the phone from her ear and opened her profile.

"Your roommate just posted it. Who's the guy?"

There it was. A picture from last week that Rosie had just now shared. Rosie was planting a theatrical kiss on Ava's cheek; Callan and Oliver were on the edges of the group shot. Ava cleared her throat. "Which guy?"

"The one with his hand around your waist."

"Oh, that's Oliver. Just a friend." Her lips burned at the lie—or the memory.

"Right. Okay. Well, you look great. I mean, the top seems different than your usual style, but…" Her mom was still dancing around it. "Oh, here, your father wants to say hi."

Ava was fully awake now. Both parents. This couldn't be good. "Hey dad."

After the small talk, he dove into it. "So that picture… where are y'all?"

The toeing and testing were maddening. "A bar. Is that a problem?"

"Maybe. I wasn't expecting you to go out drinking. You're 19."

"Well, the legal age here is 18, so…"

"That's not the point. Look, Avie, it might be part of the experience and all, but you need to focus on your classes."

"I am, dad. There's plenty of hours in the day."

Her mom sighed. "Ava, if you're going to have a drink, could you at least wear something more appropriate? You know better."

"Excuse me? Since when do you criticize my clothes?"

"Since whenever you started wearing things like that," her mom said. "Do you think that was the most modest choice?"

"I can wear what I want," Ava said. "And for the record, I don't plan on staying single my entire life."

"What? How does that— The kind of guy who hits on you for what you're wearing is not the kind of guy you marry."

"I'm not trying to get married. Jesus, relax."

"Ava Claire—" her dad cut in. "watch your mouth."

"Okay, this has been fun, I think I'm gonna go now..."

"Hey, did you ever find a local church?" her dad asked quickly.

"No. But I watch Grace online." She had only missed a couple of weeks.

"Will you watch today?"

Ava wavered for a moment. By the time she decided she should lie, the pause had stretched on too long and she knew only the truth would work. "I'll try. I have a ton of homework this weekend."

"Okay... Watch it when you can. Avie, don't forget what's most important."

"I won't—I haven't."

"We love you," her dad said.

"Love you too."

She was free. From the phone, not from the mountain of guilt her parents had piled on. They were going to walk all over the tiny bit of happiness she had found in Scotland. Ava climbed out of bed with a groan.

She had just gotten out of the shower when Rosie walked in. "Rosie, you got me in trouble," Ava said, unwrapping the towel from around her hair.

"Well, aren't ye a wee crabbit?" Rosie tossed her purse and a bag of groceries on the floor. "What are ye goin' on about?"

"That picture of us and Callan and Oliver. My parents freaked out."

Rosie tossed her head back and laughed. "Do they want you in a nunnery?"

"Apparently."

"I'm not taking it down. For yer own good."

"How is that for my own good?" Ava asked.

"There are boys in Texas who think yer celibate. I'm letting them know yer not." Rosie tapped her forehead and pointed at Ava. "Planning ahead, hen."

"Is this about Jack?"

"It wasn't," Rosie said. "But now it is."

Great. "He thinks of me like a little sister."

"Not anymore," Rosie said with a wicked wink.

Ava pressed her lips together tightly. Thinking of Jack and Oliver in the same context wasn't natural. It wasn't the way she treated her friends. "It won't work. He only likes blondes." *Like Val* slipped unwelcome into her mind.

Rosie skipped across the room and draped an arm over Ava. "Then can you please bring the infamous Jack here? I happen to know a blonde who might be interested."

Ava poked her in the ribs. "Back off, Tinker Bell." Rosie only tossed her head back in a contagious laugh.

The laughter couldn't shake off the guilt her parents had left, though. Ava threw herself into homework for distraction, drawing up proposals for hypothetical clients. This was where she was at ease: in imaginary spaces created for imaginary people. Imaginary people were simple, with needs and wants that fit neatly into one category or another: like the modern high rise guy or the natural retreat lady. She could be the invisible god hand over a space, crafting someone else's sanctuary. If only it was possible to make one for herself.

Chapter 12

Ava was walking away from her last class on Wednesday when her phone buzzed. She answered it with a smile.

"Happy birthday to you, happy birthday to you," a clamorous choir of parents and brothers sang out.

"Thank you, thank you, that was awful," Ava laughed. Her brothers each gave a quick hello before their mom shooed them all out the door for school.

"I can't believe my baby isn't here for her birthday," her mom said with a moan. "This is the last time I'm ever letting that happen."

"It's harder on us than you, I'm sure," her dad said.

"It's hard here too," Ava said, before wishing she hadn't. "But we can have a late celebration in a couple of months."

"Buy yourself some double fudge brownies, baby."

"They won't be the same as yours, mom."

"Of course not, but that will make you appreciate mine all the more when you get them."

Ava laughed. "Okay, sounds like a plan."

"We wanted to send you a present, but the shipping was insane, so we're emailing a gift card instead. Is that okay?" her mom asked.

"Absolutely. I'm a broke college kid, you honestly cannot give a better gift."

Her mom laughed. "We know, we see the bank account."

"Don't worry, I'll get a summer job," Ava said.

"You're perfectly fine. In fact, go get an extra present on us," her dad said. Ava could imagine the look between her parents.

"Do you have any plans for the day?" her mom asked.

"Not really. I might get my roomie to go out for dinner with me." And more, but they didn't need to know that.

"That sounds lovely. Take a tour around the city or something."

"I will. We have another road trip planned for this weekend. Out to the islands on the west coast."

"Send lots of pictures," her mom said.

"Will do."

"Okay, we'll let you go, hon," her dad said. "Call if you need anything."

"I will. Love you guys."

"Love you too, sweetie."

Ava hung up and stared at the door to her building. The person who talked to her parents about double fudge brownies wasn't the same as the one who walked into that room anymore. Glancing at her phone, she couldn't help the disappointment at the lack of other notifications, despite the knowledge that it was still early back home. No texts. No voicemails. Nothing on social media. She sighed and pocketed the phone. And the old friends.

The moment she walked into her room, it erupted into streamers and girlish cheers. "Happy birthday!" Rosie, Molly and Liliana all shouted in union.

A wide smile broke across Ava's face. "What? Oh my gosh, y'all are too sweet."

"Welcome to your twenties, hen." Rosie kissed her cheek. "You might only get one birthday in Scotland, so we're going to do it right."

"Yes, please, I am up for anything," Ava said.

The girls cheered again and someone popped a bottle of champagne. They poured it into clear plastic cups.

"Classy." Ava giggled.

"That's how we do it." Rosie lifted her cup in a toast, the plastic clink not nearly as satisfying as glass.

"So we're starting the drinking at three today?" Ava asked.

"Don't worry, we know your tolerance," Molly said with a laugh. "We'll break it up with dinner and shopping."

"Oh, you girls are good," Ava said, her spirits instantly lifting.

They finished the champagne and Rosie declared it was time to shop. They all headed downstairs to pile into their rideshare. It took them north of the touristy downtown and into a ritzy shopping district.

"Okay, meet in an hour," Rosie said. "I'll be helping Ava get some decent clothes."

Ava glared at Rosie, but willingly followed her into the large department store. Their tastes could not be more different. Even knowing she was there for something lavish and sexy, she still gravitated towards practical, modest tops while Rosie pulled out the most garish things she could find—all silk, lace, and tiny straps.

After repeatedly shooting down each other's choices, they found some middle ground and Ava ended up in the dressing room with a pile of dresses and tops. She stepped out awkwardly in each one, waiting for Rosie's approval. If they disagreed, Rosie sent a picture to Molly and Lilianna for extra opinions.

The moment she tried on the black dress, Ava's breath caught. This had to be the feeling a bride has when she finds *the dress.* She would never get away with wearing a v-neck this deep at home, but it was perfect for Scotland. She walked out of the dressing room and gave it a twirl.

"Oh, that's the one!" Rosie cried. "It's pure barry. You have to. You *have* to."

"It's £150," Ava hesitated. "That's crazy for a dress I'll hardly ever get to wear."

"Spend £150, look like a million. That's a good trade."

Ava squealed. "Right?" The dress was timeless. She spun by the mirror again. Black sequins sparkled like dark diamonds over the dress. It hit midway down her thighs in an asymmetrical hemline. The long sleeves gave it a touch of modesty.

"It's cut a little low—" Ava said.

"But that sash," Rosie said, running a hand over the wide black satin sash across her waist. "I never knew ye were a perfect hourglass, make the rest of us look downright hackit. You'll have the braws by the balls."

Ava frowned and shook her head. "I don't think I want that."

"Aye, of course ye do," Rosie winked at her. "You're buying that dress or I'm kicking you out of my room."

Ava laughed. "Okay, fine."

"Now, what about the green top?"

"I'm blowing the budget as is."

"Och, fine, next time."

They met with the other girls and caught a ride back to their dorm to get ready for dinner. The bathroom turned into a familiar crowded mess of curling wands and makeup. Ava attempted to give shape to the kinks that made up her wavy hair. She did a full face of makeup and let Liliana put on a deeper lipstick than her usual.

"It's time," Rosie said, with all gravity, pointing to the shopping bag.

Ava pulled on the black dress in privacy and gave it one more spin. She did have assets, didn't she?

"Oh, I hate you," Liliana said when she stepped out. The others chimed in. "You have to wear heels with that, though."

"I can't walk in heels," Ava pouted.

"Don't wrinkle your makeup," Molly said. "I have some low ones you can wear."

"What about the black booties?" Ava asked. Her dressing team stood around weighing their options and testing them on her. They finally agreed she looked like a newborn calf in heels and conceded to the booties.

Soon they were at the restaurant, ordering small meals to save room for the night ahead. Liliana ordered a bottle of wine for the table.

"You girls make being in my twenties seem pretty fabulous," Ava said. "But you know when I get home, I won't be able to drink for another year."

Liliana and Rosie booed.

"I've heard American students have their ways around that," Molly said with a tease in her eyes.

"They do, but not the ones who live with their parents," Ava laughed.

"You're 20," Liliana said. "It's time. Here's to Ava moving out this summer."

She lifted her glass and Ava met it. It was her birthday. She would cheer to anything tonight. The girls talked about 20th birthdays and the ridiculous escapades that Ava could never top. Their male waiter seemed to be havinghave fun with the table, offering flirty comments and the other girls fed into it.

Rosie was laying out the bar-hopping plan for the night when Ava's phone buzzed. Jack was calling. Rosie snatched it away before Ava could answer. "No way, no Texas tonight. This is a Scottish birthday, lass."

"Rosie—" Ava reached for the phone but Rosie stuck it in her pocket.

"Call him later. It's time to go. There are people who want to see this fine thing in person." Rose pointed over Ava's body and Ava suddenly lost confidence in the night.

"We don't have to do all this—"

"Oh, yes, we do," Rosie said as she looped an arm through Ava's and pulled her from the table. "Let's not keep the night waiting."

When they made it to the first bar, half of the rugby team was already there, including Oliver, in black jeans, a green button up and black sports coat, topped with a cream scarf. He looked like he had walked straight off a GQ photoshoot. Ava's annoyance at Rosie began to melt away.

"Happy birthday, beautiful," Oliver said, smiling confidently as he leaned in to plant a soft kiss against her cheek. She could hardly remember how to swallow, much less speak. "You look incredible. May I claim you for the night?"

"Ye nah gonnae do that," Rosie said, leaning hard on her accent and covering for Ava's inability to speak at the moment. "She's everybody's here. Too much for ye to handle, anyway. Ye can hae her later."

"Deal," Oliver said, nodding to Ava. He turned to hug Liliana and Molly.

Ava elbowed Rosie in the ribs. "Why would you do that?"

"It works, hen, trust me," she said with the smile that knew too much.

Their group grew larger at every bar until Ava didn't recognize half the people at her birthday party. It didn't matter. Drinks were landing in her hands faster than she could order or down them as Rosie worked her around the room. She tried her best to follow Benj's advice and took them only from people she trusted.

"Good grief, Rosie," she said, before another introduction was made. They were at their fourth bar and the alcohol was building her courage. "I am not a show thing."

"Hae ye seen yerself?" Rosie asked with a raised eyebrow. "I'm just making sure every boy gets a chance to meet the birthday girl."

"Okay, I think they've had a good show," Ava laughed. She knew Rosie's motivations were not selfless. Rosie was calculating and working the room herself as well. Callan was noticeably absent. "You know, we could visit with the other girls here, too."

"Ye want to meet the ladies?" Rosie asked, her mouth twisting upwards.

"Shut up," Ava elbowed her.

"That's 'haud yer wheesht' to ye," Rosie giggled. "A'right. Go see Oliver then, I'm going back to that fine ginger over there."

Ava tossed back her champagne in one swallow. The room was warm and heat pricked her cheeks. She scanned it for a moment to gain her bearings. It was hard to focus with the music rattling her bones. Her eyes landed on Oliver, talking to a girl she didn't recognize. Ava bit her lip and looked around the room for someone else. Liliana was being absorbed into a boy's mouth and she couldn't find Molly. A couple of rugby guys she recognized were at the bar, looking bored.

"Hey." Ava walked up to them under the pretense of returning her glass to the bartender.

One of them cocked his head and appraised her coolly. "Ah, the birthday girl. Rosie let you go, eh?"

"I'm on parole."

He laughed. "Well, I guess it's my turn to buy you a drink then."

"No, it's mine," a voice said from behind her. Ava turned and found herself two inches from Oliver.

The guy she had just been talking to shrugged. "Missed my chance," he said and raised his glass to her as he walked away. His friend left with him, and Ava was alone with Oliver.

"Champagne again?" Oliver asked, with one hand on her back, at the line of skin exposed by the cut of her dress.

The electric touch of skin sent her heartbeat off the charts. "Um, sure. No, actually, whisky."

"And Coke?"

"Just whisky."

"That's my proper Scot." The way he said it made her laugh. After ordering two whiskys, he lifted his glass towards hers. "To the birthday girl."

The smoky warmth filled her lungs, burning her throat and soothing her heart rate. Her legs were tired. She had been walking for hours and needed to sit down, but there wasn't an open seat at the entire bar.

"Is it 'later?'" Oliver asked. "Are you mine now?"

"I think so," Ava said, refocusing on his dark eyes. "Rosie's abandoned her post at least."

Oliver traced a finger along her jawline and it felt cool against the heat in her face. "Looks like you've had a good night."

"I have. Thanks for being part of it."

"I can make it better," he said, with one eyebrow raised in challenge.

"How's that?" she asked with a teasing smile. She should have taken flirting lessons years ago.

Oliver leaned over and caught her smile with his lips. She set her glass of liquid courage on the bar and reached both arms around his neck, bold enough to pull him closer, to taste more of him—the man that held all the confidence she craved for herself.

"Ye caught her," Rosie said, clapping her hands as she stepped up to them. Ava shot her a look.

Oliver straightened but kept a hand on Ava's back. "Any more bars on your list tonight?" He asked Rosie.

"Naw, this is the last good one before our place," Rosie said.

Oliver looked back at Ava. "I'll walk you home whenever you're ready."

"Go on, that's all the alcohol Ava can handle," Rosie said with a grin.

Ava laughed. "I'm okay, I'll wait for the rest of you girls."

"I won't be back tonight," Rosie winked. "And you have class in the morning."

Ava pursed her lips. "True…"

Oliver caught the bartender's attention and closed out his tab. He offered his arm to Ava, and she slipped her hand around it. Ava walked out of the bar as "that" girl for once; the one who might make others jealous, rather than always being the one watching and wondering.

"How's school?" Oliver asked, his voice breaking the rhythmic sound of their feet hitting the cobblestones. He slipped his arm away from her and held her hand instead.

The cool night air did little to clear her head, but she didn't mind. The buzzing warmth helped her maintain her confidence. "Mmm, good. Midterms are coming up though, and now I've missed an entire night of studying."

"You cannot think about studying on your birthday. Against Scottish rules."

Ava laughed. "Okay, what are the other Scottish rules I need to know?"

"No talking about midterms on a date either."

"You're the one who asked about school," Ava said, glancing up at him. "And calling this a date is against American rules."

"Ouch," Oliver said, with a playful frown. "Why?"

"You can only call it a date if you asked someone out beforehand. Not if you just run into them at a bar."

Oliver laughed, stopping short as he tugged Ava close to him. He brushed a hand along her cheek. "Hmm. I'd like to ask you out on a walk tonight. Are you free?"

Ava laughed again. The world around her was dancing, but she knew this was a moment she would want to remember. The first time someone asked her out, even if it wasn't exactly a real date. Even if they had already kissed. Things were out of order. No, they were in Rosie's order. Rosie was right after all.

"Sure," Ava said, nudging him with her shoulder. "Just a short one, a block or two."

"Perfect," Oliver said. Ava laughed again and Oliver cut it short with a quick kiss, short stubble scratching her cheek. The sensation was foreign but welcome.

They walked at a meandering pace. The cobblestones were vicious tonight, tripping Ava on the way and she tightened her grip on Oliver's hand as he caught her. When they reached her building, she fidgeted with the keys, struggling to unlock it. When she finally opened it, she turned back to Oliver, hesitating.

"I have to see you safely to your room," Oliver said. "Scottish rule."

"It's on the fourth floor. Are you sure you want to make the climb?"

"I'm on the rugby team, doll. I'm a little offended you don't think I can make it up four flights."

Oliver wrapped an arm around her waist as they climbed the stairs and she leaned into the support—the stairs beneath her were expanding and shrinking unevenly.

When they reached her room, he ran a finger over the daffodils on the door. "Narcissus… Very pretty."

"Thanks, I made it," Ava said as she finally unlocked the door and swung it open.

"You're quite the talented thing," Oliver said with a smile, stepping into the room behind her.

Ava turned towards him, unsure what to do next. "I had fun—"

He stopped her with a soft kiss. "You're absolutely beautiful," he whispered against her lips as his arms wrapped around her and closed the gap between their bodies. One hand traced the bare skin of her back, sending an electric current through her body and sucking the air from her lungs. Ava broke the kiss with a gasp as his thumb brushed against her ribs.

"You deserve to be touched," Oliver whispered into her ear as he kissed her neck. He pressed into her, closer than anyone had ever been, and pulled her further into the room. "Come here."

Ava hesitated. The room shrank, crowded with the two of them. "Um, I'm not sure—"

"What?" He turned back to her with a smile wrinkling at the edges of his eyes. "I enjoy being together, don't you?"

"Of course..."

"So does it have to end? Let's have a bit of fun. We can watch a movie or something." His subtle, lilting accent was mesmerizing. Its spell worked on her.

He lifted her onto the bed and laid next to her. His body stole the majority of the small bed. Something was missing... A movie. Ava tried to sit. "My laptop—"

Oliver pressed her back and rolled on top of her, kissing her again. "That's a'right doll, we'll get it in a minute."

His body was heavy and she couldn't catch a full breath. Her head spun until she was dizzy. Whether from alcohol, the weight against her lungs, or the kiss, she couldn't tell. The need for fresh air overwhelmed her.

"I'm sorry, I can't—" she couldn't form full thoughts, but she pressed her hands against Oliver's chest, trying to lift some of the weight off of her.

He groaned and leaned into her. "Yes, you can. You keep touching me like that and I'll teach you the rest." His hand ran over the neckline of her dress.

Ava's hands fell away from him. Her heartbeat was too loud—surely anyone in the building could hear it, it was all she could hear. "Oliver, move." He pressed down more firmly on her hip and tugged her dress up. Panic rose like a wave, engulfing her and pulling her under its weight. Things had gone from strange and new to an absolute nightmare.

"Stop, stop, I don't want this." She wanted to shout it, but all she heard was a panicked whisper. She fought to move away but her muscles didn't seem to work.

"Naw, doll," he said with a smile and thickening accent as he brought his lips back to hers. One hand held her head in place. "It's too late for that. Any tease knows they have to finish it."

Ava shook her head and salty tears slid down her cheeks. She hadn't planned to finish anything—this was supposed to be fun. It wasn't anymore. Her body locked in place. Her muscles were useless. She had built her own trap and now she was caught in it.

"Oliver, please, don't—" Her words caught in her throat and drowned her.

The decision was no longer hers.

Chapter 13

As the first gray light came through the window, Ava sat up, unsure if she had woken or simply become aware of the light. Had she slept? She wasn't sure what her body had done. Her stomach hurt with a deep, aching pain and Ava curled over it. Oliver had left with a promise to have more fun together again soon. Nothing about last night was fun. *"Do you not know that your body is a temple?"*[6]

Ava climbed down quietly. Rosie still wasn't back, but she needed to be silent. Lest she wake anyone, anywhere, who might ask anything. She checked the lock again and tiptoed into the bathroom. Watching her movements in the mirror as she dressed, Ava pulled on Jack's black TGU fleece and wrapped her arms around herself. She tried to recognize the body she saw. The body that had felt confident and sexy so briefly now felt cheap and sleazy. *"Do not arouse or awaken love until it so desires."*[7]

All the stupid purity pledges. All the stupid lists she had made in middle school about an ideal man. All the stupid prayers for a future husband. All the stupid promises that virginity was some measure of purity and worth. *"Flee from sexual immorality."*[8]

Ava could only flee from herself. She grabbed her backpack, needing the distraction of school and headed to the architecture building. The bag hit against a faint bruise on her shoulder. Another faint one sat at the base of her neck, where the fleece zipper landed; it had a distinct thumb shape. The walk was eternal, her bones ached, and fear creeped back in—he could be anywhere. *"Expel the wicked person from among you."*[9]

The brass doorknob to her classroom wouldn't turn. Inside, it was still dark. Ava looked around and numbly realized she hadn't checked the time when she left her dorm that morning. Class wasn't for another hour. Stupid. So stupid she couldn't even check the time. *"Control your own body in a way that is holy and honorable."*[10]

She leaned her forehead against the cool wall, trying to think straight. The walk back to her dorm would take 15 minutes, and she didn't want to be in that room. She would just stay in the building. *"The sexually immoral person sins against his own body."*[11]

Ava took the stairs to the graduate student coffee lounge that all the undergrads snuck into. Nobody else was here yet. Good. Mindlessly going through the actions, she started a pot of coffee and sat in a chair. The stairs, the walk… She was exhausted. And sick. Nauseous. She doubled over, laying her forehead on the table. *"If anyone destroys God's temple, God will destroy him."*[12]

"Wow, you like your coffee weak."

Ava's head snapped up and filled with dread. She would know the voice anywhere. And the back of his cropped black hair. Benjamin turned, holding the coffee pot with murky water in it.

It took a moment to realize what was wrong. "I—I guess I forgot the coffee."

Benjamin laughed and set it back down. He wore a bright blue hoodie with a black jacket over it and black jeans. The color scheme echoed his eyes and hair; pockets of light against a dark sky. He pulled a chair back from the table, scraping it across the floor. Ava cringed and dropped her head back down.

"What's wrong with you? Don't tell me Ava Sanford is hungover."

"No," she whispered. *Don't play the guessing game. It's worse.* Her stomach flipped again. The chair scraped the floor as Benj stood. At the sound of a cabinet opening, Ava lifted her head just enough to open one eye. He pulled a first aid kit out of the top cabinet, opened a bottle, and set two white pills in front of her.

"All they have is Tylenol. But it should help. I'll make some real coffee." His smirk was firmly in place.

Ava moaned. "I'll just throw it up."

Benj made a face. "You're that sick?"

Talking to him was too much work. It made everything worse. Ava groaned and dropped her head into her arms. Benj sat back down and propped his feet on the table.

"What'd they put in your drink last night?"

"What?" The sudden jerk of her head made the headache explode, and she pressed a hand to her temples.

He lifted his hands in surrender. "Dang, I was joking. Are you okay?"

Ava stared at him for a moment. His smirk was gone, along with the sarcasm. The one and only time in her life that she had Benj's undivided attention was the one time she didn't want it. Tears burned her eyes and slipped away before she could stop them.

"I'm so stupid," she choked out quietly and the tears multiplied.

Benjamin looked around the room uncomfortably. He grabbed a napkin from the counter and passed it to her. She tried to dab at her eyes and nose but her sinuses were too far gone for ladylike behavior.

"Hey, Ava, you're freaking me out. What's wrong?"

"Oliver—" was all she managed.

Benj blew out a breath. "Don't tell me you slept with the rugby guy."

A sound somewhere between a sob and a strangle escaped her lips as she nodded.

"Dang, that was fast. So, what's wrong? Morning after regret?"

Ava shook her head. "I didn't want to do it," she croaked out.

"Everybody has a regrettable one-night stand at some point," Benj shrugged. "It happens. You'll feel better tomorrow."

"No, I won't, Benj," she said. How could he take it so lightly? "That's not me."

"It's just sex, Ava," he said. "Now you're part of the club—a bigger, better one, trust me."

It's just sex, Ava. The words rang in her head and she realized she had heard him say that before.

It's just sex, Ava. Maybe if she chanted it enough times, she could wash away 20 years of purity culture, convincing herself that virginity and sex meant nothing. That not having any "firsts" left for a future husband was okay.

It's just sex, Ava. Benjamin stood and poured a cup of fresh coffee. He brought it to her, brushing against her shoulder. The touch cut through some of the fog with a strange tension she couldn't name.

"Let's skip class today," he said.

"What?"

"You're a hot mess. Unless you want everybody asking why, you should probably skip. We can find something else to do. You just need a distraction. I promise it'll help."

Ava's heart beat faster. He was right. She couldn't go to class in her current state, and she didn't want to spend the day alone, crying in her dorm room. Those were good enough reasons.

"Okay. Let's do it." She rubbed the tattered napkin over her nose one more time and stood, inches from Benjamin. Forgetting anything else, and needing the contact of someone familiar—needing the touch to replace Oliver, to cover the wounds like a salve—she hugged him. His arms came around her for a long, wonderful minute. A minute in which she could almost forget about Oliver. And Cassandra.

They slipped out the back of the building as students began to file in the front. Ava couldn't carry her backpack all day, so they stopped by her dorm. She left Benj downstairs while she dropped off her bag. Ava brushed on some makeup to cover as much of the redness and puffiness as possible. She changed her oversized tee and fleece for a silver sweater with a knotted bow at the bottom, and added a black and white houndstooth scarf. Just because she was a failure didn't mean she had to look like one.

"You never skip class," Ava said as they walked east to Holyrood Park. The pain was still in her stomach, but her joints were warming up to movement again.

Benj shrugged. "I guess I just needed a good reason."

Ava smiled and focused on the cobblestones underneath her feet. Maybe a day with Benj actually would help. As long as she didn't think about anyone else. Anyone at all. In their own world, they were safe.

They reached the edge of the park and Benj led them around to an entrance on the north side, next to a small loch. After stopping to admire the swans, they continued into the park. She could almost pretend to forget about last night.

"What's that?" Ava asked, pointing at a pile of rocks.

"Muschat's Cairn. Some kind of burial or memorial for a lady. Her husband killed her in the park."

"What the heck?" The pain in her stomach churned and threatened to rise. Ava pressed a shaky hand into the base of her throat. "I didn't need to hear that, Benj."

Benjamin laughed. "Sorry, bad tour guide." He caught her hand and held onto it as they walked towards the base of a hill.

Unsure why he reached for her hand, Ava tried to downplay it. Maybe he had noticed it shaking. How long had she wanted his touch? Until now. A day when she didn't really want anyone's touch. But if anyone could help her forget last night, it would be Benj. He could steady her hand today.

He let it go as they started the climb up the hill, a gently sloping walk along a worn, grassy path. It was a rare sunny day, with temperatures somewhere in the 50s and a brisk wind, but it felt glorious. Ava was in no rush and Benj seemed fine with that. When they made the first curve around the hill, Ava turned towards the city, shrinking behind them, but Benj stopped her with a finger on her jaw.

"No peeking until we get to the top. Eyes on the hill."

"Okay, tour guide," Ava smiled and kept her eyes on Benjamin, ignoring the rising pain in her ribs.

They made it to a large flat area, close to the top. Benjamin made her promise to keep her eyes on the hill again. It was hard not to look around, there wasn't much to see but tall grass and a few scattered hikers.

They soon started a more difficult climb over a steep, rocky pass to the very top of the hill. It held her focus as she picked her way along the stones behind Benj. He stopped every so often to offer a hand. She took it, even when it wasn't needed.

At the last crest, Benj hopped over it, reaching a hand back for Ava. As soon as she stepped up, he told her she could look around now.

It was breathtaking. The city spread out in miniature; the vantage point turned enormous chapels and towers into children's toys. Behind the city, the sea sparkled brilliantly in the sun. She even found the loch they had passed earlier, though the swans were invisible from this high.

"This is gorgeous," she said.

Benj flashed a rare genuine smile and tugged her towards a large rock outcropping. They climbed on top of it and sat down, letting their feet hang over the edge. The wind whipped her scarf and hair.

"It's so beautiful," Ava repeated, soaking it in.

"So are you."

Ava's eyebrows shot up and her mouth dropped open for a split second before she pressed her lips together again. She laughed but couldn't bring herself to look at him. "Jack should have told *you* to remember you had a girlfriend," she mumbled.

"Excuse me?" Benj straightened and regret instantly hit her chest. When Ava glanced at him, his blue eyes were a cool steel and his smirk was back in place. "So he told you to remember I have a girlfriend? Why would he have to tell you that, Miss Texas?"

"Haud yer wheesht," Ava smirked back.

Benj caught her hand in his and leaned in close. The smell of his cologne wafted off of him, as intoxicating as any drug. He approached her so slowly, she thought she would pass out waiting. *You could move away.* The thought floated in and out of her body; but the body wasn't hers.

His lips met hers as his hand reached into her hair. Words like 'frigid,' 'daydream,' and 'experience' floated disconnected through her mind. Ava tried to reach towards him, but her hand was caught under his. She tried to twist towards him but couldn't move, caught between Benj and the edge of the rock.

The world closed in on her. Air was gone. Panic struck her body. It was a bolt of lightning that struck white hot, hitting all the sore places.

Ava gasped and yanked back. She grabbed at the rock with her hands and pulled her feet up but they missed their landing spot, scattering a stone down. Her soul fell off the edge and she couldn't tell if her body followed or not. Benj grabbed her arms and in her panic, Ava shoved at him.

"What the hell, Ava," he shouted, physically stopping her. The pressure of his hands on her only drove the hysteria higher.

"Let go," she said, as tears spilled over. "Please let go."

"Move back from the edge first." His voice was cold as stone as he gritted the words out.

The empty body followed direction, sliding to a more even landing spot.

Air came back. At some point, Benj had let go, and she sat alone, a few feet away from him. Her hands shook and her body refused to relax. When she looked up, through watering eyes, she found him staring at her.

"Were you trying to kill me for kissing you?" he asked.

She shook her head like an idiot who still couldn't breathe enough to speak or defend herself. Defenseless. Weak. "I'm sorry," she choked out. She was too raw for a salve after all.

With her head hanging low, she heard Benj move closer. The warmth and scent of him was too heavy, too intoxicating. She turned her head the other way, trying to breathe. Ava stripped her scarf off, needing the air to hit her.

As slowly as if it had to make the entire climb up the hill again, her spirit found its way back into her body. She focused on her feet first, making sure she could still feel them. She worked her way up, mentally reaching her arms, crossing them to touch them and make sure they were hers. Finally, she lifted her head. Benj stared straight ahead.

"I'm sorry. I shouldn't have panicked."

"Could you at least wait for solid ground next time?"

Ava tried to laugh, but it wasn't genuine. "Yeah, I'll try to plan it better."

"Note to self, don't kiss Ava on cliffs." He lifted his arm around her shoulders. It felt heavy.

He shouldn't be kissing her anywhere. "Aren't you still dating Cassandra?"

He dropped his arm and his typical smirk returned. "That's my problem, not yours."

Ava frowned at him but didn't press the issue.

"Are you ready to hike back?" Benj asked. "I'm starving."

"Yeah… Let's go." Ava stood too fast and the ground tilted underneath her. She grabbed onto Benj's arm instinctively.

"You okay?"

Ava turned towards him and leaned into his chest. His arms came around her again. What an idiot. She stood here, panic-stricken because he had kissed her, knowing he had a girlfriend at home, yet wanting to kiss him again, if only to wash away the memory of Oliver.

After a deep breath, she pushed back gently and Benjamin let her go, with a small smile. They made their way back down the hill quietly. By the time they reached a cafe for lunch, Benj had clearly decided to pretend the panic had never happened. Ava did her best to keep up. Maintaining the act was crucial today.

Chapter 14

Benj offered to keep her distracted all day and into the night, but Ava was exhausted by the time dusk rolled around. She dreaded going back to her room, but she needed sleep. It wasn't possible to avoid the place forever.

The four flights of stairs stretched like a mountain before her and she thought she would throw up halfway through it. She finally made it, on feet like lead. Quietly unlocking the door, she poked her head in before entering. It was empty. Ava pushed the door open and walked inside, shutting it and double checking the lock behind her.

She headed straight for the bed, kicking off her shoes as she went. Only one step up, her arms started shaking. *"Let the marriage bed be undefiled."*[13] The stupid sheets were there, tangled, marked, most certainly defiled. She hated them with a sudden ferocity. Anger coursed through her, energizing her as she ripped the sheets off the bed, shoved them into a trash bag and tossed it to the foot of the bed.

Jack's black fleece that she had tossed on the bed earlier today got tangled in the sheets. Now it hung one limb out of the bag, begging to not get the cut. Ava sank to the floor next to the bag and tugged it free. She wrapped it into a ball and laid her head on it, trying to remember what home felt like. What Jack smelled like. But the scent was gone. The fleece was a hollow shell.

It was barely after six when Ava checked the lock again and wrapped in her plush cream blanket. She stared at the wall until sleep took over. A restless, uncomfortable sleep. There were sore spots every way she turned. Rosie came into the room at some point but Ava pretended to be asleep.

She wasn't ready to face her. To hear more about how undateable she was. How frigid.

• • •

Skipping one day of classes might be forgiven, but two days would push it. Ava forced herself into the motions Friday morning, walking through campus with senses both dull and on fire. Every part of her was aware that Oliver was somewhere on this campus.

She made it through the dreaded architecture class with Benj, Sloane and Grayson. Benj was slightly nicer today, waving when she arrived and making sure she walked with their group on the way to their lab with Garcia. It was all an act. Her body was on autopilot.

The day was so close to being done. Bed was beckoning. Classes were done and the lab was just about to be dismissed when Professor Garcia called for Benjamin and Ava to stay after class. Ava nearly tripped on her own feet. Benj looked just as surprised as she felt. The rest filed out quickly.

Garcia asked Benj to wait in the hall before he turned to Ava. "One of your teachers told me you missed a midterm yesterday, and I need to know where my students are. Can you tell me what's going on?"

"A midterm? No—" She would never miss a midterm. Environmental Design's midterm was next week, but… Visual Communications. Her interior design class. The warmth drained out of her face and Ava knew the color had gone with it. The midterm was yesterday? Twenty percent of the grade, gone? Was there extra credit? Could she take it late? Ava groaned and dropped her bag onto the floor, leaning onto Garcia's desk as her brain fought an onsetting fog.

"And your Environmental Design professor said you and Benj weren't there yesterday either. Where were you?"

How could she answer him? Was there some salvageable part of the truth, some broken piece of it that could suffice? She shook her head slowly, searching her own stories for something that made sense.

"Ava?"

"I don't... I can't—" Tears were falling before she realized she was crying.

Garcia sighed and pulled a chair to the side of his desk so Ava could sit down. She dropped into it heavily and focused all of her attention on breathing. If she could just breathe, she could get back in control. Of something.

"I was sick," she whispered.

Garcia pinched his nose for a moment. He patted her knee and wordlessly stepped into the hallway.

When he returned five minutes later, the fog was in full control. She stared blankly at the wall, barely noticing when Benj entered the room behind him. Garcia knelt next to her, and she blinked twice as her eyes refocused. "Why didn't you tell me? That's what I'm here for. If what Benj said is true, I'll need to report it."

"What?" Her eyes flicked up to Benjamin. He shrugged and revealed nothing else.

"Date rape is still rape," Garcia said softly.

The word made Ava's stomach turn. What a horrible word. "What? No. It's not like that."

Date rape? That's what Benj had told Garcia? After he had just spent an entire day telling her to get over it? Blood rushed into her head.

"Are you sure? It can seem confusing at first—"

"I'm sure." She had the childish urge to plug her ears and shout. Instead, she stood and grabbed her bag, its weight threatened to pull her back to the ground.

"Ava, UE has a counseling center—"

"No, thanks." All she wanted was to stop talking about it.

Garcia sighed and planted a hand firmly on his desk, leaning over it. "I'll talk to your teacher and see if you can make up some of that grade."

Ava thanked him absently and bolted for the door Benj held open. He kept pace alongside her as she hurried out of the building, craving the air. The moment the cold hit her, it cut through the mental fog and Ava spun on Benj. "What did you tell him?" In her mind, the words were angry, offended. Aloud, they were meek.

Benj shrugged. "Skipping class is one thing, but he said you missed a midterm, so I told him the truth."

"The truth? Which truth?"

His usual smirk returned and Ava suddenly resented it. "Whichever one is most convenient. You should be glad, I saved your grade."

"I don't care about my grades." Not right now.

"Yes, you do."

Ava wanted to scream but her voice only cracked. "Don't tell me what I care about."

Benj laughed and looked her up and down slowly, and somehow she felt as naked as she had two nights ago. He snickered and shook his head. "You're a mess." With that, he turned and walked away.

More of a mess than he could possibly know. Students passed her as she blocked the middle of the sidewalk. Ava begged the cracks in the sidewalk to swallow her. Somehow, her legs found the will to keep walking. They carried her to her dorm building because there was nowhere else to go.

After two nights of barely sleeping, Ava was exhausted. Mentally and physically. She sat outside of her dorm building for several minutes, building the strength for the stairs. The strength for facing her room. Or worse, Rosie.

The moment Ava opened the door, her heart sank.

"There you are, hen," Rosie said, popping her head out from the bathroom. "I was just starting to think Oliver had up and stolen you."

He did. She had no strength left for this. Ava dropped her backpack to the floor and sank down next to it.

"What's wrong with you? Are ye sick?" Rosie asked.

Ava nodded silently. Rosie pulled a water bottle from their mini fridge and handed it to Ava, who drank it gratefully, cooling the bile in her throat.

"What's wrong?" Rosie sat cross-legged on the floor in front of her. For a brief moment, she looked like she had the capacity to have a serious conversation.

Words were hard to find. "Oliver."

"What?" Rosie looked bewildered. "Don't tell me he's no good in bed."

"I didn't want to sleep with him."

Rosie wrinkled her small face, and the seriousness was clouded by pixie dust. "Yer aff yer heid. Of course ye did. You were dressed like sex and walkin' home wit the hottest guy on the team."

Home. Is that what this place was? "I didn't think walking home meant sex."

Rosie laughed like it was a joke. "Yer too naïve. Don't let old Puritan Ava get in the way. Scotland Ava had a fantastic birthday, thanks to her good friends Rosie and Oliver."

Ava searched Rosie's face, trying to find the secret to her nonchalance, trying to ingest it for herself. If she could just stop caring, she would feel better. If she could be completely and solely Scotland Ava.

"But there is such a thing as consent," she muttered to herself.

"Then just say yes next time," Rosie giggled. "He at least used protection, right?"

"I don't even know," Ava said. Details were fogged over.

Rosie sighed and shifted through her things until she found a small box. She opened it and dug out a pill, holding it out to Ava.

Ava pushed it back. "Already on birth control."

"And I thought you were a virgin," Rosie laughed.

"Anemia," was as far as Ava's explanation could go. She didn't want to address the "was" part of her virginity. It didn't matter anyway. Oliver would be the first and last. She was unloveable. Only a shower seemed achievable right now—a cold shower that would clear her head, the noise of the fan and the water drowning out any thoughts.

Chapter 15

Friday had started too early and would end too late. Jack had led a campus tour through the athletic department facilities that morning before classes and work. Now, Natalie had convinced him that an evening at Draft Haus with the other student staff would build morale. As he sat at a high top in the old building, he wasn't sure the place was capable of such lofty goals. Draft Haus had all the markings of former glory—too many tables that usually sat empty and a stage that hadn't seen a live band in years. But even in its dilapidated state, it was still the closest thing to campus and they had cheap beers.

Jack mostly listened to the gym gossip; the guy that went to the gym three times a day, each time with a different girl; the cheerleaders who ran until they threw up; the people who came in and never touched the equipment, only walked around and talked to anybody who would listen.

"You're not innocent either, Victor," Natalie said. "You say you're going to workout after every shift and then always end up with sudden illnesses or homework."

Jack laughed. Natalie had a terrifying knack for pointing out anyone's flaws and nobody wanted to be on the receiving end. But Victor could handle himself. He spun the conversation to pick on Jack for refusing to touch an elliptical.

"Those are for girls," Jack said, offending everybody and earning himself a smack from Natalie. They were a fun group—a change of pace from the students at Grace. A touch of another reality. One that kept him humble. They reminded him of the life he had lived when he played football, and the reasons to give it up.

The group complained about classes before switching to spring break plans. Most of them were staying in town, several were working. It was beach week, there was no need to leave. Thousands of college students around Texas would be arriving on their doorstep and bringing the party with them. Victor and Dallas started comparing hookup stories from past spring breaks before Natalie and Jack ended it.

When everyone ordered a second round of drinks, Jack switched to water and ignored the snide remarks. He had a one drink policy. A carefully crafted policy, after watching his dad drink, and testing it out for himself in high school before he started going to church. He was ready to call it a night when he overheard his name in a conversation between Natalie and Dallas. He leaned over. "What do I hate?"

"Your major," Natalie said. "Dallas is thinking about changing his to business too."

"I don't hate it," Jack said.

"Yes, you do," Natalie said, waving him off. "What are you going to do with it?"

"The business school has the highest rate of job placements for grads."

"Fantastic, go get yourself a job you hate," Natalie said and cocked an eyebrow at him. "Name one business class you've enjoyed."

"Sports Management."

"Right, because you enjoy sports, not business."

Jack shrugged. "Everything's a business. It'll come in handy somewhere." It was a line he repeated to himself after every mind-numbing class, that, if he was being honest, he did hate.

Dallas started asking questions about the business program and Jack toed the line between answering them honestly and maintaining the appearance that he enjoyed it. He didn't have to love his major. He just needed a decent salary one day.

"What are you going to do for the internship requirement?" Dallas asked.

"I haven't found anything I'm interested in yet."

"Of course not," Natalie said.

Jack finally caved. "Look, I would change it if I could. But I'm already behind. I don't have the time or money to stick around another year."

"You know there's a scholarship for kinesiology majors working in the athletic department, right?" Natalie asked. "Professor Anderson would write you a recommendation in a heartbeat."

He didn't know. Jack studied her for a second. She was being serious. How much was that scholarship?

"Why didn't you go into kinesiology to begin with?" Dallas asked.

"Sports are unreliable," Jack said. He had put everything into football in high school and walked away with nothing but a scar. "I'd rather have a real job."

Natalie was one of the few who knew him well enough to know why he said it. "Nobody's asking you to be an NFL player, Jack. But what about coaching? Or personal training?"

Jack gave a short laugh. God and football couldn't coexist. "I don't exactly want to stay in college for the rest of my life."

Natalie pointed at him. "I'm calling bull. One more semester wouldn't kill you if it means a career you'd actually enjoy." Natalie never held back. And she was rarely wrong.

"You can minor in business to keep those credits," Dallas said.

Jack nodded and took a long, slow sip of water, waiting and hoping for the conversation to change on its own. It didn't. They waited. "I'm thinking about it."

Natalie cheered. "Just do it Jack. Do *something.*"

"I do everything."

"Do something you *want* to do."

Did he even know what that was anymore?

• • •

Jack woke early Sunday morning with a start. His mind had been racing in a dream but he couldn't remember what it was about. He tossed in bed for a little longer before giving up the fight for sleep. His body needed to move.

Church wasn't for another three hours, so Jack pulled on black joggers and a gray TGU t-shirt. He paced the apartment for a moment, an electrical current buzzing through his body. And it only had one cure. He grabbed running shoes and his phone and shut the door behind him.

His apartment complex backed up to the city soccer fields and the mile-long track that circled them. He started the first lap, letting his mind focus solely on his breath and pace.

In the second lap, full thoughts began to form. Something was missing. His mind replayed the past week, searching for it. On the third lap, he found the missing thing and tried to ignore it. The fourth lap forced him to accept it.

Ava.

Sweaty and breathless, he jogged back to the apartment, showered and changed into jeans and a blue polo. He couldn't avoid it anymore. Jack found Ava's name on his phone and blew out a breath. She hadn't answered his phone call on Wednesday. He could chalk that up to birthday celebrations. But she hadn't responded to his text Thursday, either. Or yesterday.

The phone rang. And rang. He hung up when the voicemail greeting started. Jack chewed on the inside of his lip. She didn't have to answer. There might be a hundred valid excuses. Why did it bother him now? He started to type out another text, but erased it. He restarted half a dozen times before giving up entirely. It was time to go to church. He needed it today.

College students claimed three rows at church—their group had grown throughout the semester, as usual. Students were settled into the rhythm of the semester and coming more regularly.

When the service was over, Jack talked to a few of the newer students for a little while. Val approached from the side and cut him off mid-sentence, asking him about lunch plans.

"There's too many of us to go to one place," Jack said, glancing at her halfway. He'd already blown his budget this week. "I think I'm skipping, anyway. Ask Talia."

"What? You can't do that. That's not fair," Val said, tugging on his arm.

Jack gave a shrugging smile to the students he had been talking to and turned to Val. "I didn't think where I ate was a matter of justice."

"I need to talk to you," she said, pulling him further from the group.

Jack followed her until they were outside of the building. He leaned against the sun-warmed brick and waited for her to say whatever she needed. Val sighed at him like he was the problem. "I have to go to my cousin's wedding next weekend."

"Okay."

"Will you go with me?" she asked, crossing her arms like it was a challenge.

A couple of young families were leaving the school building and one waved towards them. Jack and Val waved back. "Weddings aren't really my thing," he said.

"Oh, come on." Val twisted the strap of her purse in her hands and had an expression that was somewhere between a pout and genuine hurt. "I need somebody to go with me. We always have fun together."

The girl was having a hard semester with family health issues. And she had remembered Jack on the anniversary of his mom's death. And he had already turned down joining them on the spring break trip next week. He couldn't turn her down again. "When is it?"

"Saturday evening."

"I have to work intramural basketball championships all weekend," Jack said.

"What time do they end on Saturday?" Val was pushing this hard.

"Five."

"Perfect," she said, clapping her hands. "The wedding's at six."

"I'll have to clean the gym and equipment after—"

"Just the reception then?"

"Okay… just the reception. Are you sure? I mean, I bet one of the other guys—"

"I'd rather go with you," Val said.

"Val—"

"Just text me when you're done with work on Saturday."

"Right... Okay."

With a victorious squeal, Val gave him a hug and bounded off back towards the building to find herself a lunch group. Jack leaned his head back against the building. How did that happen?

Chapter 16

Rosie woke Ava Saturday morning with a shove. "'Mon sleeper, Molly's ready to go."

Ava sat slowly in confusion. The light had already been coming through the window when she had fallen asleep this morning. Time had become irrelevant. "Go where?"

"Are ye off yer trolly? Or did ye have a bevvy without me last night? To the isles."

Ava had forgotten about the road trip. With a swear, she threw the blanket off. Getting out of town would be a good thing. She rolled out of bed and threw her things into a backpack, adding clothes and toiletries with little thought. Rosie watched until the bag was sufficiently stuffed before dragging Ava out of the room.

Winding roads, nodding daffodils, gorse-covered glens and half a dozen lochs passed through the window. Scotland was waking up to the first touches of spring and one rolling green hill led to another. Music blared through her headphones, providing a perfect conversation barrier. Ava forced herself to focus: another little town. Another distant castle. These were good things. There was no reason not to appreciate them. The girls were doing this largely for Ava's sake—she had pushed for road trips. She needed to enjoy it.

They stopped at Inveraray Castle, a Gothic Revival masterpiece. One she should appreciate. Grey stone. Four towers with steep cone tops. Three floors in the main building, each with seven windows. Neoclassical rooms. Perhaps her soul couldn't feel beauty anymore, but she could still process details. Details were attainable.

The paths through the gardens were laid out in the cross of the Scottish flag. Japanese cherry blossoms were beginning to unfold along the path. Shrubs were carved into perfect shapes. Details.

"What's wrong with you?" Molly asked as they walked silently through the grounds. "You've gone quiet."

"I'm tired," Ava said. It was true. "I haven't been able to sleep lately."

"They've got a cafe in the castle if you need some coffee."

"Yeah. That would be good."

Molly stopped short. "You're acting weird."

"Sorry."

Molly hooked an arm through Ava's as they continued the walk. "I studied abroad last semester. It got hard around this point. The excitement wears off and you still have so long to go. You'll get back into the swing of it soon though. And then you'll never want to leave."

Ava wanted to grab her, to cry on her shoulder, to tell her everything. But she couldn't keep talking about it, spreading it around. Nobody seemed to understand what the problem was—it was hers alone. Everybody she knew could be classified into two groups: the ones who wouldn't see the problem, and the ones who would judge her for it. Her mind was preoccupied with categorizing people.

Ava nodded in reply, unable to trust her own words to form properly right now.

They made it to Oban by the late afternoon. Ava declined dinner, opting for a nap instead. Not that napping at six in the evening made any sense, but she was exhausted. In the comfort of a hotel room, with crisp white sheets that smelled like lavender, she managed to fall asleep for the first time since Wednesday.

• • •

The next day, the girls got an early start to the Isle of Mull. Nobody had to wake Ava this time, she'd been lying awake in bed since three in the morning—the consequences of going to sleep at dinnertime. After crossing to Mull on a ferry, they drove straight to a port on the far end of the island.

Molly parked the car, and they bought tickets for a smaller ferry to the Isle of Iona, a spot none of the girls had been to before. Ava followed the girls through the motions, finding a seat on the ferry. Last night's sleep hadn't been enough. Her body felt like it was filled with rocks.

The ferry trip to Iona was short. The island didn't allow cars, but it was small enough to walk. The girls wandered through the small town, popping into the handful of shops that lined the single main street. The shops were tiny and crowded, stuffed to the brim with trinkets, drying flowers, and smelly cheese. There wasn't room to breathe and Ava excused herself, opting to stay outside instead.

Up the block she caught sight of a stone ruin. Ava crossed through an empty grassy lot to the ruins and ran a hand along the stones, tracing a deteriorated wall. Moss poked through the stones. Broken columns spoke of once-beautiful archways. Walking the perimeter of the ruin, it was clear it had been a religious building of some sort.

Ava came to the front of the ruin and found a historical plaque. A nunnery. A slow smile forced its way onto her face and a dry laugh escaped. Of all the places she would be drawn to—

"There you are," Rosie's voice rang out. "No shopping for Miss Texas? Don't ye want a souvenir?"

"What?" Ava asked and lifted a hand to shield her eyes. Two months in Scotland and her eyes had forgotten how to handle sunlight.

"Never mind," Rosie said. "Come on, Puritan, you'll like the abbey."

They walked along the unused single-track road towards the abbey. Iona Abbey was one of the oldest Christian sites in Western Europe. The birthplace of Christianity in Scotland. Beautiful, historic, good. Though she wouldn't share a single photo of it, lest she supply the TGU students with even more ammunition for the mission trip joke. This part would be a secret. Another.

The abbey was still in use, shared by various religions on the tiny island. The last service of the day had ended half an hour ago, so the girls wandered into the main chapel. The medieval stonework contrasted sharply with the 1970s-style wooden chairs and hardback hymnals. Molly and Rosie moved on quickly, heading into the adjacent courtyard, but Ava stayed.

She walked through the chapel slowly, tracing her fingers over the chairs, a lingering warmth filled the room that had been inhabited so recently. Patches of new stones filled in spaces on the walls, their brightness glaring against the historic gray ones. At the far end of the room stood a white granite altar, the stonework cold under her fingers as she traced the faint green lines that ran through it like scars.

A door slammed somewhere not far away and jolted Ava from her reverie. She hurried towards the exit and found herself in a tiny courtyard lined with rows of double pillars. A priest walked towards her, and the once-comforting sight of a clergyman suddenly terrified her. Ava rushed through the courtyard towards an exterior door.

Shoving the door open, she tripped over a stone step, landing on her hands and feet on the gravelly path outside. Ava sucked in a sharp breath and clasped a hand to her knee. Blood seeped through. The sharp sting in her knee was an antidote to the fog in her mind, lifting it suddenly.

With new clarity, the island now seemed over-saturated: a crisp blue sea behind the abbey, and emerald green hills in front, dotted with white specks of sheep. The air was light and peaty, with a faint hint of salty sea mixed with subtle farm smells. A cool breeze blew against her sun-warmed cheeks. Had it blown all day? Ava brushed her dirty, bloody hand off on her already-ruined jeans and touched her own cheek gently, as if discovering it was still there.

A lowing in the distance drew her attention, and she crossed the church grounds to find a fenced pasture. Two brown highland cows were standing near the fence, watching people pass by. Hairy bangs nearly covered their eyes, and small horns stuck out on either side. Ava reached out towards one and it bellowed, a deep, homely sound that made her laugh.

"Miss Texas," Molly shouted.

"She does still smile," Rosie said quietly as they joined Ava.

"They're so cute, you guys," Ava said, touching the snotty nose of the cow.

"That must be your cowgirl side," Rosie said, shrinking back.

Molly gently touched the cow's forehead. "You've been in the city too long, Rosie. Don't forget you grew up around these hairy coos."

"And I left as fast as I could." Rosie muttered, lifting her hand to pet the cow but when he let out another bellow, she drew it back and declared it was lunch time. Ava turned to follow them when Rosie grabbed her arm and stopped her.

"What happened to you?" Rosie asked, frowning at Ava's leg.

Her jeans were ripped at the knee, where she hit the gravel. Blood and dirt were caked in fine lines on the exposed skin. "I tripped," she shrugged.

"You need to clean that, hen," Rosie said, like a scolding mother. She ushered Ava into the hotel restaurant just a few yards away.

The girls found a table while Ava went to the bathroom to clean her leg. She bit her lip as she dabbed a wet paper towel at the scrape. The jeans were already partially ruined, so she tore them a bit further to get access to the cut, flicking out bits of gravel. With her knee finally clean, she realized her lip was now the part bleeding.

Ava lifted a fresh paper towel to her lip and stared at herself in the mirror. For a moment she had felt like more than a shell. For a moment, she had been present again. But she saw it slipping away—the more she stood here and thought about it, the more her eyes dulled, and the further her soul went. She threw the paper towel in the trash bin and sprinted from the bathroom, determined to stay in her body as long as possible.

"Yer boyfriend called," Rosie said, pointing to the phone Ava had left on the table.

"Boyfriend?" Molly asked, looking between them.

Ava picked it up—two missed calls. One from her mother and one from Jack. And a text from Talia, but it was just a meme. Ava swiped the notifications away. Molly repeated her question.

"Not a boyfriend," Ava muttered.

"He wants to be," Rosie said with unfounded confidence.

Rage vibrated through her, anger directed solely at Jack. Ava's words spewed like lava. "If he wanted that, he should have said something before I left."

"Maybe he needed to miss you," Rosie said.

"Then he'll always miss me. Because he's missed his chance." If he had asked her out before she left, Oliver would have never been in her room.

"Ah, now that's gallus," Rosie said. "I like it."

She didn't want to think about Jack. She wanted to throw her phone out the window. After forcing down a few pieces of the fish and chips on her plate, Ava washed it away with water. She passed the rest off to Molly and Rosie, her stomach tightening with each passing moment.

When they finished lunch, the girls meandered back towards the ferry and caught a ride to the Isle of Mull. They had a long day of driving ahead of them. An hour drive across Mull. A ferry to the mainland. And three hours back to Edinburgh.

Hours in tight, enclosed spaces. Ava pulled her jacket off at the thought of it and stood at the front of the ferry for the ride back to Mull, abandoning her seat next to the girls. She needed to store up the cold, it eased her stomach and throat. The wind whipped the water, carrying tiny droplets to sting her face until a wet chill settled into her, soothing her with shivers.

Chapter 17

Jack's thumb hovered over the picture on his phone. He told himself to swipe past it but he couldn't stop staring, wondering if he would have even recognized her if it hadn't been for her name. Other birthday photos had already been posted, but this one was a close-up. Chocolate brown hair fell over half of her face and covered part of the neckline of a black dress that dipped precariously low. She leaned over her roommate's shoulder and smiling behind too much makeup. It highlighted her almond-shaped eyes, though it didn't cover the flush and shine that hinted at too much alcohol.

He hadn't spoken to her in 10 days. Their text message conversation looked like he was talking to a wall. Yet she obviously had time for friends there. And for going out. Her roommate tagged her in pictures that didn't seem to follow any chronological order, but he knew there had been another road trip. Ava hadn't posted anything herself in days. That fact alone bothered him, and the unsettled, electric feeling he'd woken with a week ago had never gone away.

A buzzer went off in the next court and Jack shoved the phone into his pocket. The intramural basketball championship had taken over his entire weekend, and Val had filled the rest with the wedding last night. Only one more game to go and he would be done. Approximately three hours stood between Jack and his bed.

As he set up the scoreboard for the next game, his phone rang in his pocket. If it had been any other name, he would have ignored it. He was working. But it was a Sanford.

"Micah, hi," Jack said, trying not to give away any surprise. He had been close to Ava's parents since junior year of high school, but they didn't call to chat.

"Hey Jack, do you have a minute?" Micah asked.

"I'm working, but I can spare one."

"Call me when you get off, then."

"Are you sure?"

"Yeah, it's fine, anytime tonight," Micah said.

"Okay… Will do."

The nagging current amped up.

• • •

It was late by the time he locked the gym and walked to his truck. It was a weird hour to call a friend's parents. Or a pastor. But Micah had said anytime and Jack needed an explanation.

"Jack, thanks for calling back," Micah said.

"No problem, what's up?" Jack didn't have time or energy for small talk.

"It's about Ava," Micah cleared his throat. Jack's hand stilled over the gear shift, waiting. "Have you heard from her?"

"Not in a few days."

"Neither have we…" Micah's tone was careful, measured. "Or Talia."

The electrical current sparked into a flame. That wasn't like Ava. She might be busy, but she wouldn't stop talking to her parents and best friends.

"I'm sorry to involve you, I thought maybe you had talked to her. I hoped someone had…"

"No, it's fine," Jack said. "Have you reached out to the school? The professor there with them?"

"I'm planning to tomorrow," Micah said. That was both reassuring and a terrible sign. "It might be overbearing, she might just be busy, but it seems odd."

"I agree," Jack said. "I've been thinking the same thing."

"And Jack, if you talk to her, could you let me know? You don't have to tell me anything else, just if you hear her voice, if she's okay."

"I will."

Jack backed the truck out of the parking lot, caught between the buzzing spark in his veins and ravenous hunger. He drove to his apartment on autopilot. After a shower and a pizza from the freezer, he plopped onto the couch with his phone. He wouldn't be able to sleep.

The first post he saw was from Ava. So she was alive, at least. She had shared a picture of an old door front, a soft pink hue, with a lantern in front. No caption. With a quick calculation he knew it had to be the middle of the night in Edinburgh, but she had only posted it five minutes ago. Jack closed the app and dialed her, prepared to leave a voicemail this time.

The sound of her voice startled him into an upright position.

"Hey, one sec, my roommate's asleep," she whispered. A door clicked shut in the background. "Jack, it's 4AM here."

"I saw you just posted, so I knew you were up," he said without apology. "Where have you been?"

She was silent.

Jack double checked his phone—the call hadn't dropped. Her silence made him nervous. He aimed for a softer tone. "I haven't heard from you in a few days."

"Yeah." She offered nothing else.

He asked how she was. *Fine.* What she had been doing. *Nothing.* She only gave single word answers.

"Happy belated birthday, by the way. How was it?"

Ava started to say something but coughed. "Um… it was okay. Not great."

Not the answer he expected. Not from the pictures. But it warranted more than one word from her and he went for it. "Really? Why not?"

"I don't really feel like talking, Jack." Her voice was so quiet, he hardly heard her.

"Wait—" He couldn't lose her now. "I'm sorry. Sorry it wasn't great."

"Me too."

Talking to her was supposed to cool the electricity in his veins, not ramp it up. But nothing she said reassured him. "Aves… What's wrong?"

"I'm screwing everything up," her voice cracked.

With a strength that surprised him, he suddenly longed to be back at their coffee shop, throwing a wadded napkin at her for saying something self-deprecating, then catching her hand before she could return it. "What do you mean?"

"Nothing. Never mind. I'm just stupid."

"That's a lie," Jack said, standing to pace the living room. "Who's telling you that?"

"Rosie. Benj. Everybody."

"Why are you talking to Benj?" Jack asked. Worry turned to anger. "I've been trying to tell you—"

"Shut up, for the love of God, shut up," Ava said, with more vitriol than he'd ever heard from her. "I can talk to whoever I want."

Jack gritted his teeth and mentally counted to five. "Okay. Of course you can."

"It's not about Benj, anyway."

"Fine. What's it about then?"

"I can't—" Her voice lost its natural cadence, replaced by an uneven, choking strain. "Don't hate me, Jack."

"I would never hate you."

"Yes. You will."

"Try me." It was a bravado he didn't believe. He listened as she seemed to wrestle with the challenge, taking a deep breath, starting a sentence and cutting it off after a single word. And repeat.

"I kissed Benj," she finally spit the words out.

So it *was* about Benj. Jack bit back every instinct, the snapping reply he wanted to give. He had to prove he wouldn't react as poorly as she expected, but he couldn't offer much else. She was making a huge mistake. The idiot she had a crush on was a wolf in sheep's clothing. He had seen enough of Benj and his type to recognize it. But she couldn't see past Benj's face to trust Jack.

"Say it. Go ahead."

"I wish you hadn't." He had plenty more to say, but Jack settled on a compromise.

"Why not?" she fired back. "Why am I not allowed to kiss someone, but you're allowed to go out with Val?"

"What? How is that even related? It was just a wedding—"

"I don't care, Jack. I don't care what it was."

"At least Val isn't in a relationship with somebody else," Jack said, forcing his voice not to rise. "Your first kiss was with a guy that has a girlfriend."

"He wasn't—" Ava started but Jack couldn't make out her words anymore.

Jack knew a first kiss meant something to Ava. Even if she had thrown it away. But the sobs were bigger than any bad kiss deserved. He shouldn't have snapped back at her. She had the power to hang up the phone at any moment and nobody knew when they would hear from her next.

"Hey, I'm sorry. I shouldn't—"

"It's not just… There was someone… I can't—"

"It's okay. Seriously, Aves…" Crying was outside of his comfort zone. Especially from Ava. And words were useless in a place where arms were meant to be. Jack ran a hand over his face. He wanted to promise her it would be okay, but he wasn't sure he believed it himself. If anybody knew life could fall apart at any minute, it was him.

"You don't know what it's like," she said. "It's just—it's so much harder, being out of that church circle—"

"Of course I know what it's like. I lived outside of it for years, it's hard and hopeless. But why are you outside of it? You're doing this to yourself."

"You don't know what you're talking about," she choked out.

"I'm worried about you."

"Don't be."

"I am. So are your parents. And Talia."

"What do they have to do with this?"

"You haven't talked to anybody."

"I don't owe y'all anything."

The tears were gone and her tone made him take a mental step back. Jack tried to walk it off and recover the lost ground. "No, I guess you don't..." Except the parents paying for her school, but mentioning that was pointless.

"I don't want to talk anymore."

Neither did he. "Okay. Fine. But please let somebody know you're alive once in a while."

"I'll try."

The line went dead. He had lost her.

Jack decided to wait until the morning to text Micah. Texting him late at night was one thing, admitting he had talked to the man's daughter at four in the morning was another entirely. It could wait a few more hours.

Sleep didn't come easily. The gnawing stress rose again. Jack found himself replaying the conversation, trying to fix it. He should have explained the wedding with Val wasn't a date. Or at least he didn't mean for it to be. Not that he had to defend it.

He should have reacted better about the Benj thing. Maybe she would have talked more. But how could he have? She was doing exactly what he had warned her not to and it would only lead to more hurt if she kept it up. Benj was far from trustworthy. Though a kiss shouldn't have brought Ava to her knees.

The days-long silence. The refusal to talk about it. None of it was like Ava. Part of it could surely be blamed on the phone. If only he could see her, talk to her in person. Watch her avoid eye contact by fidgeting with a bracelet. See her stall, twirling a long wave of hair around her finger. She had never been able to lie to him in person. Face to face, she would cave the instant he raised an eyebrow at her. But here, he was 5,000 miles away and completely useless.

• • •

After talking to Micah, Jack spent the next few days stewing. The pastor he admired and respected was wrong, and Jack was sure of it. Micah had told Jack to give Ava "space." He had given some long explanation about how they had pushed their own lifestyle on her too heavily. "As hard as it is, Ava needs a chance to choose her own path." So Micah and Rebecca had decided to give her space. Worse, they asked Jack to do the same. Jack had never argued with a pastor before and he hadn't done it well.

The last thing Ava needed was to lose contact with her family and friends, and rush into the arms of Benj and anyone like him. But could Micah be so wrong? The man was usually right. Surely he knew something Jack didn't. So they settled on the terms: Jack wouldn't reach out, but if Ava contacted him, he would talk to her.

He only lasted three days. He kept his phone in his hand all of Wednesday afternoon, waiting for Ava to call for their usual talk, fully aware she wouldn't. He went to Bible study at the Torres' house and tried to act normal. He ate dinner quietly. When it was time for the Bible study, Jack couldn't handle it anymore. He excused himself and stepped outside, giving in and tapping her number. He expected the voicemail but was surprised by a different voice instead.

"The incredible Jack," a voice rang high with a song-like quality. Ava's descriptions of a pixie roommate made more sense the moment he heard it. "This is Rosie."

"Hey, is Ava there?"

"Ava's busy right now. I can take a message."

"I could leave one on the voicemail for that, I'd like to talk to Ava."

"Well ye need to do more than talk, don't ye?"

He was a fish, taking the bait. "What does that mean?"

"Haven't ye ever seen a movie? Aren't you supposed to jump on an airplane, show up with flowers and land a giant kiss on her?"

"What? We're not— she's my friend."

Rosie laughed. "Right. Well, we Scots have got her in good hands. Mate of mine gave her a little practice. She might have a move or two to teach ye when she gets back."

The buzz in his veins shot into his heart. *Scots. Mate of mine.* That wasn't Benj. "Who are you talking about? Where's Ava?" And how many people was she kissing?

"Don't worry, ye'll get her back for yerself in two months," Rosie said. "What was yer message?"

"Nothing."

"I'll pass that right along."

"Forget it," Jack said. He pocketed the phone and stalked into the Torres' house, unable to hold a decent conversation with anyone in the group.

Micah was right. If Ava wanted to kiss every guy in Scotland, she needed space to do it.

Chapter 18

Wednesday night came like the toll of a bell. Ava watched her phone, waiting. If Jack didn't call, it would confirm her deepest fears. That nobody wanted her. He hadn't texted her again since their last talk. Nobody had—not Talia, not even her parents. They had all given up on her so easily. They had moved on. She wasn't worth anyone's time.

Not that she wanted their attention—it would only come with judgment. Even their cold, flat faces on the wall were judging her. When the hour for Jack's phone call came and went, Ava yanked the pictures off the wall, ripping them and throwing them into the trash bag at the foot of the bed, where her old sheets still sat.

The plush cream blanket was a makeshift sleeping bag. Ava told herself she would wash the sheets but hadn't found the energy or willpower to do it. If she had even a single friend in this city, just one person to ask for help… Only an idiot was incapable of doing such a little thing. Sick of the reminder, she set the bag of sheets and photos outside of her room for trash pickup. She could get new ones.

When she climbed back onto her bed, the textbook lay there, entirely neglected. Ava reread the paragraph on Ludwig Mies van der Rohe for the fourth time. It never sank in. Every time, she reached the end of the paragraph and couldn't remember what she had just read. The next time she looked at the clock, it was 11. Jack wasn't calling. It had only taken the mention of a single kiss—that was all it took to lose him. One kiss he disapproved of. Thankfully she had stopped the truth-telling there.

Ava tossed the textbook to the ground and hopped down after it. Another shower would help. The second today. She scrubbed her skin in the cold water, willing it to sink in and numb. But she didn't have time for it to reach those places now. Rosie would be back soon and Ava had to be asleep by then, or pretending at least.

Working quickly, she pulled her razor along her legs and armpits. It snagged on her left ankle, catching a swath of skin in its blades. Ava cursed as the water turned red along the floor of the tub. All that blood from such a small patch. So she wasn't hollow.

A laugh let loose as she watched. She used to hate the sight of blood. A razor cut would have had her playing the wounded soldier at home. Here, it was just another sign of incompetence. Here, nobody cared.

The sting on her leg worked where the water hadn't. In fact, it worked better. Rather than numbing, it brought her back to life. Ava finished her shower with a fresh appreciation for every part of it—the coconut scent of her shampoo, the fizzing suds in her hands, Edinburgh's crisp tap water. When she stepped out of the bathroom, she didn't even mind that Rosie was already back. In this moment, she was refreshed. Truly.

Rosie called over to her without looking up from her study spot at the foot of her bed. "Oliver wants yer number. Can I give it to him?"

Ava never knew a moment could be so short lived.

"No, of course not. Are you crazy?"

"Are you still hanging on to this?" Rosie asked, finally looking at Ava with a bored expression. "I'm not losing my friends for you and your petty problems. You might get to leave at the end of the semester, but I'll still be here with whatever you screwed up. Oliver is pure barry."

"I don't want to talk to him, or see him, ever again," Ava said.

"I'll just tell him he has to ask ye himself," Rosie said. "And I thought we had made progress on yer being so frigid. No wonder ye haven't dated anyone."

"We're done talking about this," Ava said, pulling out headphones to end the conversation. She hadn't dated anyone because no one could love her.

• • •

By the time Ava arrived at her morning architecture class with Benj, her bones were aching. The wet Scottish air had turned her into an elderly person, complaining about the pain in her joints if she walked more than a few yards. She was so weak. Everybody else on the TGU team had adjusted fine. Why couldn't she?

There was a test that morning and Ava had never finished the paragraph in her textbook, much less the chapter. The words swam on the page as she forced herself to check boxes and take her best guesses. The room spun around her. Professor Garcia had tried to talk to her after their last lab but she had only laughed it off and said she was fine. After he saw the grade on this test, he would know she had lied.

Usually she knew some Bible verse to help calm her during tests, but today she only remembered the worst ones. "*Expel the wicked.*"[14] "*Have nothing to do with such people.*"[15] "*Weak women, burdened with sins.*"[16] The book that once held such comfort was now the source of rising nausea.

She hastily finished the test, handed it in and hurried out of the room, desperate to leave. A hand caught her just outside of the classroom door.

"Hey, slow down," Benj said.

Ava straightened to meet his eyes and held onto his hand, letting it steady the tilting building around her.

"Shoe's untied," Benj said with a nod towards the floor.

Staring at her shoes, she barely remembered putting on the canvas sneakers. Benj looked at her like she had gone completely dumb. She had.

"Forgot how?" he asked as he leaned down. His hand brushed her ankle and she twitched in pain. Benj's hand stilled and he flipped the cuff of her jeans, revealing the cut. "What happened to you?"

"Shaving accident," Ava said, the sting brought the spinning room to a still. "Like a sixth-grade girl."

He didn't laugh. Benj stood and stared at her wordlessly for a moment. "Let's get coffee," he said, holding his hand out.

Ava weighed it—a half-mile walk and an hour of talking. What a lot of effort for someone who might or might not acknowledge her in tomorrow's class. *For a guy that has a girlfriend.* More guilt was the last thing she needed right now. "I'm sorry… I can't…"

"Hey girl," Benj's voice was gentle, his touch at her elbow even more so. He was the last person on earth who saw her. "Come on. There's a great spot on campus you'll love."

Staying on campus would be easier. And rejecting him meant giving up the only person who didn't hate her. Ava took his hand, warm and solid, and turned her brain and guilt off. It was getting easier with time.

Thankfully Benj didn't seem much for conversation today either. They walked between the buildings towards the campus gardens. The large lawn that filled in with students on rare sunny days was sparse today. Benj led her past the lawn, towards a grove of trees. He stepped off the path and pushed back a branch.

A small forest enveloped them. Inside of the grove, a bed of pine needles and old leaves made a soft, natural floor. The buildings that encroached all around the park disappeared, along with the sounds of traffic. Benj tossed his backpack on the ground and laid back on it.

"How do you find all the best spots?" Ava asked, as she sat next to him.

"Exploring," Benj said with a shrug. "Don't you ever just wander the campus?"

"I tend to stick to the map. Stay on the path."

"How's that working for you?"

"Not so well."

They didn't say much else, enjoying the sound of the wind in the trees instead. A squirrel chattered at them before hopping away through the trees.

"You missed class on Tuesday," Benj said.

"Yeah, I wasn't feeling good… It's gonna show on the test for sure."

"We should study for the next one together."

"Thanks," Ava said. "But I wouldn't be a very good study buddy. I don't have much to offer."

"What happened to the color-coded highlighters and notes?" Benj asked with his half-dimpled smile.

Ava shrugged. "Too much work." She watched the trees move above her but became aware of Benj's eyes on her. She glanced down and caught him staring at her, but he didn't look away.

"Are you okay?" he asked, his tone oddly serious.

"Yeah."

Benj turned his eyes back to the trees. "Do you talk to anybody from home much?"

"Not really." *Just one.* Which brought back the reminders of everything Jack had said and Ava tried to force her brain off again. The guilt. The needless, baseless warnings about Benj. How could Jack hate him so much?

An hour slipped quietly, and they both had classes to attend. Benj stood and pulled Ava up with him as they brushed pine needles off their clothes. There were a dozen stuck to the back of Benj's navy sweater and Ava plucked them out, keeping a hand on his shoulder.

The moment she released him, he caught her by the elbow and turned so they were standing only inches apart. He leaned down slowly and brushed a kiss to her forehead. Her heart fluttered and the world tilted around her. Guilt swallowed the peace she had gained in the last hour. But why? Something this small didn't warrant guilt. She had done far worse.

Ava turned her face away from him and, before either said anything, a shape in the pine needle floor caught her eye. A small, round bird's nest that almost blended into the ground. Three speckled eggs sat inside, unaware they had fallen from the sky. "Benj, look."

With his hands on her shoulders, Benj leaned over Ava. Somehow she both relished and resented his touch. "Wind must have knocked it down." He stooped down and reached towards the nest.

"Don't touch it!"

Benj raised an eyebrow at her. "They're broken."

"The one in the middle might not be." And she didn't want to find out for sure.

"The parents won't come back for it now."

"Leave it alone." Ava pulled on his arm, a surge of protectiveness rising for the fragile things.

Benj shook his head and laughed at her. "It's just snake bait now, Ava."

Chapter 19

The gym was dead all morning, only a handful of students made their way in. Even the athletes got spring break off. It made Jack's shift easier, yet ten times longer. The music echoed off the walls, the sound of a lone weightlifter racking the weights was the only diversion. Jack wasn't usually the get-ahead type, but sheer boredom had him studying ahead and outlining papers two weeks before they were due.

The chime at the front desk beeped, alerting him to someone coming in. Jack raised his head and found Val, walking in with a paper bag in hand and a smile. Long blonde hair swung over a flowing top that was definitely not gym attire.

"Hey, what are you doing here?" Jack asked. She should be on her way to Austin with the Grace students for a week of concerts.

"We're leaving in half an hour, but I thought I'd see if I could change your mind about coming one last time."

"Sure, let me just walk out and get fired real quick."

Val laughed. "I know, I know. That's why I brought you breakfast instead." She lifted the paper bag and passed it over the front desk to Jack.

"Thanks," he said. Bringing him breakfast was a little too friendly, even for Val. Jack pulled two breakfast tacos out of the bag. "Want one?"

"No, thanks. Got any plans for the week?"

"Some coworkers are talking about a beach bonfire tonight. And I think a few others from Grace are going to try to get together later this week too."

"Sounds fun. I bet the beach will be packed."

"Filled with beer cans and future skin cancer patients."

"Such a pessimist," Val said with a laugh. "Just don't end up stuck in the gym all week."

Jack shrugged. "I'll find something."

"You should," Val said, reaching across the desk briefly to touch the back of his hand. "I better get going. Have a good week, Jack."

"Thanks. You too."

He watched her walk back out the gym for a second, looking away before she caught him. She was getting too close. Breakfast tacos almost made it acceptable.

The clock on the wall ticked backwards until it finally jumped forward and marked the end of his shift. Jack passed the baton to Victor, who reminded him about the beach bonfire. It was the closest Jack would come to a real spring break, so he agreed.

He started to drive home before deciding to use the rest of his day for something else. He followed the highway north, crossing several bridges on his way to the wildlife refuge. It wouldn't be busy out there. Jack drove through the park until he found a trailhead with an empty parking lot. He had just gotten out of the truck when his phone rang with an unknown number. Jack ignored it and started on the trail. The phone buzzed again with a voicemail. But this was a break from humanity for a moment.

Jack reached the top of a small hill in the otherwise flat landscape. The view stretched over tidal flats to the bay. The hike would only be better with something to eat. He enjoyed the view as long as possible before his stomach took over and he turned back. When he got to his truck, he pulled the phone from his pocket and checked the message.

"Hey Jack, this is Benjamin Rath. It's, um, call me back."

His fingers tripped over themselves as he tapped the number and slammed the phone to his ear as if force would speed up the phone call.

"Jack Shields," Benj said, too casually.

"Benjamin. What's up?"

"You're friends with Ava Sanford, right?"

"Yes, why?" The words were like sand in his teeth. Anything Benj had to say about Ava couldn't be good.

"Have you talked to her lately?"

It was a test. Jack couldn't risk the wrong answer. "Why?" *Get to the point already.*

"She's kind of having a hard time. I was just wondering if talking to somebody from home would help."

"What's going on?"

Benj hesitated before answering. "Actually, forget about it. I'll talk to her."

"Don't—" the word fired out before he could stop it. Challenging a guy like Benj would only make him worse. "Don't worry about it. I'll um, I'll reach out to her."

Again.

Benj laughed and his tone cooled. "I just thought I'd give you a heads up."

"Thanks," Jack said.

Benjamin ended the call and Jack climbed into his truck. He didn't know Benjamin well enough to have any idea what that conversation actually meant. But he knew it wasn't good.

• • •

The last time Jack's dad had known about his plans on any given day was high school graduation, when Jack had plastered the date on the refrigerator, hung his cap and gown in the living room, and texted multiple reminders. So when his dad called and said he knew it was spring break and wanted Jack to come over, Jack assumed the worst. "Is Lion dead?"

"What? God, no. I've got a bad transmission and could use an extra set of hands."

It still seemed strange, but Jack agreed. Sweating in a garage was the only way they could spend more than a couple hours together.

Wednesday afternoon, Jack's dad popped open two beers, and they started pulling parts out of the Pontiac Firebird that was older than him. The girlfriend wasn't around today, at least not yet. Lion watched them from his spot in the shade.

"Who'd you go to that wedding with?" Jack's dad asked from underneath the car.

Jack laughed. "What? Don't tell me you're on social media now."

"Yvonne made me do it," his dad said, muffled by the engine between them.

"Sure, blame it on the girlfriend."

"Your girlfriend got you to go to a wedding, pretty sure that's worse." His dad rolled out from under the car and wiped the back of his hand across his forehead. He stood next to the shop fan, letting it blow his shirt out around him.

"She's just a friend."

His dad threw him a withering look.

"Okay, she might think we're more, but I don't."

With a huff, his dad went to the front of the car, shining a flashlight into the engine. "I should've raised you better than that."

The hair on the back of Jack's neck raised and even Lion lifted his head. *You should have raised me at all.* "What the heck is that supposed to mean?"

"It means I don't want you to end up old and married with a kid before you realize what you want out of life."

The blood in his veins heated. Was his dad calling him a mistake? "Like you did with mom?"

From the side of his face, Jack saw his dad's jaw clench. His dad reached out, lifted the hood off the prop and slammed it closed with a metallic bang. Turning slowly, he pointed a finger into Jack's chest. "Your mother was the one thing I got right, son. And if she was still here, you wouldn't be leading any girl on."

Jack stepped back. "If she was still here, maybe I would know what I wanted. But I don't have any idea."

His dad crossed his arms and locked him in with a look. "Yes, you do. You're just too scared to go for it."

So now he was a mistake and a coward? "Fine. Maybe I am. Maybe losing everything at 12 years old does that to a kid."

His dad scoffed. "You still had me."

"No, I didn't. Not for the last nine years. And I don't know what you're doing right now, but you're too late. I'm 21. You missed your chance. For this." Jack waved a dismissing hand at *this*—whatever parenting attempt was happening right now.

Turning on his heel, his dad stalked into the house. Silence hung heavily in the air. For all the times he had wanted his dad to play the part, he wasn't expecting or welcoming it today. His dad was the expert at coasting through life. That's where Jack learned it, the fallback when decisions failed. And Jack had failed plenty.

Looking at the ceiling of the garage, Jack blew out a breath to cool down. His dad had tried and he had shot it back in his face. He swiped a hand over his face.

Lion lifted his heavy self and made his way to Jack, plopping back down on top of his feet. Jack squatted to scratch his head. "What's up with dad, buddy?" Lion only yawned.

Before Jack had decided whether to go inside or leave, his dad returned. He came into the garage carrying two water bottles and passed one to Jack. With one hand freed, he lifted it in surrender. "You're right. I wasn't much good without your mom. But don't be like me, Jack. Don't let life just happen to you."

Jack studied the water bottle in his hands. Deaths *just happen.* ACL tears *just happen.* "But it does just happen. No matter what you do. And it knocks you off track. So why bother?"

"Because if you're on the right track when it happens, it'll be that much easier to get back on it." His dad started picking up the wrenches lying around the car. They were obviously done for the day.

They put everything back into the tool chest and wiped their hands off on a grease-stained yellow towel. The conversation turned to lighter things, mostly sports and cars while they cleaned. Before Jack left, his dad insisted on the usual truck check-up.

"You're gonna need a new air filter soon," his dad said, popping it back into place. He rubbed his shoulder and stretched his neck. "I'm sorry if I missed my chance. But I hope you got enough of your mother in you to listen to reason."

Jack huffed a small laugh. "You're still talking?"

With a grin, his dad gave his shoulder a light push. "Yes, the old man's still talking. I've got some time to make up for."

Arms crossed, Jack took a wide stance. "I'm listening."

"Decide what you want and go for it, Jack. And don't waste your time on the wrong stuff. The wrong job. Or the wrong girl."

Jack studied Lion for a minute, trying not to picture the right girl, the one slipping out of reach. He simply gave his dad a nod. This new attempt at parenting was weird for them both and his dad wasn't the most reliable source of life advice. But he was trying, for once. "Thanks, dad."

"Come out again soon. We'll tune up that A/C before summer hits."

Air conditioning was only an excuse. With a handshake and a back pat, they silently agreed to keep trying.

• • •

Jack cleaned up at his apartment, scrubbing black grease marks off his arms and legs for half an hour before heading over to the Torres' house. There wasn't an official Bible study meeting during spring break, but Katie and Isaac had invited anyone staying behind to come for dinner. Jack, a couple of college kids, and a young family made it.

They ate a potluck of Italian food and talked about everything from spring break traffic to making a group trip to a baseball game. One of the college students asked Isaac where Micah had been last Sunday, when they had a guest speaker.

Isaac shrugged. "Pastors need a day off too."

"Because of Ava?" someone asked. Jack's head jerked up too fast. He had missed who asked the question but kept his eyes trained on Isaac for the answer.

"What's going on with Ava?" a young mom asked Katie.

Both of the other college students laughed and one of them answered, "She's turned into some crazy party person now."

"We don't do this," Isaac cut them off. "We don't talk about anybody in our group behind their backs."

"If you think she might be struggling, feel free to pray for her," Katie said, softening the awkward silence Isaac had left. "Jack, how's work going?"

Jack gladly changed the topic and tried to share snippets of gym antics despite the boring week.

When the meal wrapped up, people slowly cleared out, with long goodbyes and lingering conversations. Jack cleared the table and began washing the dishes while Isaac walked people out and Katie chased little kids to the bathtub. The house was mostly empty and Katie was getting babies ready for bed when Isaac joined him in the kitchen.

"Thanks for helping man," Isaac said as he grabbed a towel and started putting dishes away.

Jack finished the last one and turned the water off. He scanned the kitchen, looking for another way to stall. Isaac turned to face him, seeing right through the pretense. "What's up?" Isaac asked.

"It's Ava. Something's wrong."

Isaac sighed. "Maybe if you talked to Micah—"

"I have," Jack said. "And we disagree. I need to talk to somebody else."

Isaac nodded towards the couch and Jack followed him. They sat at opposite ends. Jack rubbed his hands together, studying the floor. It might be gossip. But it was necessary. "I hardly even know her anymore. She's making some bad decisions and I want to help her, but how?"

Isaac paused and responded slowly. "It can be hard to recognize someone when they're depressed."

Jack studied the rug on the floor for a moment. Was she depressed?

"There's not much you can do. Other than pray for her."

"I have been, but I still feel like I need to do something about it."

"Like what?" Isaac asked.

"I don't know," Jack said, rubbing a hand over the back of his neck. "Micah thinks she just needs space, but I'm telling you... That's not it. She's isolating herself and it isn't going to help."

Isaac's daughters came running into the room for goodnight hugs and kisses. Katie followed with baby Gabe in her arms.

"Sorry to interrupt," she said to Jack.

"No, I'll get out of your hair," Jack said and started to stand.

Katie waved him back down into his seat. "You're fine." She passed Gabe to Isaac while she followed the girls to their bedroom.

Their conversation paused while Isaac bounced the baby on his knee, dipping him back and making him giggle. Katie came back a minute later and retrieved the baby with a kiss on Isaac's cheek. "Thanks for getting him all worked up before bed."

"Anytime, babe." Isaac waited until Katie was out of the room before turning his attention back to Jack. "So, what are you going to do?"

"If I knew, I would be doing it," Jack laughed. "I just wish I could talk to her in person."

"So go."

Jack shook his head, surprised at Isaac's serious tone. He ran both hands through his hair. He had thought about it. Even his subconscious had taken on the idea, dreaming about it at night. But it was impossible. "Me and my big fat bank account? I've already looked into it. I don't think I can."

"Do you think you should?"

"Yes." The answer slipped out without a second thought and the moment he heard it aloud, he knew it was true.

"Then go. God will take care of the rest. If He's calling you to do something, He'll make a way. He always does."

Jack gave a doubtful grunt. "How do you know when He's calling you?"

Isaac studied his hands before answering. "When you won't have peace until you do it."

Chapter 20

"That's it," Rosie said, slamming the door behind her and making Ava jump. "I'm scunnered wit ye diddy. Yer all peely wally, fun as a poke."

"Rosie, I cannot understand a word you're saying," Ava said, sitting up in her bed.

"I am tired of your moping," she said, dragging each word out. "Get out of bed, yer goin' out."

"Going out is the reason I'm in this mood."

"Well, is sittin' in yer bed fixing it?" Rosie asked. Ava refused to answer. "That's what I thought. Goin' out isn't yer problem. It's locking yerself in this room, and yer doing more of the same to try to fix it. So get yer arse out of bed."

She had a point. Ava groaned and climbed out of the bed. She never slept anyway, despite the hours she spent trying. "It's all pointless," Ava mumbled.

"Of course it is. 'Eat, drink and be merry,' right? It's even in yer Bible."

Ava tilted her head. "You're right…"

"See, I know a thing or two," Rosie said with a wink. She shoved Ava towards the bathroom, commanding her to shower and shave. Ava stripped off her leggings and Jack's TGU pullover. Rosie had largely ignored her lately. It was refreshing to at least have some interaction with her again, even if it was only to be bossed around.

Everyone at home ignored her. No one had reached out, except for one text from Katie Torres asking for prayer requests. Ava never responded.

Her resolve grew in the shower. She might as well enjoy her time in Scotland to the fullest. She would be home soon enough and nobody there would even speak to her. Why not eat, drink and be merry? Or at least drink? While she could. With the few who didn't judge her.

Rosie promised to keep it a girls-only night. She said it would be in honor of Ava's reemergence into the world. Ava sighed and put on one of her own shirts, opting for a pale sweater over any of Rosie's tops.

Sleet fell as they left, fogging their breath and hazing the street lights. Ava buttoned her coat to the throat and tugged on a beanie, ignoring Rosie's protests about ruining her hair. The sleet would ruin it if the hat didn't. It was half a mile to Double Cross, and the ice cut through her jeans as they walked. Ladies' night meant half-price beers, and Ava had warmed up to the taste over the last two months.

Molly met them a few minutes later. She took a seat next to Ava and elbowed her playfully. "Good to see you dressed again."

"I've been getting dressed." Ava rolled her eyes but felt lighter already. Rosie was right, leaving the room was a good idea. Even if she checked the front door every few minutes, tracking the faces of everyone who came in and out of the bar.

Rosie dragged them into a game of darts along the back wall of the bar while they drank. It was more fun than Ava expected and the girls got plenty of digs at each other. On two separate occasions, guys offered to teach them, or tried to join in the game; but Rosie's dedication to girls' night proved strong. If anything, she seemed to enjoy the power trip of turning them down.

After the second one walked away, Rosie pointed at Ava with a dart. "That one was a blond, hen. I hope you realize how much that means to me."

Ava covered her heart with her right hand. "Your sacrifice has been noted."

Rosie tossed the dart at the board, barely catching the edge of it. Molly threw her arms up in a cheer and they chalked in a 20 on the scoreboard according to their invented scoring system that worked better for their skill levels. They ordered a second round of beers, not without complaint from Rosie about having to pay for their own drinks, and started a new game.

They finished their third round of beers and a third game, during which they had improved enough to keep real scores. A different numbness settled over Ava—a kind she had missed. The kind that made her warm and giggly. She laughed, told stories, and spoke in full sentences again. She had missed this.

When Molly called it a night, a twinge of disappointment hit Ava. They all had classes in the morning and needed sleep, but it meant this moment of feeling alive would end.

"What day is it?" Ava asked, suddenly confused.

"Wednesday," Rosie said with a pat on Ava's head like she was a child.

"So tomorrow is Thursday. Class with just Benj. Okay, fine, I'll go to class tomorrow."

"What have you done to her?" Molly asked Rosie with a laugh. Rosie only shrugged and smiled.

When they stepped outside, the sleet still fell, a welcome chill compared to the warmth of the bar, and Ava left the buttons on her coat undone.

"I'm glad you came out," Rosie said, grabbing Ava's hand as they walked.

"Me too." Ava leaned her head on Rosie's shoulder. "Thanks."

"Anytime, hen. We'll do it again soon."

• • •

When Rosie texted two days later that they were going to St. Bart's, Ava finished her homework as quickly as possible to start getting ready. She wanted to be warm again. If she was rejected at home anyway, she might as well enjoy Scotland. And if she was already burdened with sins, she might as well use one to feel better.

Rosie came bursting into the room, always in a rush. "Yer still in pajamas!" She tossed her backpack and started rummaging through the closet.

"Joggers, thank you very much."

Edinburgh was caught in a late winter cold snap. Ava hadn't seen the sun in over a week. She reached for a sweater when Rosie looked over and gave her quick disapproval. After having the next two tops shot down as well, Ava realized this was not girls night. Rosie tried to convince her to wear the silky red shirt, but Ava didn't want anything to do with it. She finally settled on a gray sweater that, according to Rosie, at least had a decent dip in the neckline.

The body that met her eyes in the mirror didn't look like hers. *Peely wally* was right—she was pale. She could blame that on Scotland. But her hair seemed to have lost its shine too, along with her eyes. Something about looking at her body emptied it even more, becoming a shell. Ava swallowed hard and shook her head. She lifted limp strands into the curling wand, trying to bring her hair and self back to life.

Getting dressed proved exhausting, and she lost the excitement of going out by the time she was ready. Rosie's energy wasn't spreading the way it used to. Everything took Ava twice as long, despite Rosie's prodding to hurry.

"I'm actually really tired—" Ava backed away, sicker by the minute.

"No, you don't," Rosie said and caught her by the hand. "You'll feel better with a drink. Trust me."

Ava stared at her for a moment, trying to find her way back to the energy she'd had an hour ago. "And if I don't..."

"You can leave," Rosie agreed.

Ava nodded and finished pulling on her shoes. Rosie looped her arm through Ava's to strengthen her resolve, or maybe pass along some energy. St. Bart's wasn't far, but the walk left her bones tired. The night ahead asked too much: ordering, drinking, talking—it was all an act. And she would be watching it from somewhere else while her body went through the motions.

Ava went straight for whisky, choosing an Aberfeldy distillery from the list and sipping its honeyed malt slowly. It filled her hollow bones and by the end of the first drink, Rosie was right—she felt better.

Now with a beer in her hand, she followed Rosie through a few introductions of other architecture students. She downed the drink quickly for warmth and confidence. Ava recognized one girl from an interior design class. She was sweet and they chatted easily.

They stood talking for a few minutes before Rosie flitted away. Off to meet more friends. She followed Rosie with her eyes and nearly dropped her empty beer glass. Her knees buckled and she gripped the table.

"Are you okay?" the girl next to her asked, reaching a hand out.

"Fine." She choked on the word, scanning the bar for another exit. Oliver and Callan were standing in front of the only door. Rosie buzzed in front of them with cheery hellos. She pointed back to where Ava stood, and Oliver's eyes met hers.

Ava's mind raced to nowhere, spinning through half thoughts as she looked for another exit. There had to be one somewhere. At the back. Ava stepped in that direction but saw only restrooms. She grabbed her phone and dialed the first name that came to mind.

"Benj," she gasped when he answered. She watched Oliver approach in slow motion. Ava paced to the rear wall, still searching for a door she couldn't find. "Benj, Oliver's here. Can you come, please? I can't do this."

"Where are you? Just leave, girl," Benj said. "I'm at Devil's Glen, come over here."

"I can't." Her sentences were at the same half-capacity as her mind. Oliver stood between her and the only way out. "Not alone. Please, Benj."

"Where are you?" he asked again.

"St. Bart's."

Benj sighed. "I'm on my way. Tell him you're seeing someone."

Ava hung up and stared at the black wall like a child in time out. Her blood was hot, her throat tight. If she turned, she knew she would see him.

"Ava."

Too late. She still didn't turn. Maybe if she kept her back to him, he would give up.

"It's been too long since I've seen you," he said, putting a hand on her shoulder. Every other body part evaporated and it was the only thing she felt. He turned her around. A black coat and green scarf were the first things she saw. Then the laughing smile in his eyes, like she was the butt of his joke. "Where have you been?"

"Busy," the shell of Ava said, as her spirit walked out the front door.

"We need a real date. Give me your number."

Ava stepped back and hit the wall behind her. Oliver's hand was still on her shoulder. Her body vibrated. She scanned the room behind him, looking for a way out. Wondering if it would make it worse to turn him down. Wondering if she should agree for now and block him later. Trying to calculate how long it should take Benj to get there. How many blocks away was Devil's Glen? How fast could Benj walk?

Oliver reached his hand to her chin and turned her face towards him. "I think I promised you another night of fun."

"No, thanks," Ava whispered, unable to muster any more of an act.

Oliver narrowed his eyes and his jaw tightened along with the hand on Ava's face. "Why not?"

She had taken the wrong approach. But she couldn't backtrack now. It was time for Benj's lie. "I—I'm seeing someone else."

"Lying lips are an abomination to the Lord."[17]

Oliver dropped the hand from her face and planted it on the wall behind her, his broad shoulders closing her in. Her body locked down. Afraid that moving away would make him mad. Afraid that any movement at all might encourage him. Her body was completely useless. He smirked, seeing straight through any bravado.

He leaned in until his face hovered just above hers. "From virgin to slut already? That was fast, Miss Texas."

Ava tried to blink it away, trying not to hear him. She focused on an empty spot at the bar several yards behind him. She had to delay, stall, distract.

"Texans are full of surprises," she said, plastering on a smile. Be friendly, play a part.

Oliver laughed and leaned back. It was working. "Who is he then?" His eyebrow raised, testing her.

"Benjamin. He's on his way over."

Oliver moved the hand from the wall and brushed it across Ava's cheek. She froze. "Too bad." He leaned back, dropping his arms. With the space to breathe again, Ava had a new goal: to be anywhere except backed against this wall. The spot at the bar was still empty. *Be friendly, stall.* She had to keep the act up. Six more minutes? Five?

"I want a drink," she said. "Care to join me?"

Oliver followed her to the bar with a hand on her lower back.

Her phone buzzed and Ava lifted it immediately, ready for any distraction. *Jack.* His name in this place, in this situation, made her nauseous. But it was a lifeline, nonetheless.

"I should answer—"

Oliver pushed her hand against the bar. "That's not the boyfriend."

She was caught in the lies. *"He who breathes out lies will perish."*[18] "This is a friend."

"Then it can wait."

Missed call.

Oliver smirked and ordered two whiskys.

Ava held back the bile in her throat. The whisky helped wash it away. She focused on chatting mindlessly, distracting Oliver, and waiting for Benj. Oliver was quiet, waiting to see if anyone would show. Every minute that passed made Ava more nervous. If Benj failed her…

Benj's face at the door was the most welcome sight of her life. It made her choke on words. Oliver followed her gaze and finally dropped the hand from her back. She waved Benj over. He unzipped his leather jacket and ran a hand over his cropped hair as he walked. Ava didn't take her eyes off of him.

Benj edged his way in, claiming the space closest to Ava. The relief he brought was challenged by claustrophobia. Benj held his hand out and Oliver shook it. Standing next to each other, Benj's lean height was overshadowed by Oliver's broad build.

"D'you wanna go?" Benj asked Ava.

"Aren't you here for a drink with your new girlfriend?" Oliver asked with a smirk.

Benj wasn't fazed. He took Ava's glass from her hand and finished off the whisky. "Had a drink. Now I have other ideas." His signature half-smile lit up one dimple. He took Ava's hand, guiding them both towards the door, but stopped short of it, grabbing her shoulders and pulling her close to him.

"What are you doing?" Ava asked.

"Puttin' on a show." Without waiting for a reply, he covered her lips with his. He tasted like beer. Benj claimed her for all in the bar to see.

Ava's free hand went to his chest and pushed him back. "That's enough."

"Just tryna help," Benj laughed. Light caught in his blue eyes as he scanned the dark bar. "I think he knows now. Com'on."

He pulled her through the doorway and Ava suddenly remembered Rosie. There was no way she would walk back through that door, though. She grabbed her phone and tapped out a quick excuse to her roommate.

"Texting your other pretend boyfriend?" Benj asked with a smirk.

"What? I'm texting Rosie."

Benj only laughed as he wrapped an arm around her waist. There was no need to pretend here, but Ava let him. His solidity stilled her liquid bones. Benj told stories about the TGU group at Devil's Glen and their drama. Ava only listened and guided their walk towards her dorm. She had no energy left for anything else. When they reached her building, Ava paused at the door. She would go the rest alone.

"Thanks for coming—"

Benj tightened his grip on her waist and his lips crashed against hers. Ava jerked back.

"Benj—"

He laughed. How did she just now see how unfocused his eyes were? He tugged her closer and whispered in her ear. "I saved the damsel. Don't I get a kiss?"

Sirens sounded in Ava's head. Benj pressed his lips to hers roughly. Ava struggled to breathe and tried to turn her head away. Benj caught it with one hand and held her in place. Fight and flight held each other in a deadlock. Ava's body froze in the limbo, her muscles limp.

When she stilled, he dropped a hand to her hips and slid it under her shirt, climbing to her bare waist and rubbing a thumb over her bottom rib. The sensation of skin on skin lurched flight into motion. Ava managed to drop her head away before Benj could catch it.

"Benj, stop—" she sobbed, pressing her head into his chest. There was nowhere else to go. How was she always wrong?

"Ava Sanford," he said, dragging out each syllable. "Come on, you've done more than that."

He was right, of course. And Rosie's version of consent floated through Ava's mind: *then just say yes next time.* Was this all there was? Ava shook her head against his chest, refusing to look up. She raised a hand to where his rested on her ribcage. "Benj, please. Let go."

Benj scoffed and tightened his hand for a second before sliding it slowly down her back and over the top of her jeans. "I thought you'd wanna play pretend a little longer."

"I'm done with it," Ava said, stepping back.

His smirk transformed into a thin laugh as he shook his head. "Then you owe me. Goodnight princess."

"Goodnight," Ava said, jamming her key into the front door, needing to get away. Tears were stinging her eyes by the time she reached the second flight of stairs. The next two stretched out like Mount Everest. Adrenaline had wracked her body, pain was the only thing left.

Chapter 21

Friday afternoon, Jack emerged from the athletic department offices after a long talk with the department director. Spring break was almost over, and so was his business major. Jack glanced at the yellow sticky note in his hand with various email addresses on it. He still had time to apply for the department scholarship, which the director all but guaranteed him, and to register for summer courses.

Jack headed outside and sat heavily on a bench. Somehow, his dad's attempt at parenting had gotten through to him and Jack was ready for a change. He'd been so afraid of chasing the wrong things, he had given up pursuing anything at all. Not any more.

The slow week had given him a chance to pray, to think, and to talk to Isaac and Micah more. They had both encouraged him to go for it. Apparently, God wasn't against football. Micah had even sent him a list of verses about races and athletes.

"Jack, if God gives you a talent, he doesn't want you to bury it," Micah had said. "You can do all things to his glory. Maybe God took football away to bring you to him. That doesn't mean he took it away forever."

Micah had also repeated words that Jack remembered from high school. Back when he had been mad about his mom's death, Micah had told him God was rarely the one to take. That was the devil's job: to steal and kill. God gave—comfort and hope.

If Jack timed everything right and took enough summer courses, changing his major would only add one semester to his graduation timeline. Then, with a teaching certificate and kinesiology degree, he would be on his way to a coaching job.

Typing an email to his advisor and the financial department, Jack said one more quick prayer before hitting send. Isaac's advice about God's calling applied to school, too. For once, Jack had peace about school. More than that, he was actually excited about it.

• • •

Hours later, Jack sat at the front desk of the gym during a dead shift, scrolling through the course listings for summer kinesiology classes, when his phone rang with a familiar number. Jack immediately did the math: it had to be nearly one in the morning in Edinburgh. He couldn't risk missing this phone call. Only a handful of students were here, he could slip away. He answered it, heading out the double doors of the gym into the cool night air. Pounding music immediately assaulted his ears. "Benjamin."

"Bro, your girlfriend is a mess," Benj said with a laugh. His words were sloppy and it was hard to hear around the music, but Jack heard enough to tense up immediately. "I'm a go save the damsel now. You should thank me."

Fire and ice ran through his veins at once. "Leave her alone, you're drunk."

The music in the background cut out and it was quiet, save for Benjamin's now too-loud voice. "See, if she's kissing me, at least she's not screwing another Scottish guy," he laughed again.

He didn't care what Benjamin had to say, he didn't want to hear it. He wanted to hang up, but he couldn't. "Leave her alone, Benj. I mean it, back off."

"Hey, bro, I'm just tellin' ya. She's the one callin' me. I can't help if she wants to do me." Benj followed it with another stupid laugh.

Violence wasn't his go-to, but Jack desperately wanted to hit something. His hand flexed and clenched at his side.

"I don't care what she wants," Jack said, cringing at his own words. "Don't touch her."

"Hey, hey, hey, look, I can play pretend boyfriend with her too. She asked for it."

Time for a hail Mary. Jack's mind scrambled. "Benjamin, I swear—"

Benjamin cussed and said something about directions. "I gotta go Jacky, I'll give her your love." He laughed again, and the line went dead.

Jack cursed at the night and ran a hand through his hair. Of course he cared what Ava wanted. Benjamin didn't. Ava's one other "Christian" friend there was cheating on his girlfriend, getting drunk, and acting like Ava was a plaything. Jack swore and paced the sidewalk again. The sidewalk here. Five thousand miles away. Where he was useless.

He dialed Ava's phone number, but it went to voicemail. He wouldn't have expected anything else. He called Talia instead.

"Hey, what's up?" She sounded confused. So was he.

"Have you talked to Ava tonight?"

"No, what's going on?"

Jack hesitated. If Ava hadn't talked to her about Benjamin, he couldn't be the one to tell her. He hadn't planned this out. He forced a deep breath. "What the heck is going on with her? She's losing it, Talia."

She sighed. "I know..."

"But she's choosing this," Jack spat the words, fighting with himself. "Nobody's making her act like this."

"Jack—something's wrong. Just... Trust me. Something's really wrong."

"What are you talking about?" The low buzz in his veins hadn't left for weeks; its strength varied throughout the days, and now it rose violently again. "Talia?"

"She'll come back," Talia finally said. "In two months. And things will get back to normal."

"Will they?"

"I hope so." Her words lacked conviction.

Jack leaned his forehead against the building. "Okay. I need to get back to work."

"Hey, Jack, she means a lot to both of us. This is hard. I'm sorry I don't have any better answers."

Jack cleared his throat. "Yeah."

"I'm getting back into town tomorrow. Let's get lunch or something. We need to talk."

"Okay. Sounds good." Jack pocketed the phone and kicked the mulch in the landscaping in front of the building for another minute. He ran a hand over his neck as he returned to the abandoned front desk, physically, if not mentally.

• • •

Saturday at noon, Talia was back in town and at Jack's apartment. Together they drove to a taco place on the peninsula. The spring break crowds were still out in full force; the energy of it was contagious and both Jack and Talia seemed to be in better spirits when they arrived.

They talked about their spring breaks and the semester ahead before Talia steered them back to Ava. The mood dropped instantly.

"What are we gonna do?" she asked, twisting the paper straw in her hands. It was a rare break in her confidence. "How do we help her?"

"Go get her."

Talia laughed. "Micah told me she needs space. And he's her dad and all…"

"But he's wrong," Jack finished.

"Yeah. There's more going on than he knows."

"Like Benj," Jack said dryly. Talia obviously knew at least some of it and she nodded slowly. "You know Benj is a bad idea, right?"

She narrowed her eyes at him. "You would think that about anyone."

"I'm serious, he's a manipulative jerk."

"Okay then, who?" Talia sat back in her seat and crossed her arms. "Who would you approve of, for Ava?"

Jack stared at her, gritting his teeth. He tried to run through a mental list to prove her wrong. There were half a dozen decent guys at Grace. Or close to it. At least, not total jerks. Or maybe they were. Jack groaned.

"Exactly," she said. "But you can't fight off every guy and then friend-zone her forever."

Jack stared at her. "What the heck, Talia?" She knew he and Ava had been friends for years. The sudden confrontation was unwarranted.

"Don't 'Talia' me," she said, tucking her short black hair behind her ear. "If you keep being the main guy in her life but you won't date her, you're wasting your time and Ava's."

"I thought this was about helping Ava, not chewing me out."

She shrugged. "I'm just saying, as her friend."

"It takes two to make a friend zone," he said, scanning the room to avoid her eyes.

"And it only takes one to ask her out."

A hard laugh left his lips without any humor. "Yeah, that would go great. She's infatuated with Benj."

"I don't think so…" Talia said slowly. "No, he was just a distraction."

"From what?"

She shrugged and refused to look at him. "Trust me." She might know even more than he did.

"Fine. Either way, she's not ready for a relationship right now, anyway."

"Maybe not right now, but what's the long game?"

"Do I need a long game?"

"Do you like her?" Talia asked. When Jack didn't respond, she took his silence as an answer. "Then yes, you need a long game. And you need to stop going out with Val, or whatever y'all are doing."

"We're not going out."

"Right. Sure. Does Val know that?"

Jack ran both hands over his face and into his hair. "You could have warned me this was Relationships 101 with Talia."

"If I had, you wouldn't have come," she said with a laugh, interrupted by her phone ringing. Talia grabbed it and frowned at the screen. She held a finger up to Jack. "Hi Mrs. Sanford…"

Jack tilted his chair back on two legs and glanced around the diner, trying not to eavesdrop.

"No, I haven't… I think Jack might have. Yeah. Actually, I'm here with him right now. One sec." Talia lowered the phone and whispered to Jack. "Did you talk to Ava last night?"

He shook his head.

Talia lifted her phone back to her ear. "No, sorry, he didn't."

"I talked to Benjamin Rath," Jack said.

She passed the information on. "Okay, sure, yeah." She held the phone out to Jack.

He took it and was met with Rebecca Sanford's voice. "Hey Jack, Benjamin is one of the TGU students in Scotland, right?"

"Yes ma'am."

"What did he say?"

Jack hesitated, looking at Talia. He stood and walked away from the table, stalling on his answer until he was outside. "Um, it… I think he was drunk."

"Why did he call you, hon?" Rebecca asked.

"I don't know. He reached out a few days ago to say Ava was having a hard time. And then last night… Honestly, none of it is worth repeating."

"Was it about Ava?"

"Yes ma'am," Jack said.

"Did you tell anybody about this?"

"No one."

Rebecca sighed. "Thank you, Jack."

"Are y'all okay?" Ava's parents were acting out of character.

"Someone called Micah with some rude things to say. It's got me worried."

If those words were similar to Benj's last night, they were more than worried. "I'm sorry." There wasn't much else he could say.

"Thank you. Come by sometime, hon. We miss you."

"I will."

Jack ended the call and watched cars pass on the street for a minute before heading back inside. Rebecca had been a substitute mom to him as long as he had known the Sanfords. He had been a high schooler who didn't think he needed a mom again, and she had been one anyway. He would do anything for them.

Chapter 22

Saturday went by in a haze. It started with Rosie barging into the room, accusing her of attempting to ruin all of her good social connections. Apparently rejecting Oliver was selfish and rude. *"I'm not losing my friends for you."* Of course not. Ava didn't want that either. But seeing Oliver was too much. Rosie grabbed her books and stomped off to the library.

Cold water always helped. So she took a shower before crawling back into pajamas and bed, where she forced herself to get through homework and essays. She napped in between projects and slowly snacked on a single granola bar as both breakfast and lunch, and now dinner too.

As she wrapped up an online assignment, her legs ached from her position on the bed. Time to move again. Leaving the room seemed too hard today. She paced the floor for a minute before deciding on another shower.

So Ava stood in the shower again, washing away the sweaty feeling of lying in bed all day. It worked, but its effects wore off quickly.

The moment she got out of the shower, Ava heard her phone buzzing. *Four missed calls.* How long had she been in there? She tapped the notifications—two from each parent. Ava toweled off quickly and pulled on joggers and a cropped tee.

Ava bit her lip as she hovered a finger over the call button. Suddenly the room closed in, crowded and tight. She grabbed shoes and Jack's TGU fleece as she headed out the door. It wasn't enough to keep her warm, but she wouldn't be out for long.

The sun sat low, lighting everything in an orange glow. Ava crossed the street, heading for the heart of campus. The wind bit through the fleece with ease, the sharp air cooling her soul. She went straight for the park and Benj's grove. It was a 15-minute walk from her dorm and the sunlight turned to a gray dusk by the time she made it there. The walk had burned off some of her nerves and Ava finally tapped the call button.

"Ava Claire," her mom answered curtly.

"Hey, mom…"

"Why didn't you answer our calls?"

"I was in the shower," Ava said. "Am I not allowed to do that?"

"Of course, sorry, I was just… worried."

"Why?"

"We got a phone call from another parent at Grace. It was about you."

"What? Who?" Her phone buzzed in her hand, Talia was calling. She ignored it.

"That doesn't matter," her mom said with a sigh. "Honey, what are you doing?"

"Nothing," Ava said. But it wasn't just her mom anymore. The echo told her she had been switched to speaker phone, and she heard her dad join in.

"Avie," he said. "We've tried to give you space and freedom to do things your way. But you still share my last name and represent our family."

"What are y'all talking about?"

"Don't forget that you're not the only one affected by your actions," her mom said. "The church sees our entire family as an extension of your dad."

"I never forget that," Ava hissed. "But I'm on the other side of the Atlantic, right now. What could I have possibly done wrong?"

"We've heard some awful things," her mom said.

Ava's stomach tightened, twisted. Talia and Jack were the only people she had spoken to since her birthday. She would have trusted them with her life. Neither would have said anything to anyone else… Right? Her phone buzzed again with a text from Jack.

"What did they hear?" Ava asked through clenched teeth.

Several heartbeats passed before her dad spoke. "Are you sleeping around?"

Her heart dropped into her shoes. "God, no, what the heck?"

"Watch your mouth," her mom said.

"Then why do people think you are?" her dad asked.

"Abstain from all appearance of evil."[19] "How should I know?" she snapped. Dark was approaching even faster in the cluster of trees and Ava hurried out of the grove. She brushed leaves from her hair as she walked, a shiver setting in.

"Honey," her dad said, cutting off whatever her mom started to say. "We love you. We want to see you do the right thing. How can we help?"

"You can't," Ava choked on the words. There was no undoing what had been done. *Sleeping around?* How fast was that spreading in Grace's tight-knit circles?

"Avie," her dad said. "Do you need to come home?"

"I can't," she said. Hopelessness wrapped its fingers around her neck. *Ava Sanford—sleeping around?* Her stomach turned.

"We want to help," her mom said. "This is going too far."

Her phone buzzed again, Jack was calling this time. "I gotta go," Ava said. Both parents tried to stop her, but she switched calls.

"Jack." She turned, heading up the street towards her building.

"Aves, hey."

"What's going on? Why is everybody calling me?" If anyone would tell her the truth, it would be Jack. But he avoided the question too. He tried to act casual, like it was a coincidence. Ava cut him off. "Did you..."

The fingers around her throat tightened and her voice cut off before she tried again. "Did you tell somebody? About Benj? That I... We kissed?"

"What? No."

"Are you sure?" She didn't listen to his answer, focusing instead on keeping her bearings despite the fog settling heavily over the street lamps and signs. "Who did you tell, Jack?"

"Ava Claire, I didn't tell anyone. It had to be Benj."

"Benj wouldn't. He doesn't care—"

"He called me last night," Jack said. A wind blew through her jacket and Ava's entire body shook. The cold was the only thing keeping the nausea in check. Why would Benj call Jack?

"Why did Benj call you?"

"It was about you."

"He wouldn't."

"And I would? Come on, Aves. Who do you really trust?"

"I don't know," she said. Her building was finally in sight. Ava reached into her pocket for the keys.

"You don't know?"

"No, I don't, Jack. I have no freaking clue who I trust." She patted her jean pockets and jacket before letting out a curse under her breath. "I gotta go."

She ended the call before he said anything else. No keys. She was locked out. Rosie was too mad at her right now. Ava texted Liliana and Molly. And then she waited. With her back to the building, she watched the fog condense and turn into sleet. This was the coldest March weather she had ever felt. The shiver consumed her muscles. Nearly ready to give up and find an open store to stand in, Liliana finally came to her rescue.

Liliana taunted her relentlessly about it on their walk up the stairs. Ava shrugged and admitted she was an idiot. An eejit. A bampot. A diddy. A walloper. Scotland had a hundred words for idiot. She was in the right place after all.

When she got to her room, Talia called. Ava groaned and answered it. They repeated the conversation she had had with Jack. Talia's honesty helped, but she couldn't point to the source of the rumors either. Ava had no protest, tripping over a handful of words instead. The cold had numbed her tongue and mind. Nothing she had to say was worth anyone's time.

People could point fingers all they wanted, but the truth lay on Ava's shoulders alone. She was responsible for this, somehow. She had only slept with one person—if it could be called that. But she had kissed "around," hadn't she? The truth could be easily confused by the time it had spread across the Atlantic.

Talia tried to calm her down, offering promises and reassurances. But it wasn't working. Ava had done this and now her parents knew. Now they were getting heat for it. Being a pastor meant being constantly evaluated, analyzed, and challenged. And now she had given the haters something to go for. Now they could say her dad failed his family. They could attack the entire church if they wanted to. Because what happened to a Sanford happened to the entire church.

The guilt crushed onto her chest, with physical weight. Ava pressed a hand to her heart. Did 20-year-old women have heart attacks? Maybe drinking made it more likely. She would deserve that too, then. She excused herself from the phone call with Talia and stripped off the jacket and shoes she had been pacing in.

Still chilled to the bone, Ava climbed into bed and let the oversized plush blanket swallow her. Desperate to build her own home, she had stolen bricks from everything around her until only ruins remained. She was left with nothing. Pieces of every role and place, and yet she fit into none of them. There wasn't a place on earth where she was wanted anymore.

Chapter 23

Church ended and the row of college students slowly filed out. There was a large group this week, at least by Grace standards. They gathered around the coffee table in the entrance, effectively blocking it off. Jack could almost hear Ava correcting them. In a past life.

There were too many of them for one restaurant to handle, so they decided on a pizza picnic at a park on the bay. Everybody pooled money and someone called in the order. They were splitting into cars when Val walked up to Jack and placed a hand on his arm. "I'll ride with you."

Stepping back, his eyes darted around the room. "Um, actually, sorry, can we talk for a sec?"

"Sure," Val said with a bright smile. She didn't move.

Okay, he could do it here. Jack lowered his voice. "Val, I think I've given you the wrong idea."

"About what?" She tilted her head to the side, fake blonde hair falling over the straps of her blue dress.

What if she didn't have any ideas at all? What if he sounded like an idiot? Or what if he ended up accidentally married with kids? "Me. Us. I mean, we're only friends. Right?"

Her smile faltered and lifted again. "Yeah. Totally. I mean, I know."

"I'm sorry if—"

"Seriously, Jack. We're good."

That wasn't what her eyes said. "Okay."

"Okay." Her smile was tight as she spun away from him. He had definitely hurt her feelings.

Jack groaned inwardly and flagged down a couple guys from the group to offer them a ride instead. Talia joined in as well. They all rode to the pizza place to grab the order, arriving at the park last, to the cheers of hungry students. Val took a seat three tables away from him.

The conversation was scattered around the pavilion. Occasionally a topic gathered enough steam to carry it around the group. Their side ended up talking about C3 events and the disastrous spring dance they had hosted.

"Remember Benjamin Rath?" one girl asked. "Last year he was the only guy who actually danced with any of the girls."

"He's in Scotland, right?" somebody from the other side caught onto the conversation. Jack tried to find someone nearby to talk about something else, anything else, but everyone eagerly followed the new direction.

"Yeah, with Ava Sanford," Val volunteered.

"Sanford? Like Micah?" one of the new students that had joined Grace asked. While Val filled her in on the connection, another girl spoke over the group.

"Ava sure seems to be having a good time in Scotland, doesn't she?" It was a sneer and almost the entire group laughed. Jack shot a look at Talia and she met it from beneath pinched eyebrows.

"I guess you're not a pastor's kid anymore when you're in a different country."

"What does that mean?"

"Have you seen her pictures? She never used to dress like that."

"I'm looking at her profile, it doesn't look that crazy."

"Look for the stuff she's tagged in."

"I had no idea she was hot—"

"No, she's like anorexic now."

"She's got some Scottish boyfriend now."

"I heard she slept with Benjamin Rath." That one trumpeted over the others.

"What?" chorused from the group.

The original commenter shrugged. "Benjamin told one of his old roommates—"

"Okay, anybody wanna go swimming later today?" Talia jumped in loudly.

"Hey Jack," one of the guys called out. "Didn't y'all date or something? Did she sleep with Benj or not?"

Val's eyes shot to Jack's, her eyebrows raised. He gritted his teeth and ran defense. "We didn't date. And it's none of our business."

"It's really not," Talia said. "Let's talk about something else."

There was a collective grumble before most of the group switched to TGU sports. Jack could tell from the tucked heads of three girls across the pavilion that they were still talking about Ava. He watched them, debating if he should break it up, when Val interrupted his thoughts, sauntering to the table in her blue dress that looked like no match for Ridley Bay's wind.

"You're pretty defensive for just being friends," she said, leaning over the table with a feigned interest in reaching for a slice of pizza.

"Drop it," Jack mumbled.

A girl on the other side of the table spoke up. "Well, apparently Ava does more with her friends than we thought."

Both of them laughed.

Frustration turned into adrenaline and Jack stood, needing to move. "I'm leaving."

The other girl whined in protest, while Val's eyes seemed to dare him.

"Hang on—" Talia stood too. "Let's do something else. Don't you have a frisbee or football or something in your truck?"

All he wanted was to leave. To not listen to this anymore. Jack squeezed the keys in his hand and let out a silent sigh. "Yeah. Probably. I'll go check."

The short walk to his truck helped cool his blood, and he found a frisbee in the back. He walked back to the group, tossing it in the air and spinning it on one finger. One of the guys on the opposite side of the pavilion stood with a hand in the air and Jack flicked it over the heads of everyone, making the girls squeal.

The distraction broke up the tirade and the subject of Ava was carefully avoided for the next hour as they played two games of ultimate frisbee. The girlier, or chattier, girls stayed on the sidelines. Talia stayed out too. She would normally play, but Jack finally understood why she didn't want him to leave earlier. And why she didn't join the frisbee game today. They were refereeing the other game going on.

Once the group started to disband, Jack claimed he had errands he needed to run and couldn't give any rides home. He sent Talia a look. She pressed her lips together and nodded. They walked to his truck.

"Thanks for staying," Talia said in a low voice. "I was worried it might get worse if we left."

Jack only nodded, preoccupied with his own questions now. As soon as the doors closed on the truck, he turned on Talia. "Did she sleep with Benj?"

Talia groaned. She dropped her head in her hands. "I don't think so. But it's not about Benj. You get that, right? None of this is really about him."

He leaned back on the headrest, staring at the nothingness at the top of the truck. "Then what is it about?"

"I'm not sure, but it's not Benj. Ava's so beat down, she needs to come up for air but I don't think she remembers which way is up."

The realization of what he had to do settled hard in his chest. "I think I'm going to Scotland."

The statement hung over them. Talia finally spoke, quietly. "She's not the same person anymore, Jack. I don't want you to get hurt too."

"Ava can't hurt me."

"Jack… I know you love her—don't." She raised a hand when he opened his mouth. "Don't deny it. And she's not acting like herself right now. She's pushing people away."

Jack stared at the park in front of them and the ocean that stretched a few thousand miles to Ava. He wanted to argue with Talia on every point but he couldn't find the words. "I have to do something."

Talia reached over the center console and squeezed Jack's hand. "Then do it."

• • •

Jack pulled up to the Sanford's house late Tuesday afternoon. Ava's younger brother Ezra answered the door.

"'Sup, bro?" Ezra asked, with a guy's handshake and back pat. He nearly reached Jack's height, though barely 16 and more lanky.

"Hey man. How's school?"

Ezra shrugged. "Being a sophomore is better than a freshman."

"Gets better every year. Is your dad here?"

"Yeah, he said you were coming. I think he's in the office."

"Thanks." Jack headed down the hallway to the door on the right.

"Hey, Jack," Ezra said, stopping Jack in his tracks. He turned around, but Ezra wouldn't meet his eyes anymore. He studied the family pictures lining the wall of the hallway and his voice dropped. "Is this about Ava?"

Jack didn't offer anything in reply.

"Joshua stinks at being the oldest sibling around here. Ava was way better at it."

"I know."

Ezra nodded without looking at him and walked away towards the kitchen. Jack turned back to the office door and knocked.

"I thought I heard you," Micah said, waving Jack into the office. "Come on in."

Jack took a seat in the yellow lounge chair facing Micah's desk. It felt formal; he had never sat in here before. They were usually a talk-on-the-couch family, but this was a more private space, which they needed today. Micah leaned back in his office chair and Jack didn't waste a minute. "I want to talk to you about going to Scotland. I think Ava needs to see somebody from home."

Micah nodded slowly. It didn't seem to be much of a surprise to him. News traveled fast lately. "Have you talked to Ava about it?"

"I've texted her, but she hasn't replied."

"She doesn't anymore, does she?"

"No..."

"I think I was wrong," Micah said, flexing his fingers against the desk. "We've been trying to give her space. But I shouldn't have asked you and Talia to do that too. I'm sorry."

Jack shrugged. "I get it."

Micah sighed and interlaced his hands behind his head. "We thought it would be good for her to spread her wings. To do things on her own. I had no idea..."

"Nobody did."

"I think the people-pleasing side of her... Went to the wrong people."

Jack only nodded, unsure what to say as they danced around the topic, around the rumors of who Ava slept with, what she drank, and worse.

"So tell me about this trip. What are you thinking? Why do you want to go?"

"She seems depressed. Lost," Jack said. Micah looked out the window, his eyebrows pinched together. Jack continued. "And one of the students there... One of the guys has been calling me, he's not the best guy, and I'm worried about Ava. I think if she reconnected with somebody from home for a few days, she might be able to make it through the semester."

"Rebecca told me you had spoken to Benjamin." Micah rubbed a hand over his face. "We talked to Talia the other day too. And honestly, we appreciate that neither of you will tell us much, even if it's currently driving us crazy."

Jack laughed. "Sorry. It's Ava's story." He didn't know much of it, anyway.

"That's why we trust y'all. Look, you have to realize you can't fix everything. Not by yourself. Only God can, and Ava has to rediscover that herself."

"Yes sir. But maybe I can help."

Just then Ava's mom, Rebecca, knocked on the door and cracked it open. "Sorry to interrupt. I'm about to set the table for dinner. Can I set a place for you, Jack?"

"Thank you, Mrs. Sanford, I'd love to, but I have to close the gym tonight. I've got to head out soon."

"Has it been that long since you were here last? It's Rebecca to you," she said. "How about a plate to go, then?"

"I can't turn that down," Jack said with a grin.

"Sweetie, Jack is going to Scotland," Micah said before she left.

Pain flashed in Rebecca's eyes—the same he had seen in Micah's. Jack looked away to give her a moment.

"Will you... Could you please take some brownies?" Rebecca asked, recovered, though the smile was weak. "It sounds silly, but she didn't get her usual double fudge brownies for her birthday. I could have mailed them, but it was so expensive and I thought..."

"Absolutely. Although fair warning, if there's going to be double fudge brownies in my bag, you might want to send me with extras."

"Will double cover the carrier fee?" she asked with a smile.

"That should do it."

Rebecca hesitated in the doorway for a second before walking away. Micah watched her for a moment before turning back to Jack, resoluteness on his face. "Jack, she can come back if she needs to. She won't really talk to us. So tell her... If she needs to come home, right now, she can. She doesn't have to stay through May."

Jack focused on the marks in the wooden desk between them. "Yes sir." He knew this family, and it was obvious. Things were bad.

Micah reached into a desk drawer and pulled out a checkbook. "I'm sure Rebecca will tell me to give you more later, but—"

"You don't have to—"

"Jack, this isn't a sight-seeing trip. This is about helping my daughter. And I'm going to help you with that. This should at least cover a hotel." As Micah passed the check to Jack, he locked eyes with him and managed a look that could shake the gates of hell. "You are getting a hotel, right?"

An entirely inappropriate laugh tried to form in Jack's chest at the misunderstanding of Jack's relationship with Ava. He forced it back. "Yes, sir. Of course. It's not... No. Yeah. Hotel." *Smooth.*

"I trust you with my daughter," Micah said, uncharacteristically stern. "Do you understand what that means?"

The laugh was gone. *Not really.* Jack could hardly trust anyone with anything. He knew Micah loved his children more than life, and that being trusted with Ava was more than he deserved. "I'll do my best to be worthy of it."

"I know you will," Micah said as he stood and crossed around the desk. Jack stood and followed him into the front hallway.

"Come get your plate," Rebecca called from the kitchen. The guys walked into the kitchen and she handed Jack a paper plate covered in foil. It smelled delicious. "Brisket sliders."

"I can't think of anything that sounds better right now." Jack said as he took it and gave her a quick hug.

"Come back for a full dinner soon," she said. "And tell me when you plan to leave, I'll make sure to get fresh brownies to you."

"Will do."

"Thank you," she said as she reached to give him a quick kiss on the cheek.

Jack waited till he got to the gym before devouring the sliders. He had a few minutes before his shift and pulled up flights on his phone. He groaned. Good thing Mrs. Sanford had offered him dinner anytime. He wouldn't be able to afford his own for another month. Jack noted the cheapest dates within a week and headed inside to ask for the days off.

Chapter 24

Rosie
Meet me at Double Cross in an hour?
Ava
I'll be there.

It had been over a week since she had spoken with her parents. And every day since had been a nightmare. The gates of hell had been unleashed. Everything everybody knew about her was either a lie or an ugly truth.

People here hated her for things she had done. Benj had been ignoring Ava all week, anger and awkwardness between them since the night he had walked her to her dorm. Sloane kept her game going too, with subtle jabs like, *"You're the most popular girl at TGU who isn't even there."* She meant the most talked about, of course. Rosie had been mad too, though thankfully pixies couldn't hold grudges for long, and soon enough she acted like nothing had happened.

People at home thought she had done even worse. Ava received messages that ranged from false-fronts of "checking up on you," to ugly notes from random girls at TGU calling her a slut. Someone had even sent her an article on the effects of a variety of drugs, which had made Ava laugh in a weird mixture of humor and despair. Eventually, she shut down her social media accounts. She blocked incoming texts from everybody in Texas. There was no point in trying anywhere.

She poured herself into studying and homework—the only reason she woke every day. Her grades were slipping regardless of her efforts, but at least failing a test wasn't as bad as being hated.

Rosie
I've got a seat for you at the bar.

The current essay she was working on was due three hours ago. Every hour late was a point off. She typed out a final sentence and scanned it briefly. She had no time for edits, but it met the word count. Ava emailed it and hopped down from the bed. The jeans and sweater she had worn all day would work. Rosie had declared this a girls-only celebration of surviving the week. They still weren't on the same terms when it came to the rugby club, but Rosie had promised to avoid them for tonight.

Ava looked in the mirror one more time and blew out a breath before grabbing her coat and jogging down the stairs to the ride she had scheduled. This didn't have to be a disaster. It could be fun. Bars might be part of the problem, but they were also one of the few places where she was still welcomed.

The drive to the bar only took five minutes, but Rosie texted her two more times threatening to give her seat away to the next hot guy that walked in. The car finally pulled up and Ava stepped out as sleet stung her cheeks. The weather had only gotten worse lately, like Edinburgh was offended that winter might try to end.

Her hand was on the door when she heard her name. "Ava Sanford." Benj's voice was seething.

She spun around and even in the fading light she could see his blue eyes flashing as he approached on the sidewalk. "Benj?"

"Don't talk to me. What the hell is wrong with you?"

"What?" Ava stepped back and did a quick scan of their surroundings—one couple walked past with raised eyebrows. A crowd of teens stood a few stores away. "What are you talking about?"

"Tell me why Cassandra thinks we slept together," Benj said. "What did you do? Run and tell everybody we slept together because of a kiss? Is this all a stupid game to you?"

"I didn't tell any—"

"Who did you tell and what did you say?"

"Benj, I didn't tell anybody," she said, willing herself to be calm enough for both of them, despite the rising heart rate. "Who did *you* tell?"

"I'm not a little teenage virgin," he sneered. "I don't have to go tell everybody when I get a kiss."

He knew she was neither of those things. But her ability to care what he thought had been more used up than her body. With nothing left, anger took over. "Screw you, Benjamin."

"You wish you could. You better fix this," he said, jabbing a finger into her shoulder.

"Cassandra is your problem, not mine, remember? Everybody back home is spreading crap about me. If I knew how to fix it, I would."

"Maybe if you weren't actually sleeping around, that wouldn't have happened."

"I'm not!" She shouted as the crowd of teens passed them. "One person doesn't— It was you, wasn't it? Who did you tell? About… Oliver?"

"That you had sex with him? You can't even say it," Benjamin laughed and shook his head. "I told a couple guys."

"What? Why would you do that?" She heard her own voice getting hysterical and the sound of the bar door opening behind her.

Benjamin's half smile wasn't cute anymore. He stepped into her space, overwhelming her with proximity as blood rushed to her head, drowning out sounds and thoughts. "They thought you were hot, and I let them know you've loosened up now."

Fight jumped up before flight locked it down and Ava shoved him back. "How dare you?"

He grabbed her wrist and jerked her to him. Before she realized what her other hand was doing, it flew out and landed across Benj's cheek. Ava barely recognized it as her own until her fingers tingled. Benj grabbed it and she was caught, panic sweeping in.

A whistle sounded from the doorway of the bar. Rosie let out a swear word slowly as she stepped between them, gently pressing Benj's hands away from Ava. "Ah dinnae see that comin' either, Cowboy. Now, if you'll excuse us..." Rosie pulled at Ava's hands.

Ava's feet wouldn't move. She couldn't look away from Benj's face. The eyes she had once desperately wanted to catch were now staring at her with raw anger. He hated her. Rosie was whispering something in Ava's ear and she finally let herself be pulled away. When she looked back over her shoulder a few yards away, Benj still stared at her.

They turned the corner at the next block and pain finally swallowed the anger. There was so much pain. Ava's strength gave out as she grabbed Rosie and heaving sobs took over her.

"What the hell was that?" Rosie asked.

Ava tried to get it out between sobs and hiccups but it wasn't coming in order. Finally breaking the dam, she told Rosie about the rumors, the people she had hurt back home, and the accusations she had launched at Jack.

When Ava finally regained control, Rosie brushed a hand across her cheeks and sighed, concern etched on her face. She only had one answer to this sort of thing. "A'right lassie, we'll get a bevvy somewhere else. It'll be a'right." She reached into her purse and handed Ava a tissue before going for a powder compact and mascara.

Rosie led her to a bar on the opposite side of campus. Ava couldn't think straight and didn't want to. A bevvy was just what she needed.

After the first round of drinks, pain settled in her temples. Ava excused herself and stepped outside to make a phone call. The night was pitch black, there were no stars, no moon, only hazy street lights. She needed to apologize to Jack, but the call went straight to his voicemail. Ava hung up without leaving a message. She deserved to be ignored.

Back inside, Rosie handed Ava a tiny glass of something blue.

"What's this?"

"A shot. To Texas, exes and sexes," Rosie said, lifting her glass.

Ava clinked to the nonsensical toast. She tried to sip the liquor and Rosie scolded her for failing to throw it back. Rosie ordered another shot, this time it was green.

"To hell, may the stay there be as fun as the way there," Rosie said.

"I don't think I can toast to that," Ava laughed.

Rosie clinked her glass anyway and Ava swallowed it in one go.

When the first bar cut them off, Rosie led the way to another one. They were all new spots to Ava, probably to avoid certain crowds. She didn't mind. They found a couple of other girls from their dorm building at the next bar. The story of Ava's slap made its rounds and one of the girls bought her another shot for it.

"To Ava's first slap," Rosie said.

"And I thought there weren't any firsts left," Ava said.

Rosie had promised to help Ava feel better. What she really meant was to feel nothing. Ava was okay with that. She tried to call Jack again as they walked to another new bar, at the west end of campus. Straight to voicemail.

The third bar was in a basement, loud and cramped. More students joined their group with another round of shots. It was finally working—Ava was numb and tingling.

And nauseous. Looking for a break from the crowds, she pushed her way to the restroom, tripping over her own feet on the way. Even the bathroom was crowded with girls who smelled like a dozen different perfumes. It turned Ava's stomach, and she backed out. The exit sign next to the restrooms promised fresh air. Ava stumbled towards it, desperate for air.

She pushed out into an alleyway, next to a dumpster. The smell of ripe garbage was too much for her stomach to handle. Ava threw up next to it. It wasn't the fresh air she needed. At least the cold helped with the heat in her face. Claustrophobia still strangled her though. If she went back into that bar, she would throw up again.

Ava didn't want to be anywhere. She threw up, losing count of how many that was. She had to get away from the dumpster. Wandering down the alley, she headed in the direction of campus. Or close enough. If there was fresh air, it would work.

The next thing she knew, she was throwing up on beautiful rose bushes. Would that ruin them? She should get back to Rosie. What was the name of that last bar? Ava looked at the dark buildings around her with vague recognition. These weren't campus buildings. It was the fire and brimstone parish. The stupid parish.

Ava tried to call Rosie. No answer. She called Jack again. No answer.

Her mind was a fog and she couldn't remember which way she had come. Or gone. All she wanted to do was lay down and sleep. And throw up again. Ava sank against the stone wall that fenced in the parish. The vomiting left her cold, and she didn't have her coat. It didn't matter. None of it did. The warmth in her head spread into her bones and she closed her eyes.

• • •

"Ava Claire!" A male voice rang out and Ava's head popped up, smacking the wall behind it.

The blast of pain in her head and the flashlight hitting her eyes combined to make her throw up again, this time on her hair and shirt. Pain or panic sent a ringing through her head and she covered her ears to make it stop, squeezing her eyes shut against the light. The man closed in on her. Ava tried to push away from him, but she was backed into the wall with nowhere to go. Her breath came in gasps.

"Aves," he whispered. She slowly opened her eyes and tried to focus. Even when she did, she didn't believe what she saw. The world tilted and Ava threw up again.

Chapter 25

Jack texted Rosie from Ava's phone, asking her to bring a change of clothes and a jacket to the hospital. She didn't respond for an hour—probably hungover. But finally she was on her way.

He waited outside of the hospital. The sun shone brightly but its warmth couldn't reach him through the cold air. He zipped his jacket as he waited. Even if he hadn't seen her in the pictures, he would have been able to pick Rosie out by Ava's descriptions. Blonde curls kept time with each step as she bounced along the sidewalk.

"The indispensable Jack?" she asked with a wide smile.

"Rosie," he said and reached for the bag of clothes in her hands. He didn't need any more of an introduction.

"Yer outside of Texas. What are ye doin' here?"

"Right now? Helping Ava get over alcohol poisoning and hypothermia."

Rosie pouted and bounced slightly, stomping a foot. "All she needs is a wee Irn Bru. It wasn't that bad."

"Wanna come see her?" Jack asked nodding towards the hospital doors.

Rosie bit her lip. "How is she?" She crossed her arms and flounced her hair. Her body was a constant motion.

"Sleeping it off. On IV fluids. Thankfully off the oxygen now."

"I was only tryin' ta help. Her term's been rubbish."

"That's why I'm here."

Rosie tilted her head to one side and her smile dropped off. "Ye should hae been here weeks ago."

Jack ran a hand through his slept-in-a-chair hair, fighting the thought that Rosie was right. "I should get back to her."

Rosie cranked her smile up a few notches. "I'm sure I'll see ye 'round." She waved before skipping away.

Jack jogged up the stairs back to Ava's room. She moaned and covered her eyes with her forearm when he opened the door. It was the first sign of life in several hours. She'd finally gotten some sleep after a night of vomiting.

"Hey girl," he said quietly, sinking into the chair next to the bed.

"Jack?" she croaked out his name, pressing the palms of her hands to her eyes.

"Headache?"

She nodded. Jack tapped the nurse call button and requested a glass of water and painkillers. The nurse was soon back with both.

Jack gave her space while waiting for the painkillers to start working. He grabbed a late breakfast at the cafeteria, getting an english muffin for Ava. It seemed like the least sensory-offending option. And she needed to eat something. She was far too light when he picked her up last night. And cold.

When he came back, Ava was sitting in the hospital bed. She looked like she'd been hit by a bus and she likely felt it too. There were dark circles under her eyes, contrasted by a surprisingly pale complexion, and a mess of dark hair framing her face.

"Do my parents know?" she asked quietly.

"No."

"Thank you." It was barely a whisper from her hoarse voice. She thanked him again when he handed her the muffin.

He wanted to ask her what she had been thinking. Why she had gotten blackout drunk. Why she had collapsed in front of a church. Why she was only wearing jeans and a thin sweater when it was below freezing outside. But Jack buried the questions—for now.

She picked at the muffin. "Why are you here?"

"I'm here to help. We can talk about it later."

She nodded absently, shredding the muffin more than eating it. "I want to go home."

"Let's get you discharged." Jack handed the bag of clothes to Ava.

"How'd you get these?"

"Rosie. Quite the roommate."

"She's not that bad."

"She let you get alcohol poisoning and walk away alone, without a coat. Not exactly great friend material."

"That's my own fault, not hers." Ava's voice was hoarse as she defended the roommate who obviously had no moral code.

Jack buried the frustration. He didn't want to argue with her right now. "I'll go get the doctor."

By the time he returned with the doctor, Ava was dressed, her hair in a messy knot, and color easing its way back into her face.

The doctor said she was good to go. But not before a long, rehearsed speech on alcohol poisoning. He seemed to enjoy the joke—American students having too much fun with the UK's younger drinking age. When the speech started to drag, Jack interrupted him with a handshake and "thank you."

They slowly made it back to Ava's dorm, in near silence. When they got to the building, she hesitated at the door, squinting against the distant sun. She reached for the bag of old clothes Jack held. "I've got it from here."

Jack frowned. He wasn't ready or willing to leave her at the door. "Can we talk?"

Her eyes darted around him, glancing up and down the street, not meeting his. She pulled her lips in tightly. "Inside?"

"I mean… It's kind of cold out here, but…"

"I guess so." It was barely more than a whisper. She pushed the door open and stopped halfway through the doorway, suddenly stuck. She stared at the stairs ahead, then out the door again, barely glancing at Jack. Finally, she walked through the door and let it close behind them.

They made painstakingly slow progress. Halfway up the stairs, Jack was about ready to carry Ava the rest of the way. But she eventually made it. Once in her room, she excused herself to the shower. Jack sat on the only seat in her room, a stiff wooden chair under Ava's bed. He never would have guessed this side was hers, if he hadn't seen her get her things from it. The bare walls and bed weren't like her. Neither were the messy piles of papers, books and clothes underneath it. Rosie's side was strung with lights and paper lanterns over her bed. The bright style looked more like the Ava that had left Texas three months ago.

When he had flown out yesterday morning, he still thought he could bring the old Ava back. When he found her last night, he worried he was too late. Watching her now, he knew he was.

Wringing her hair in a towel, Ava walked into the room to grab a blow dryer. A white shirt hung over her too-thin frame and her jeans clung to her hips with the last of their willpower. She wasn't eating enough. Jack was in over his head.

She left the room again, and Jack used the time to pray. Because Micah was right——he couldn't fix this himself.

When she came back, her hair hung in loose waves down to her ribs. Her makeup covered the dark circles under her eyes. She looked fine. Beautifully fine. If he didn't know her, he could have bought into the appearance. But he did know her, and her eyes were empty.

Ava leaned against the bookcase. "Why are you here?"

"I knew something was wrong."

Ava crossed her arms, studying her feet. "That doesn't explain it."

Jack moved to stand next to her. "Sure it does."

She sighed and leaned her head on his arm. "How did you find me last night?"

"You called me."

Ava stiffened and moved away from him. "I don't remember," she admitted quietly.

"Left a message." His phone had still been in airplane mode when she called. Her speech had been slurred and irregular as she rattled a frustrated apology and talked about the church that sounded like death. Jack shrugged. "I was heading to my hotel and redirected the cab to the closest parish to campus."

"I still don't get it. How'd you know?"

"I know you."

"No, you don't," Ava whispered.

Any argument there was a lost cause. She was right. He was in the room of an absolute stranger, trying to save her. He wanted to call Isaac, Micah, anybody smarter than him, anybody who could handle this better. But he was trapped in this moment and continued with silent prayers instead.

"Everything is still there," she said, her voice cracking as she buried her head in his shoulder. Jack lifted his arm around her and held her there. She wasn't normally this touchy, but nothing was normal right now.

"What is?"

"Everything I wanted to drink away."

Jack brushed her hair back and waited. For her to say more. For answers to prayers. Either. Both.

"Benj thinks I told people we slept together," Ava said, muffled by his chest. "I didn't. We didn't. Please say you believe me."

"I believe you." It didn't address what else she might have done. There were plenty of other rumors. He couldn't let himself think about them right now. Seeing her like this, he couldn't hold anything against her.

"We kissed. That's it." Ava covered her face with her hands. "Benj is the one who told everybody at home."

"I know."

"I'm sorry."

"Me too."

"You have nothing to apologize for."

"Then I'm sorry that all of this has happened," he said.

Ava opened her mouth but went for a silent nod instead. The mental image of her body crumpled on the ground last night forced words out of him. He said it as softly as possible, handling her like glass.

"You can't drink things away, Aves."

"Then how do I get rid of them?"

"We'll figure that out. But you can cross drinking off the list."

She scoffed and tilted her head back, studying him with eyes that were still slightly red and swollen. "I learned that. No need to remind me." There was the slightest lift on her lips, a hint of a smile. He wanted to bring it out in full.

Jack poked her lightly in the ribs. "They're starving you here, but I won't let them do it to me. Where do we get lunch?"

A gentle smile spread warmth into her face. "You're always hungry."

"That reminds me..." Jack grabbed the backpack he'd been hauling since yesterday and unzipped the top. He pulled out a plastic container and handed it to Ava. "Double fudge brownies. Happy belated birthday."

Ava laughed, and the sound was the first sign since he'd arrived that Ava was still in there somewhere. "Did you save me any?" She popped it open.

"Your mom sent extras. I already ate mine, the rest are yours."

Ava held the container out to him. "Valiant effort, but you can't resist another."

"Eat one with me then."

They sat on the floor with desserts in hand. Ava barely ate half of hers before setting it back down. She suggested a bistro down the street for lunch. Jack stood and pulled Ava up by the hand. She groaned and pressed a hand to the side of her head.

"You need coffee," he said. "Let's go."

Ava grabbed a coat and hat while Jack zipped his own jacket. She frowned at him. "You're gonna freeze."

"You survived it last night."

"Shut up." She reached onto her bed and grabbed a black fleece, tossing it to Jack.

He caught the familiar Athletic Department pullover. "You still have it."

"Of course I do," Ava said with a wrinkled brow and a laugh.

Jack shrugged. He wasn't sure why it surprised him. She seemed so distant, so far removed from the girl he had given it to. It was weird to see signs of that girl here. "You never replied when I said I was coming. I figured you didn't want to see me."

"You never told me you were coming..."

"Yes, I did. I texted you half a dozen times."

"Oh. Right." Ava dropped her head, staring at her feet. "Sorry. I, um… I blocked a lot of people on my phone."

The girl he considered his best friend had blocked his number. The girl who was now a stranger. Jack tried to ignore the twinge in his chest. "Why?"

Ava shrugged. "Everybody hates me."

"That's not true. You don't believe that."

"I don't know what I believe."

He wanted to shake those words away. They hurt to hear. And Jack couldn't tell her what to believe. But he could help her find it again. He pulled the fleece on and zipped his jacket over it. He made a face. "It smells like girl now."

Ava smiled and willingly took him up on the topic change. "Whatever. It's an improvement over the gym sweat it used to smell like."

Jack took the mature route; instead of replying, he stuck his tongue out at her.

When they got down stairs, Jack quickly realized Ava was right. The afternoon sun hadn't warmed the day at all. If anything, it was colder. By the time they arrived at the bistro, Ava's hands shook as she reached for the door, either from cold or exhaustion.

They ordered and took their food to a bench seat near the window. Ava sank into the seat heavily, with a sigh. She went quiet, poking around the salad she had ordered.

"Are you gonna eat?" Jack asked.

Ava's head jerked up and she blinked at him several times before squinting at her plate again. Did she even see it? Her eyes were red. She nodded and stuck her fork into a strawberry in the salad, lifting it to her lips and lowering it again. "Actually, I'm still a little nauseous. Do you want it?"

"Do you want something else?"

"No, I'm good. I'll eat later." She managed a bite or two in the time it took Jack to eat his sandwich.

On their way out the door, Ava offered to play tour guide around Edinburgh.

"You're exhausted, Aves."

"I'll be okay."

"Your body just went through hell. You need some recovery time. And I still need to check into my hotel."

"Oh… Right. You must be tired too. Sleeping in a hospital. And jet lag. Actually, how are you still awake?"

Jack shrugged and ran a hand over a scratchy jawline that needed a shave. "The tour can wait till tomorrow."

They walked back to her dorm together quietly. When they got to her room, Jack reached for his bag when Ava stopped him.

"Thank you." She stared at her hands. "Thank you for being here."

"Of course."

"No, I mean it, this isn't something you would normally do. And it means a lot." Before he responded, she reached her arms around his neck and hugged him tightly, the fresh scent of her hair tickling his nose. She stepped back quickly, still not meeting his eyes.

Jack gave her arm a quick squeeze. "Get some rest."

Chapter 26

Poisoning her body had taken its toll. Throwing up half the night and spending the second half in a hospital bed attached to an IV had left her exhausted. Ava went straight to bed and slept all of Saturday afternoon away. It was the hardest she had slept in a month.

She woke in the evening, the nausea finally gone, though a low headache persisted. Her stomach hurt, but for once, Ava thought it might actually be hunger instead of stress. She called Jack, and he answered on the second ring.

"Hey, do you wanna get dinner?" Ava asked. A sudden wave of shame slammed her. Jack might not want to see her again today. He had just seen her at her worst. He wouldn't want to be around her anymore. "I could make something here. But, I mean, it's okay if not, if you had other plans."

"Aves, I'm sitting in my room flipping through a dozen BBC channels. What plans do you think I have here?" Jack laughed.

"I don't know." She still didn't understand why he was here at all.

"I'll head over. There's a grocery store by the hotel, want me to pick anything up?"

"I've got pasta and sauce."

"Sounds vegetarian. I'll grab some meat."

"You're such a guy," Ava smiled. "Call me when you get here."

Her half of the room was a mess. Having Jack in it earlier today made her see it again. She still slept cocooned in the cream blanket on a bare mattress. She had taken down any signs of family and friends—they didn't want to be on her walls, anyway. And she certainly didn't deserve to have

Jack here. The hunger started to change back into anxiety, her stomach knotting itself closed again.

Ava sorted the books and papers on the bookcase into somewhat decent stacks. She tossed loose clothes into a bin, blushing when she realized there had been a pink bra sitting right on top of the bookcase. She didn't have many guys in this room. There had only been one other. The knot tightened.

By the time Jack arrived, Ava was more than ready for the conversation to distract her. Ready to relax again. But he didn't have the same effect this time. Maybe because she had slept and actually saw him clearly this time. Maybe because he had slept too and cleaned up well. Maybe because the guilt seeped back in. Her hands were shaking again.

"Does anybody ever play?" Jack asked, pointing to the ping-pong table against one wall of the lounge area.

"Never."

"Perfect. That's what we're doing after dinner."

"You know I'm terrible at it."

"That's okay. I like to win."

Ava laughed, and the nerves took a step back. *It's Jack. Just Jack.* Just Jack in black jogging pants and the black TGU fleece that fit his body very differently than hers.

She focused on chopping onions and bell peppers while Jack put the beef in a pan. He was his usual self, somehow completely at home even in a new setting, and started juggling the tomatoes.

"Thanks for the show, jester," she said, rolling her eyes at him and stealing the tomatoes. Jack bowed dramatically.

"Well, isn't this cute," Rosie's voice called from the front door. "Playing house?"

"Making dinner," Ava said. "Want some?"

"Nope, going on an official date with Callan tonight."

"Wait, official? Really?"

"Official, for the second time." Rosie gave Ava a kiss on the cheek. "So, which of us gets our room tonight?"

"Rosie," Ava groaned. "I'm sleeping in my bed. By myself. No boys."

Rosie shrugged and turned to Jack. "Too bad. I like this one, hen. Even more than Cowboy."

"Who's Cowboy?" Jack asked.

"Nobody—" Ava said loudly, before Rosie answered. Rosie raised her eyebrows at Ava and laughed.

The humor left Jack's face, and he turned his attention to the stove top. "Well, now I know who it is."

Rosie hopped onto the countertop, sitting next to the stove and closing in on Jack's space. Jack didn't budge. She took the spatula from his hands and scooped a bell pepper slice for herself with it.

"Feart not, inviolable Jack," Rosie said, her voice dripping with honeyed Scottish twang. "She slapped the daylicht out of Benjamin."

"Ava wouldn't slap anyone."

"Och, she's done plenty o' things ye would nae hae thought," Rosie said with a laugh.

Jack turned towards Ava, holding her gaze as he raised an eyebrow. "I'm sure she has."

"Great, thanks, Rosie," Ava said. "You're not wearing that to dinner, go change."

Rosie hopped down, using Jack's shoulder for support. She blew a kiss and skipped up the stairs. Dinner was ready and Ava's stomach was back in knots. Jack plated everything in silence and they sat down across from each other. He didn't say a word.

"What?" Ava asked finally. "What do you want me to say?"

"Nothing. I want you to eat."

"I lost my appetite."

"Why?" Jack dropped his fork on his plate. "Why would you lose your appetite? Over Benj?"

Ava pushed her chair back and stood. "Why are you here? If you came to rub it in my face and let me know I'm a failure, then you can leave. Because I don't need that."

"What do you need?" he asked in an even tone.

Ava stared at him for a moment. Neither of them had any answers. She moved to put pots and pans in the sink and fill them with water.

Before she realized he had followed her, Jack's arm reached around her and switching off the faucet. Ava's lungs switched off too. She turned, blocked against the countertop by Jack's arms on either side of her, crowding in. "Jack, don't—"

"Talk to me."

Her breath was shallow. "Don't, don't—" Ava pressed a hand against his chest as her vision tunneled, darkening around the edges. He didn't budge. Pain rose through her back, tightening around her neck. Ava dropped to the floor to escape him, pressing against the cabinets, the knobs digging into her back. She pulled her knees to her chest and buried her head in them, trying to remember how to breathe.

Jack squatted in front of her. "Aves, babe?"

She shook her head against her knees. He was still too close, too warm. Her lungs were empty, and she forced words out with the last of her air. "Move. Please. Move."

The air opened around her when he left. She focused on breathing, on making her lungs work again. Jack would never hurt her. It was stupid to react this way. But this body wasn't hers. She couldn't control it. The pain settled into her heart.

When she finally looked up, Jack sat on the floor too, his back against the cabinets opposite her. Watching her and looking like he held the weight of the world. "What are you not telling me?" he asked quietly.

His eyes scanned hers. If he could figure it all out on his own, she would let him. But she couldn't talk to him about it. "Why are you here, Jack?"

"To help."

"Why? Why do you care? I'm worthless." Ava tilted her head back, staring at the ceiling.

His eyebrows pinched. "How can you say that?"

"Nobody will talk to me. Not even Talia."

"That was your dad. He told Talia and me that you needed space."

"Space?" Ava barked out a laugh. "My dad told my two best friends not to talk to me while I was going through hell?"

"Yeah. He admitted he was wrong."

"But you went along with it?"

"I shouldn't have. I'm sorry."

Ava groaned and stood. Jack joined her. She walked over to him and pressed her forehead into his chest. He lifted his arms around her for the second time today. It felt like home. The first piece of home she had felt in three months. She didn't want it to end.

"I kinda killed dinner," Ava said without moving.

Jack brushed a hand through her hair and an involuntary shiver ran down her spine. But it wasn't threatening. "It's okay. Italian is good reheated."

Ava propped her chin on his chest, tilting her face up towards him. "You're not this nice. Where's the Jack who likes to taunt me?"

Jack frowned at her. "I'm saving it all for ping-pong."

Ava laughed and pushed back from him. "Then let's go, Shields. I'm ready."

Jack finished his dinner in a few bites while Ava cleaned, promising to eat later. He won the first two rounds. Ava changed the rules for the third: her points counted as double, his were half points on one side of the table and negative points on the other. She finally won.

Before he left, Ava made him narrow down what he wanted to see in Edinburgh tomorrow. They decided to start on the Royal Mile in the morning. With a plan in place, Jack waved goodnight and headed for the dark street. Ava watched from the doorway. It was drizzling and he lifted the hood of his jacket as he walked away, a shadow that disappeared quickly.

• • •

Jack stood in the hotel lobby when Ava walked in. She only half-acknowledged him, keeping her eyes on the ground. Shy again. A shy Ava was confusing, frustrating, and endearing all at once. But she had warmed up last night; she would again today.

"I turned down the hotel buffet, and now I'm starving," he said when she was within earshot. "Where's this breakfast you promised?"

"It's not too far." She gave a barely there smile.

She led the way to a diner on the edge of the Royal Mile. A light snow drifted down and the entire city looked like it was straight out of a movie. Curving streets, cobblestones, and the occasional storefront painted bright yellow or blue—as if it could make up for the gray sky overhead.

Ava stole the menu from his hands and ordered for them both: a full Scottish breakfast, a bowl of oatmeal, and two coffees. Their waiter brought out the plates and set the massive one in front of Jack. At least she knew he could eat.

Jack scanned it for familiar items. "Eggs, ham, baked beans, sausage link… biscuit?"

"Tattie scone—potato scone," Ava corrected.

"Tomato and… mushroom?" Jack guessed at the black round. Ava nodded. There were two more unidentified objects on the plate. "Sausage? And lump of coal?"

"Haggis and blood sausage."

"Neither of those sound edible."

Ava laughed, and some shyness seemed to melt away. "Sure they are. Here, at least. Maybe not in America. Sheep entrails stuffed in a stomach and sausage filled with dried blood. Bon appétit."

"Fine, I'll try it. But only if you do too."

Ava confidently leaned over the table and stuck a fork in the haggis. They tapped their forks together and took a bite. It wasn't actually as bad as he expected. The blood sausage was worse—salty and tasted like, well, blood. At least the rest of his plate was edible. Ava even finished her oatmeal. It was the first time he had seen her eat.

After breakfast, they wandered the Royal Mile, poking into kitschy shops to escape the cold, and pretending to shop for tartans and kilts. At one point, Ava bought a kitchen towel with a hairy highland cow printed on it. Jack couldn't help but comment on having a hamburger's former self displayed in her kitchen. It actually brought a laugh out of her, along with a smack on his arm.

They stopped at a street corner where a man played bagpipes. The haunting sound echoed off of the buildings. Ava relaxed as they walked, and her smile came easier. She shared random facts about the city, pointing out various architecture styles. Playing tour guide suited her.

Reaching Edinburgh Castle at the end of the mile, they joined a tour group as the last of the snowflakes fell. At an overlook point, they fell back, letting the tour continue without them. The clouds were lifting, revealing a sweeping view of the crowded city, a crush of buildings broken by an occasional church steeple or bell tower rising above the rest. The view was backed by low mountains, covered in a dusting of snow.

Ava leaned on the stone wall. "Isn't it beautiful?"

"And cold."

"I do miss the sun." It peeked through the clouds now, too shy to make a full appearance.

"When are you coming back?" Jack asked.

"Forty days."

"You sound like a prisoner with a court date."

"Pretty accurate description. When do you leave?"

"Wednesday."

Ava grabbed his arm and rounded to face him. "What? No, that's too soon. Reschedule it. Stay through next weekend."

"I've got classes and work, Aves."

"No, Jack, please."

She sounded desperate. Jack steadied her with his hands on her arms and made sure he had her attention before speaking. "Come back with me."

Ava took a step back. She opened and closed her mouth twice before answering. "I can't do that."

"Yes, you can. Your parents want you to." Especially if they saw her now.

"And waste this entire semester?" Ava's voice was hoarse.

"It's not a waste, not if you need to come home. Forty days is a long way to go."

She leaned her arms on the wall, surveying the city before dropping her head onto her arms. "It's so long. You have no idea."

"So don't stay."

A shiver ran over her body before she spoke again. "I can't go home. It's going to be horrible there. How will I face everybody?" That was the real fear, more than wasting a semester.

"Will it be any easier in 40 days?" He leaned onto the wall next to her. Ava shook her head. "You have to come home eventually. Your family and Talia and I will all stand by you."

"My parents won't."

"Your double fudge brownie parents? Yes, they will."

"My 'your actions impact the entire church' parents? I don't think so. They're mad at me. And they have every right to be."

"They love you and they want you home."

"Leaving early would give everybody one more thing to talk about."

"Ava Claire, I don't care what anybody's talking about." Jack straightened. "I—We care about you. And I can't leave you here. I don't think you should do this for another day."

Whatever "this" was. Leaving Texas, he thought his mission was to encourage a depressed friend who was making bad decisions. Over the last 36 hours that had changed. Every minute with her made him more determined to get her home. Praying to get her home.

Ava wrapped a hand around his arm, leaning into his side. "I can't go back and pretend everything is normal."

"I'm not asking you to. I'm saying go back before things get worse."

"How did I screw this up so badly?"

Jack had wondered the same thing at times, but he wouldn't admit that. "It was a swing and a miss, Aves. But it doesn't matter. Let's just go forward from here."

The sun burst through the clouds now, making 45 degrees feel tolerable as they continued their tour. With the day warming, they walked through a city park, stopping for fish and chips at a street vendor and eating on the park lawn. All evidence of the snow was gone and kids ran around in pants and t-shirts, obviously used to this climate. Jack and Ava laid back on the grass and let the sunlight warm them.

"Maybe I don't ever have to go home," Ava said sleepily, with an arm over her eyes. "Let's be gypsies and traipse through Europe."

Jack laughed. "I've heard homelessness isn't as glamorous as it seems."

She only hummed in response but he could see a smile on her lips.

When they were ready to leave, Ava gave Jack the choice between another castle, a historic district, or a botanical garden. Jack picked the gardens, based on the amount of effort required—Ava was more exhausted than she would admit.

"Are you sure?" he asked again. "Don't push yourself too hard. We can just hang out."

"Of course I'm sure," she said as he helped her stand. "I want to make the trip worth it for you."

"I didn't come expecting anything, Aves."

She studied him for a moment, with an unreadable expression. "I still don't get it. How are you here? This isn't like you."

Jack shrugged. "Maybe it is now."

Ava reached up to his hair and brushed off a leaf.

"That was my souvenir," Jack said with a frown.

A laugh lit her face. It was the brightest he had seen her yet. "That was such a dad joke. Let's go before you say anything worse." She grabbed his hand and tugged him towards the street.

If lame jokes made her smile like that, he would come up with a thousand more.

Chapter 27

After incessant prompting from Jack, Ava called her parents Sunday night. He was right, they didn't care about wasting a semester. They wanted her to come home. Home beckoned like a lighthouse; simultaneously calling her in and warning her away. The decision was impossible.

There was only one thing she knew for certain: she couldn't face Benjamin on Monday morning. His rage would be far worse than being ignored. She skipped classes, to Jack's protest, but he was skipping for her, so Ava finally won without having to admit the real reason. Molly let Ava take her car, and they drove out to Loch Lomond and Trossachs National Park. Driving through the area with Jack, Ava hated to imagine leaving this beautiful place early.

The drive had to end before either were ready though. She had an appointment with professor Garcia that afternoon. As she drove into campus, her stomach sank. The sight of her dorm building ate away at her. The thought of running into Benj or Oliver on campus made her want to throw up. Actually, there were plenty of reasons to leave early.

Ava asked Jack to walk with her to the meeting. She told him she wanted to show him the campus and the buildings. Not that he was playing bodyguard.

The walk through campus was eternal. Any tall male with dark hair that passed by put her on edge, every muscle tensed for fight or flight, though Ava knew she would only freeze. The stress and adrenaline had her body vibrating by the time they reached the architecture building. Somewhere along the way she had stopped talking, stopped pointing out buildings. She didn't have any words now.

Jack moved towards a stone bench outside of the building and Ava grabbed his hand. The entire TGU group could be inside those doors. She wasn't going in alone. Jack raised an eyebrow at her but followed her in silence.

When they got to Garcia's temporary office, Ava asked Jack to wait for her in the hallway. She knew she was acting weird and owed him an explanation. But she couldn't give one right now.

Ava stumbled through the story to Garcia. She was… sick. And her parents wanted her to come home. He stood against his desk with his arms crossed and his head down, focused, taking in her broken sentences and questions.

"You can probably finish a couple of the classes online," he said. "But the other two… Your grades have been slipping. You might be better off taking an incomplete than finishing them."

It was more than she had hoped for. "Would they really let me? Finish online? I would hate to waste everything."

"These things happen, Ava. Probably more often than you realize." Ava wasn't sure if he was talking about going home early, or the incident she refused to discuss, but the blush she'd been wearing since walking into his office deepened. Regardless of whether he had the details right, he pitied her, which was both vindicating and shameful. Turning to study the calendar on his desk, he silently counted out weeks. "The final decision is up to your instructors, but I can contact them about it. They should understand."

"Am I… Is this a mistake?" she asked, finally sinking into the wooden chair in front of the desk. "I should stay, shouldn't I?"

"What would it take to get you through the next five weeks of classes?" Garcia asked.

"I have no idea." The only answer that came to mind was Rosie's: *a bevvy*.

"There might be some consequences," Garcia said. "You could lose some financial aid. But five weeks can be a very long time when you're dealing with mental health issues away from home."

"So long," Ava mumbled.

Garcia stood and paced to the small window. "Ava, if I may, I think you might be better off finishing the classes online. I think I failed you this semester, I'm sorry."

"You're failing me?" her voice squeaked like a preteen boy.

"No, goodness no." He chuckled. "No. I mean, I failed to manage the group well. I didn't realize how much bullying was going on until too late."

Ava's cheeks were burning. He obviously meant Sloane, but thinking of it as bullying was humiliating. Wasn't she too old for that?

"And I should have sent you for more help after… the midterm. I know you said you were fine, but I don't think that was true."

Far from true. She hated it. "Yeah… I think I want to go home." And accept that she was a child after all.

Garcia sat at his desk and they worked out the details. He sent emails to her professors and the study abroad coordinator at TGU. Then he sent her a referral for TGU's counseling center. Ava left his office with a new weight: the looming mountain of home. Would it really be any better?

Ava led Jack the long way back, pointing out buildings on the half-hearted campus tour. They had just reached her room when her phone rang. Garcia was calling.

Both interior design professors immediately agreed to Ava finishing online. The study abroad coordinator had dropped the two architecture courses and was updating her status already. She was cleared to leave.

Ava held herself together through the conversation. The moment she hung up, she sank to the floor, as unwanted tears blurred her vision. Jack sat next to her and pulled her into his side. "Aves?"

The tears had to run their course, shed mostly against his shoulder, before she could answer. Numbness set in, with a headache to cover the heartache. "It's official. I'm a failure."

"No, you're not." Jack kissed the top of her head. It was so sweet and unlike him, a few more tears escaped.

Ava brought her hands to his arms and pressed them around her, willing him to stay there as long as possible. It pushed the friends-only rules, but she would be back to the old rules soon enough. She could break one more while she was here. And his arms were a better home than the one she had to return to.

• • •

"What did Rosie say?" Jack asked, flipping through a stack of papers next to Ava as they packed her side of the dorm.

"She was livid. Angry fairy dust all over the place. And she blames you."

"I can handle that." Jack passed two interior design papers to her. He put the rest of his stack in a trash bag.

"She wants to go out tonight. One last hoorah to say goodbye."

Jack reached for the last pile. "Do you want to?"

Ava shrugged. "I guess I pictured it happening that way. But nothing has happened the way I thought it would."

"We can go if you want. Just, maybe with a drink limit."

"Obviously." Ava pushed him. "It might sound weird to you, but I want to end on a better note than what happened Friday."

"Maybe a short hoorah."

"Maybe. Far from campus."

"Why far?"

Ava only shook her head. She pulled out a bin from the bookcase with hats, scarves and gloves. "Will you grab the clothes in the closet? My stuff is on the left."

The closet burst open, clothes fighting each other for air. There was no dividing point, so he started with the far left, shoving the clothes back. A few hangers fell off the rod, joining a pile on the floor. Jack bent down, one shirt he recognized as Ava's, and he tossed it to her. There were a couple more shirts that looked more like Rosie. And underneath those, a sparkling black dress he had seen in a picture.

"This is yours, right?" He held it out. No reply. Jack poked his head around the closet door frame at Ava and repeated the question.

She stared at him. "Throw it away."

"Are you serious? This thing looks expensive." He turned it over, looking for the problem.

Ava stood, looking at him like he held a snake. "Throw it away, Jack."

"You looked great in it." More like drop dead gorgeous in the birthday photos.

Ava snatched the dress, breaking the hanger with the force of it. She shoved it in a trash bag. "I said throw it away."

"Wow, okay. Since when are you the kind of person who can only wear an outfit once?" Surely Rosie or somebody else could wear it at least.

"Shut up. I'm serious. Stop talking about it."

Jack surrendered and proceeded cautiously through the rest, pulling out clothes and waiting for the next item to be trashed. Nothing else was. Ava's half of the room was almost entirely in two suitcases when Rosie showed up.

"Hey lovers," she said, ripping off her coat, scarf, hat and gloves and tossing them on her bed. She pecked a kiss on the cheek to both of them. She wrinkled her nose at Jack. "I can't believe I'm letting you steal Miss Texas."

"I'm not stealing anything," Jack said.

Rosie hummed a disapproving sound. "So, dinner first? All together or just the two of ye? Meet up after?"

Jack looked to Ava. He had his preferences, but this was her decision.

"Dinner all together sounds good," she said. Not his preference.

Rosie stepped into the bathroom and banged on the attached room's door. Another girl's voice sounded, and she stepped into the room, tall and pale, with short dark hair.

"—Why can't I invite Harris?" she asked Rosie before she saw Jack. She turned on a huge smile for him. "Hello, you must be Jack."

Jack shook her hand as Ava introduced him to Molly. He tried to find a way to step back in the tiny room as the three girls started arguing about who else could be invited. Apparently Ava was fine with inviting Molly's boyfriend but not Rosie's, and it made Rosie mad.

"Harris is actually nice," Ava whispered. "And if Callan goes, how do I know his friends won't show up?"

"Nice, huh? For your information, 'Callan's friends,'" she said with air quotes while shooting a devilish grin to Jack. "Are no different than the immutable Jack."

"Yes, they are," Ava said.

"Fine," Rosie said, lifting her chin. "No boys then."

"I'm not going without Jack," Ava said.

"What about Cowboy?" Molly asked.

Rosie eagerly recounted the slap story and Jack tried to hide his eavesdropping by paging through more papers. A red-headed girl, Liliana, joined them, somehow finding space in the small room. She shook Jack's hand and held onto it too long.

"Miss Texas, are all the boys back home this cute?" Liliana asked. "Why did we even bother you with our Scots?"

Rosie and Molly laughed.

"You guys are vultures," Ava said dryly.

"Well, this has been fun," Jack said, squeezing past Liliana to stand next to Ava again. "I'm hungry. Are we eating anytime soon?"

"Let's go to Finnigan's," Rosie said. Without any warning, she pulled her shirt off her head.

At the first flash of skin, Jack whipped his head away and found Ava's face inches from his. He raised his eyebrows at her and she laughed.

"Sorry, I should have warned you about her," she whispered. "Rosie—there's a bathroom for a reason."

Rosie laughed as she rummaged through the closet next to him. "The innocent Jack, then."

Maybe not innocent. Nor immune. Intelligent, perhaps. Jack used the excuse to study Ava's face. They weren't usually this close. Specks of gold flecked her brown eyes in a way he somehow hadn't noticed before. Too soon, she gave him the all-clear.

Rosie had changed into a strappy red dress that practically screamed bars and beers. She tossed Ava a sheer white top and Ava tossed it back. "No, thanks."

"Och, 'mon hen, ye packed yer only decent tops. And ah ken ye won't wear a dress." She tossed another shirt, covered in black lace.

Ava analyzed it for a minute, her eyes flicked up to Jack. He aimed for complete indifference but there wasn't much else to look at in the room and he was failing. "Fine." Ava headed into the bathroom to change.

Rosie shrugged at Jack and put on a fake pout. "Sorry, Jack, I tried to get her in something sexier."

He shook his head and pulled out his phone, wanting to escape the estrogen-charged room. The girls danced through the bathroom with hair tools and makeup brushes. He didn't expect Ava to be part of it, but she blended right in. Jack realized his white sweater and black puffer jacket were about to be completely outdone.

Ava came back into the room wearing jeans and the black shirt, its sleeves and sides cut out with lace. She sat on the suitcase below Jack and leaned her head onto his lap. He wasn't sure if the affectionate side of her was a new-Ava thing or just a Scotland-Ava thing. Hopefully the former. Jack rested an arm on Ava's side. The lace proved a minimal barrier between his hand and her skin, though, so he quickly adjusted his position.

Ava complained that Rosie would take another lifetime to get ready and Rosie yelled something incomprehensibly Scottish from the bathroom. Once everyone was finally ready, Jack was starving. Rosie and Liliana led the pack north, away from campus.

After a surprisingly enjoyable dinner, they walked back to a bar they had passed on the way. Ava said he needed a proper Scotch before leaving and ordered them each a whisky neat.

"To quitting," Ava said, lifting her glass to the table. The girls responded with a mixture of laughs, pouts, and raised beers. Ava waited for Jack.

He lifted his glass. "To beginning." Amused, he watched Ava sip her whisky. She could probably drink him under the table, if given the chance.

Rosie ordered a round of shots for the table. Jack turned his down and Ava followed suit. Rosie pouted for a moment before sending the shots off to two guys at the bar. A beer and a shot were all it took for Liliana to start touching his arm and knee. Jack leaned away and finished his whisky. "You ready to go?" he asked Ava.

She frowned. "It's early."

"It's after ten. Our flight leaves in a few hours."

Ava glanced at the front door of the bar for the hundredth time that night. Waiting for someone? She looked back at Jack and shook her head. "I'm not ready."

They sat through another round of gossip, name dropping, and stories of college antics. Nearly all the stories were alcohol-fueled. Ava quickly steered them away from anything involving her name. Half an hour later, she initiated the departure. Ava hugged each of the girls, hanging onto Rosie the longest. They were whispering various things to each other. Jack stood and pulled his jacket on. When Ava turned away from Rosie, she looked ready to cry. She slipped into her coat and grabbed his hand. Jack squeezed it and used his other hand to wave to the group of girls.

They stepped outside into the cold. "I know you don't get it, but she's my friend," Ava said, a quiet crack in her voice.

Jack interlaced their fingers. "I get it."

Their walk back was quiet, but he wouldn't force her to talk.

"It'll be another year before I can go out and get a drink again," Ava said.

"They took off the age limit for water and coffee back in the states."

"Jack—" she punched his arm.

"There are other ways to have fun."

"I guess." When they turned onto the street that led to her building, Ava stopped short. "What am I going to say to everybody at home?"

"Don't say anything if you don't want to. Being liked isn't the most important thing in life."

"You would know."

Jack poked her in the ribs, she laughed and tugged his hand forward until they were within view of her building. She stopped again. "I can walk the rest by myself."

"It's right there, Aves, I'll walk you." He wasn't leaving her on the dark street.

"I'm okay." She turned to him with a smile and tugged on his jacket zipper. At that moment, he knew this was Scotland Ava. It wasn't the real Ava, the new one.

"It's dark—"

"I'm fine. My walks are usually safer alone than with a guy anyway."

Jack stilled. "What?"

Ava's laugh was light. "Never mind. Just go. I'll see you at six?"

"Bright and early." His voice sounded dry. His mouth matched it. "Aves, are you okay?"

"Yeah. Goodnight, Jack." She stepped back and gave him a small wave. Jack didn't move until she made it to her building. They would be home soon. And everything would be different.

Chapter 28

The first night back in her room in Texas, Ava woke with a start. Her heart raced and she couldn't remember where she was. She flicked on the lamp and forced her brain to accept that she was at home. After three flights and 18 hours of traveling, the return felt like a dream.

She had taken a walk of shame across her parents' front lawn, expecting the worst. But the big family drama never happened. There had been a late dinner, forced happiness and light talk about the weather. It was like the last three months hadn't even happened. Like nothing had changed, but everything had.

Ava woke again. This time she hunted through the sheets, looking for the one thing that would help her sleep. It wasn't there. Ava hopped out of bed and dumped out her suitcases, searching for the black fleece, before she remembered Jack had it now. With a sigh, she climbed back into the sheets, waking again and again. Each time sinking a little deeper into her reality.

By the time sunlight overtook the lamp, she was still exhausted. Ava laid in bed for hours. The room held her down, burying her in the clutter of another person. Someone who had pictures of friends on the walls, awards and certificates framed on the desk, and a porcelain angel on the bookcase. Someone who disapproved of the girl in the bed now. The Texas spring sun hit her bed, warming it beyond comfort. The quilt closed around her throat. Ava threw it off the bed and shivered under the sheets.

At noon, her mom knocked on the door and asked if she wanted any food. Ava turned her down. It all tasted like paper, anyway.

When she finally crawled out of bed, her body ached. The pain radiated through her bones. She needed to do something. Anything. Her eyes landed on her suitcase and the piles she had pulled from it last night. She began unpacking and organizing. It took the entire day.

To be polite, Ava joined the family for dinner. Her parents asked a few light questions about Scottish scenery and cuisine. Ava might have believed their act if it weren't for Joshua and Ezra: they were too quiet. The chatter about sports, band practice, and high school drama was noticeably missing. Everybody listened to Ava for the first time ever; and she had nothing to say.

Bed was her reward for making it through the day. Ava craved the peace of sleep. She wrapped herself in the plush cream blanket and slept. Jet lag woke her at 3AM.

Friday she hid behind online classes. She needed to bring the grade up to justify staying in class. But the words in the textbook swam and the quiz module online looked like it had been written in a foreign language. Ava stared at the screen. She had been smart once, right?

Unable to handle any more homework, she stretched and paced the room. It was cluttered. Crowded. Filled with crap. Ava slipped downstairs unseen and grabbed two large trash bags. She needed breathing space. New space.

Camp t-shirts, childish mementos, and a dozen books and journals filled the first bag in a matter of minutes. Anything that screamed *you failed* went in. The angel with the broken wing went in and out of the bag multiple times before Ava settled for hiding it in a drawer.

She took all the dresses out of her closet and shoved them into a bag to give to Talia. Folding the quilt on the bed, she tucked it out of sight. Next, she stripped the walls, tossing photos or stashing them in a desk drawer.

By Saturday afternoon, the room was naked, with room to breathe. The holes on the gray walls cried, puffing out plaster. That night she skipped dinner. The cleaning had left her exhausted and numb. Nobody said anything. They were probably relieved.

Ava was ready to go to bed before dark. But if she slept now, it would be restless and interrupted. So she forced herself to stay awake and earn the night of unconsciousness. She scrolled through her phone, logging back onto social media after weeks away from it. Rosie, Molly and Liliana had gone to Scotland's east coast, where dramatic cliffs dropped into the sea. Benj posted a picture of half the TGU students in a bar in Glasgow. Everybody was still there, succeeding at everything she had failed at.

A knock at the door distracted her. It was Ezra, the third Sanford and the one most like her. He stepped into the room without waiting for an invitation. He whistled as he looked around the room. "Mom and dad wouldn't let me take this room all semester because it had your stuff. And now you throw it all away, anyway. Freakin' sisters."

Ava smiled. "Tired of sharing with Joshua?"

"It smells like a cologne store in there. I probably have lung cancer."

"Gross."

"He's gonna ask a girl out this weekend."

"No, he is not," Ava said. Her younger brother would beat her to having a real relationship. It hurt more than she could admit to Ezra.

"Yep. And she's a cheerleader." Ava shuddered in mock horror. Ezra plopped his gangly self onto the foot of her bed and leaned back on his arms. "I'm glad you're back."

Ava reached over and tugged on the too-long dark hair that fell in his eyes. Only four years younger, she still remembered playing like he was her baby. She still saw him that way. "Me too." It was good to have him back. Even if there was still an intangible ocean between them.

Ezra recounted high school stories while Ava played wise advisor. When he eventually left, it was actually a decent hour to sleep. And she slept the best she had yet.

But then it was Sunday. And the Sanford family revolved around Sundays.

"I'm not going," Ava said when her mom stood in her doorway, asking if she wanted a ride.

"Why not?"

"I feel sick." She'd hidden on thin lies all week long, but she would need a good one to skip church.

"Honey, I've raised three children, I can tell when they're faking being sick."

"I have horrible cramps, mom." It was a scapegoat. One that worked well in a family that was mostly male. Her mom paused. She started to say something but changed her mind and left.

The next week passed in a daze. Jack texted a few times and invited her to hang out. The risk of running into someone she knew was too high, so she turned him down. She made it out of her room for a visit to the TGU counseling center that she told her parents was school-related. It had been an exhausting experience. Talia had stopped by unannounced once. She had filled Ava's room with her personality and presence. Ava did her best to laugh at bad jokes, chat about every random topic and take silly selfies with ugly filters. It was a beautiful distraction, but she was empty by the time it ended.

And then Sunday came again. It always did.

This week, Ava planned to claim a headache. But her dad showed up at the doorway this time.

"Avie, you're not sick." He stepped into the room. "Why aren't you coming to church?"

She didn't want to hurt her dad. He embodied love; but love wasn't enough to make her face the church—the college students. "I don't want to see anybody."

He sat on the bed next to her. "It won't be that bad."

"Yes it will, dad. I know what they've said."

"So go and show them it wasn't true."

Ava wanted to choke. He shouldn't be this confident in her. Too much of it was true. "I'm sorry, I'm not going."

"Look, coming back from time overseas can be hard—"

"This isn't reverse culture shock."

"Then what is it?"

Ava shook her head. It didn't make sense. Her dad was a family counselor. So many others went to him for help but she couldn't bring herself to say a word.

He sighed. "There are still expectations here, Avie. If you live in my house, you go to my church."

"Then I'll move." The words were out now, taking on their own form, and she would live and bleed by them.

"Where?" His voice stayed level, but she had thrown him off. "How are you going to afford that? We're not paying for you to live somewhere else."

"I'm looking for a job. I'm not going to church."

"Ava…" He didn't have anything else to say. Neither did she. Ava reached for her laptop and headphones. Her dad hesitated at the door. "I love you."

The choke sat in her throat as Ava opened the resume document she had started. She had to finish it. She had to be on her own. Even if all the jobs sounded exhausting, paid minimum wage and required too much experience. She had to prove she could live on her own without becoming a complete mess. Maybe then she could face people.

The house had been empty for half an hour when someone pounded on the door. Church should have started 10 minutes ago. Ava hopped up and peeked out the window to find a familiar truck parked in the front. With a groan, she pulled a hoodie over her tank top and tripped down the stairs. She yanked the door open. "What are you doing here?"

"Come to church with me," Jack said.

"Did my dad send you?"

"Nobody sent me. But hiding isn't going to help."

Jack reached his hand to her shoulder and Ava shoved it away. "Yes it will. Things will die down in the summer. Half the students will leave."

He stuck his hand back into his pocket. "Come on, Aves. Why'd you come home if you're just going to stay in your room?"

"You tell me. You're the one who made me come back."

"I didn't make you do anything."

"And I'm not going to let you."

Jack sighed and swayed back on his heels, glancing towards the street before turning back to Ava. "I'll be there with you."

"You're not enough."

The words were physical and knocked Jack back a step. "What?"

She instantly regretted them. No one else's opinion of her was worth hurting him. "Jack—"

"No," he cut her off. "Of course I'm not."

He turned and walked away. The second man she had seen walk away from her this morning. Ava retreated, closing the front door before Jack reached his truck. She slid down the door and sat on the cold tile, staring at the empty house. *"If I have all faith… but have not love, I am nothing."*[20] She had neither. What was less than nothing?

She did have one thing: the ability to make people walk away, to make them hate her.

• • •

Only the Sanfords knew why he was late. Jack had been there early today to help set up. He had seen Rebecca's red eyes. Her smile quickly covered it as she shook hands and welcomed volunteers. But after a few words with Micah, Jack had decided to give it a shot. It was a mistake.

"You're not enough."

Worship had ended by the time he got back to church. Rather than joining the college kids, Jack stood with Isaac at the back of the auditorium. Micah stepped up to preach and his eyes locked with Jack's in a split-second realization that Ava still wasn't there. But even at home, she wasn't there. Not really. She wasn't anywhere.

The moment they had pulled up to her house after the flight back, she had shut down. Closed off. Apparently even her parents were on the chopping block. Maybe he did make her come back too soon. Maybe it had been the wrong thing to do. Somehow she was just as far away now as she had been in Scotland. And angrier.

She had a point: summer break would help kill off the thrill of rumors. But what she didn't know was that every Sunday she skipped made them worse.

When the service ended, he hung back as the auditorium cleared out. Val stopped as she passed by him. "Staying?"

"I'm gonna help clean up."

She shifted the purse on her shoulder. She had been cold towards him since the "just friends" conversation. "How was Scotland?"

Jack hadn't posted about it, but enough people had noticed his absence from work and church to find out, anyway. "Quick visit."

"And Ava came back with you?"

"She came back on her own." At least, he'd thought she had. He wasn't sure anymore. The auditorium was nearly empty and Jack started picking up left-behind notes and coffee cups. Val stuck with him, cleaning alongside him.

"Why isn't she coming back to church?"

"Maybe she's still jet lagged."

Val stopped and straightened, waiting for Jack to face her. "Jack, are you sure you don't want to talk about it?"

About the rumors she was eagerly trying to gather information for? "No, thanks. Really, Val. Give her some space." Like he probably should have.

She sighed and stuffed a napkin into a coffee cup. "I guess you're not coming to lunch."

He couldn't. He didn't have the willpower. Talia was handling that for now. And if he couldn't do it, how could he blame Ava? Jack shook his head.

"Going to see Ava?"

"No." That much was honest.

Val hummed and raised a single eyebrow before turning to leave.

Jack finished cleaning every row while the band cleared equipment off the stage and someone started a vacuum. Micah made his way back into the room and silently joined Jack in tying up trash bags.

They were at the dumpster at the back of the building before Micah spoke. "Didn't go well?"

"I guess I did the wrong thing," Jack said. "She blames me now."

Micah crossed his arms and seemed to read the entire story on Jack's face. "It's not your fault. She's crushed by guilt, failure, maybe. I think she's just looking for someone to carry some of that blame."

Jack wanted to be a good friend, but if she was only looking for an enemy, he wasn't going to be there. "I can't be that person."

"Don't be. Somebody else already handled it all a couple thousand years ago. She has to rediscover that herself."

Chapter 29

Ava
I was a jerk. I'm sorry.

The second text this week. The first had gotten lost between intramural tournaments and studying for finals. This one came while he was supervising the rock wall at the gym. He wasn't allowed to text here. Jack stuck the phone back in his pocket. He couldn't fix this. No matter how much he wanted to, he wasn't enough to handle it all for her.

It was a busy night, with students burning off end-of-semester stress. When the gym closed, it took longer than normal to clean everything. Natalie and Jack stacked weights, shut off televisions, and did a quick sweep through the locker rooms. Natalie jetted out the door the minute they finished.

After locking up, Jack headed to the truck. Several yards away, he realized someone was sitting on the back tailgate. Someone he always wanted to see, even if it meant a long night. Bracing himself, Jack rounded the truck and pulled himself onto the tailgate next to her.

"Heart attack on a bun." Ava passed him a paper bag. "With extra jalapeños."

The tiredness evaporated and Jack chuckled as he pulled the triple-meat hamburger out of the bag. The new Ava still remembered his order. Jack passed her the fries and started on the burger.

"Natalie gives out your schedule pretty easily," she said. "Probably would have given me your social security if I asked."

"Planning to steal my identity?"

"And be the new Jack Shields with a Pottery Barn credit card."

Jack laughed and shook his head. It was so easy to slip back into joking with her. To act like everything was normal for a moment; but he never knew when the moment would end.

Their legs swung over the edge of the tailgate and Ava kicked Jack's foot. "You're not texting me back."

"This week has been crazy busy."

"I'm sorry about what I said on Sunday. I didn't mean it. I was freaking out."

"It's okay."

"No, it's not. Of course it's not. Please say you'll forgive me."

Jack wanted to hug her, to hold on to her before she disappeared again, but this wasn't Scotland. He went for an elbow nudge instead. "Of course."

"I'm being a terrible friend," Ava said. "But just cause I'm miserable doesn't mean I should drag you down too."

"I don't want you to be miserable. Tell me how to help." She only shrugged. "Aves… Have you thought about talking to anybody about it?"

She nodded slowly. "Yeah. I have, actually. At the university's counseling center. Professor Garcia suggested it, maybe for leaving early or something."

"How'd that go?"

Ava studied him for a minute before leaning back in the truck and grabbing a basketball. "The lights are still on."

"The courts technically close at nine."

"I don't see a fence."

Jack laughed. "I'm sorry, who are you again?" But he didn't wait for an answer. He hopped to the ground and lifted Ava down unnecessarily. She landed next to him and spun away quickly. This was Texas.

The night was warm and unusually still. The sound of the basketball hitting the court reverberated, but no one was around to hear it. They shot baskets randomly, without tracking points. After a few minutes of teasing each other's worst shots, she finally answered his question. "Counseling wasn't as bad as I thought it would be."

Jack jogged after a missed three-pointer. "They made me see one at school when my mom died."

"Did it help?"

"I didn't think so at the time." Jack threw the ball to Ava. "But looking back, it did."

"Nobody gets it." She made a shot from the free throw line. "Nobody knows what it was like over there."

"They might never get it." Jack caught the ball and dribbled it up the court. "Most people don't know what it's like to lose your mom as a kid. But that doesn't mean you give up on people. Or God."

Ava attempted to steal the ball, and Jack spun on her. "I made the shot, it's mine—" She grabbed his arm.

"Foul," Jack shouted. "Major foul."

"These are street rules," Ava said, yanking the ball from him.

"More like no rules," Jack said, poking her in the ribs.

Ava laughed and missed her shot from the side of the court. "That was your fault."

Jack made the rebound; he couldn't help smiling. "I missed this."

"Me too."

They played until two guys walked onto the court and started a game on the other half. They invited Jack and Ava to play two-on-two but Ava declined before Jack could. With a silent look, they agreed to head out.

"See? We're not the only ones breaking your nine-o'clock rule," Ava said as they walked to the parking lot.

"Guess not." Jack tossed the basketball into the bed of the truck. "Where's your car?"

"The lot was full when I got here. I'm down by the fields." She gestured towards the dark street that ran to the intramural fields.

Jack opened his door. "Get in." But Ava didn't follow suit.

She fidgeted with the bottom of her UE t-shirt, twisting it in her fingers. "I can walk. It's not that far."

The moment of normality ended. Jack leaned back against the truck with his hands in his pockets. "Aves… Why do you not trust me anymore? What did I do?"

"What?" Her eyes met his. "I do trust you."

"Really?"

He watched her, partially hidden in shadows, debating her words. "I think it's me I don't trust."

Somehow, that made sense. Jack straightened and extended his hand, not daring to hope she would take it. But she did and stepped closer to him. "Can you trust me enough for a ride to your car?" he asked, resisting the urge to touch her hair. They were already on thin ice.

Ava finally nodded. Jack kept her hand in his as they walked around the truck. He opened her door, and she climbed in. Jack let out a silent sigh, relieved at the sight of something that used to be completely normal.

Two minutes later, they pulled up to her car—alone in the dark parking lot. Ava didn't move to get out though. "I got a job. More like an internship, but it pays decently."

Blindside. "Really? Where?"

"It's with a wedding venue just outside of town. Doing event design, working with the florists and stuff."

"That sounds perfect for you."

"I mean, it's not exactly interior design, but I think it'll be great, anyway. I just can't believe they hired me."

"Of course they did, Aves. You're great at that stuff."

A smile lit her face too briefly. "Hopefully I am. I start next week."

"Through the summer?"

"It might extend into the fall," Ava said, staring out the window. "Or else I'll find something else in the fall. I'm moving out."

Blindsided twice. "What? You just got home."

"I want to be on my own. And do it better this time."

"Are you sure about this?" he asked. She nodded. "Where are you going to live?"

"I don't know yet. I wanted to get a place with Talia but she's stuck in her lease."

"You could wait. Save up."

"I can't. I want my own place. Besides, I have to go to church until I move out. Part of my plea bargain."

Jack said nothing. Her mind was obviously made up, and there was no point in disagreeing. Ava opened her door and Jack got out too, crossing to her side. "So you'll be there this Sunday?" he asked, secretly hoping it would take weeks to find a place. At least long enough that she would want to come back on her own.

"Yeah. Kill me now."

"You'll be fine, I promise."

The streetlamp reflected in her eyes as she looked at him. Eyes that were dark, rich, and full of doubt. This time, he didn't stop himself before reaching a hand up to brush her hair back. The second he did, she was Scotland Ava, stepping into his arms, with an unspoken promise that they didn't have to lose all of this.

• • •

Sunday came. It always came again. Ava spent the entire morning getting ready for church. She chose the least noticeable outfit possible: jeans and a nondescript black tee. There wasn't time for breakfast. The thought of going back to church had tied her stomach into knots since yesterday, anyway.

Never in her life had she missed church more than a couple of weeks in a row. Now she pulled up to Grace after four months away. The school building where they met was too brown and basic to deserve an architectural name; nothing like the beautiful cathedrals in Edinburgh. Beautiful but hollow.

She had hoped Jack would offer to go with her, but he never did. It was probably too embarrassing to be seen with her. She was alone. So she timed her entrance carefully—three minutes before the service started. Late enough that she could head straight to her seat without socializing, early enough that there weren't too many people in the auditorium to see her.

She took a side door to bypass the welcome team and coffee table. But the doors into the auditorium were guarded by greeters. Ava pulled her phone out and buried her attention in it as she slipped into the nearest door. The greeter was someone new who didn't recognize her.

With the auditorium darkened, and her head down, Ava made it to the front row without being noticed. Not the best row for hiding, but it would be the least conspicuous. Sanfords were expected to sit with their parents or their friends. And Ava wouldn't be joining the college students. Her brothers were off with friends. She would be the one and only Sanford descendant at the front today, like a child.

With vague awareness and a refusal to lift her head, Ava mentally noted the sounds of people entering the building. Acute senses told her when Jack got there. He was talking to someone.

Ava's mom slipped into the row next to her and squeezed her hand. "I didn't even see you come in."

Her dad joined them shortly after worship started and stood on the other side of Ava. For a brief moment, the two pillars on either side of her lifted the weight off. Where she expected suffocation, she found breath instead.

Ava sang along out of habit and politeness. She studied it all, analyzing the changes in the worship band—the new bassist she didn't know and the college girl now on piano. They had changed the lighting set up too.

The third and last song began, and the weight came crashing back down. It was her favorite worship song—had been. Surely her dad had chosen it; probably as a kindness, but now it was more like an attack. Ava stared silently at the words on the screen. They didn't sink in anymore. As the song came to an end, her dad squeezed her shoulder and kissed her head before gathering his Bible and notes. At least he wasn't ashamed to acknowledge her.

Micah Sanford never taught topically. He always taught through the Bible and today was no different, though Ava wondered how his series was timed so perfectly. She wasn't sure if the message of forgiveness was aimed at her or the congregation. It seemed to be both.

"Therefore I tell you, her sins, which are many, are forgiven—for she loved much."[21]

Every time she had read the story before, she read it from the perspective of the disciples. The ones sitting next to Jesus, learning about forgiveness and love as moral ideas. She had never pictured herself as the woman on the ground, Mary, wetting Jesus' feet with tears. The one being used as an example.

Yet in the verses surrounding it, she found more of the same. The wrong roles, over and over. She had seen Jesus as a peer she nodded alongside and cheered for, but now she found herself at his feet. Stories she thought she knew by heart she found to be strangers.

The pastor's kid, completely unworthy, the marked and ashamed one, standing here, in front of everyone. A Sanford who couldn't carry the name. A Sanford who couldn't even remember how to pray.

When her dad finished the sermon, the worship team came up for another song. Ava wanted to stay for it. She wanted to feel at home here. But she didn't. Because everyone standing behind her also knew she was unworthy. If she waited too long, she would be trapped by them.

Without a word, Ava slipped out of the row. Keeping her head down, she ducked to the far side of the room, opposite of where the college kids sat, and made her way to the back. She pushed through the door, gasping for air she had lost.

"Ava Claire."

Ava spun around at the sound of her dad's voice. He looked at her like a daughter, but he didn't know her. She was neither a peer nor a daughter. Another wave of guilt slammed into her. Ava pressed a hand to her mouth and shook her head.

He folded her into a hug. The dam she had built during the service quickly crumbled and a sob broke free. Two auditorium doors opened as the song inside ended and her dad pulled her into a side room. He whispered prayers for her as they stood in the quiet room.

"Stop, it's okay," Ava said, pushing him back. "Go greet everybody."

"They'll be fine." His refusal to leave only refreshed the guilt.

"I'm sorry, dad," she choked out without explanation. "I'm so sorry."

He was unshaken. And eventually she felt the weight lifting again. Until he held her by the shoulders and ducked his head to look her straight in the eyes.

"Avie, nothing is too big for God to forgive. Or redeem."

Ava dropped her eyes and stepped away to pull a tissue from her purse. Her throat was dry and hoarse when she spoke again. "Why did y'all name me Ava? For Eve? Because that's a terrible namesake."

Though the question came out of nowhere, her dad took it in stride. "When did Eve get her name?"

Ava's brow pinched, not understanding the question.

"It was after the fall. After they brought death into the world, she was the promise of life. Her name, 'to live,' showed faith in God's redemptive plan."

Ava twisted the tissue in her hands. If God had a redemptive plan for Ava, he hadn't revealed it yet. "There's tear spots all over your shirt," she said quietly.

"You should see your makeup," her dad said with a grin.

The door behind them opened before she could reply, and her dad wrapped his arm around her protectively. Isaac Torres popped in and immediately backed out with an apology.

"You should probably get back out there," Ava said.

"Will you wait and get lunch with us? Just you, me and your mom."

"Sure." Her stomach was unknotting and now she was starving. "Italian?"

"You got it."

"Sorry about your shirt." Ava swiped at the smears of mascara on his striped button up.

"Worth it." He kissed her forehead. "I love you."

When he was gone, Ava rested her forehead against the cool wall for several minutes. There was so much she needed to ask forgiveness for, she was becoming quite experienced at it. And still had so far to go.

Chapter 30

As exhausting as a new job was, it proved a helpful distraction. Somebody else was counting on her to get out of bed each day, so she did. Even if it meant hours of socializing and forced smiles, it slowly began to bring her brain out of the fog.

Everyone's lives were carrying on. Only Ava had been left behind. It was her own fault. She had turned down invitations from both Jack and Talia. Work and online classes were all she had strength for. There was an upside to it: she finished the days exhausted enough to truly sleep. And sleep offered a few hours of escape.

When Sunday showed its ugly face again, she had been steeling herself up for it for three days. Ava planned to stick with the same routine as last time: arriving in time to walk straight to her seat at the front.

But this time, the greeter at the door was more observant. "Is that Ava Sanford?" A chipper voice sang out.

Ava's stomach sank and she debated pretending she hadn't heard, but it was too late now. She turned to see Val, all legs and blonde curls, in a floral sundress.

"Val," Ava said, painting on a smile. The fog suddenly blew back. Hadn't Val and Jack gone out together? Why hadn't Jack said anything about her? Were they still going out?

"I heard you were back." Val gave her a weak hug. "Did the semester end early in Scotland?"

Val instantly found the hole in her heart and began picking at it. Ava needed this conversation to end quickly. "No… I'm…"

Before she had a chance to finish with an excuse, Val waved to someone else. Ava glanced over her shoulder. Jack was walking in with two guys, one was his roommate and the other a new face. He waved back at Val and didn't seem to see Ava. He wouldn't. Associating with her here would make him look bad. The hole tore open wider.

"Sorry, I think I missed your answer," Val said with a smile that reminded Ava of the Cheshire Cat.

"I was just ready to come home."

"I'm sure you needed to," she said with a pout.

Ava gave her a tight smile and walked into the auditorium. The sound of laughs made her look back halfway down the aisle. Jack and the guys were talking to Val. Her heart was still spilling blood.

The music started the moment Ava made it to her seat. Her entry was too late. How many people had seen her come in? Was it dark enough to hide her shaking hands? Her mom was already in the front row and smiled at Ava. She wasn't sure if she managed to smile back. Panic crowded her mind and she couldn't reason it away. Music. Lyrics. Sing. She would be okay. If she left right after the service, she would be fine.

The music helped, cooling the raw edges of her soul. Her dad spoke through the parable of the sower. Once again, Ava identified with an entirely different cast in the story than she was supposed to. But somehow her dad still managed to speak hope into it.

When the sermon ended, the band resumed their positions for a closing song. Ava's dad rejoined her, putting an arm around her shoulders. She tried to sidestep it, but her mom stood too close, blocking her in. This was her only chance at a smooth exit—before the song ended. Turning to grab her purse, she bumped into her chair, knocking the purse through the gaps in the chairs and into the row behind her. Nancy Newton, a family friend who was more like a grandmother, picked it up and handed it to Ava with a big smile. She reached over the chair and hugged Ava as the song hit its final notes.

"It's so good to see you again, dear," Nancy said over the music. "How have you been?"

The lights came on in the auditorium and Ava was trapped. Her hands started shaking again. "I'm good," she said, painting the smile on again.

"How was your time abroad?" Nancy asked.

Out of the corner of her eye, she saw another family approaching. She was at the front with her parents; the worst, most popular spot to be after church.

"It was good," Ava said, relying on standby phrases instead of answers. If it was rote, she wouldn't have to think about it. But the answer picked at her every time she used it.

"Richard, look who's back." Nancy pulled her husband from his own conversation.

"Miss Ava Sanford," his voice boomed as he reached out a rough handshake. Ava cringed at its echo.

She tried to answer their questions with the same words: *good, fine, okay.* Her mother joined the conversation and started filling in the blanks.

"Well, she grew up on us while she was gone," her mom said with a light laugh. "She's looking for her own place now."

"Is that so?" Nancy said. "Our garage apartment will be available at the end of the month, if you're interested. We would be honored to have a Sanford stay with us."

Not this one. But Ava couldn't pass up the opportunity. Gaining courage, she asked for more information. It was a small studio over their garage, and she could actually afford the rent without a roommate.

"That sounds amazing," Ava said, hope sneaking into her. Ironically, her prayers to avoid church might be the fastest prayers ever answered.

"Come by this week and we'll show it to you," Richard said.

Ava arranged a time as her mom turned to talk to another family. A young couple was talking to her dad. She slipped around them to escape. Newfound confidence and excitement lasted up until the auditorium doors, where a horde of people blocked the exit. Students crammed around the coffee table just outside of the doors. Ava took a deep breath. Head down. Phone out. Walk through it.

"Hey girl," someone reached out and squeezed her shoulder without warning.

Reflexively, she pushed the hand back before she even saw whose it was—Fisher, one of the college guys. She had known him, but not well enough for him to touch her. Ava tried to step back but bumped into someone else—a girl from her small group last semester; she glanced at Ava without the slightest hint of recognition.

"Look who's back," Val said from the group around the coffee table and waved Ava in.

Whether she moved of her own accord or was jostled there, Ava couldn't say. It was a disconnected nightmare. Her heartbeat washed out the sounds. Ava focused on the faces. She knew them. Most of them. And she categorized them: friend or foe. More like fake friend or ignoring her. Some wouldn't look at her. A couple of them welcomed her back. And there was Jack, standing next to Val. Silent. Cold. He wasn't on her side here, not in front of everyone else. Without Jack, she couldn't do this.

Someone asked why she came back early. Ava gripped the purse strap running across her body, digging her fingernails into her palm. "Homesick for you guys." Ava forced a smile. It was met with a smattering of fake laughs. The words came from somewhere else as her mind searched for an escape route.

The girl next to her turned in towards the group, physically cutting Ava off. "Val, are we still doing barbecue for lunch?"

"Sure." Val turned her attention to a few others in the group and asked if they wanted to go. "Are you coming, Jack?"

Ava caught his eyes flit to hers before he turned back to Val and agreed to join them for lunch. The invite never came to Ava. The group was closing her out and taking Jack with them. This circle no longer included her. She should have left long ago.

A path to the side door opened and Ava spun towards it. Halfway there, she heard her name again. Madison, one of the freshman girls, was heading towards her. They had hung out a few times last semester.

"I'm glad you're back," Madison said with a smile. *Fake friend.*

"Thanks, me too."

"Listen, I heard you were having a hard time in Scotland. We should get together and talk about it." Madison's tone edged away from friendly.

"Thanks, but I'm doing pretty well." Ava worked to stay polite as she felt her stomach knot.

"Mmm. Well, listen, I was just thinking... You might want to reach out to Cassandra and apologize."

The rollercoaster dropped and her stomach jerked. "What?"

"Look, I'm friends with her, and this breakup was hard on her. I don't know what all you did, but it wasn't very Christ-like."

They had broken up? Because of the rumors? Christ-like? Nothing she had done was Christ-like. Bile rose to take the place of oxygen. "Madison, I didn't..."

Madison put her hands up. "It doesn't really matter. I just think it's the least you could do, don't you? After everything? Just take a step in the right direction."

Ava nodded absently, conceding to sins she never committed and others she never confessed. Madison gave her a fake smile before striding back to a group of girls. They stood there, talking in hushed voices as Ava attempted to force her numb legs into action.

When she finally made it outside, the hot May sun boiled her blood. Had Texas always been this hot? Had her blood turned Scottish? Her stomach twisted tighter. And tighter. And hotter. It pushed up and up. She needed to throw up, and the parking lot was a horrible place to do so. Too many people to see a Sanford do something unacceptable. But she couldn't make it back inside to a bathroom now. There were too many people everywhere.

Propelled by need, her legs rushed to her car. Tucked between the back of her car and the front of another, she threw up. She hadn't had breakfast, there wasn't much to lose, but liquid fought its way out. Ava stood and slumped over the hot metal of her car, desperately missing the cold of Scotland.

"Whoa, mija," Talia's voice was close, and Ava turned to see her shocked expression. "Are you okay?"

"Where were you?" Ava asked, angry and unsure of whom to trust. She reached into her car for a bottle of too-warm water to rinse her mouth.

"Volunteering in the nursery. Jack told me to go check on you. What happened?"

Jack. "Nothing."

"Then what's going on? You're not… You're not pregnant, are you?"

Ava spun on Talia. "What did you just say?"

Talia tried to wave it off. "Never mind."

"Is that what people are saying?"

Talia looked trapped. Her black eyes jumped around the parking lot. "I mean… Some people knew you were back in town. And then you didn't come to church for a little while and… Never mind."

Ava ran a hand over her face. Would this ever end? "I'm not."

"Are you sick?"

"Of course I am. So freaking sick Jack can't even stand to talk to me."

"That's not true." Talia tried to reach out a hug, but Ava needed space, not support that was too late. Ava pushed her back as a movement to her right caught her eye. Jack was approaching. Anger rose wildly, like a beast that feasted on panic.

"Hey, are you okay?" he asked, touching her arm lightly.

Ava flinched away. "Don't talk to me. If you won't talk to me in front of other people, then don't talk to me anywhere."

His brow wrinkled and he stepped back. "What are you talking about?"

"You know exactly what," she snapped. Even Talia moved back. The beast was driving them away. "You're just like Benj."

Jack's hands clenched at his sides. For a moment, it looked like he was going to walk away, but he stepped closer. "I am nothing like him. I was trying to help."

"Ignoring me isn't helping."

"Ava Claire." He ran his hands through his hair, tugging on it. "I'm trying to stop the rumors."

"What is that supposed to mean?"

"They know Jack went to Scotland," Talia cut in. "You don't think they're talking about him too? About the two of you?"

Talia took out Ava's monster with one swift blow. Ava's eyes flicked between the two of them. "What? You didn't tell me."

Jack shook his head. "You don't need to worry about it. It's all junk, anyway. But I thought it might be better if I kept my distance. I didn't want anybody to say anything."

"You're not embarrassed of me?"

"Never. It won't happen again."

His expression was so sincere, Ava nearly stepped into his arms. She had been spoiled by access to him in Scotland. But Talia was there, along with any wandering eyes in the parking lot. She pressed the water bottle to her cheek. The heat was smothering. "Shouldn't you be going to lunch?"

Jack hesitated for a moment, and Talia answered for him. "One of us has to go. We sort of help… moderate."

"Do you want to come?" Jack asked.

"Not at all," Ava said. "It's okay. Y'all go."

After promising Talia she meant it, Talia gave her a quick hug and said they would get coffee later in the week. Jack waited for his turn.

"I'm sorry, Aves," he whispered as his arms closed around her.

"It's okay."

He held her tightly, but let her go too soon. Ava wanted to grab his arms and make him stay. A smile and wave were all she managed. She started her car and blasted the air conditioning. Pulling her knees to her chest and tucking her head in, Ava did the only thing she could. She prayed. And it wasn't proper, it was pleading.

• • •

"Well, she's definitely not pregnant," Talia said as they climbed into the truck.

"I told you." Jack shook his head. "I can't believe you asked."

"Thankfully you showed up when you did. I think she was about to kill me." Talia let out a small laugh. It died quickly, and they rode in silence to the barbecue spot Val had picked. Talia fidgeted with her seatbelt. "She's not like, bulimic… right?"

The image of a shivering, vomiting Ava slumped over in the dark in Scotland came rushing back and Jack cringed involuntarily. Nobody but Rosie knew about that night. "What? Don't say stuff like that."

"I wouldn't—not to anybody else. But I thought if you knew something…"

Jack rubbed a hand over his face. "I don't think so. I think she's too stressed to eat sometimes. And she has panic attacks. But it's not an eating disorder."

"Okay. I'm gonna go to her house again as soon as I'm done with finals. I'll be able to help."

Jack smiled at her confidence, always sure she could handle anything. He had thought he could fix it, too. By now, he wasn't sure what they were even fixing. Their old friend wasn't there anymore.

They joined the picnic tables at the back. Nobody talked about Ava in front of Jack. Because he was part of the conversation now. He didn't care enough to do anything about it, showing up every Sunday was enough. The students compared upcoming finals and portfolio assignments to see who had it worse. If he joined in, Jack could top them all, because his came with an extra 30-hour work week. But he didn't. Thinking about it was exhausting enough.

"Anybody doing summer school?" Val asked. Only a small handful were.

"Jack's starting kinesiology this summer," Talia volunteered for him.

Val turned to him, bright and smiling. Her attitude towards him varied by the day. Or hour. "That's exciting."

He shrugged. It was the first class he had ever looked forward to, and it scared him. "More like relieving. I don't have to pretend to like business classes anymore."

Insincerity glossed over Val's smile and she tilted her head. "One less thing to pretend about." It changed by the minute, then.

When Val looked away, Talia shot him a secret eye roll. "So you decided God's not anti-sports?" Talia asked.

"Yeah. And I'm hoping he's not anti-me." Because there had been times in his life when it seemed that way.

Talia snorted a laugh. "He's very pro-you. That's why he won't let anything get between you and him."

Jack was only beginning to grasp that version of God.

Chapter 31

The third week of church was an improvement. For unspoken reasons, both of her brothers joined the Sanford row at the front. Maybe they knew it was the last week Ava was forced to go before moving. Regardless, having them there fortified her. She wasn't the ringleader of the college group anymore, but she still led the Sanford kids. And in this role, she was home again.

Even Joshua, the too-cool senior graduating next week, stayed by her side as they made their way out of the auditorium. He was a solid half-foot taller than Ava now and had taken on a new and absolutely adorable protective personality.

Jack skipped the distant act this week, too. He cut straight into the Sanford horde—the only one her brothers seemed to deem worthy of slipping into the ranks. He gave her a side hug. "I'm glad you came back. I'm trying a new approach this week. Promise."

"Last week's was stupid."

"That's what they call me," Jack said with a bow that made her laugh.

"I doubt that. How'd finals go?"

"Good so far, one more and then I'm free for a week before summer school."

"What? You never take summer classes."

"I do now, to catch up. I changed my major."

"Jack Shields." Ava gave him a light shove. "Why didn't you tell me? What is it now?"

"Kinesiology."

And he hadn't even told her. Or had he, and she had been too preoccupied with herself to notice? "I'm pretty sure you have a lovely, brilliant friend who told you to major in that two years ago."

"I have no clue who you're talking about," Jack said with a grin.

"What do they call you again?" Ava teased before giving him a second hug. "I'm happy for you."

He reacted more brotherly, no doubt due to the company, by attempting to rub a knuckle in her hair before she slapped his hand away. Jack laughed and casually asked for her lunch plans.

"It's a family lunch today."

"He can come," Joshua said, cutting out of another conversation.

"He's practically one of us," Ezra joined in.

Ava raised her eyebrows at Jack. "Apparently you're family."

Jack made a face. "No thanks, pastor's kids are weird."

Ava laughed at him. "Okay, get out then. Are you free on Saturday? I need your truck to move my dresser."

"Is that code for something gross?" Ezra asked.

"Shut up," Ava punched his arm.

Jack couldn't cover the smirk on his face. "I'm free in the afternoon. Text me when you want me to come over."

"Will do."

He gave her the slightest smile and squeezed her arm before walking away.

Ezra leaned over and whispered, "Ava and Jack sitting in a tree…" into her ear.

"I love you, but I'm not above killing you," Ava said quietly.

Thankfully, he waited until they piled into Ava's car before continuing the taunting.

• • •

By Saturday morning, Ava had her entire room in boxes. She had finished her two online classes with good-enough grades and now her focus turned to moving out. Her counselor had helped her mentally and emotionally prepare for the transition. Even her family seemed to be taking it well. Her mom had taken her out shopping yesterday for a few basics: cookware, paper goods, curtains.

The studio apartment was partially furnished with a bed, futon, coffee table and a dining table for two. Her dad and Ezra had helped her transport most of her smaller things to the apartment. The only things left were her dresser and bookcase, and none of the Sanfords had a truck.

Jack showed up in the middle of the afternoon, with the heat already sweltering. Late May on the coast was impossibly humid. Ezra and her dad were running errands, so the task was up to Ava and Jack.

Jack stood in her room and surveyed the furniture. "You're sure about this?"

"That I want my bookcase and dresser?"

"That you want to move."

"Absolutely," Ava said. "You have to see the place, it's got the best coastal craftsman vibe."

"I don't even know what that means."

"That's because your vocabulary is limited to lame guy-isms. Come on, I'm ready to join the land of the broke college kids living on their own."

"Definitely broke. Okay, dresser first."

After a few failed attempts to load the heavy wooden dresser, Jack and Ava switched places and he managed to lift it into the truck bed single handedly. "Where are the Sanfords with muscles?" he asked with a huff as he shoved it forward.

"Found better things to do once it hit 90 degrees."

"Smart men, why didn't I think of that?" Jack studied the truck for a minute. "Okay. Bookcase."

By the time they had both pieces in the truck, Ava was breaking into a light sweat. She did one last sweep through her room and bathroom, taking the two remaining boxes to her car. She led the way through town as Jack followed her to the apartment.

"Nice view," Jack said as they hopped out of their cars.

The Newtons lived right on the beach. Either they had cut the rent for her or God had swooped in and provided it. There was no way an apartment with a beach view could be this cheap, even for a tiny studio. This place was a gift. And this time, she wouldn't waste it. *"By wisdom a house is built."*[22]

They were halfway up the stairs with the dresser when Jack threatened to stop being friends. "Why don't you have the lightweight junk from IKEA like the rest of us?" he asked as he took over the majoritymostmost of the work again.

"Because it's an heirloom," Ava whined. "Don't hurt it."

They managed to maneuver it around the tight turn on the landing and into the front door. The bookcase was smaller and easier. Ava made Jack help her rearrange the furniture three times before she was satisfied.

"Okay, there are a couple more boxes in my car. And then I promise to buy you dinner."

Jack followed her out to the car. When Ava popped open the trunk, he snatched the tape gun next to the boxes, pointing it at her. "Stick 'em up or I'll tape you."

"Not if I get you first—" Ava lunged for the tape dispenser.

Jack swiped her arm with packing tape. Ava grabbed it from him, trying to stick his arm, but he turned. She caught his back instead, marking his shirt with a line of tape. Jack caught her wrist as he pulled the tape gun from her hands.

"Not fair," Ava laughed, twisting away.

Jack caught her other wrist, and the laugh died. He pressed her hands up against the car, pinning her under him. The ground fell beneath her. She couldn't move. The lights went out. White hot liquid shot through her veins. Her muscles turned to jelly. She was trapped in a bed in Scotland.

"Let go," she said. Or thought she did, but she couldn't hear anything, not even her own voice. She was caught in a vacuum. Without oxygen. He didn't let go.

"Let go!" With a burst of strength, she shoved her arms against him as best she could, knocking him off balance and he stumbled back a step.

She couldn't breathe. The air was so hot, so thick. Stifling. She doubled over, choking, wanting to vomit, unable to do anything. She had to get to cold air.

"Hey, I was just—" Jack was saying something.

Ava put a hand out, looking for support. She found the car, its metal burning her hand. This wasn't Scotland. There wasn't anywhere cold. Only hot. So hot she wanted to die. Jack caught her hand, but she jerked away from him. "Don't touch me."

"Aves, I'm sorry—"

Her ears were ringing as she backed away from him. She focused on his mouth but couldn't quite hear him over the rushing in her head. Her vision was tunneling. She needed air. Cold air. Somewhere. Inside. There was cold air inside her apartment. She just had to make it there.

Without realizing she had moved, she found herself tripping up the stairs until she was inside. The air conditioning was blowing, but it wasn't cold enough.

Ava yanked open the freezer and gulped the air. It wasn't enough.

She tripped into the bathroom, searching, seeking, needing the cold. She flipped the shower on and stripped. When she stepped into the icy water, it sucked the air out of her lungs, the last she had, and her vision darkened again. Ava leaned against the wall for support until it passed.

The water washed away the weight on her chest. The moment it lifted, she threw up in the shower. Panic stole everything and threw it away until she was empty. The water ran over her hair, dripping into her eyes, offering to replace the oxygen her lungs couldn't find. The cold seeped into her, warring against the burn in her throat.

Finally, shivering set in. She could feel again. In a moderated, controlled way that made more sense. But now there was embarrassment too. And shame. What would Jack think? So she made herself stand in the icy water, shivering, for as long as she could. She deserved it.

Eventually, she cut the water off. There were no towels. Of course. They were in a box somewhere. She grabbed her t-shirt and used it to pat herself dry. She put on the rest of her clothes and stepped out carefully, making sure Jack hadn't come inside. Nobody was there. She was alone.

She found the box of clothes easily and pulled out a wrinkled, oversized tee.

Fully clothed, she sat against the wall and let regret wrap around her chest and wring her dry.

• • •

The light had changed by the time Jack sat in the truck bed again, the garage in front of him had taken on a strange orange glow. He had paced a hundred laps around the driveway, climbed the steps multiple times before retreating again, and reached for his phone to call Micah, Talia, or Rebecca. But he had done nothing. Nothing at all. Except terrify Ava.

Maybe he should leave. He twisted his key on and off of its keychain, debating it, when he heard the apartment door close. Ava came down the stairs in a new shirt. Her hair was wet, and her eyes red. Still unsure of what to say, she walked up and sat on the tailgate next to him.

"How long have you been waiting here?" she asked. "I lost track of time."

"A little while." Over an hour.

"You didn't have to stay."

He could still hear her voice calling herself worthless. The idea was tucked into so many things she said, and he hated it. "Aves, what did I do?"

"Nothing," she said quietly.

"That's obviously not true. Did I hurt you?"

"No. No, it's just… It's stupid."

He reached a hand over and held hers, begging her for the truth. "You never lied to me before." Or if she tried, it never lasted this long.

Her head spun towards him with a brief guilty glance before she turned away again, pressing her lips together tightly. "You're… a lot stronger than me." Of course he was. He always had been. But it shouldn't scare her.

"What are you not telling me?" Jack wasn't sure he wanted to know, but he knew he needed to. Ava leaned against his shoulder and shook her head. "Do you want me to leave?"

"No." She wove an arm through his to reinforce it and keep him there. At least that wasn't a lie. "I still owe you dinner."

"Don't worry about it."

"No, come on, let's get pizza."

"Are you really going to pretend nothing happened?"

"Yes. And so are you."

Jack sighed and reached out to her, slowly so he wouldn't scare her, and brushed still-damp hair away from her face. "Pretending isn't working, Aves."

It was the wrong thing to say. Ava looked away immediately, but he caught the hurt in her eyes. "I'm sorry," he said. Ava moved into his arms and he gladly held onto her. Their bodies cast long shadows on the garage door. She didn't have to tell him anything.

Eventually Jack carried in the abandoned boxes from her car while she ordered a pizza. They rode together in his truck to get it, talking about summer school and work, pretending everything was normal. Jack had been offered a position with the Athletic Department running their summer camps for youth in the city. Ava told him more about the event design job. They were both taking summer courses to make up for time they had lost, between changing majors and dropping courses.

When they got back, the last bits of color were streaking the horizon. They picnicked on the beach behind the Newtons' house. The sand was still hot from the sun.

"You're the only college kid I know who gets to live on the beach," Jack said. "I think I hate you."

"I'm spoiled rotten."

"Tell me about it, Miss 'It's-An-Heirloom.'"

Ava laughed and shoved his arm weakly, he let it knock him back onto the sand. Two stars were shining next to the moon, the first ones of the night. In his peripheral, he could tell Ava was watching him. She finally laid back on the sand next to him. "I'll have sand in my hair for days."

Jack scooped a handful of sand and drizzled it over the hair laid out behind her.

"Jerk." Ava swatted his hand away. "I'll put sand in your pizza."

"You wouldn't touch my one true love."

Ava snickered. "I thought that was your truck."

"Hmm, second true love then."

Ava rolled onto her stomach and propped herself up on her elbows. "How many true loves are you allowed to have?"

"At least half a dozen."

"Name 'em."

"Truck. Pizza. Hamburgers. Sports. Jesus. This isn't in order."

"That's five."

"One more? Putting sand in girls' hair."

"You're a weirdo," Ava laughed and put her head on his chest.

"We all are, Aves." Jack wrapped a free arm around her. "I'm just honest about it."

Ava only hummed in response as she shifted closer to him. The moment felt stolen, in the dark on the beach, and he was claiming too much. Talia's lectures were in his head. *It only takes one to ask her out.* But she wasn't ready to date, and he wasn't ready to jeopardize their friendship. So they would keep playing pretend.

Until Ava hit him with a question out of left field. "What's up with you and Val?"

Jack sighed. "She needed a plus one to a wedding in March."

"Nobody actually *needs* a plus one. That's a move."

"Yeah… I figured that out. So a couple weeks later I told her we were only friends."

"How'd that go?"

"Some days we're good, other days she's kinda crazy."

He heard Ava's smile. "Quit making girls go crazy, Jack."

"What? I don't."

Ava sat up as she started listing the girls he had dated. The relationships that had all ended poorly—from burned photos to posters with his face placed around campus. Jack laughed and pulled Ava back to his chest. She could recount them all she wanted, but he hadn't dated anyone since she graduated high school. At least, not intentionally. Val didn't count.

"Okay, so there were a few," he said. "I haven't made you crazy, have I?"

"Not yet." Her hand ran a lazy line down his arm.

Jack pressed a hand into her waist, claiming too much. No part of him wanted to move away, but he managed to push away and sit. Ava hurried away too quickly. The rolling hush of the waves filled the night.

"Will you come to church tomorrow?" Jack asked.

"I don't know."

"What if we ride together?"

"And what would people say about that?"

"I don't care. Believe it or not, there are more important things in life than being liked by everybody."

"True," she said, facing the shoreline. "Do you really want me to go?"

"Of course."

"I can ride with Joshua or Ezra."

Jack followed her gaze to the waves. That plan made more sense. Even if he didn't like it as much. "Will you?"

"If I don't, are you going to show up pounding on my door again?"

"Absolutely."

Ava dropped her head back in a laugh. Long, dark hair fell behind her like a waterfall, with sand dripping from it. "Why did I let you find out where I live now?"

Her smile made it hard to come up with a witty reply. "Because you trust me," Jack said. He had to believe it was possible, at least.

Ava cocked her head to one side and studied him for a moment. "That's true."

Jack grabbed the pizza box and stood, holding a hand out to pull Ava up. He pulled her close and dropped his voice. "I'm sorry for earlier."

"You're fine."

"That's what they call me," he said, giving her hand a quick squeeze before dropping it.

Chapter 32

Nobody forced her to go to church that Sunday. But she had already texted Joshua and he would be picking her up any minute. She couldn't back out now. Ava stood on the small landing she used for a front porch, sipping coffee as she watched the lazy waves on the bay and willed their peace into her body.

The only thing making her go to church was herself. And the notebook next to her bed that she had filled last night with every verse she could find about grace. There were dozens. "*Grace and truth.*"[23] "*Grace upon grace.*"[24] "*Purpose and grace.*"[25] She knew where she wanted to be. Where she wanted to feel at home again.

Joshua's car pulled into the driveway and Ava deposited her mug inside before hurrying down the stairs. His car smelled like an exploded bottle of cologne. After teasing him for it, Ava switched to quizzing him about the new girlfriend. It would help distract her from her own nerves.

"How'd you meet her?"

"Ridley Bible Church."

"Is that where she goes? What were you doing there?"

Joshua shrugged. "Yeah. They have a big youth group, a lot of kids from school go there, so I started joining some of their stuff."

"Wait, and dad doesn't mind? What about the whole—'in my house, at my church' thing?" Ava asked.

"Your impression of dad sounds like a dying frog. I always go to Grace on Sundays. He doesn't really care if I go somewhere else during the week."

"Luck of the second born." Ava crossed her arms. "Parents are harder on the first."

"You never even tried to go anywhere else."

"I didn't think I was allowed. Besides, I wouldn't. I'm the favorite."

"Nope, that's Ezra now."

Ava scoffed. She knew for a fact she wasn't the favorite anymore, but it was a bragging right she had to claim anyway. "Is this girlfriend graduating now too?"

Joshua gave her a side glance and tapped his fingers on the steering wheel. "Next year."

"Ooh, robbing the cradle," Ava said. Joshua pushed her face away in response. "Ugh, don't get your nasty boy hands on my makeup."

Joshua didn't bother to respond as he pulled into the parking lot for church. Ava unbuckled and reached for her purse but Joshua stopped her before she got out. "Hey—"

"What?"

Joshua stalled, fixing his hair in the rearview mirror while he spoke. "One of my friends has a sister in the Grace college group."

"Okay. And?" Ava prompted but Joshua still hesitated. Her stomach started turning. She had eaten breakfast, what was she thinking? "Spill."

Joshua tapped the wheel again for a minute before speaking. "Are you okay?"

"Is that really all you want to ask?"

"Yes." Her brother always meant what he said. Every muscle relaxed, including her stomach. *Don't cry before you even get into church.* Ava reached across the center console to hug him.

She could only answer his honesty with her own. "I'm getting there."

"I'm sorry I was distracted the last few weeks," he said, staring out the windshield. "School was busy. But I'm on your side, Ava-cado."

"Thanks, Joshie Woshie."

"Call me that again and I won't let you meet my future wife."

"Slow down, boy. I'll call you what I want and she's still in high school."

Joshua laughed and hopped out of the car. Ava came around the front of the car and he pushed her arm. "Last one inside has to clean the toilets." He broke into an all-out run towards the church.

"I thought you were on my side," Ava yelled after him. There was no way she was running in the parking lot. She didn't have a chance of catching him, anyway.

"So much for going to church together," she mumbled under her breath as she walked towards the building. But he had still lifted her spirits. Distracted her. Gotten her here.

Ava made it through the main doors and a few brief interactions with acquaintances. She slowed her step as she neared the front row. Jack, Talia, and two other students from the college group sat in the second row, directly behind Ava's brothers. Out of place, but all with friendly smiles.

Ava took her place in the front row, shooting Jack a look. He just smirked. She leaned over her seat to hug Talia. "What are you doing?" Ava whispered as the worship music started.

"Mixing it up," Talia said.

The sermon was painful this week. Her dad made his way through Luke 8, with targeted verses. She knew the verse about a light not being hidden. She had memorized it. She was supposed to be the light. That was her role. But she had forgotten the verse after it. *"For nothing is hidden… nor is anything secret that will not be known and come to light."*[26] Her dad made eye contact with her multiple times throughout the sermon. He always did, with everyone. But today she didn't want to be included.

Yet as she sat there, surrounded by her family and remaining friends, she knew she would come back next week. Because every time her dad's sermon cracked at her heart, something seeped out and freed itself, and something found its way back in. Ava sensed home somewhere inside of her. The place where she would feel loved and free again. She would find it.

When the service ended, instead of being trapped at the front talking to strangers or interrogators, she was talking to other college students again. Talia invited her to join them for lunch at a burger place on the peninsula.

"Sorry," Ava said, unsure how she really felt. "I didn't bring my car—"

"Ride with me," Jack interrupted.

Ava glanced at him and instantly dropped her eyes. Eye contact with him seemed forbidden right now. Because they were at church. Because his ice-blue eyes seemed to emanate their own light. Because he had jumped away from her when she touched his arm last night. She only nodded.

"You guys should see the place Ava got," Talia said as they walked outside. "She practically has her own beach now."

The conversation surrounded her like a cloud as they drifted through the front hallway and out to the parking lot. Ava caught a look that Val sent her way—it was far from friendly. But Jack was right. There were more important things.

• • •

It was Jack's idea to sit up front and Talia was more than willing. They recruited a couple of trustworthy students to join them. His roommate Quinton couldn't care less where he sat and had always gotten along with Ava. Talia knew Isabella would gladly move with them without asking a single question. Fisher had joined of his own accord when he saw Jack and Quinton sitting there. They weren't trying to divide the college group, but Jack was tired of the rigid routines. The strict grouping. Somehow he had become their moral compass after all.

Ava rode in the front and Talia joined them, in the back seat, on the drive to the burger joint. Talia spent the entire drive trying to convince Ava to come to C3's summer kickoff event. They hosted a huge bonfire every year after graduation. Talia's main selling point was the s'mores and Jack wasn't sure if she really loved s'mores or if she was harping on getting Ava to eat. He tried to warn her off with a look in the rearview mirror but never managed to catch her eyes.

"I don't know," Ava said, turned to the passenger window so Jack couldn't see her face either. "The C3 group… That's a lot of people."

He knew she had one in particular in mind. *Cowboy.* The study abroad students were scheduled to come home this week. And there was no telling if she wanted to see him or not. She probably did. Jack tightened his grip on the steering wheel.

"Don't you think she should go, Jack?" Talia tried to drag him into it.

"She can do whatever she wants."

"Thank you," Ava said.

"You'll be fine," Talia said to Ava. "Nobody will mess with you as long as you have me with you. I won't leave your side."

For an uncomfortable moment, Jack realized he couldn't promise to stay by her side. He didn't want to be there if it meant watching Ava flirt with Benjamin all night.

"I'll think about it," Ava promised.

"Go show everybody you're not pregnant," Talia said. Jack cringed and tried again to send lasers through the mirror.

Ava surprised him with a laugh. "One more mention of that and I'm going to load your purse with pregnancy tests when you're not looking."

"Okay, can we not talk about this?" Jack asked.

"You're a kinesiology major now," Talia said. "Get used to bodies."

"Yeah, athletic ones."

"Are you saying pregnant women can't be athletic?" Talia asked with a mock gasp.

"Strike two, Tal," Jack said, holding up his fingers. "Say the P word one more time and you can both hitchhike the rest of the way."

"You're adorable," Talia laughed and leaned forward over the middle console to share a conspiratorial smile with Ava.

They managed to make it through the ride without saying "pregnant" again, while tormenting him with every other maternal word they could think of. Talia started with womb. Ava offered a few but was mostly quiet.

The students that sat with them in church today were at lunch too. Ava warmed up throughout the meal. Talia kicked Jack's foot under the table when Ava offered him the second half of her burger. He turned it down, and she managed a couple more bites.

Before leaving, Ava invited everyone to her apartment for a beach day sometime soon. For a moment, they could almost slip back into the roles they had all played months ago. But before the old, take-charge Ava came out, Scotland Ava shied away and hid the invitation behind a few layers of excuses and ambiguous dates. It was the new Ava.

"What about Saturday?" Jack asked, stepping in. She agreed. It would be good for her to get back in her element. Plus, if the bonfire was a bust, there would still be something enjoyable about the weekend. Whether it would be a bust for him or for Ava, he wasn't sure. That depended on Benj.

Chapter 33

The Texas gulf was on the cusp of summer. A breeze cooled the otherwise hot and humid night. Ava decided on denim shorts and a white, cotton long sleeve for the evening. She turned slowly in front of the mirror, making sure the shirt wasn't too tight or too loose. She skipped makeup and left her hair in a low ponytail. Appearing as plain, uncontroversial, and not-pregnant as possible was her survival plan for tonight.

The C3 bonfire had been on her mind all week, lurking like a monster in the closet. She never should have agreed to it. Her counselor thought it would be a good idea to get back into social activities, but this was too big of a jump. Ava paced the apartment with one eye on the clock. She had to stop backing out of things. Across town, Talia waited for a ride. So, doing what she did best, Ava turned off her brain and walked out the door.

They got to the beach as the C3 staff was starting the bonfire. Talia led the way towards the event, wearing a yellow maxi dress that looked like the sun itself, while the real one sank low on the horizon. Christian rap music played on a speaker, mostly drowned out by wind, waves, and the crackle of fire.

Talia kept her promise, staying close to Ava. Faces of former friends, new friends, and new foes swirled around her. But there were also new rumors, which helped Ava's lose its appeal. Ava mostly smiled and laughed, but kept words to herself.

Nearly an hour passed before Jack finally showed. His brief hug infused Ava with enough strength to leave Talia's side. She went to get a water bottle from a cooler. Stars were beginning to speckle the sky over the ocean as Ava took a sip to cool the smoke burning in her throat.

The moment she lowered the water, she caught sight of a familiar form in the light of the bonfire. *No.* The one person she had been most terrified of seeing here. Somehow she had convinced herself it wouldn't happen. But there it was: the face she had slapped. She could still feel his hand on her ribcage, squeezing, blocking out air.

Ava's heart rate doubled. She had to get to Talia or Jack. But Benj was standing there, blocking the way she had come.

Like a nightmare, her feet barely moved. She tried to circle the other way around the fire. *Don't freeze, don't freeze.* The air around the bonfire was thick and heavy with smoke. She didn't want to be here anymore. Ava stepped away from the fire, trying to breathe. If she could just make it to one friend, any friend, it would be better than being alone.

It was too late. When she looked back towards the group, she saw Benj's outline framed by the firelight behind him. "Leaving already?"

Her heart fell into her feet as he reached her side. "Girl, you've got that disappearing act down. Can't believe you left Scotland without telling me."

Ava shrugged and gave a quiet apology as she edged away towards the darkness, trading safety in numbers for less listening ears.

"Just couldn't handle anymore, huh? You missed some great stuff." Benj reached a hand out towards her. "We should go get a drink and catch up."

Ava tried to sound casual. "I'm good, thanks."

Benj laughed and slung his arm over Ava's shoulders, the weight crushed her. "I'm pretty sure you still owe me, damsel."

Rosie's voice played in her head: *"Then say yes next time."* Her soul left, simply quitting, emptying her. "Benj, I'm sorry. Can we drop it, please?"

"God, are you still heartbroken about Oliver?"

The name drained the blood from her head, leaving it light. Ava shook her dizzy head.

"Have you told your pretend boyfriend why you're all…" He waved his free hand towards her as if her entire being was summed up in one mistake.

Nausea set in as her stomach twisted into another knot. The reference to Jack left her feeling even more alone. She could disappear, vanish, and no one would even notice. *"I will never leave you."* A wave of anger replaced the fear and Ava shoved his arm away. She gasped for the air that opened around her. "Why would I tell him?"

"Dang, Ava, that's cold." Benj crossed his arms and closed in on the distance she had created. "If Jack went all the way to Scotland, I think you owe it to him to tell him."

"Tell me what?"

Ava's heart did a flip through her entire body, unable to decide where to land. She turned to see Jack walking towards them, clearly unhappy.

Benj's face transformed into an insincere smile as he gave Jack a typical guy handshake-back-pat. "What's up, man? You shoulda told me you were in Scotland. We were havin' a great time over there."

Jack was clearly on the defense. "Short trip."

"Too bad." Benj winked at Ava like they shared a joke. "This girl tells me you don't even know the real reason she left."

"I know enough."

Benj laughed. "I don't think you do. Did you meet Oliver?"

Jack looked at Ava, his face was cold, unreadable. "Who's Oliver?"

Ava searched for words but her mind went blank, and she was sure if she opened her mouth, she'd be sick.

Benj whistled. "Not even a name? Dang, I thought y'all were close."

"Drop it, Benj," Ava said. It was weak, just like her.

"Look, I'm just tryna to help. Figured you'd want to know who your girlfriend slept with and she'll never be able to say the word 'sex' for herself."

Ava saw Jack clinch his hand into a fist at his side before flexing his fingers out again. "She doesn't have to tell me anything she doesn't want to."

Benj raised his hands in mock surrender. "Okay, whatever, thought you should know it was just a little breakup that made her psycho. I mean, I'm there too—Cassandra lost it on me. I'm tryna save you here. This one's trouble." Benj finished his statement with his eyes roaming lazily over Ava.

"We're done talking about this," Jack said, edging between them to block off Benj's line of sight.

"God, you two deserve each other," Benj said with a laugh. He shook his head, shot one last disapproving look to Ava and sauntered back to the bonfire.

Ava could only see Jack's back as he watched Benj walk away. Every second that he refused to look at her was a knife. She had to explain this to him somehow. "Jack..."

He didn't even bother to turn around, only looking over his shoulder at her, his expression still cold, angry. "Not right now, Aves." Then, with his hands in his pockets, he left her.

Ava wrapped an arm around her core, watching him walk away from her. She was so sick of herself and the hurt she brought. This would never go away. Her sins were her shadow and she would never escape them. The only thing she could do was disappear.

The fire was too hot, too bright, and too crowded. Ava craved the darkness of the night, and the coolness of the sea. Ducking her head, she crossed a small path through the dunes. The moment she reached the edge of the water, a dry sob cracked across her chest. She was unloveable. A shiver took over her as she sank to her knees. This was her place: alone, breathing ocean water instead of air. Ava pressed her arms tightly into her stomach to hold herself up. If she lost it in the noise of the wind and waves, she might never find her way back.

• • •

Jack had tried not to watch Benj cozy up to Ava. It was the exact reason he almost didn't come tonight. But when his eyes flicked back to them and he caught Ava shoving Benj's arm away, he immediately jumped in, without a second thought. He had handed curiosity the knife and if it killed him, he deserved it.

Now he stalked back to the bonfire, needing to move, needing to get away from it all. He passed through the group, reaching for the keys in his pocket when Talia grabbed his arm. "Hey, where's Ava?"

All the anger at Benj's manipulation and Ava's lies rose, threatening to spill over. Jack yanked his arm away from Talia without bothering to look at her. "I don't know."

Talia stepped in front of him, undeterred. She lowered her voice. "Benj is here."

"For the love—" Jack clasped his hands behind his head and glared at the black sky. "Why is it always about him?"

Talia's lip curled. "What is wrong with you? Ava didn't want to see him. He was a jerk to her in Scotland."

"Then I guess she likes that."

"Jack Shields—"

He cut off her tirade. "She already saw him. We all got to chat. Did you know about Oliver too? Did you let me go to Scotland just to rescue her from a bad breakup?" A temporary boyfriend Ava never mentioned? Someone she had jumped into bed with and then told Benj all about? It wasn't fair to be mad at Talia, but fairness didn't change it.

Talia's mouth dropped open before shaping back into a frown. She punched Jack's chest lightly. "Stop. I don't know what Benj told you, but it was a lie. You need to talk to Ava."

Jack laughed harshly. "What good would that do? She lies to me too."

Talia raised up on her toes to gain an extra inch closer to his face. "Snap out of it. You love her and right now you need to help me find her."

"Love? Really, Tal?" Jack shook his head. "Look, I can't do it anymore. I have tried to help her and I can't. She's not the same person anymore."

"You think I don't know that? She's my best friend, I know she's not the same. But that doesn't make her less valuable." Talia looked like she might cry and it put ice on Jack's anger. "Not all change is bad."

"Name one good thing about this."

Talia blinked back tears, rapidly swallowing the anger. "How do you not see it? She's gentler. And kinder. She slows down and listens more. She watches out for people—"

"Okay. Okay." Jack rubbed his hands over his face. He was worn, mentally and emotionally, and now he felt like dirt too. "I'm tired, okay? I can't keep doing this."

Talia squeezed his arm. "It's hard. But she's gonna be okay. She's worth it."

"I've never doubted that she's worth it. I doubt that I'm enough."

"Maybe you're not. But God is. And right now, he's using us, so we're gonna be enough." Talia took a deep breath and Jack knew she was convincing herself as well. She craned her neck to scan the crowd again. "Jack, I'm seriously worried about her. We need to find her."

Jack sighed. "I think I saw her head to the beach."

"I'll check the parking lot. Text me if you find her."

They split and Jack called Ava; no answer. The further he got from the fire, the more Talia's stress worked into his veins. He crossed the dunes and the roar of the waves got louder. The beach was dark. A sliver of moonlight reflected on the waves. Jack walked closer to shore, staring into the night, looking for the outline of anything against the vast blackness of the sea.

Several yards from the shore, he finally caught sight of something white reflecting the moonlight. As he got closer, he could make out the shape of a person, kneeling by the water, white shirt flapping in the wind. Once he knew it was Ava, he texted Talia. Then, he waited. Unable to move forward. Was God really in this? God took away everything Jack had ever loved. Why not Ava too?

No. God gives.

The enemy was the thief. And Jack was the only one here to fight him tonight. He had to be enough.

The sound, or a moonlit shadow, must have hit her as he walked forward, because when he was a couple feet away, she jerked up to standing, her hands raised to stop him. He recognized the panic in her eyes. It was the same look she'd had when he helped her move. The look she'd had in front of a parish in Scotland. "Aves, it's me," he said in a low voice, not moving.

Her eyes focused, and she finally saw him instead of looking through him. "Jack?"

How many times would he have to do this? He sent a silent prayer for strength. "Let's get back to the group, babe."

"Jack," her voice cracked, and she crossed the sand to him. She leaned her head into his chest. She was shivering, far more than she should be for the temperature. "I didn't want to, I didn't…"

Jack lifted a single arm around her. "You don't have to tell me anything." Especially about this. He didn't want to know after all.

She straightened to look at him and he dropped his arm away from her. "Yes, I do. Please, listen to me."

Facing the waves, he backed away. "What do you want to say?"

"I didn't want to…" Ava stuttered over a few words before deciding on some. "To sleep with him."

Jack glanced at her. "Who? Oliver or Benj?"

"I told you I never slept with Benj."

"Apparently there's a lot you haven't told me."

There was enough moonlight to see the hurt in her eyes. "I'm trying to now."

Jack sighed. "Okay."

"I didn't want to sleep with him—Oliver. I swear. I tried not to."

The ocean seemed to roar in his own ears. He did not want to talk about this. "Don't say that unless it's true." He didn't want bad excuses.

Ava raised a shaking hand to cover her mouth while the other pressed into her stomach. She shook her head and turned away from him, taking two steps before dropping back to her knees.

He had crossed the Atlantic for her. Now he couldn't seem to cross a yard of sand. The sound of a sob finally hit him, harder than the smack he would get from Talia if he returned without Ava. *Dang it.* Jack stepped towards the waves and knelt next to her. "Come on, Aves—"

"No," she shook her head, her voice wavering. "You don't get it. Nobody gets it. Maybe I'm wrong, I don't know."

Dark water lapped the shore in front of them and its rhythm seemed to speak. *Listen to her. Listen to her. Listen to her.* Jack leaned his elbows on his knees and laced his fingers. *Okay.* "Hey, I'm sorry. I'm listening."

She took a few deep breaths and seemed to steady. "Just hear me out. Then you can decide if you hate me, or blame me, or don't believe me, or whatever."

Jack nodded.

Her voice was quiet against the noises of the night. "Oliver was Rosie's friend. I let him— I let him walk me home, on my birthday. I had kissed him, before that, another time. But that night I let him into my room. But the rest, I didn't… I didn't know 'watching a movie' was guy code for something else."

Jack's heart stopped beating. Guy code?

"I was drunk. And that was stupid. That's my fault. And I don't really remember everything. But I did try, I really did. I told him to stop, and he said I was too late. He wouldn't let go. I did try, to push him back… But I just… I froze."

It had all been there, faint scars running under the surface, invisible bruises. Hearing it, though, was like watching a nightmare come true. A new, different anger built in his chest.

"It's stupid, I should have done more. But he was so much stronger. And he took everything the wrong way. He said it was normal…" Ava choked and shook her head. "He said to stop crying. That he wouldn't leave until I had fun. So I just tried not to… I didn't know what to do."

Jack dropped his head into his hands and swore. The cracks in her voice fueled the rising rage.

"Benj found me in a student lounge the next day. I was kind of a mess. He figured it out. Rosie too. She said I was being naïve, that I should've gone along with it. They acted like I was crazy. And I didn't want anyone else to know. I was just… so ashamed."

And he had almost bought into Benj and Rosie's narrative tonight. He had accused Ava of lying. He had turned into the same jerk. Jack stared at the waves, searching for answers. "Did you report him?"

"No."

With another curse, he stood and paced the sand, pulling a hand through his hair. Rage and adrenaline needed an outlet. Something to destroy. "Why didn't you tell me?" When they were still in Scotland. When he could have done something about it. About him. To him.

Ava stood, facing the water. "It's embarrassing."

"It's rape!" His voice was too loud and Ava took a step back.

"I hate that word," she whispered, shrinking in on herself.

"Aves," he said softly as he stepped closer to her. He wanted to hold her, to pull her back together, but he couldn't without permission.

"I'm sorry," she said through tears. She still wouldn't look at him. "I'm sorry, Jack."

"Stop, babe. There's nothing to apologize for. This wasn't your fault."

"I did… I let him in the room. I was stupid."

"That doesn't justify what he did. Being in a room doesn't give anyone the right to touch you." Jack fought the urge to yell it. "I've been in your room a dozen times. Have I ever touched you?"

Ava wouldn't look at him. Her arms were wrapped tightly around herself. "You don't want to touch me."

Jack instinctively reached for her, holding her shoulders and the truth slipped out before he could stop it. "That's not true."

Closing the gap between them, Ava buried her head in his chest. His arms enveloped her and he whispered a dozen apologies into her hair. "I'm sorry, babe." He would do anything to change this.

He leaned back and framed her face with his hands, gently lifting it. "Look at me. You know it wasn't your fault, right?"

She scanned his eyes for a second. "Rosie said the dress—"

"The dress doesn't matter."

"But I let it go too far. He said it was too late…"

What Oliver said, and when, and where, came rushing unwelcome into his mind and Jack forced it all away. "That's a lie. It's never too late." She had believed so many lies and he would tackle every single one until they were gone.

She opened her mouth, probably to argue with him, but closed it again. Her hands covered his, still resting against her cheek. Her face was so close, so soft. If only he could keep her this close. "Why do you believe in me so much?"

Because he loved her. Talia was right, and this was the worst possible moment to acknowledge that. Before he risked doing anything stupid, he dropped his hands, sticking them in his pockets. "Because I know you, and I know the truth, Aves."

Hair blew into her face and he wanted to brush it back, to see her more clearly. Instead, an uncomfortable image came to mind. Ava, wide eyed and terrified. "Last week, when we were moving your stuff, did I scare you?"

Ava dropped her gaze and nodded.

He couldn't let her associate him with this. He would never touch her like that again. "If I had known, I wouldn't have— Ava, I would never hurt you."

"I know I'm safe with you. It's… a reflex, a knee-jerk reaction." She gave a short, sharp laugh that cracked. "I just never knew it would leave scars like this."

Slowly, he reached for her and pulled her in close again. "Are you still seeing a counselor?"

"Yeah. I haven't told her quite as much as I just told you though."

"You should. When you're ready." He pressed his lips to the top of her head and Ava knotted her fingers into his shirt. "Thank you for telling me."

"I wish I had sooner." Her voice was muffled in his shirt. "I'm sorry about Benj."

Jack shook his head and pushed Ava back an inch as he tried to scan her and find everything he needed to know. "Are you okay? Did he hurt you?"

"I'm okay. I'm working on not freezing up."

That wasn't reassuring at all. "I can go kill him."

Ava smiled. "I prefer you not in jail."

"I prefer you not being hurt by someone."

"Me too." She ducked her head back into his chest. "Jack—I'm okay. I really am."

Jack forced his hands not to touch her hair, her back, her waist. Not to replace every touch on her with his own. "I want you to be more than okay, Aves."

"I will be."

Chapter 34

Telling Jack was terrifying. Telling her parents was downright horrible. Jack had encouraged her to do it though, and she knew he was right. So the next day, Ava postponed her planned beach party with the Grace students and drove to her parent's house instead.

She couldn't look them in the eyes throughout the story. It was everything dads warn their daughters about; though the dad version featured dark alleyways and vans with blacked-out windows. Ava's story lacked a man in a trench coat and a knife to her throat. Hers was weak. And she included it all—seeing Oliver again, Benj kissing her, the slap. Even the night Jack found her. It was time to dig the skeletons up and let their bones breathe.

Her mom started crying well before Ava finished. Her dad switched to counselor mode—it was probably easier for him to handle it from that point of view. He repeated things her counselor had said: the guilt and shame were her attempt to claim fault; she felt safer, more in control, if it was her fault. But the guilt and shame were strangling her.

"It doesn't help," Ava mumbled. "I'm ruined."

"Nothing and no one can ruin you," her dad said. "God has more than enough grace for you."

Her cheeks were burning, but they weren't going to have this conversation more than once. They were going to talk about this. Now. "But what about all the purity stuff?"

He sighed and pressed his palms into his eyes. "Purity comes from the heart, it can't be taken away from you. It's an ongoing effort, not a one-time thing."

That wasn't what she meant. Ava shook her head. "But that doesn't change anything. I'm still… used."

"Used?" Her dad's tone rose a notch. He swallowed and brought it back down. "Ava, you're not a car. If you're basing your worth on virginity, you've turned it into an idol."

Anger rose at the mixed messages of her life. "Are you kidding? If it's an idol, that's your fault."

"Ava—" her mother started to scold her, but her dad stopped it. The words hovered in the air, turning it sour, while her dad just stared at her. Ava forced herself not to squirm in her seat.

Finally, he stood and reached for Ava. "Maybe it is. Come on, let's take a walk."

"Am I not allowed in the house anymore?" she asked dryly.

"You're always welcome. But you and I could use a little fresh air." The two of them went outside while her mom stayed behind. Ava glanced over her shoulder at the house. Her dad looked back as well. "She needs a minute."

This would take more than a minute.

They reached the end of the street without another word and turned to circle the block. "You're not saying anything."

"I'm looking for the words, Avie."

Maybe it would be better if he didn't find them.

They made it halfway down the next street before he spoke again. "Maybe you're right. Maybe I let the pressure of being a pastor weigh too heavily on our family. Hon, if I taught you that your worth was based on what you did—or what others did to you—I'm sorry." They had stopped walking and faced each other.

"It's just part of leading a church."

"No. Leading a church should never get in the way of leading my family." He gripped her shoulders, and she leaned in for a hug. "Your worth can never be stolen, Avie. You will always mean the world to me."

His embrace was so familiar. When she was younger, it held the power to fix everything. How she missed those days. Ava took a deep breath and pushed back, against the pain in her heart. "What about God through? What if he doesn't want me back?"

Her dad smiled and turned to continue walking down the block. "I can guarantee you that will never happen. God takes it all: new, used, even completely broken down. No wrong turn is so far off you can't get back on track."

A knot tightened over the words in her throat. "What if I can't find my way back?"

Her dad's step faltered and he cleared his throat. Twice. "Avie, sometimes the sheep wander. That's what the shepherd's for. God seeks us out in the midst of sin and shame. He never gives up. He sought out Adam and Eve, didn't he?"

Ava leaned against his arm and sighed. Hearing the words was like seeing an old friend again, both nostalgic and new. When they made it back to the house, her dad stopped on the front porch and they leaned over the railing, side-by-side.

"Avie, it wasn't your fault."

"But it's not just that. I made other mistakes too, dad." There were drinks and kisses and words and plenty of other things that weren't pure. "And I was already saved. What if I lost that?"

He gave his all-knowing smile and squeezed her shoulder. "Thankfully grace relies on God's goodness, not yours. His love was never based on your righteousness to begin with. You can refuse it, but you can't lose it."

"I can lose other things," she said, mostly to herself.

"You didn't lose it. It was stolen from you." He picked at a piece of flaking paint on the rail. "And healing from that is hard. I'm glad you're seeing a counselor. And God can help too."

She couldn't help the scoff that slipped out. "I'm sorry."

"It's okay, I can handle it."

She sighed and watched the trees sway in the wind. "If God's so helpful, where was he in Scotland?"

He rubbed his hands together. "Honestly, I'm going to be wrestling with that one too. But you should ask him, hon. God can handle questions."

Ava nodded. So many of his words she had heard shared with others. They were never supposed to be for her; but they were now. He didn't seem to mind.

"By the way, you're not the only one at our church who has gone through this," her dad said with a nudge. "I can think of a couple women who would be willing to share their stories. It might be good to talk to them."

"I think our church has already said enough about me. I'm not sure I should spread it further."

He straightened, his fingers tight on the railing. "I'll deal with that. I've got a sermon series I'm working on now."

Ava laughed and stretched her arms over the rail, letting the sun hit her hands between the dancing shadows of the oak tree. She knew the answer to her next question, but needed to hear it, anyway. "Do you still love me?"

He put an arm around her and squeezed, kissing the side of her head. "Always and forever. And so does God."

• • •

Summer started with a rush—summer classes and the new youth outreach job swallowed Jack like a rogue wave. Every morning he ran summer camps and every afternoon he attended kinesiology class. The new job required more hours, which meant trading his social life for breathing room in the budget.

The next weekend, he was ready for a break. It quickly filled in though. Saturday morning he was at his dad's house, replacing the brake pads on his truck. By lunchtime, he was back at his apartment, working on an assignment he hadn't even glanced at all week. He skimmed through the readings required for the essay while scarfing down a sandwich. Thankfully kinesiology came more naturally to him than any business paper had.

His roommate Quinton walked into the living room as Jack finished the first page. "Aren't you going to Ava's?"

"What?" Jack's head popped up. Quinton stood there in swim trunks with a beach towel over his shoulder. Realization slowly dawned. The rescheduled beach party. Ava hadn't held it last week, after the bonfire incident, and he had been so busy, they had barely spoken since. "Dang it."

"Do you want to ride together, or…"

"No, go ahead." Jack sighed and dropped his pen onto the textbook. "I'll be there soon."

By the time Jack got there, an hour later, three cars lined the street. He jogged to the beach behind the house. Everyone else was already there. Ava was laughing at something Talia said when she spotted him. The laugh quickly died to a smile. She'd been quiet last time they'd seen each other too, the Sunday after the bonfire. It had changed something in their friendship. For him, he could no longer ignore the fact that he loved her. But he wasn't sure what had changed for her. Either way, he couldn't risk losing her. He had to play it cool.

He greeted everyone with high fives or fist bumps—including Ava, awkwardly diverting from a hug.

Despite the slight frown she wore, she looked good: rested, fed, and sun-kissed. "Where have you been?"

"Essay. These summer classes are brutal."

"You're not the only one in summer school." Ava cocked an eyebrow. "Besides, this whole get together was partly your idea."

She turned away but Jack caught her arm. "I'm sorry I'm late."

Ava stepped out of his touch before answering. He couldn't help filtering her actions through a new lens. Was she mad, or did she not want to be touched like that? Jack stuck his hand in his back pocket.

"Whatever." She shrugged. "We had pizza. There's some left in the kitchen if you want it."

She returned to the group conversation and Jack hesitated a moment before taking the stairs to her apartment, two at a time. A green and white wreath greeted him at the door. He grabbed a piece of pizza from the boxes on the tiny table in the kitchen. A small angel with a broken wing stood on the kitchen counter, watching him. The entire space was crisp and clean, whites and creams. Ava had decorated it since the move. It wasn't bright and colorful like her old room, it was new Ava.

Jack took another slice with him as he jogged down the stairs. When he was back, they started a game of sand volleyball. Having a smaller group was a good change of pace. Everyone played and talked about summer plans—a mix of summer school, jobs, camps, and family vacation plans.

The sun blazed and everyone was ready to cool off in the water once the volleyball game ended. Ava was the only one not in a swimsuit. She wore athletic shorts and a tank top. It was still the most skin she had shown since coming home.

None of the girls went past their knees in the water, while the guys swam further out. When they got tired of trying to drown each other, Quinton decided to force the girls in. "They just have to get their stupid hair wet and they'll swim," he said, paddling back towards the shoreline.

Knowing Quinton well enough to read his plans, Jack kept pace next to him. He headed straight for Ava as water dripped from his hair into his face. He reached her just in time to block her from Quinton's attack. With a splash and quick tug, Quinton had pulled Talia into the water. After a decent return attack from Talia and Isabella, Quinton's plan worked, and they were both swimming out further. Ava stood back, laughing at their antics.

"Don't want to swim?" Jack asked.

Ava smiled. "What? You're not here to wrestle me down?"

"I won't make you do anything you don't want to."

The smile dropped and she groaned. "Jack, stop acting weird."

"How am I acting weird?"

"You're treating me differently."

"I am not."

Ava glanced at the others and lowered her voice. "You won't even get within arm's reach of me. Do you really think I'm that horrible now?"

"What?" He couldn't let her think that. "No, not at all. That's not it."

"What is it then?"

Jack blew out a breath and ran a hand around his neck. He had to find the perfect limits to the truth. He hesitated too long.

Ava waved it off. "Forget it. Can we just go back to normal?"

"Which normal?"

She looked down, chewing on her bottom lip. "Before I ever left."

"No." That was impossible.

Her eyes shot up to his. "What?"

"I can't do that and neither can you. But we can figure out a better normal."

"Avoiding me isn't better."

But what if that was the only way? "I never want to scare you, Aves."

Ava turned to face him directly, squaring off shoulders that were half the width of his. "Jack, you probably will sometime. And you have to be okay with that. I am."

How could that be okay? Her eyes answered him. *Because it's inevitable.* She was willing to risk a panic attack. And one day, he would risk their friendship. "Fine. But you have to promise me you'll tell me what I do wrong. Or just hit me."

Her serious expression turned into a laugh easily. "Better take that back, Shields. I signed up for that self-defense class you told me about."

"Good, then it'll hurt."

"You bet."

Jack's gaze wandered past her to their friends in the water. There were definitely a few glances in their direction. He went with the best casual grin he could muster. "Get in the water, Aves. And make it look like I made you."

One side of her mouth lifted before she bit down on the smile. Without a word, she spun around him, shoving at his back in a terrible attempt to push him into the water. In a calculated risk, Jack scooped her up and tossed her into the next wave, praying it wasn't too much.

She resurfaced with a fake gasp and splashed him.

• • •

The next day, Ava joined their new, smaller group of Grace college students in the second row. A few more had joined their ranks and now the college group seemed equally split; old and new, right and wrong. Some had been gossipers before, but if they were ready to move on, so was he. Just in case though, Jack sat next to Ava, ready to block her from anyone who might try to slip in an ugly word.

But nobody bothered. And now that the groups were equally split, it seemed less like standing up for Ava, and more like excluding the others. After the last worship song ended, Jack pulled Ava aside while the others headed out of the auditorium.

"What do you think about inviting more people to lunch? It's such a small group in the summer, anyway."

Honey brown eyes studied his for a moment. "Like who?"

"I didn't have anyone specific in mind. I just don't want the group to be split."

Her gaze flicked towards the doors, calculating. "Will you stay with me?"

"Always."

She looked back to him. "Then anybody can come."

He gave her a quick shoulder squeeze. That trust meant everything.

When they got to the foyer, the lines were blurring, students from each seating section were talking to each other. Ava's brothers joined her and, when she was tucked safely between them, Jack left her side for a second cup of coffee.

Val caught him the moment he was alone. "We've missed you at lunch the last couple of weeks," she said with a pout.

"Then come with us today," Jack said.

"Who's us?"

"You know who."

Val sighed and put a hand on his arm. "I'm worried about you, Jack. Some of the decisions you're making don't seem like you."

"Right, because I'm actually making decisions." He crossed his arms to pull away from her touch. "That's all it is."

"No, it's not." She scowled. "Let's get coffee or something this week. I want to talk."

"We can talk here."

"Seriously? Come on, Jack. You're spending time with the wrong people."

Jack caught Ava's glance at them. He reached for the back of his neck. "It's called Grace Church, Val. Could you show a little?"

Val's jaw tightened. "That's not what this is about."

"What is it then?"

Val lifted one eyebrow. "You. Fisher. Quinton. Word spreads that a girl's easy and all the guys in this church line up."

Jack straightened, every muscle stiff. "Excuse me?"

"Who's first?"

"That's way too far," Jack said through clenched teeth. "You do know whose church this is, don't you?"

"Not mine," she said, turning away before he could. They were both done with this conversation. And the coffee tasted like dirt.

His blood still boiling, Jack sliced through the Sanford guards to Ava. He started to reach an arm around her and awkwardly redirected it to his hair. Distance didn't come naturally. Not when he wanted to protect her from everyone around them.

"Is Val coming to lunch?" Ava asked, glancing at him with an innocence that came from a kind heart, not a lack of experience.

"No." Not today, maybe never.

"Oh… Are you okay?"

"Great," Jack said with a smile he didn't feel.

They decided on a new sandwich place for lunch. Ava had her own car today and got there first. When Jack arrived, the seats nearest her were claimed by Talia and Fisher. *Fisher?* Jack found a spot at the far end of the table with Quinton and a few other guys.

"Are we doing a service week again this summer?" someone asked Ava.

"Yep," she said. She looked at ease in this role again. "I think they're announcing it later this week."

"What is it?"

Ava shrugged.

"We know you know." Talia elbowed Ava. "We're gonna find out soon, anyway."

Ava smiled. "Fixing up a place. Painting and stuff. Somewhere cool."

"Spill," Jack said and threw an ice cube from his drink at her.

Ava swatted it away. "Fine. It's for a women's trauma center. For domestic abuse survivors."

"Are you serious? That is so much cooler than picking up litter at the park," Talia said. She laid an arm over Ava's shoulders and gave her a side hug. "I'm glad you're back. You get us better projects."

Several people at the table agreed with Talia. Jack caught Ava's eyes and the slightest, shyest smile crossed her lips.

Chapter 35

Summer was in full swing by the middle of June. Ridley Bay had traded its college students for hordes of tourists who never knew where they were going. Traffic crawled along the small streets making Jack late to church. The sun was already blistering as he climbed out of his truck and headed into the building.

Their new seats weren't very forgiving for late arrivals, but thankfully the worship band was still playing. Jack slid into the row next to Talia. Ava was sandwiched in the middle already, too far from him. Micah taught through Luke, about evangelism and sending lambs to the wolves and treading on serpents. Somehow, after five years in this church, Jack had never heard any of this.

Growing up, he had watched his mom read the Bible every morning. Once he became a Christian, he promised God he'd read through the Bible after he graduated. That deadline kept shifting further. Conviction burned in his chest. Pursuing his passions was fine, but he had to keep things in the right order. There was no other first. Jack stuck the sermon handout into his Bible as a bookmark. Even if it took him the rest of his college career, he would read it. There would never be a perfect time.

When the service ended, Jack found his way to Ava's side. Ezra had dropped from guard duty. Only Joshua stuck with her every Sunday now. He and Jack walked on either side of Ava.

"Hey man, what are you doing tonight?" Joshua asked him over Ava's head, as they stepped out of the auditorium doors.

"Why, are you asking me out?"

Ava poked his side. “He’s taken, lover boy. Got some cheerleader girlfriend.”

“Nice,” Jack reached a fist bump around to him behind Ava. He didn’t miss her eye roll.

“We all get to meet her tonight,” Ava said. “She’s coming over for family game night.”

“You should come,” Joshua said. “You’re practically family.”

“He just wants some other non-Sanford there to take the pressure off,” Ava said.

“We need an even number of players,” Joshua said, rubbing the top of Ava’s head. She swatted at him.

“I’m not a wingman,” Jack said. “I will destroy you at every game in front of your new girlfriend.”

Joshua glared at Ava. “You need better friends.” Jack and Ava both laughed.

Micah joined them and gave Ava a quick hug. “Looks like you two are making my son the butt of a joke.”

“He wants Jack to come to game night so we won’t grill Sophia too much,” Ava said.

“It might help Sophia relax if she’s not the only non-Sanford there,” Micah said.

Joshua waved dramatically towards him to emphasize the point. Jack caught Ava’s smile. “I’ll be there,” he said.

Ava was riding with Joshua back to her parents’ house for lunch, so Jack skipped out on the college group lunch and went to his apartment to cram in as much homework as possible in a single afternoon. And the first chapter of Genesis.

That evening, he pulled into the Sanfords’ driveway 10 minutes late. Rebecca assured him there was no “late” in this house. Joshua wasn’t even there with the new girlfriend yet. Jack and Ava forced their way into the kitchen, against Rebecca’s protest, to set the table and wash cookware.

Finally, they all sat around to an awkward but delicious Italian dinner. Sophia was somewhere between Joshua and Ezra’s ages and peppy enough to handle the entire thing. Or oblivious enough. It was a thin line. Jack kicked Ava under the table every time she choked on her water at something dumb Sophia said.

He held to his promise through the first two rounds of games, soundly beating Joshua or his team each time. Ava and Ezra joined in on the attack, working together to beat him, despite the glares Joshua sent them behind Sophia's back.

The third game was Joshua's pick though and apparently he was the master of strategy games. He finally had his big win. Ava chose charades on her turn, but wanted to play without keeping score. Of course.

Three siblings, two friends and two parents made for an actual game night. A louder, more chaotic one than Jack had ever had as an only child. He liked the pace of it—the sibling banter and the parent refereeing.

It was late by the time each sibling and Sophia had had their pick. They offered Jack a game of his choice but he had to be up at the crack of dawn for another sports camp in the city. He stretched from the couch and apologized for being the one to call it quits.

Sophia said she had to go soon too. She and Joshua stepped out onto the back porch. The moment the door was closed, Ezra and Ava started whispering about how long Sophia would last. Rebecca put a quick end to it and started moving snack trays from the coffee table into the kitchen.

"Hey, do you have time to drop me off at my place?" Ava asked as they walked to the kitchen carrying forgotten cups and bowls. "I rode here with Joshua earlier but I don't think I want to be in the car with those two now."

She added a shudder for effect and Jack chuckled. "Yeah, of course."

They dropped dishes into the sink and Rebecca shooed them out. Ava grabbed her purse from the front hook and gave everyone goodbye hugs. Jack pulled the keys from his pocket and walked out the door with her close behind.

The moment he stepped out, his eyes landed on a truck. His truck. Almost unrecognizable in the light hitting it from the porch. His heart fell to his feet. A rush ran through his mind, clearing thoughts like a straight line of wind and he was left with only one instinct: *keep Ava away.*

• • •

Jack stopped short and Ava ran into him. "What—"

He spun on her, towering over her and pushing her back. "Go back inside." His tone was firm. Cold. Every bit of warmth and fun from the evening evaporated.

"Jack, what the heck?" Ava said, pressing her hands against him. He had been unpredictable ever since the bonfire, but this was beyond rude.

Jack lifted her face in both of his hands and cut off her protest. "Ava, sweetheart, go back inside."

The tone turned her blood cold. He stood broadly, blocking her view out the door. "What's wrong?"

"Give me a minute. I'll be right back. Stay inside."

She agreed out of sheer confusion, if nothing else. He closed the door behind him and Ava stared at its white wood. She could ignore him. She could open that door. Stress was weaving its way through her, trying its knots. The moment she reached for the handle, the door opened again and Ava stumbled back. Jack caught her arm and pushed her further inside the house, closing the door.

He held her elbow, pulling them both down the hall. "Micah, can you come outside for a minute?"

"Sure," her dad said, glancing between the two of them as Ava ripped her arm away from Jack with a scowl.

"Stay here," Jack said under his breath. The two men walked out of the house while Ava stood awkwardly halfway between the front door and the living room.

"What's going on?" her mom asked with a pinched brow.

"I have no idea." Ava mentally pressed back against the stress that worked through her like a poison, consuming her.

"Jack's gonna propose," Ezra said with a smirk and no ability to sense a mood. Ava smacked his arm while her mom told him to be quiet.

Her mom hesitated a moment, looking towards the door. "Come help me clean," she said and pulled Ava towards the kitchen. Ezra followed.

Nobody said anything else and the clock on the wall seemed to come to a complete stop. Ava wandered into the living room and gathered the last few stray napkins and utensils. The front door finally opened, and both men walked in grimly. Ava made it to them first.

"What was that about?" She crossed her arms and blocked Jack's path. He didn't even look at her.

Her dad reached out and eased Ava back. "Give us a minute honey."

The stress began feeding into anger. "I gave you five. What's wrong?"

Her dad looked to Jack instead of responding. Jack ran a hand into his hair. He finally turned to Ava, but his expression gave nothing away. "Somebody vandalized my truck."

"What?" Ava's voice rose an octave and she stepped towards the door. Jack stopped her with a hand on her arm.

"You don't need to see it," he said quietly.

"Why not?" Her veins went heavy with dread. "Jack?"

Before he answered, Ava heard her dad's voice on the phone. He was giving their address to someone.

"Is he calling the cops?" Ava asked. Jack nodded. Ava reached for his arm, as if it could hold her up against the weight of stress. "Why can't I see it?"

Something flickered across Jack's face. He brushed Ava's hair back, keeping his hand where it landed behind her head. "Trust me." He never touched her like this, especially not with her family there to see. And it meant something terrible. Ava searched for truth somewhere in his clouded eyes.

Joshua and Sophia came through the back door in a whirlwind of laughter. It died immediately. Her mom explained the situation to Joshua; he was out the front door before she finished.

"They said they'll be here in half an hour," her dad said, putting the phone down.

Her mom wrapped her arms around her dad as he pinched the bridge of his nose. Ava glanced at the others. Sophia looked utterly lost. Ezra seemed to be trying to find a joke to make.

The front door slammed and Ava jumped half a foot in the air. Jack wrapped his arms around her from behind, pulling her back into his chest. Ava's hands landed on his arms and held them close.

"Who would do that?" Joshua shouted from down the hall. "Who hates you that much?"

"Enough," her dad said, moving to cut Joshua off as he stormed into the kitchen.

"'A slut?' Are you kidding me?"

The word hit Ava like a slap. *"From virgin to slut already?"* Panic wrapped its fingers around her throat and began to squeeze. Her legs were weak; she might have sunk to the floor if it weren't for Jack's arms around her.

"That's enough," her dad's voice raised to a near boom, an unusual sound from him. It only made her wonder what the rest said.

Joshua raised his eyebrows at their dad before looking at Ava and Jack for a moment. He stalked out of the room without another word. Ava turned to face Jack with a hand against his chest, using his strength to hide the shake as she feigned indifference. "It's about me?"

He studied her for a moment before answering in a low voice. "It's about us."

"Us? What do you mean?" She moved towards the front door again, needing to see what everyone else had. Jack held onto her hand and pulled her back. Anger rose to cover the panic and Ava spun on him. "I deserve to see it too."

"You don't need to."

Ava landed a fist against his chest. "Stop trying to decide what I can and can't handle."

Jack's face was ice cold as he wrapped his hand around her fist and pulled her towards the back door. "Let's talk."

She followed him numbly as they stepped onto the back porch and into the warm, humid night air. The moment the door closed behind them, she jerked her hand away from Jack.

"Why do you have to keep me at arm's length from everything?"

"Why can't you trust me enough to protect you?" Jack countered.

"You don't have to do everything by yourself, Jack."

"And you don't have to know everything."

"For the love..." Suddenly she understood the urge to beat one's head against a brick wall. Jack was about as dense as one. "Are we just gonna talk in circles?"

Jack sat on the wooden porch swing with a sigh. Forearms on his knees, he stared straight into the dark yard. Holding the world again. "Nobody needs to see that truck, babe. We'll cover it as soon as the cops check it out."

Ava sank onto the swing next to him. "If you won't let me see it, at least tell me. Please."

He evaluated her before caving, with a shake of his head. "It's graffitied and keyed. Two windows are broken."

Ava tried to swallow but her throat stopped working. "What else does it say?"

"Nothing worth repeating."

"Jack."

"More of the same stuff."

"Same as what Joshua said?"

"Yeah."

She nodded slowly. Oxygen caught in her throat. But she had to prove that she could handle this. "I'm sorry—"

Jack cut her off as he pushed up from the swing and crossed the porch. "That's why I didn't want you to know. You're going to feel bad for something some psycho did. None of that stuff is true, Ava."

"Stop believing in me so much," she snapped back. "When will you realize I'm a mess and give up on me?"

"Never."

"Why?"

Jack faced her, arms crossed, as determined as she was. "Because you're worth it."

Ava stared at him, wishing she could wrap her mind around his words, wanting them to be true. Before she found an answer, her dad knocked on the doorframe. "Hey Avie, I think you need to call the Newtons and have them check on your car before the cops get here."

Ava looked to Jack—he was unshaken. Guilt and panic were racing each other, and all she wanted was to hear his words again. When her dad stepped back inside, Ava began fumbling through the contacts on her phone. Her thumb reached Richard's number and hovered, shaking.

Jack joined her, standing at her side. "Do you want me to talk to him?"

Desperately. Ava shook her head and tapped the number. Within minutes she confirmed that her car was fine. She went inside to report it while Jack called his dad.

"They probably don't know where you live then," her dad mumbled.

Ava steadied herself with a hand on the kitchen counter. "It was supposed to be my car? And they found Jack's instead?"

"I don't know."

It was meant for her. It was about her, about things she had done. "*From virgin to slut already?*" The weight of dread pressed back onto her, tying stones to her joints and dragging them down. Ava swallowed and stiffened against it. *Lies. They're lies. This isn't the truth. "The truth will set you free."*[27]

When Jack came inside, his face was somber. It wasn't the way Jack was supposed to look. He stood across the kitchen from her, arms crossed. Was he mad at her? He had every right to be.

A knock sounded at the front door and both her dad and Jack moved to answer it. Ava stepped into Jack's path and stopped him. "I'm sorry."

"It's not your fault." He squeezed her shoulders and walked past her towards the two police officers at the front door.

Lies.

Chapter 36

Jack woke early, sore and tired from a rough night on an air mattress in Micah's office. Micah had convinced Jack and Ava to stay there last night, so they had shuffled things around until Ava was sleeping in her old room and Jack was downstairs. But it wasn't really the air mattress that kept Jack awake all night. It was the feeling of being attacked and targeted. It was knowing someone out there wanted to hurt them. It was the reminder that anything he loved could be easily stripped away.

The world outside was still dark when he slipped out of the room. The sound of hushed voices reached him halfway to the kitchen. A light above the stove lit Ava and Micah in a soft glow, coffee mugs in hand.

"Hey," Jack said, running a hand through sleep-mussed hair as he reached for a mug behind Ava. She moved away without looking at him. They had barely spoken since the cops arrived last night.

The cops hadn't left much hope behind. The next step would be checking with neighbors to see if anyone had a security system that might have caught something. Jack's insurance wouldn't cover the damage, but his dad said they could fix the body. Replacing two windows would cost a few hundred dollars.

Micah excused himself to get ready. He would follow Jack out to drop off the truck at his dad's house and give him a ride back to work. They had to leave early, both for work and the cover of dark as the truck paraded through the city.

Whoever had tagged it hadn't taken anything. But the broken windows made it an easy target for theft, so he and Micah had emptied the truck last night. They'd brought everything inside, including the black athletic department fleece Ava was wearing now.

Jack poured his coffee and turned to face her. "Nice jacket."

Ava looked down and toyed with the quarter zipper. "Oh, yeah, sorry… Is that okay? I mean, I can, I'll give it back, I just got used to it in Scotland…"

He had to try not to laugh at her, shy and rambling about a jacket. "Keep it. It looks better on you."

Her eyes flitted to him, then back to studying her coffee. She zipped the fleece again. "I want to pay for the windows."

"You're not going to do that." Jack set his mug on the counter and put his hands on her shoulders. "This isn't your fault."

She set her mug next to his and looked up at him, the low light couldn't hide the evidence under her eyes that she hadn't slept either. "My dad thinks they probably came for my car and found yours instead."

Better his than Ava's. "I'll take one for the team."

"Jack… I'm not worth this much trouble."

If there was anything he could do to take that thought away from her, he would. Hidden in the dark kitchen, Jack brought Ava into a tight hug and kissed the top of her head. "You're worth everything, Aves," he whispered. Even risking their friendship.

She didn't reply, but settled in closer to his chest, pressing her fingers into his back.

A door closed somewhere in the quiet house and they both pulled back. "You're not responsible for this," Jack added.

"I know. But I still want to help make it right."

Jack squeezed her arm for a split second before Micah walked in and they each moved further back. He finished his coffee, and both men gave Ava a quick hug on their way out.

• • •

Jack pieced together borrowed rides throughout the day until he made it back to his dad's house that evening. Lion greeted him as happily and cluelessly as ever. Jack was still rubbing the old lab's ears when his dad walked out from the garage.

"Who'd you piss off?" his dad asked, wiping his hands on a yellow shop towel.

"Don't know yet." Did it even matter?

"No ideas?" His dad rubbed the back of his head as he walked around the truck, examining it again. Jack had ideas, but they weren't worth voicing. "Whose initials are these?"

"Ava's."

His dad nodded slowly.

"It's not what it looks like," Jack said quickly. "We're not sleeping together or anything. It's stupid rumors."

"Well, let's see what we can get off." His dad walked back into the garage and returned with rags and wax. "Hopefully this works. If not we'll have to strip some of the paint."

They tackled the graffiti first. The bright orange was more glaring than the keyed inscriptions. Jack started on the driver's door while his dad went for the side of the bed. Parts of it came off fine. Some left an orange stain. Between the two of them, they had the majority of the words and phallic symbols off within a couple of hours.

The tailgate still held the outline of a five-letter word, the edges refused to come off and it was embedded into the creases. His dad brought out a lacquer thinner to remove the remaining stains and stubborn spots. Fixing the paint after this might be a bigger job than they anticipated.

Yvonne offered vegetarian quesadillas for a dinner break. Nobody mentioned the truck while they ate. When they finished, Jack and his dad went back out to work on the keyed initials. They buffed and polished until it was dark.

"Amazing how fast you can do the damage and how long it takes to fix it," his dad muttered, bringing out a clear coat.

Jack repositioned the spotlight they were working under and swiped an arm at the sweat on his forehead. The heat hadn't disappeared with the sun. "Thanks for doing this, dad."

"Of course. That's what I'm here for."

The formerly white truck was a patchwork of shades—stripped, dull paint and sections of creamy, pale orange. They didn't have the touch-up paint they needed to even it out, but it could at least be driven through town now. The windows were still taped and waiting to be replaced at the shop later in the week.

"I'll have to order the paint. I'll call you when I've got it," his dad said as they cleaned their equipment. "And next time bring Ava too."

"If you're planning to put her to work, I gotta warn you, she's got the muscle power of a mouse."

His dad laughed. "No, I like her. If I remember correctly, she takes the edge off you."

"I don't have an edge."

"Yes, you do."

"Then I inherited it from you."

His dad laughed again and rubbed at his shoulder. "Yeah, that's probably true."

Jack reached out a side hug before climbing into the truck. "Thanks again, dad."

"Hope they find out who did it."

Jack gave a half-hearted nod. Knowing might only make it worse.

• • •

Panic followed Ava through the week like a shadow, but she was determined to keep it contained. She fought against it every minute, pouring herself into work, school, counseling, and re-reading all the Bible stories she had never understood before. Truth was worth fighting for.

The rest of her time was filled with family. Her dad convinced her to spend another night at their house. And another. He didn't want Ava back at her apartment until they knew who had attacked Jack's truck.

But it wasn't his fear that fed Ava's panic-shadow. No, the panic fed on the fact that she hadn't heard from Jack all week. He had to be mad. He came to mind too frequently, and each visit brought guilt that seeped into the cracks. Ava patched them with an arsenal of verses. *"My grace is sufficient for you."*[28]

Thursday afternoon she poured herself into work, calling a dozen vendors after a bride decided to change her colors at the last minute. She had grabbed her keys and walked out for the day when her phone rang again. Ava sighed and answered from her headphones, expecting another vendor to be calling back late. "This is Ava Sanford."

"Miss Sanford," Jack's voice rang out in a ridiculously formal tone. "Do you have scheduled dinner plans for the evening?"

The weight of the day washed away. "No dinner plans, but I have a self-defense class in two hours. Should I pencil you in?"

"Burger Bay in 15 minutes."

"Thirty minutes, I need to change first."

"No way, I'm already heading over there right now. And if you're not there in 15, I'm ordering a heart attack with extra jalapeños for you."

"Ew, don't you dare. I'll be there."

The panic shadow faded as she drove. At 15 minutes on the dot, Ava parked next to Jack's truck at the back of the parking lot. It was the first time she'd seen it, but there wasn't much left to see. The paint was a little roughed up, though there were no discernible markings. The windows had been replaced.

She walked into the building behind a group of college guys wearing board shorts and nothing else. It was the type of place that had a "no shirt, no shoes, no problem" sign on the door, not the type of place for her slacks and floral silk blouse. Jack stood inside the door and he looked her over with a grin.

"I don't think I've ever seen you in heels before," he said as he reached for a quick hug. "It's weird."

"Everybody's weird, right?"

"That's my girl." His face burst into a full smile that could stop a girl's heart. "You were extremely close to getting the Jack burger. The surfer wannabes saved you."

Ava tried to shush him before anyone heard but Jack only laughed at her attempts. At least he was smiling.

After they ordered, they found a booth and sat across from each other. "How's work?" Ava asked.

"Great." Jack rolled a straw wrapper into a paper ball and flicked it back and forth in a game of finger soccer. "Only one bloody nose at sports camp today, so overall a pretty successful day."

"Gross."

"Not so bad compared to Goldfish Kid."

"Stop—" Ava put her hand up. "I don't want to know."

Jack smiled. "I'll wait until after you eat."

"What a gentleman," Ava said, intercepting his finger soccer ball. "How's the truck?"

He shrugged. "Been better. Been worse."

"Any news on who did it? Some girl you made crazy?"

"Nope. Probably for the best."

"What? I need a name so my dad will let me go back to my apartment."

"Whoever did it could get in serious trouble. I'd rather this all be over and move on." The lighthearted demeanor was gone, and a heavy weight settled over him. Pushing it wasn't the best move.

"Oh, that reminds me. Maybe this will help." She slid an envelope towards him.

"What's this?"

"Money for the windows."

"You're not paying for that." The envelope slid back and forth on the table.

"Fine, then this is an advance on paying you back for your trip to Scotland."

"Ava Claire, when have I ever made you feel like you had to do that?"

"Never. But I've been an expensive friend lately."

"Just don't make me bail you out of jail anytime soon."

A waitress interrupted them with two baskets overflowing with burgers and fries. Ava's appetite was ever-fluctuating and currently it lapsed. She poked around the fries. "You better take that envelope or I'm donating it to the waitstaff."

With a groan, Jack pulled it to his side of the table. "I'm not using this. I'm saving it for your bail. Or your birthday. Whatever comes first."

"Wow, high expectations of me, huh?"

A crooked smile lit his face. "You never know. We all make mistakes."

"Not like I have."

"That's not true."

"Well, if your only options are bail or a birthday gift, are you sure you want to stay friends?" Ava laughed, wishing the question were a joke and not a spoken fear.

"Yes." His ocean blue eyes were sincere as they held hers. "Nothing, no mistake, can change your worth. Or who you are."

Ava opened her mouth to argue but nothing came out. His words echoed through her mind, shining a light in dark places. *That's love.* Not Jack's. That was God's love. It was love for her very being, not for what she did, or what anyone else did to her. It had been a nice thought, an ideal she couldn't accept. But now she could see it. If Jack still liked her, surely God could too.

"And you like who I am..." Ava whispered. To God.

"Duh." Jack's eyes narrowed at her, annoyed at his own confession.

God probably wouldn't say duh to her. Then again... maybe he would. Maybe his love was such a given, he had the right to. Ava couldn't help but laugh. "Do you think God likes us?"

Jack frowned at her. "I think you have low blood sugar or something. Eat your food."

Ava laughed and pushed a french fry around, trying to rekindle her appetite. It still wasn't working. She looked up again at the boy who saw all her flaws and still liked her. The boy who made her wonder if God might still like her too. She pushed her basket of fries across the table. "Scoot over."

"What, didn't like the view?" Jack asked as she moved into the bench seat next to him.

"Mmm, now I can see the surfers better," Ava said with a raised eyebrow.

Jack elbowed her side. "I'll tell them you want a picture when we leave."

Ava pushed him back. "Then I guess we're never leaving. Get comfortable."

"You know that's not a threat, right? Spending the night on a bed of greasy fries is my dream come true."

"Who's the weird one now?" Ava laughed and leaned her head on his shoulder. They were always toeing the line. This might be too far, but currently, it seemed natural.

Talia said not to let him get too close without commitment. It was the exact opposite of Rosie's advice. Maybe they both had a point. Maybe she and Jack would forever be in limbo. But for now, in this moment, Ava didn't care. Being close was enough. Enough to bring back her appetite. And she was famished.

Chapter 37

After nearly a week at her parents' house, Ava woke in her own apartment Saturday morning. Her brothers were more than ready to have their own rooms again, and she was ready to not smell like a teenage boy. Together they had convinced her parents it was perfectly safe. She would never admit the nerves or the amount of times she had double checked the lock.

It had been an emotionally exhausting week and Ava was ready to be home. The little studio had truly become a new home. A sometimes lonely, quiet home, but a home all her own. A place that held the promise of respite from a world of stress.

A lazy Saturday morning was exactly what she needed. But her body had other plans. Ava woke early with a start, unsure of what she had been dreaming, but knowing she couldn't go back to sleep. When her eyes flicked to the lock on the door and she forced her gaze back up to the ceiling.

With a sigh, she rolled over and started scrolling through her phone. A post from Molly quickly pulled Ava down a rabbit trail back into a life she never loved and the friends that had built it. It felt like another reality. But it wasn't. It was forever a part of her.

And there he was. In a picture with Rosie. With that mocking smile.

Ava closed out the app and stood up, moving slowly. *Stupid.* She slumped the few steps from her bed to her kitchen and grabbed an apple. She turned it in her hands for a moment. Like Eve with the forbidden fruit, she wanted too much. Ava set it back and grabbed a water bottle instead.

The panic shadow had left. But the shadows of guilt and shame never would. The tangles of truth and lies never would. The fact that Oliver's own words had been carved into Jack's truck reminded her that she would never be able to escape Scotland.

"Slut."

And God wasn't in Scotland.

The walls were tightening, and the floor creaked under her pacing. No amount of feng shui could get rid of this feeling. Ava dressed quickly and rushed out the door. It was time to demand an answer from God. She took the stairs at a quick clip, striding towards the beach with determination, as if God would be waiting there on the shore to answer her.

Her pace faltered as she reached the water's edge. God wasn't there, of course. No one was. The beach here was private; some neighbor occasionally walked it, but not a soul was in sight this morning. She was alone. Clouds hid the sunrise, and a flat light illuminated the beach.

With humidity in her hair and salty air in her nose, she headed south along the shoreline, the sand warm under her feet. Blowing out a breath, she asked him, out loud, since no one else was around to hear it. "Where were you God?"

Nothing.

Could she even still hear from God? Why was he a *"soft whisper?"* Why wasn't the God of the universe a booming, powerful noise?

"Where were you God?" Ava asked louder, letting the morning waves cool her bare toes as she walked. "Where were you in Scotland? Where were you when Oliver… How could you leave me?"

"I will never leave you nor forsake you."[29]

"But you did. If you had been there…" Ava trailed off as another Bible story came to mind. She was Mary again, the one who wept at Jesus' feet. *"Lord, if you had been here, my brother would not have died."*[30] If God had been there, things would have been different. If God had been there, she wouldn't have given in to Rosie's lifestyle. She wouldn't have gotten drunk and kissed Oliver. If God had been there, she would have come home the exact same as she had left. Side by side. Never at his feet.

Ava stopped walking and sank into the sand. The warm grit blanketed her legs. The Bible stories hurt. They cut into her, telling her she would never be enough. She would forever be Eve, believing lies and walking in death. The rest of Mary's story played through her mind. Jesus waiting, not saving her brother Lazarus in time, weeping, and finally, raising Lazarus from the dead.

I weep for my beloved.

It wasn't a whisper, it was merely an instinct. Squinting against the gray clouds, no miraculous sign met her eyes, no shining cross or extended hand of God. Ava shook her head. It wasn't the voice of God. It was a spin on the story. That part of the story was famous for holding the shortest verse in the Bible. *"Jesus wept."*[31] Every kid used it in memorization contests because it was so easy.

I weep for my beloved.

Regardless of whether or not it was the voice of God, hot tears burned in her eyes. Jesus had wept over something he knew he would soon fix. He wept because he felt their pain and he loved them. Ava twisted her hands together. "You don't cry for me. I'm not your beloved."

I weep for my beloved.

Her fingers curled around fistfuls of sand as a heave escaped her chest. Why wouldn't the thought go away? Raising a handful of sand, she drizzled it out and watched the pieces fall, scattered in the wind. Words were tight, squeezing out of her throat. "Do you love me?"

You are my beloved.

The still, small voice spoke into her heart more powerfully than any megaphone ever could. It came as an awareness, a light in a dark place.

Jack's words, promising nothing could change her worth, came back to her. Her father's words, promising God loved her, came back. Finally, they began to sound true.

"You love me," Ava tested the words quietly, like a child taking her first tentative steps. When she found solid ground beneath them, she repeated them louder. "You love me."

You are my beloved.

With no righteousness of her own, with every mistake she had made and with everything Oliver had stolen, God loved her. It weighed on her heart, pushing her deeper into the sand as her head dropped low. She didn't deserve this love, but she received it anyway. Overwhelmed and awed, she received it as a silent cry released itself. God loved her.

As with Lazarus, he had allowed bitter things to happen. He had allowed free will in a fallen world. Like Lazarus too, he had a plan to redeem her. *"... so that the Son of God may be glorified through it."*[32] If she could only believe, he promised she *"would see the glory of God."*[33] She didn't have to know the plan right now. All she needed to do was believe.

"I believe."

Sunlight came pouring onto the beach as the clouds parted, lighting her face and flooding her with warmth. Pressure suddenly lifted off her lungs like a swimmer coming up for air and she laughed. She was free.

That's where God was in Scotland. Weeping with her, waiting for her, loving her. He hadn't forgotten her and he certainly hadn't given up on her. He had a plan to bring beauty from the ashes. She had a defense, a sanctuary, and a purpose. She had the only love she ever needed. She was free indeed.

• • •

Saturday afternoon Jack headed to Ava's apartment to pick her up. For some reason, she had agreed to go with him to his dad's house while they finished painting the truck. He couldn't help the restlessness that buzzed inside. The cops had called yesterday with news about the vandalism and now that he had a name, he wanted to be near Ava more than ever. Just in case.

The Newtons' house appeared at the end of the row, and he spotted the security cameras they had installed this week. It helped some, but last night was still the first time Ava had been alone again. Thankfully her car looked perfectly fine.

Jack took the stairs two at a time and knocked on the door. Ava answered with a thousand-watt smile—more than fine. "Come on in, I'm almost ready." She left the door opened and went back in for shoes.

There was no way he would ruin that smile with a name now. He buried the restlessness and tapped the red and white flowers on her door. "New wreath?"

"Daisies, for the Fourth of July."

Jack leaned against the kitchen counter next to her highland cow towel and closed his eyes, letting the nerves die down. When he opened his eyes, they landed on the angel figurine on the table, watching him. He lifted it, brushing a finger over it. It didn't seem like something Ava would have, or keep, with its chipped wing. "Where'd you get this?"

Ava glanced over as she hurried around the space, grabbing water and putting away lunch. "My dad gave it to me when I got baptized."

"Who broke the wing?"

"Ezra."

"Why didn't you glue it back?"

"The piece shattered."

"And you didn't get a new one?"

"Why? What's wrong with this one?" Ava gave him a funny look, but he only shrugged. "This one has character. It doesn't have to be perfect to be valuable."

Jack ran his thumb over the nub of a wing. "Good point."

"What's up with you today?"

He set the angel on the table again, not sure why it kept catching his attention. "Nothing. You ready?"

"Are you okay?"

"Yeah, let's go."

Ava narrowed her eyes at him before deciding to let it go. She grabbed keys and locked the door before following him down the stairs.

"Does your dad even remember me?" Ava asked as they pulled onto the road.

"He'll never forget you after what he saw on the truck."

Ava groaned. "Great, so am I going for a lecture or to finish the paint job?"

"Not sure, but I'm not letting you touch my truck."

Ava rolled down her window and reached a finger out. "I'm touching it."

Jack pushed her arm. "Are you 12?"

She laughed and tilted her head back against the headrest, obviously happy with herself.

"You're in a good mood," Jack said.

She sat straighter and turned towards him. "I am. Wanna know why?"

He hadn't seen her this peppy in a while and he wasn't sure if it was mania or joy, but he was willing to ride along with it. "Sure."

"Because Jesus loves me. Like, actually loves me, for no good reason. And nothing, no mistake, no one can steal that."

Jack couldn't resist her contagious smile. "Girl, there are slow learners, and then there are the ones that take 20 years…"

Ava shot him a fake pout. "Better late than never."

"True." And just to touch her, he pushed her face away as she swatted at his hand.

Twenty minutes later, they were bumping along the road to his dad's house. Lion hobbled up to meet them as the truck came to a stop. "Lion!" Ava hopped out of the truck, kneeling to his level as he licked her face.

"Ava Claire Sanford," his dad's voice rang out as he stepped out of the house with a beer in hand. "I learned your full name with all those initials."

Ava stood and groaned dramatically. "I'm sorry about all of that. Thank you for helping Jack."

"I'm good at one thing and that's cars," he said as he shook her hand. "I need that truck to break down once in a while to get Jack out here. The darn thing runs too well."

Ava smiled. "Glad I could help, then."

His dad surveyed the truck and started pulling out the paint supplies. Before they started, he lifted the beer in his hand. "I need another. Anybody else want a drink while we work?"

"I'm good," Ava said. Jack echoed her and his dad disappeared inside towards the kitchen. Ava leaned close and lowered her voice. "You can have a beer, Jack. I'm 20, not in AA."

Jack smiled. "You didn't get that invite I sent you?"

"Shut up—" Ava tried to smack his arm, but Jack was too quick.

His dad reappeared in the doorway and took a long drink of his beer. "Well, nothing else to do but get started I suppose."

Jack followed his lead, and they were soon covering the patchwork job on the truck. Ava offered to help, but he turned her down before his dad could agree. She found a spot in the shade of the oak tree, petting Lion. His dad talked with her on and off about her major as they painted.

"Eventually I want to work on houses, helping people love their home," Ava said.

"How do you do that?" his dad asked, stepping away from the truck, conveniently more interested in chatting than painting.

"It depends," Ava said. "I think everyone has a different idea of what home should feel like."

"And what do you think home feels like?"

"Somewhere peaceful, where I can rest. Somewhere I'm loved."

"You gonna help or not?" Jack called from his spot at the tailgate, where he was applying a clear coat.

"I'm gonna talk to the lady here, like a gentleman," his dad called back. He turned back to Ava, but his voice was loud enough for Jack to hear. "He could still learn a thing or two from me, if he wasn't so stubborn."

"I wonder where he got that from," Ava laughed.

His dad scoffed. "You were right, Jack, she's got a mean streak."

Jack came around the truck scowling. "I never said that."

Ava and his dad both laughed. Jack grabbed a towel and brushed his hands off, joining them in the shade of the house. The sun was scorching by now and he downed a water bottle in one go.

"What about you?" Ava asked his dad. "What does home feel like for you?"

"Home's where the heart is, right?" his dad quipped before striding away, ready to paint again as soon as the conversation became too personal. Convenient.

"I'll get him one of these days," Ava whispered with a conspiratorial grin.

Jack gave her a quick pat on the shoulder as he walked past her towards the truck. "Don't hold your breath."

With his dad working again, they managed to finish quickly. An hour later, the truck was good as new—or close enough. Ava and Jack waved goodbye and headed into town. The drive was quiet; she seemed as tired as he was.

Ava stretched slowly in her seat and then suddenly bolted upright. "Wait—you didn't answer it."

"What?"

"What does home mean to you?"

He had purposefully chosen not to join that conversation. He shrugged. "I don't know."

Turning in her seat, she gave him her full attention; her gaze intense as he kept his eyes on the road. "I'll wait."

She would have to. There were versions of home in his life, pieces of it. He had never given it too much thought. "I guess it used to be with my mom. For a while it was a football field."

"Where is it now?"

Now it was scattered. Parts were with his dad and Lion, parts were at his apartment, and another part sat next to him in the truck. "I don't know anymore. I would say somewhere safe. Something you can't lose. But that doesn't exist. You can lose anything. I guess you were right, we should have been gypsies after all."

Ava chuckled under her breath and pulled her hair over her shoulder, raking her fingers through it. "Well, you're in luck. I've got some ideas about things you can't lose."

"Like what?"

"You can't lose God. Even if you try, he won't leave you. And honestly, once you know that, the rest… isn't so scary. Because you're safe. I mean, you'll still get hurt, but that perfect, eternal home isn't going anywhere."

He wanted to tease her, to thank her for the speech. But he couldn't. The words were burrowing into him. She was right. He had tried to lose God after his mom's death, but God had still found him. "Yeah. I know."

"Of course, that means when we want someone to blame, God's right there. And we waste so much time pointing fingers at him instead of turning to him and trusting him."

"Okay, okay, pastor Sanford, cool down. I'm learning that. It takes some time though."

Ava gave him a sincere smile that quickly turned mischievous. "And you said I was the slow learner?"

"Whatever, this is advanced stuff, this isn't 'Jesus loves me.'" Jack poked her in the side and she squealed and curled up before attempting retaliation. Jack caught her hand. "No poking the driver."

"Not fair."

"It's fair because I hold your life in my hands."

"I'm trusting God—" she jerked her hand away and jabbed him in the ribs. He could have easily caught her hand again, but if he did, he wouldn't want to let it go. Although, suddenly, that didn't seem as risky as before.

Chapter 38

Sunday morning, Jack was back at Ava's apartment, this time for church. Despite her reminders that she could drive herself, he claimed it was somehow better for the environment and she hadn't questioned it.

When she answered the door, hairbrush in hand, she looked flustered. Without bothering with a hello, she tugged on the bottom hem of her blue and white shirt. "Is this shirt okay?"

"You look great." It was true, it always was. The summer sun agreed with her complexion and highlighted her dark hair, both of which contrasted well with the bright top.

She ran the brush through her hair again. "Are you sure? My dad's going to have the service team stand in front of the church so they can pray for us."

Jack made a face as he stepped inside. "Can I pass?"

"No way. If I'm going up there, you're going with me."

"Fine. And yes, I promise the shirt looks good."

The service project at the women's shelter started tomorrow. It was a week-long event and Jack and Ava had both taken off work to focus on it. They would be painting, moving furniture, landscaping, and whatever else came up. It would be a good change of pace from the middle school sports camps and kinesiology midterms, plus working beside Ava all week.

Then again, that was part of the problem. The more time he spent with Ava, the more he wanted. Every minute together he spent fighting the desire to reach out, to hold her, to finally admit he was madly in love with her. It had to wait though. At least until after the project. Because if she wasn't ready, if he was wrong about how she felt, if he ruined their friendship, he needed to be on the first flight out of the country, not working beside her all week.

"Jack? You ready?" Ava waved a hand in front of him. "Let's go."

His morning run hadn't done much to clear his head. Shaking it off, he followed her down the stairs and into the truck.

They were halfway to church when Ava broke the silence—and the roaring debate in his head. "Is Val okay? I haven't seen her in a couple weeks."

Hiding an inward sigh, he glanced at her. She would read into it, and she wouldn't be wrong. "I heard she's checking out Ridley Bible Church for now."

Acknowledgement and disappointment danced across her face. "Because of me?"

"Because of you, the culture at Grace is changing for the better. If some people don't want that, they were in the wrong place."

Ava glanced at him, surprised, before turning her gaze out the window again. "Thanks."

When they arrived at church, they tag-teamed to make sure the entire college group sat together. The split needed to end. They had a smaller group these days, which could easily be blamed on the summer. Students would return in the fall, new ones would show up, and they would be here, in the front, learning grace.

As the sermon closed, Micah talked about the upcoming college service project. He asked the volunteers to stand at the front. Jack hesitated but Ava grabbed his hand and pulled him along. Most of the second row emptied out, including Fisher, who once again navigated to Ava's other side.

Micah started praying for them and from the corner of half-closed eyes, Jack caught Fisher drape an arm over Ava's shoulder in a pseudo-prayer-hug move. Ava flinched. Before Jack could lift a hand, she had shrugged Fisher's arm off and stepped in front of Jack. Intuitively moving into the space she left, they rearranged the line silently.

Jack radiated all the cold rejection possible towards Fisher. Was this what he had to look forward to all week? Watching Fisher try to make a move on Ava? What if Ava fell for it…

Without hearing a word of the prayer, it ended. A quick look to Ava didn't reveal much of how she felt. She was smiling and stepping off the stage to hug Katie Torres. Fisher vanished off stage in a heartbeat. Jack answered a few questions from other church members about the service project but mostly pointed people back to Ava.

The auditorium had thinned out; Ava was already gone. Jack and the others on the project team followed their routine—meandering to the coffee station to talk about every restaurant in town before picking one of their usual spots. He reached the double doors first and pushed one open, running straight into Fisher—who was talking to Ava.

"Oh, hey, there you are." He fumbled through words. She didn't look upset. At all. Was he wrong about something there?

She smiled back like the stars were hers for the taking. "Hey. Did y'all decide on lunch?"

"Not yet." Jack glanced at Fisher and thanked God when Fisher's face gave it away. The slightly annoyed expression and eye aversion said he was the one who was wrong, not Jack.

Jack couldn't do this all week. He sent a silent look to Ava and tilted his head back slightly. She raised an eyebrow but followed him as they slipped away from the small group of starving students.

The welcome table offered a perfect excuse to busy his hands, and he set to stacking sermon handouts. "Can we get lunch, just the two of us? We need to talk about something." This was about who vandalized the truck. Nothing more.

They cleared the table and tossed the items in the storage bin below. "That sounds serious."

"As a heart attack."

"Jack," she whisper-scolded. "You can't joke—"

Talia skipped up just in time to save him. "Hey, we're thinking Mexican. Remember that place with the picnic tables?"

Ava's eyes flitted to Jack. "Yeah, y'all should totally do that. I've got a lot of homework to do before this project starts though, so I think I need to go."

Talia gave Ava a deadpan stare. "Whatever. Enjoy your lunch with Jack and we'll study later."

"Shut up."

Talia let out a laugh as she walked back to the group.

Jack smirked at Ava. "Did you really think you could lie to Talia?"

Ava shrugged and grabbed the bin. He took it from her and carried it to the storage closet, desperately looking for any more jobs to do in the front hall. He suddenly wanted to stall as long as possible. This was about telling Ava what the cops had found. Nothing else. He wouldn't ask her what she was talking to Fisher about. He wouldn't tell her he loved her. There would be a perfect moment and it wasn't now; not right before the service project.

"Are you on cleanup duty or what?"

Jack nearly jumped at the sound of her voice. This was ridiculous. "Nope. Let's go."

Then again, there were no perfect moments.

• • •

It didn't matter where they went, but Ava was surprised when Jack drove straight out of town and crossed a bridge to the peninsula. Something was off. He wouldn't stop tapping his fingers on the wheel and he was unusually quiet. It tempted Ava's imagination to go wild with "what ifs" but she held the reins tightly.

He turned into a fried chicken spot but didn't park. "How about a picnic?" he asked, heading towards the drive through.

"It's 90 degrees outside."

"And?"

Her curiosity broke loose, and she decided to run with it. "Perfect for a picnic. But I'll need a giant iced tea."

"You got it."

She would be a sweaty, frizzy-haired mess before long.

Fifteen minutes later, they were driving down the sandy beachfront until Jack found a relatively empty spot. *As far away from people as possible. What on earth does he want to talk about?* "You're not going to kill me are you?"

"What?" Jack huffed out, finally turning his full focus on her.

"I mean, you brought me to some deserted spot without telling anyone where we were going..."

"Stop watching TV."

Ava laughed and grabbed the tea. They hauled their picnic into the truck bed, facing the water and the wind. It could have been a comfortable silence if it weren't for the nervous energy Jack still emanated. It made it impossible to eat, despite being starved. She had to get him to talk. "What's going on?"

Jack stopped mid-bite. Not a good sign. He brushed his hands off and leaned onto his knees, watching the waves. "One of your parents' neighbors turned in security camera footage."

That explained his nerves. Ava inhaled salty air and seaweed, grounding herself like she'd been taught in counseling. "And?"

"They identified the car that was there."

The nerves were contagious. "Spit it out, Jack. Whose was it?"

His eyes locked on hers and she couldn't read them. Apprehension? Care? He spoke softly, like he was handling a child. "It's registered to Greg Herzog."

Herzog. Cassandra's last name. Benj's ex. Ava swallowed against the dryness in her throat. *This isn't your fault. This isn't your fault. This isn't your fault.* "Cassandra?"

He nodded. "Her dad's car."

"I'm sorry." She raised a hand to stop his protest. It might not be her fault, but she had contributed. "I'm only saying I'm sorry. Now you say you told me so."

"What? Why?"

"You warned me about Benj."

Sky-blue eyes held hers and a slow smile spread from his lips to his eyes. "I can let that go. After all, we've both learned something more important."

"What's that?"

"Ava can make girls go crazy, too."

"Shut up," Ava said with a laugh and elbowed him. "I didn't make anybody crazy if they weren't already."

Jack squeezed her arm. "Exactly. You're figuring it out, Aves."

"Thank you, Mr. Know It All." Ava took a long drink of tea. "So what now?"

"A couple of court dates. She'll probably have to pay a fine."

"Will this ever end?"

"This? Maybe. But then life will find something else to throw at us."

Ava only hummed an agreement. It was true. She could handle that though. After a forced bite or two of food, her appetite returned and they talked and ate. But Jack was still fidgeting. There had to be more.

"Okay, there's something else on your mind. Spill."

"What?"

"You keep starting sentences and trailing off. What else do you need to say?"

He stalled, cleaning up lunch and tying off the bag instead. "Nothing. I'm looking forward to the project this week."

"Jack Shields, I may not be able to tell a lie, but neither can you." And her imagination was getting the better of her again. Was he mad about something? Would he finally admit he was mad about the truck? "What is it?"

He let out a breathless laugh and ran a hand through his hair, streaked blond now by the summer sun. "It's about Fisher."

The base of her neck warmed, and not from the heat of the sun. That whole thing had been awkward—the deadweight arm, the way she couldn't handle surprise touches, the hope that no one else in church had seen it. "That was embarrassing."

"What were y'all talking about after church?"

An uncomfortable discussion she'd rather not repeat. She wasn't sure if she had handled it right. "I told him I'm not a hugger…" *And that he needed to give me space.*

Jack laughed. "Is that true?"

Not exactly. "Maybe for unexpected hugs from people I don't know well."

"And how do you feel about hugs from people you do know well?"

Ignore it. Ignore the silly flutters and thoughts about Jack's hugs. She didn't need them. *You are loved. You are complete.* "You already know how I feel."

"Not about some things."

"Like what?"

"How you feel about me."

Her breath halted. *Keep breathing, he didn't mean that the way you're thinking.* "What do you mean?"

With a swing of his legs, he hopped down from the bed of the truck and turned to face her. "I'm sorry, I can't keep doing this, Aves. I keep trying to wait and stay away because I don't want to ruin our friendship but I can't do it anymore."

His words jumbled in her head and she wasn't entirely sure if she understood him. Did he not want to be friends anymore? Or did he want… she didn't dare hope for the alternative. "What are you talking about?"

"I want more than this." He waved a hand between them, and with that, her heart left the starting line at a full sprint because the best-case scenario was suddenly possible. Jack turned away from her. "But I don't know if you feel that way or not."

"Jack—" Ava breathed out a laugh. When he still didn't turn around, she jumped down from the truck to stand in front of him, to look at him and make sure this wasn't some weird joke. He looked sincere. And nervous. Ava scrambled for words. She had dreamed of hearing this; why had she never dreamed up an intelligent response? "Of course I do."

"Really?" His eyes shot back to hers, vulnerable this time. "You have to tell me the truth, babe. Because I'm crazy about you."

Was this really happening? The biggest, dumbest, most uncontrollable smile broke across her face and she ducked her head to hide it. "Jack Shields, I've liked you since I was 15. Of course it's true."

"As more than a friend?"

"Yes!" Was he actually that clueless?

Jack let out a heavy breath. "Good."

"Good? Really? That's it? What… Do we shake on it now or what?"

A sheepish grin lit his face. "I have better ideas than that."

Her heart tripped over itself as he stepped closer, wrapping his arms around her and pulling her into her favorite place. Burying her face in his chest, she breathed in Jack. "I'm absolutely a hugger when it comes to you."

Jack chuckled, a motion more than a sound. "And I'm absolutely in love with you, Aves," he whispered.

The words knocked the air from her lungs but she was willing to let it go. She pushed back to look up at him. It was real. He was real. That was the first time she had heard those words. When she thought she didn't have any firsts left, this one seemed to reset the count on all the rest.

"Sorry, too much?"

She couldn't help but smile as she reached to touch his face, testing it. The touch that was once forbidden was suddenly hers for the taking. "Not at all. Honestly, I've waited so long for this, you have some catching up to do."

In an instant, they both moved closer. His hand framed her face as she pressed up on her toes and reached her arms around his neck. Jack tilted his face closer but stalled an inch from her lips. All the friend rules were gone. "Is this okay?"

"Yes."

"Are you sure? We don't have to—"

"Jack," Ava laughed. "Kiss me."

His smile was so close, she felt it. "Somebody's aggressive."

Before she could protest, their lips met. It wasn't stolen; it was given. And apparently she had plenty of firsts, because this was the first time she had ever been kissed like this. Like she was something to savor, not use. The kiss was slow, gentle, and sweet. Without fear or guilt.

When Jack dropped his forehead against hers, Ava hung onto his shirt, as if grasping the moment itself, holding her heart from bursting. His smile threatened it. "So, you'll go out with me?" he asked.

Her heart didn't burst. It took right off, soaring with the birds. A grin built steadily as she tilted her head and studied his face. The face she knew so well but had never been so close to. The face she loved, and loved to tease. "Actually, sorry, I was thinking Fisher and I—"

"Ava Claire—" Jack wrapped his arms around her waist and lifted her off the ground, spinning her around as she let out a laugh.

He set her down and caught her face again, leaning in close. "You were a dork when you were 15," he whispered before kissing her.

Ava could hardly contain her smile enough to kiss him. Everything she had ever known was backwards, upside down, and exactly right. And far better than she had ever imagined. She was home.

Readers Discussion Guide

1. Ava recalled several Bible verses throughout the book. Her memorization of verses was sometimes comforting and other times condemning. What made the difference? For an interesting example of using scripture, read about Jesus' temptation in the wilderness in Matthew 4:1-11. How can scripture be used incorrectly? How can you prevent misusing the Bible in your life?
2. Rejection and loneliness are painful experiences that can cause depression and anxiety. How would you encourage someone struggling with this? What are some practical ways to seek community in times of disconnection?
3. Before the assault, Ava began to explore a new lifestyle with her roommates. Was it a lifestyle she wanted? Was she being true to herself and seeking freedom, or caving to pressure?
4. Ava believed much of her worth was tied to her sexuality. Where do beliefs like this come from? How did this belief impact her before the assault? How did it affect her afterwards?
5. After the assault, Rosie tells Ava that she was "dressed like sex." What other victim-blaming was represented? Ava felt guilty for choices she made prior to the assault. Should her actions and decisions be part of the conversation at all?
6. While Ava learns to forgive herself, little is said again about Oliver. Does she still need to forgive him? Report him? Or take another action?
7. Benj was an inconsistent character. At times, he seemed to support Ava, and other times he seemed to attack her. Did you identify any motivators for his behavior? Have you personally experienced relationships with people like this?
8. Because football had once become a god to Jack, he thought being a Christian now prevented him from participating in it. How did he eventually break this limiting belief? Can you think of examples of

other extra-biblical rules or limitations we add on, due to cultural or personal beliefs?

9. Jack and Micah were often voices of opposition to Ava's own thoughts and what others were saying. In many ways, they represented the love and grace of God, helping Ava to see truth more clearly. Who is someone in your life that has helped you understand the goodness of God?
10. Men like Benj, Jack and Micah provided various types of feedback and support for Ava after the sexual assault. How can men be a positive or negative presence for a woman recovering from trauma?
11. Ava experiences a breakthrough with God, understanding his view of her better and accepting his grace. Is this the final step in her journey? Where do you see her healing journey going from here? Will the assault impact her relationship with Jack?
12. Some studies say one in four women will experience sexual assault in their lifetime. Many people in Ava's life did not know about the assault, and it is likely there are silent survivors around you as well. Without knowing everyone's story, how can your language and actions be sensitive to this? If you have experienced assault, do you need to seek support? (Please refer to the resources page.)

Resources

If you or someone you know needs help regarding a sexual assault, please contact the Rape, Abuse and Incest National Network at RAINN.org or 800-656-HOPE (4673), or the National Sexual Violence Resource Center at NSVRC.org. If you want to learn more or find Christian-specific resources, visit Wetoo.org/resources.

References

1. Psalm 91:11, English Standard Version
2. Ecclesiastes 4:9, ESV
3. Psalm 73:23a, ESV
4. 1 Peter 1:24-25, ESV
5. 1 Corinthians 5:9-11, New International Version
6. 1 Corinthians 6:19, ESV
7. Song of Solomon 8:4, NIV
8. 1 Corinthians 6:18a, ESV
9. 1 Corinthians 5:13, NIV
10. 1 Thessalonians 4:4, NIV
11. 1 Corinthians 6:18b, ESV
12. 1 Corinthians 3:17, ESV
13. Hebrews 13:4a, ESV
14. 1 Corinthians 5:13, ESV
15. 2 Timothy 3:5b, NIV
16. 2 Timothy 3:6b, ESV
17. Proverbs 12:22a, ESV
18. Proverbs 19:9b, ESV
19. 1 Thessalonians 5:22, King James Version
20. 1 Corinthians 13:2b, ESV
21. Luke 7:47a, ESV
22. Proverbs 24:3a, ESV
23. John 1:17b, ESV
24. John 1:16b, ESV
25. 2 Timothy 1:9b, ESV
26. Luke 8:17, ESV
27. John 8:32b, ESV
28. 2 Corinthians 12:9a, NIV

29. Joshua 1:5b, ESV
30. John 11:32b, ESV
31. John 11:35, ESV
32. John 11:4b, ESV
33. John 11:40b, ESV

Acknowledgments

This story would not have happened if God hadn't breathed new life into old dreams, spinning my career path around and planting this story in my heart. From the earliest inspiration to the toughest days of rejection, He has carried this story to completion.

Many thanks to my husband, Scott, for his unending support and grace. From our trip to Scotland to wrangling our girls while I edited, I couldn't have done it without him. Thank you to my mom for not only teaching me to read and write to begin with, but also for her wise advice and encouragement throughout this process. Thanks also go to Leslie, Lydia, and Lori, for being my first readers and forever cheerleaders, and to my dad, for his wisdom and legal counsel for situations both real and fictional.

Thank you to the people who walked through the publishing process with me. The Black Rose Writing team, for believing in me and catching the vision of this story, and the fellow authors who supported me with early reviews. I'm also thankful for the friends who read the story early on and helped improve it, and the church community that prayed for me.

Of course, there are many more—the Webbers, who declared God would work through my writing, the college professors who refined it, and the in-laws who babysat when deadlines got tight. It's impossible to name them all, but incredible to see God weave it together. Thank you all.

About the Author

Anna Daugherty lives in Central Texas with her husband and two young daughters. She graduated with a degree in journalism from the University of Texas at Austin and spent most of her twenties writing and editing for local and international publications. Then, God reawakened a long-buried passion for fiction, and she is now pursuing her lifelong dream of being a novelist. When she isn't typing away at the computer, you can find her running—either for a 5K or because she's chasing a toddler escapee.

To connect with Anna, find bonus content, and check for updates on future books, visit Daughertyanna.com. Your reviews and support are deeply appreciated.

Note from the Author

Word-of-mouth is crucial for any author to succeed. If you enjoyed *Outside of Grace*, please leave a review online—anywhere you are able. Even if it's just a sentence or two. It would make all the difference and would be very much appreciated.

Thanks!
Anna Daugherty

Made in the USA
Coppell, TX
29 July 2023